ARTHURIAN TALES:
AMBROSIUS AURELIANI

Leon Mintz

Erie Harbor Productions
Pontiac, Michigan

Arthurian Tales: Ambrosius Aureliani

Copyright © 2010 Leon Mintz.

Printed and bound in the United States of America. All rights reserved. No part of this book may be reproduced or transmitted in any form or by any means, electronic or mechanical, including photocopying, recording, or by an information storage and retrieval system – except by a reviewer who may quote brief passages in a review to be printed in a magazine or newspaper – without permission in writing from the publisher.

Single and bulk purchases are available regarding Ambrosius Aureliani.

For information, please contact:

Erie Harbor Productions
223 West Cornell Avenue
Pontiac, Michigan 48340
www.erieharbor.com

_____

10 ISBN: 0-9717828-5-7
13 ISBN: 978-0-9717828-5-3
Library of Congress Control Number: 2010934064

_____

My many thanks go out to Dan, Jen, John,
and the ladies of New York for helping to
to point out the errors of my ways.

Please do not fault them for not finding them all.

Note from the Author

For the most part, modern names of the various locations have been used in <u>Arthurian Tales: Ambrosius Aureliani</u>. The notable exception is the use of Aureliani instead of Orléans. The intent is to reinforce Ambrosius' connection to this Gallic city, or more specifically to a villa in the nearby region. The reason for this is further explained in the section entitled <u>The Making of Arthurian Tales</u>.

It is truly hoped that the general reader will not find it necessary to read anything after page 352 to enjoy <u>Ambrosius Aureliani</u>. If it is needed, then I have failed as an author.

The point of the pages past the end of the story is to explain why certain key elements in Arthurian legends were portrayed in non-traditional fashions.

<u>Ambrosius Aureliani</u> is this author's vain attempt to present a historically plausible, "World-Restorer" scenario for King Arthur while utilizing a vast majority of the sources in a synchronized manner.

Note from the Narrator

Greetings. I am Merlinus or simply Merlin. It is the latter that I have been called of late. The trappings of Rome have fallen away like the features of a fading leper. The sights are horrid, and the losses sting with great regret. And though I am a Roman at heart, I have not lived under Roman rule in quite some time. Still, I possess documents revealing my legal claim to a large imperial villa on the shores of the Loire River near the city of Aureliani. It was many, many years ago when I first received that vast estate.

During the consulship of Constantius and Constans, a Roman senator and my father made a deal. In this deal, the Spaniard signed over his Gallic lands to me. In return, my father vowed to escort another nobleman's daughter and her newborn son to Barcelona. In addition, after a short stay, Father would bring her back to her home in Armorica. That was the plan.

But then, Father caught an ill vapor and died before he could execute his part of the deal. I stepped forward to fulfill Father's obligations to the senator. It was at this point that I became privy to the other elements of the plan. Father had agreed to exchange the daughter's child with the son of the self-proclaimed restorer of Rome, King Adaulphus. So I did what Father had arranged to do.

Shortly after this secret switch took place, the daughter's child became ill and died. Her baby was mourned as if he were Theodosius, the son of King Adaulphus and Princess Placidia.

So the son of the *Restitutor Orbis* lived on as Ambrosius. It was not until years later after gray strands had crept into his brown hair that he died. Many may scoff at what I write, but they are fools if they do. Life is not always simple, and I have no interest in telling lies. So become aware of the truth about Ambrosius Aureliani by your own free will or stumble into enlightenment as I did.

CHAPTER 1

The sun poured across the eastern horizon as I neared the end of my long walk. My destination was a certain church near Barcelona. The overpowering sun rolled over me. I closed my eyes, but still I could not block out its light. Blindly, I kept going until I tripped over a stone. On my hands and knees, I looked up and saw the church.

A line of people flowed through the church to pay their respects to the dead child. I joined their line and entered the church. Its center aisle divided two rows of benches. Ten of them, wooden and backless, sat in each row. People filled them all. Some stood behind them, waiting for an available seat, while others observed from afar. I took a seat when I could. The church had never held so many mourners at one time.

Some time later, Princess Placidia entered. The hurt in her face tore at my heart. I looked away, knowing I had caused it. Or, at least, I was partly to blame. I tried to forget about the young lady kneeling in front of the silver-plated baby casket. I tried to forget her beautiful face, her slender cheeks, soft dark eyes, raven hair, and olive skin. She moaned, reminding me that she was still there, crying her last good-byes to her baby, Theodosius. I felt nauseated. My hand trembled as it rested on my knee. I wanted to vomit. Sweat slithered down the sides of my face.

Her king, Adaulphus, stood behind her. He looked more Roman than Gothic. He sported a black toga with gold sashes. Though not tall in stature, Adaulphus was distinguished in beauty of face and form. Placidia's weeping grew; King Adaulphus placed his hand on her shoulder. She looked up at him with sad red eyes. Tears streamed down her soft cheeks. They had shared a lifetime, though they were together only four years.

For the first time in centuries, barbarians had sacked Rome, and this man standing behind the Roman princess had led them. As the brother-in-law of Alaric, Adaulphus fought and killed many Romans. He had captured countless prisoners for his Lord Alaric, but none so precious as Placidia. After Lord Alaric had perished in Italy, Adaulphus took control of their mobile empire. Though barbaric and Arian, this great man left few doubting his self-proclaimed title of the restorer of Rome.

Originally seized from her home as a hostage, in time Placidia fell in love with Adaulphus. From the plunder of Rome, he gave her wedding gifts of jewels and gold. Together, they had united the greatest elements of their cultures. Now, they mourned their fate. The hope of a grand dynasty had passed like the spirit of the child in the closed coffin.

Imperial pleas and threats arrived continuously, all centered around Princess Placidia. Many of them came from men like Germanus, the Bishop of Auxerre. The bishop stood in the inner imperial circles. He was a friend of Budicius, a Spanish senator and cousin of Emperor Honorius.

Already that day, I heard the whispered words of divine judgment, as if the death of baby Theodosius was God's wrath against the Roman-Gothic union. His death fulfilled the prophecy of Daniel. Though joined, there would be no future heirs to keep the two empires together.

What would the masses say if they knew Theodosius lived? What would they say if they knew that the baby boy was being kept out in a nearby villa waiting for me to take him to the fringes of Armorica?

I needed to leave. I stood. My movement caught Germanus' attention, and he looked at me. The bishop had a light complexion. His face was long but not ugly. He was well-groomed, not a single black hair out of place. He kept it short. It glistened from oils in his hair. His beard ran thinly along his jawline. His regal attire revealed that Germanus spent more time primping than praying. His moral demeanor, which I had witnessed, didn't seem to warrant such a pious position. He smiled, knowing that I was leaving, finally, for the villa. Earlier, he had told me that I shouldn't have come to the service, and I should have left for Armorica instead.

I had inflicted the queen and her king with something worse than pain. I wanted no part of my father's circle of friends now. My father's friends were not mine. Sadly, I questioned the true character of my dead father. I had been suddenly pulled into this conspiracy with his death less than a month ago. Now it was my duty to complete what he had begun. With his dying breath, my father begged this from me: "Save the family."

I didn't return Germanus' smile. It melted into a frown, and he moved toward me. I didn't alter my pace as I made my way to the aisle. Germanus caught up with me before I could reach the doors of the church.

Though only fourteen, I was noticeably taller than the bishop.

"Why the long face, young Merlinus?" Germanus whispered.

Still walking, I glanced at him with the same sour expression.

"You act like you've done some terrible injustice," he hissed lowly.

"Haven't I?" I replied.

"No," Germanus replied. "Your actions shall save Rome and all of Its Glory. You've shown that you're a true citizen. As true as Caesar."

"He was a dictator. Spare me your lies. The Empire is in greater peril than ever, if you think a baby could cause it to self-implode," I barked as we stepped free of the church and into the light of day.

"You must see that if we didn't do this, the Empire would be torn apart. None of the nobles of Rome would honor Adaulphus or any son Placidia might bear him, not even one named after her great father, Theodosius. For God's sake, Adaulphus is a barbarian. And worse yet, Arian."

"What's not barbaric or unholy about our actions?" I asked.

"The boy is not dead," Germanus answered.

I continued to walk in the direction of Budicius' villa where the baby, Theodosius, was kept.

"Do we have a problem?" Germanus called out as he stopped.

"If we did, that whole church would know by now," I replied.

"Good," he replied, "so, don't worry. Your family shall be rewarded for serving the Empire in this task. Budicius is a wealthy landowner. He has the ears of Honorius' advisers. His Gallic holdings near Aureliani are immaculate. Your father would be truly honored."

"My family is the only reason I am going through with this," I declared.

My words and hard stare melted his false smile once more. Convincing him of my intent, I turned and continued in the direction of the villa. I had made a terrible error in judgment, and now I had to deal with it.

As I walked, I wondered why they insisted on handling it this way. If the child was a threat to imperial authority, then why not kill the child or leave him at the crossroads where some animal would do what the authorities couldn't. Maybe Father was supposed to kill the child, and they thought that he had told me to do the same. He had never mentioned such a thing.

CHAPTER 2

After some time, I finished the long walk to Budicius' villa near Barcelona. I toiled over how my father fit into this dark conspiracy. I saw his part as the enforcer. Father had retired from the legion, but lacked the luxury that he sought. Father had convinced Mother that this imperial assignment would secure our family's future. Mother and Father had argued over the issue for some time before she finally conceded. He was dead now, and I stood in his stead.

Slaves tended to the upkeep of Budicius' land as I arrived. Several worked the large garden next to the outer wall that enclosed the living quarters and several barns. Others washed clothes while still more fed the tame fowl and wandering livestock. My appearance went unnoticed, or at least not acknowledged, by the workers.

When I had first arrived weeks ago, I was amazed and envious of this large, winged-corridor villa. The long buildings subdivided into the living quarters, kitchen, dining room, and audience chamber. They enclosed an immaculate courtyard. Fine ceramic tiles covered the various buildings' roofs and the rim of the outer wall. Many fine horses resided in its stables. Budicius had everything that I wanted. At that time, I wished to obtain a place such as this. Eventually, if I owned such a posh villa, then I would have achieved my dreams.

Now I knew that I might be on a path leading to material success, but I had strayed far from being an honorable man. I traded integrity for an income and sold grace to feed my greed. The workers felt the same as I did about this place. Sick of it. I made my way to the inside.

"Merlinus," a loud thick voice called out. "Where have you been?"

I saw Budicius. He had dark olive skin and short black hair. It was thinning heavily on the top of his head, giving the impression that it was tonsured. He walked toward me with an honorary *cingulum* draped over his white toga. The richly ornamental belt identified people of more pomp than power. His cold gray eyes glared at me.

"I was at the service," I replied.

"There was no reason for you to go. You should have left at dawn."

"Theodosius and I shall leave in the morning," I replied.

Budicius backhanded me. My bottom lip bled, cut from his jagged ring. I tasted blood in my mouth.

"Don't you ever call the baby by that name. His name is Ambrosius," Budicius hissed. "Don't make me regret honoring an old friend's dying wish."

Anger raged in me. I wanted to lunge at him and pound his face with my fists. Thoughts of my family barely restrained me from attacking him. Instead, I said nothing and walked away.

"Am I understood?" He barked as if I were a slave.

I wasn't powerful, but I was still proud. I refused to reply.

"I said —,"

"I heard you the first time," I walked off toward my quarters.

Ahès sat quietly holding Theodosius in her arms. The baby boy slept peacefully. She cared for him as if he was her own. He was a good baby, quiet most of the time. His pudgy legs lay motionless. I looked at the birthmark above his right ankle as he slept in her arms. Affectionately, she brushed away a lock of hair that hung over his face. She glowed with innate beauty. She was a vision with her long brown wavy hair, small frame, and soft curves.

Ahès had fared childbirth well. The extra weight gained from carrying a child had turned the girl into a young woman. Her plump breasts enticed my glance many times. She did not strike me as being promiscuous as Lord Grallon had portrayed her. The innocence was stripped from her soft brown eyes, though. However, I didn't see the wanton glare I expected. Instead, when she showed joy, her smile was genuine and warming. Her beauty was naturally enchanting. Her thin eyebrows accentuated her high cheeks and full lips. Her small ears were hidden under her long curly locks of dark brown hair.

With a whisper, she asked, "Where have you been?"

I just shook my head as I walked toward her.

"Oh, what happened to your lip?" She asked.

"Politics," I plainly replied. I sat down on the bed next to her.

"Huh?"

"It's not important," I added. "How long has he been sleeping?"

"Only a short while," she whispered with a smile.

She had been too free with herself; too free for her father's liking. For this reason she was sent to Barcelona. Ahès and her baby had to travel here with me. Now her baby laid in the silver coffin at the front of the small church near Barcelona. It fit all too well. Grallon, Ahès' father, rid himself of a bastard grandson and the Empire lost a great threat to their authority.

How many people were involved? Whom could I trust? Would my deeds even be honored? Did they have to be? How could I force them?

I walked over to the table in the corner of the large rectangular room. I stared at the sealed documents, which I had viewed often since I had received them from Budicius. The property rights listed on the scrolls would provide substance and safeguard my family well beyond my own lifetime. What more could I do for them? All I prayed for was their safe journey to our new home in Aureliani.

CHAPTER 3

"Lord Grallon is aligned with unscrupulous associates. His ties run deep with imperial salt, *garum*, and wine," Ahès whispered after laying the baby down. "You and I are mere victims in this debauchery."

"Only you are," I declared. "I am as foul as the fish in spoiled garum."

"Your actions come from noble intent," Ahès stated.

"That's easy to say, but that still doesn't justify the means."

"Merlinus, you are up against something much larger than any one person. Budicius, Germanus, and Grallon are all part of the imperial network. They are part of the elite. Your father never was. He was an errand boy like you are, now."

Ahès didn't mean to sound cold but her words cut me. She walked over to me and then caressed the back of my arm with her hand.

"You've done the right thing under the circumstances," she added. "Though tainted by treachery, take this moment and secure a future for your family and the child."

"What if I leave the boy at the crossroads?" I questioned.

"I believe they expect as much from the likes of you, a poor provincial struggling for the sheer survival of his family. How easy would it be to neglect the delicate care of a child?" Ahès remarked.

The fate of the child lay with me. My father's associates' hands were clean and the Empire was safe for now. No. I wasn't making it that easy for them. Theodosius would make the trip west to the Bay of Douarnenez. Lord Grallon would be forced to deal with the child. He would have to bring an early demise to this child, for I would not.

"What are you thinking? Don't be foolish, Merlinus. You lack an army for your dreams of justice. Long, spirited speeches do little to stop short, shiny swords."

Placing her hand on my shoulder, she asked, "When do we go?"

"In the morning," I answered.

"I thought Budicius said we were leaving today."

"We're leaving in the morning."

Several days had passed since Ahès, the child, and I had left Budicius' villa with some of his men. Traveling light, we covered much ground. At first, we traveled northeast from Barcelona toward Narbonne on the Via Domitia. We rendezvoused with an armed escort at Alenya. Then, we cut cross-country with the regiment of Alans. Budicius' lead man, Valerius, wanted to avoid the Goth-controlled town of Narbonne.

Ahès cared for the child. She took a big burden from me. She made the journey easy. From what Lord Grallon had said, I figured she would be more of a problem than the baby. Instead of keeping a close eye on her and the child, I kept it on Valerius and his crew of merchants.

Valerius was an ox of a man, about two hundred and fifty pounds. His body had no fat, from endless work on the docks. He kept his head shaved but maintained a wide beard trimmed short. It was mostly gray revealing the merchant's age. His arms were thick and his chest was wide. He was so much like a bull that if Valerius went to the mithraeum, he'd be wise to remain on the benches or he might be sacrificed in the *tauroctony* instead of the wild bull.

My limited contact with Valerius and his crew left me feeling that they were like thin ice. On the surface, they were cold and expressionless. But if crossed, they would consume all that risked it.

Stopping for the night, the wagons had been drawn up into a circle. The sun had fallen behind the mountains long ago, and with it the temperature. Now the remanence of its light had all but faded away. Already, I felt the deep chill in the air. It was much colder than any night so far. I gathered up wood and placed it in the center of the camp.

"What do you think you are doing? No fires. There will most likely be no fires for the next couple of nights," Valerius ordered.

"What? What about the baby?" Ahès questioned.

"That baby is not my concern. Besides, I am not the one that delayed our departure from Budicius' villa. Direct your anger at Merlinus. He's the one that held up our departure. I wanted to leave several days before we did. Merlinus refused to leave earlier.

"This is no-man's land," Valerius added. "Survival goes to the sharpest. We can't expect protection from anyone out here. We are on our own until we reach Alaigne. There will be no burning fires to show the demons of the night where I sleep."

I thought to when we first went to Barcelona. That time, the rendezvous point was at Alaigne, which was twenty-five miles southeast of the Garonne River. We had traveled cross-country that time, also.

"Why wasn't this an issue the last time we passed through here?" Ahès questioned.

"We were traveling in the middle of the summer. Therefore, a fire wasn't necessary. You didn't notice it, but we did the same thing at the time," Valerius stated.

"It's true," I remarked.

I drew near her.

"I brought extra blankets. It will be all right, Ahès."

Finally we reached Alaigne without incident. We stayed there for the night. As we joined their festivities and enjoyed their warm hospitality, the people acted as though there was nothing to fear. We toured the Alan settlement. It was truly enlightening to see how my people lived as they had before serving the Romans. I was twice removed from the old way, the ageless Alan traditions, nomadic in nature. My grandfather was the first to fight for Rome from my family's clan.

Ahès halted before a small group of people huddled around an old man who was sitting on the ground. He had a long white wiry beard. He mumbled words, and I struggled to gather his meaning.

"What did he say?" she asked. "What is he saying now?"

"Shh," I remarked. "I'm trying to figure it out."

The old shaman directed his comments at a boy who sat facing him. The boy appeared nervous. He wasn't even half as old as I was. His long black hair was pulled back from his face in a ponytail. His eyes opened wide as he waited for instructions from the old shaman. Though his face revealed fear like a misbehaving child about to be caught, the boy did not look away. Instead, he waited with his small hands in his lap.

" 'Your future waits for you,' " I translated the old man's words for Ahès. " 'It shall find you if you lag too long. Pick up the osier sticks. Roll them in your hands until I say stop, then drop them. From them, I shall glimpse into the world beyond here and see you in the days of tomorrow. Your future shall be seen.' "

"What's the young boy's name? How old do you think he is?"

Ahès asked, cradling Theodosius in her arms while he slept.

"I don't know," I remarked.

"The boy's name is Draco. He's my younger brother and he's only six years old," remarked a young girl. "My name is Metelli."

She had long black hair and wore a cloth that tightly bound her head. The tail of the fabric hung down behind her as her hair did. This custom had clung to the people, though they were far from their traditional home in Central Asia. She finished with a shy smile that quickly slipped away. Ahès smiled, seeing the girl's interest in me. Although having the customary drawn head, she was still pretty to my Roman eyes.

Pointing at Ahès, I politely announced, "This is Ahès. And I am Merlinus. It is a pleasure to meet you, Metelli."

With a bright smile, she added, "Draco begins his journey on the warrior's path tonight. He must wander into the darkness of the night and maintain an all-night vigil. Besides his own wits, he shall have no assistance except for what the shaman tells him now."

She fell silent, waiting for her brother to cast his destiny. Metelli and Draco had several similar features. Besides the indigenous dark eyes and hair, they shared the same high, thin cheeks and short noses. Both had long narrow ears, which their long hair would conceal if they weren't in ponytails. The young boy quickly rolled the thin, straight sticks in his hands, but he seemed uncertain if he should keep up his pace. His eyes were fixed upon the old man. One eye twitched.

"Stop!" Commanded the old man.

Draco's eyes grew wider. His nose flared. He dropped the sticks. They scattered across the sand in-between the boy and the old man in a random manner. One stick from the bundle stuck straight up while another slowly fell. Many of them crisscrossed each other.

"You'll serve a good king, but save a greater one," the old man said. "Your future waits for you now. It is here. Watching, watching us."

The old man turned and looked directly at Ahès. She smiled and he leaned back from Ahès' glance. Spooked, the shaman got to his feet and left without a word. The group of people scattered along with Metelli. Only Draco remained. He said nothing. He stared at us, studying us. And then, the young boy got to his feet and sprinted off into the night.

"What just happened?" Ahès asked.

"I don't know," I replied. "We should return to our wagon."

The next morning, our group picked up the Roman road from Narbonne to Toulouse. Far enough between the two cities, there were no issues with the Goths. Our crew was vulnerable. Vandals still insulted authority in the area, whether it was imperial or Gothic. Although mostly driven farther south, some lingered, leeching a living like common thieves.

Our travels took us northwest to the Garonne River. The group met up with the ships that would sail us to Armorica. With careful timing, the ships past Toulouse at night. It was a Roman town, but the Goths held more and more influence there since they sacked Rome four years ago.

The boat sailed for the sea. The journey was peaceful and helped to clear my thoughts. Though winter approached, the weather wasn't poor. A breeze sped us on our way and took the edge off the strong sun. All seemed consumed by their own thoughts or tasks at hand. Few spoke, only Ahès remained vocal. She sang to the baby, whispered soft words, and treated his every need. She had grown attached to Theodosius. It was great for the child, but I worried for her. What would happen once we made it to Armorica? Did she think she could keep him? There's no way Lord Grallon would allow Ahès to keep the child. What would happen with the child, then? Who would care for him?

I felt sadness. She glanced at me. My expression soured hers.

"What's wrong?" She asked.

"Nothing."

"It has to be something. That look is from something."

With no one in listening distance as we stepped off the docked boat, I said, "What will happen to the baby once we reach your father?"

A surprised look formed on her face.

"You're not keeping him? Since you said you weren't going to leave him at the side of the road, I thought he was going to Aureliani."

"I was simply told to bring the child to your father," I replied.

"You're not keeping him?" she asked again.

"No."

The baby squirmed and fussed slightly. He drew Ahès' attention.

"Oh, it's okay, baby. It's okay," she cooed. She fluttered his lip with her finger. "See, it's okay, baby."

"It's hard to say what will happen," I remarked. "Grallon might give him to the church."

"If that was the case, Bishop Germanus would have taken him.

Grallon would want to keep him away from educated eyes, though. He might give the child to a peasant family to raise." Ahès stated.

"Is there a chance that he might . . ." I paused as I thought the worst. Looking up from the baby, she peered at me to see my intent.

"No. I don't believe he would do that. More likely than not, he will end up pawning the boy off on my stepbrother, Vortimer," she answered. "Maybe I can talk him into allowing me to raise him."

"Maybe," I replied. Though, I doubted it even as I said it.

Lord Grallon would not allow such a scandal to live dormant under his roof. He had used his daughter in this conspiracy; he would not allow anything to go to chance.

With the baby in her hands, Ahès and I stood on the shore waiting for the men to unload the wine. They moved quickly as night grew more complete. It had been a long journey. The crew and ship had labored against the tidal bore of the Garonne River. The sea wasn't any easier. Still, we had reached the Bay of Douarnenez safely.

Grallon had not come to the shore to greet us. His men stated that Lord Grallon traveled to Vorgium. They expected that he would return by late tomorrow or early the following day.

"Merlinus and Ahès, go ahead and get on the lead wagon," Valerius ordered. "The driver will take you to the villa. We will follow after we unload the rest of the wine and load the garum and salted pork."

"Okay," I replied.

I took the baby. Ahès climbed onto the wagon. I carefully handed the sleeping child to her, then got on. The driver set the oxen in motion with a snap of his wrists. The wagon rolled forward with a light tug.

At a slow pace, we moved away from the sea and inched toward the villa. The night consumed the remaining light. Stars brilliantly lit the sky by the time we reached the villa.

Servants quickly gathered with torches in their hands as the wagons pulled through the gatehouse. After climbing down, I reached for the baby. Ahès got down, afterwards. Though tired, she smiled at me as I held the boy peacefully. I gave the boy back to her without a stir.

We walked quietly through the courtyard. Torches filled the open lawn with a strong flickering light. An older woman led us to our quarters.

"Sweet dreams, my lady."

With a smile, she added, "You, too."

CHAPTER 4

The next morning I rose early. My thoughts kept me from sleeping. I wandered through the quiet villa. Eventually I exited it by following the scent of the sea. I stood at the back end of the Roman building. The outer perimeter walls ran north and south and abruptly ended at the sea cliff. There was no outer wall running east and west to serve as protection at the back of the villa. Instead, the sea and a large statue stood guard. Curious, I walked up closer. A massive marble man towered at least fifteen feet tall. He held his hand out as if to stop the sea while in the other one he grasped a trident. From the tailbone of the statue a fish's tail curled out around the man's right leg forming part of the base. Standing directly in front of the statue, I read the inscription on its base:

<u>To the divinity of Augustus and to Neptune Hippius, Caius Varenius Varus, of the Voltinia tribe, curator of the conventus of Roman citizens for the fourth time, has erected this.</u>

I hadn't seen the statue's equal. I glanced once more toward the sea. From my elevated view, the harbor and this villa appeared lower than the bay in the distance. The harbor's shoreline stretched toward the northern horizon and nearly touched in the center. Its rising slope formed a natural dam. The docks and the area around bustled like a thriving city.

"The sight is enchanting if you have any love for the sea," a man called out from behind me. Turning I saw Grallon.

He stood regally dressed. It seemed odd seeing him this way, so early in the morning. His wavy hair was gray with remnants of black roots. It gave Grallon a dignified look. He had a narrow face and greenish-blue eyes. A thin beard covered his soft features. Even though I was extremely tall for my age, Grallon was still taller. This made him at least six and a half feet tall. He had a thicker frame, also. Thoughts of him snatching me and pitching me off the nearby cliff didn't seem unrealistic. A silver cape of fur draped his broad shoulders. A cardinal red cloth lined the inside of it. His silver wool tunic had red plates of light armor fastened to it. He looked as though he was dressed for an imperial procession.

After slightly bowing, I remarked, "Good morning, Grallon, lord of Vorgium."

"Greetings, young Merlinus," he replied as he walked toward me. "I hope all has gone well?"

"As good as can be expected under the circumstances," I remarked. "I don't believe Valerius will report that things went as smoothly as they did. Our Alan escorts never filled me with a moment of doubt. They knew the lay of the land as if they had held it for a lifetime. No one was hurt or even harassed."

"Good. Then everything went as well as can be expected. Something always comes up and the plan must be altered to fit the present conditions. That's life," Grallon said as he walked past me. He walked closer to the cliff. I moved up but stayed out of arms length.

"You see this? Mark yourself as one of the fortunate few. For many have not seen things like these and some never will. Only powerful men of the Empire have stood where you do."

"And servants," I added with light conviction. The silence and the look from Grallon made me think I would have been better off saying nothing. Father said to never correct a superior.

Seeing no malcontent in the sharp remark, he fired back, "Even emperors have been called from the farmer's fields."

He turned back toward the sea, dignified with his hands drawn together behind his waist.

Without looking back at me, he called out, "Your father would be proud of you. You have handled things in the best possible manner. There is just one more thing I would like you to handle. If you agree to it, I will order a generous supply of salted pork and garum to be sent to Aureliani, today. In addition, a small chest of coins will be included."

"What task could warrant such an offer?" I inquired.

"Nothing you haven't done already," the lord of Vorgium remarked. "I wish you to sail to the western shores of Britain. I have honorary holdings there. I gained them when I served in the legion sent by General Stilicho. Instead of leaving when we turned away Britain's enemies, I stayed. The bulk of the men returned to the continent. Recently, in return for honorable service, I've given much of the lands to my men who still fight for me. At the holdings near Gloucester, I have stationed my son, Vortimer. I want you to sail with the child, Ambrosius, to Gloucester. Once there, simply give the boy to Vortimer. And then, you shall be richly rewarded."

"You have lands in Britain?" I asked.

"Yes," Grallon said in a strong, proud tone. "I have many holdings here and on the island. Even in tough times, I have prospered. Times are changing. People must adapt or die in poverty. I have served the Empire well and I have been rewarded with wealth and prosperity. I am more powerful than Carausius and less blinded by pride than he was. Learn from my example, Merlinus. Use the Empire. Don't fight against the system. It has consumed kingdoms before us. It has consumed Christ. It could easily consume you or I if we step out of line. So don't, and you could gain all the riches you desire, as I have."

After pausing for a moment, Lord Grallon added, "Let me level with you a moment. Few have realized it and I have done nothing to inform more, but I have never stood with my sword drawn on a battlefield.

"I served my time as a quaestor in the army," Grallon said with a smile. "I helped to coordinate the transporting of Stilicho's army to and from Britain. I am a rare Roman. I am renowned for my sea legs. Instead of taking payment for services rendered, I obtained parcels of imperial lands in various ports on the island, and on the shores of Armorica.

"In addition to these imperial grants in London, Portchester, Topsham, and Tintagel, there are family holdings in Demetia and Gloucester. And as I said, it is to Gloucester that I want you to take the boy. My son, Vortimer, stays at the villa in Gloucester."

"That's it?" I asked.

"That's it," Grallon replied. "Do this and you shall be richly rewarded."

"Done," I quickly replied.

CHAPTER 5

I watched and listened as Ahès and Grallon argued on the shore the next morning.

"You can't send Ambrosius away. If you do, I'm going with him."

"You can't, child. What would you do, live as a slave mother, raising Ambrosius as your own? Impossible."

"Absolutely," Ahès cried out. She broke free of him. Ahès waded out into the water as the boat pulled away from the shore. Her eyes stared at me. Her lips shivered from the chill of the water. Still, she trudged through the deepening tide.

"Ahès, turn back before the waves pull you under," I called from the boat as I held the baby. With no expression, he looked up at me.

"Ahès, stop," Grallon ordered.

She did not halt. High waves rolled over her, as her hand frantically clawed at the stern of the boat. She spat out water and gasped for air, but still she reached for the boat.

"Give it up, Ahès," Grallon shouted as he walked out into the waves after her. "Don't force me to drag you in."

"I shall wreak havoc upon your city if you force me to stay."

"Young lady, I'm your lord and father," Grallon barked, charging deeper into the rushing water. In no time, he was out nearly to Ahès.

Her nails dug at the side of the boat. The ribs of the boat flared up at such an angle that it made it difficult for Ahès to climb aboard.

Not wanting her to drown, I called out to her, "Let him go, Ahès. Let Ambrosius go."

Releasing what little hold she had of the boat, we separated quickly as the drift of the sea set in. Ahès sank like a rock underneath the waves. Moments passed, but she did not surface. Lord Grallon watched for her. His face grew more frantic. He reached down into the water, first with one hand then with both. Calming himself, Grallon stood still and scanned the water. Spotting her silhouette, he shot into the water and a moment later hauled her up from the depths of the dark blue sea.

The oarsmen got situated and worked the sea. The high waves heaved the boat up and down as it crawled across the choppy water. The rough ocean wore on me. I tried to keep Ambrosius as comfortable as possible. I turned into the center of the ship to help shield against the splashing waves. Still, its mist was inescapable. In time, we made it to the mouth of the Severn and eventually docked near Gloucester.

No one was waiting for us. The docks were bare and deserted. The merchants acted like nothing was wrong. I moved away from the shore. My eyes followed the road up toward the horizon. In the distance, a wagon rolled toward us.

After some time, the large oxen-driven cart arrived near the docks. I moved to climb aboard. He yelled something. I struggled to understand. The words had to be in one of the Brythonic dialects.

"What are you doing?" the husky driver barked in broken Latin.

"Are you not from the house of Vortimer?" I questioned.

"Yes," the heavy-set man replied as he lumbered down from the wagon's seat.

"Well, that's where this child and I are heading. I am here by order of Lord Grallon. Vortimer will be expecting my arrival."

After an odd look, the driver looked back and replied, "This may be true, but you cannot ride. There is no room. You will have to trail behind the wagon."

"Won't it be a long walk carrying a baby," I declared.

"That's not my concern. I'm just here for the wine," the man stated.

"You can't be serious," I barked back at him.

"I am," the man replied as he walked by.

"This is insane," I began. " I will not –."

With a tug on my arm, I stopped talking. Glancing down, I saw the baby pulling at my sleeve of my wool overcoat. The grumbling man's words faded in the breeze. The wind blew a cold hard truth. Winter was settling quickly. I took the excess cloth of my tunic and cradled the baby in it so I would have both hands free while walking. I marched from the wagons and headed for the crest forming the immediate horizon.

Where had I promised to take this child? Though I would not personally kill him, was I not ensuring his doom by bringing him here? I walked to the town of Gloucester. Though not far, I struggled to swallow the fact that no one was sent to greet our arrival. *But why would they? Vortimer could not be too happy.*

Luckily, it wasn't difficult finding lodging there.

For the next three days, Vortimer refused to meet with me. We walked out to his nearby villa. Each time, we were greeted by the same servant, Allectus: an elderly man with refined manners. His slate gray hair was trimmed short. The lines of age were quite visible, though his face lacked all other emotions. He had no facial hair to conceal this. Each time I asked for Vortimer, he repeated his same response.

"Lord Vortimer is unable to meet with you, today. I shall inform him that you have called upon him."

Each time, I gave the same reply, "Please inform your master that I shall call upon him tomorrow."

"I shall," he answered before closing the door.

On the fourth day, as I walked through the courtyard toward the front entrance, the door opened and Allectus appeared.

"Greetings," I called out to him.

With a reserved nod, he acknowledged our presence.

"I —," I started.

"He will not see you," Allectus cut in. "He has instructed that you leave the child with me."

"I —,"

"Young man, my lord, Vortimer will not see you," the old servant added. "You have done all that you can for the child. It's time for you to get on with your life. Go to your new home in Gaul and seek peace."

After hugging the baby, I kissed his forehead. Unfortunately, I had my own attachment to him.

"Take care, Ambrosius," I added.

Allectus took the child. The servant turned and walked away. As they entered the villa, Allectus closed the door without looking back. A strange emptiness invaded me. I had thought that once I was done, a burden would be lifted from my conscience. I was wrong. I didn't feel free. I felt worse. The uncertainty of his future pained me. I could do nothing to alleviate it. I lacked the resources to buy his freedom. I truly doubted that Grallon would allow me to do that, anyway.

With nothing left to do, I walked back to the inn where I had stayed the last few nights.

CHAPTER 6

I debated my next step. *How should I get to Gaul? Taking a ship from here would be outrageous. I could walk to Dover, see the island and then catch the short ride to Gaul from there.* I left the room and went downstairs. I sat at a table and ordered some roast and ale.

Nearly finished with my meal, I noticed two soldiers enter the quiet inn. Their eyes scanned the empty tavern. They were looking for someone. They saw me sitting in the back corner of the wide room. I looked back at my plate to finish off the final bit of roast. As I glanced back at them, they moved straight for me. My hand casually dropped below the table. My fingers slowly inched over the hilt of my dagger hanging on my right hip.

Why were they here for me? Were they Grallon's men? What did they want? It couldn't be good.

The soldiers stopped at my table. Remaining silent, I looked up. A dagger and a gladius mounted their right and left hips. Both wore red tunics underneath their *lorica segmentata.* This legionary-style armor was fashioned from a leather vest and protective bronze bands. Each man sported a cardinal cape fastened to their shoulders by golden brooches. They wore red trousers to stand the damp chilly weather.

The soldier on the right had short black hair and a thick beard like Hadrian. The other was clean-shaven and had wheat-colored hair.

"Greetings, young man. I'm Falco and this is Bellus," stated the soldier to my left in Latin. They were both bigger than I and well armed.

"Hello," I replied as I glanced at both of them, gauging their intent. I grew nervous in the silence that followed. The bartender behind his counter stopped what he was doing when he noticed their presence. His concerned look matched my feeling.

"Sorry about interrupting your meal. My men and I have recently been transferred from Lord Grallon. We're heading for York. We've been instructed to contact you. I am to inform you that you may travel with us to York. Once there, you may leave for Aureliani on a ship scheduled to depart in a short while. Your service has been greatly appreciated. Would you want to travel with our detachment?" asked Falco.

I said nothing. His offer made me leery. Grallon had said nothing about any men going to York. I didn't know what to say. Was this a trap?

"You are Merlinus, are you not?" Falco impatiently asked.

Bellus laughed and declared, "Falco, I don't think he trusts us."

I didn't.

Falco laughed and added, "You're right, Bellus."

"If we meant you harm," Bellus began, "who's stopping us from doing what we want with you? Who are you to anyone in Gloucester?"

As he finished, Bellus glanced around the tavern to see if anyone was stepping up in my defense. Looking at the bartender, Bellus smiled as the man's glance fell away as if he hadn't even seen us.

Seeing his point but sensing no ill intent from them, I asked, "When are your men pulling out of Gloucester?"

"Tomorrow," Falco answered.

"So are you interested in going to York with us," Bellus asked.

"Yes."

The next morning, shortly after sunrise, I met up with Falco and his men at the tavern's stable located behind the inn. The group contained fifteen men including Falco and Bellus. All of them were several years older than myself.

"Greetings, young Merlinus," Bellus called out from some distance as soon as he had noticed my approach.

"Hello, Bellus. How are things?" I asked.

"As well as can be expected," he replied with a light nod.

"Good," I added.

"So are you ready to head for York?" Falco said with his hand outstretched to greet me.

"Yes, sir," I replied as I grasped his hand.

"Good. We shall ride to Fosse Way and take that northeast to Lincoln and from there we will ride north to York," Falco finished.

"Will we make it to Lincoln tonight?" I asked.

The majority of the men laughed.

"No," Bellus added. "It will take a few days to reach Lincoln. It's over thirty leagues from here."

"Mount up, men. It's time to ride out." Falco shouted.

Days later, after spending a night in Lincoln and continuing north, we arrived in York. People from miles around crowded the forum, selling, buying, and bartering goods and services.

"So, have you ever been to York?" Bellus asked.

"No. Actually, my arrival in Gloucester, two weeks ago, was the first time I set foot in Britain," I declared. "I like what I have seen so far."

"If that's the case, you should go with us to meet Duke Coel. He resides in the palace of Septimius Severus. He was the emperor that had the palace built over one hundred years ago."

"It would be all right if I went?" I asked.

"Sure. Why not?" Falco remarked as he dismounted.

"I will gladly go," I remarked.

"Good."

Proceeding through the bustling town, we headed toward a spectacular stone building at the north end of the forum. Ten white columns supported the portico, six for its façade and two for each end. Servants greeted us as we walked under the open awning.

"Welcome, Falco," called out one of the male attendants.

The four servants wore white ankle-long tunics. Each had a gold-embroidered V-shaped collar with a matching tassel belt. Leather-strapped sandals clad their feet.

"Lord Coel has been expecting your arrival. Your men may leave their mounts with us."

"Very good, Cato," Falco replied.

As I handed over the reins of my horse, Cato looked at me oddly.

Seeing the young man's expression, Bellus laughed and added, "This young man is with us."

"Of course," the young man commented as he took the reins from my hand. "Please accept my apology."

"There's no need for it," I answered.

Cato nodded and led the horse to the side of the building with the other men's horses. I followed close behind the small group of soldiers as Falco led the way into the magnificent palace. Numerous sculptures filled the grand building ranging from alabaster busts to larger-than-life statues. As we neared an open room that housed one of these colossal emperors, a regal attendant approached us. He appeared as the others did, in a white linen tunic with gold tassel belts and leather soles. He was older and taller than the others. He also had their bowl-shaped haircut.

"Greetings, Falco and Bellus. Lord Coel shall be glad that you've brought him so soon," the young man announced.

A sinking feeling consumed me. I glanced at them, and their shifting eyes confirmed my suspicion. Instantly, my pace slowed. Noticing the change, a regretful look formed on the attendant's face. He knew he had said something he shouldn't have. Before anything could be said, a man appeared as if he had walked out of the statue behind him. The sculpture was a mirror image of the old man. I stopped some distance from him. His attendant stood to the right while Bellus and Falco were at my left. He was a man of average height, an inch over five and a half feet. He commanded respect with his presence. He had lived twice as long as most folks. "He's one of the last Romans remaining on this island," Falco had stated before we made it east. Though old, Lord Coel gave no impression of being frail. Instead, his manner presented a good-natured, youthful vigor. He appeared more as a scholar than a soldier. He wore a light gray robe with flowing sleeves and a V-cut collar. Bands of royal blue lined the edges. He wore a thin white tunic underneath the robe and a wide black leather belt drew them in around his waist. Because of his snow-white hair and beard, Coel looked like he could be Grallon's old uncle.

Smiling at me as if we were old friends, he bellowed, "Greetings, young Merlinus. I hope your travels in my province have gone well."

"All is well so far. Your lands seem quiet civil."

"Ah yes, we're far from the troubles of Spain," the duke said. "Do you know why I asked you to be here?"

My fear deepened as I naively replied, "I thought I had come of my own free will."

The old man smiled and, while glancing at Bellus, Falco, and his attendant, he remarked, "Leave us."

They bowed their good-byes and walked out the way we came. It was a strange feeling that overtook me. I didn't fear for my life. In no way had this man tried to intimidate me. In fact, it was quite the opposite.

"Will you take a walk with me?" The man asked.

I nodded yes.

CHAPTER 7

Lord Coel led me through a labyrinth of corridors. The treasures of the palace became more and more splendid as we went. More gold-laced vases, gold diadems, and gold-tipped spears for the statues. It appeared as though they had problems with flooding. I noticed water damage at the base of the walls. Various attendants smiled as we passed them. He saved his words and didn't speak.

He took me to the central courtyard of the palace. Full-grown trees lined its borders, and a fountain stood center stage. With her hands up in the air, the female stone statue looked like a Y. Water poured out from her raised palms and splashed into the pool below her. It was nearly winter and still birds sang in the courtyard, drowning out the noisy sounds of the street.

"This is where I go to get away from the craziness of the world," the old man remarked as he stepped out onto the grass. I stopped as I took it all in. Its beauty was breathtaking, a serine oasis within the busy town. Though no tropical paradise, its tranquility soothed me.

"This courtyard is incredible," I replied. Glancing back, a pure joyful smile brightened his face.

"I'm glad you appreciate such things. That says something about your character. Also, your coming to Britain really says something."

"I don't understand," I remarked. "Why does my coming to Britain say something about what type of person I am?"

The duke smiled at my question. I noticed an attendant approached us.

Turning, Coel remarked to the boy-servant, "Balbus, fetch my young friend and I some fresh water from the well."

"Yes, my lord," the young attendant replied.

"Would you like to take a seat?" He asked.

"No, thank you, sir," I smiled as the grass comforted my sore feet. Only sand would have felt softer on my leather soles. "I actually would prefer to stand."

"What I have meant was, you didn't leave the child's welfare to chance and brought the child to Britain," he added.

"What child?" I asked.

He smiled. Taking a couple steps toward the approaching attendants, the duke took the two silver goblets off the serving tray. The young man turned and walked away. The duke handed the cool, long-stemmed cup to me. The water chilled my throat as I took a long drink.

"How old were you when Rome was sacked?" The old man asked.

"I was ten. I was living in Lyons at the time," I declared.

"Everyone remembers where they were when the news reached them. I was having a banquet at the time. It was a grand celebration.

"So, you are only fourteen, now? You've done a lot of growing up since then," the duke declared.

"Yes, a lot of things have changed. My father died earlier this year. That was more difficult to deal with."

"Your father was a good man. He served Rome well. It's unfortunate what happened to him," the old man remarked.

"You knew my father?" I asked. I couldn't hide my surprise.

"Yes, we served in the imperial legions together. I imagine you don't know this, but I knew your father even before that. Your grandfather served under King Crocus back when the Alemanni chieftain was still alive and stationed in the Vale of York. My father was a magistrate of York. This is how your dad and I crossed paths.

"Your father and I joined the legions at the same time when we came of age. Ironically, we swore allegiance to a dead emperor. The same year we joined the British ranks, Maximus was executed in Aquileia.

"In truth, it mattered little. Rome was and is always in need of able, fighting men and willing to pardon some when misled by usurpers. It's usually the leaders that lose their heads just as Marcus, Gratian, Constantine, and Gerontius have recently demonstrated. And those are just the British honorable mentions. Revolt seems to be Rome's greatest export at the moment. It is being churned and cured everywhere as we speak. This chaos is not isolated to this island. At the moment, the Irish and the Picts remain checked at the fringes of the western shores of Demetia and the northern frontier. But this was only after much hardship and bloodshed.

"Your father and I served in defending this province. We both rose to leadership positions when the regiments sent by Stilicho arrived to help against the plundering Picts and Irish."

"I wonder why I never remember living in Britain," I remarked to Lord Coel as he drank his water.

"By the time you were five, your father's unit had been withdrawn from Britain to counter the hostilities of Radagaisus and his Gothic army. Your father gained great honors in the battle of Fiesole serving under Stilicho. At the time, he only had a few more years to serve before retiring from the legion. But all that he had rightfully gained was wrongfully stripped away and confiscated when the Vandal Roman general met his demise and your father was punished through association. Your father kept his life, but lost half of his pension. That is the only reason that he got sucked into this mess with Grallon and his imperial cronies. I wish your father would have accepted my invitation to return to York. He was too proud for that. He thought it was a handout, but it wasn't. I would have been thrilled to have your father fighting by my side once more. I still could use him if he were still alive."

"I wish you would have been able to convince my father otherwise," I remarked.

After a short laugh, he added, "I bet you do. I bet you do."

Lord Coel paused as he looked skyward. For the first time, I noticed the coldness hovering in the courtyard. The standing torches and braziers threw off only so much heat. The stone walkway in and around the courtyard was hypocaust, which most likely kept the fountain water from freezing.

"I've seen and done many things but know much more. I know that you escorted Grallon's daughter and a child from Barcelona. I know that you brought this child to the Isle and have given him to Vortimer. I have been told rumors about the boy. Are they true?" The man asked.

"That all depends on what they said," I replied.

The smiling, old man nodded in agreement.

"I will stop needling you, son," the old man remarked. "I already know if I ask you what the boy's name is, you will say that it's Ambrosius when it's Theodosius. I could use this to know that you are willing to lie to me, but the truth doesn't save a martyr."

He let his words sink in. His candidness amazed me. It set me at ease, but I didn't say anything. Instead, I waited.

"The sacking of Rome was like a pebble dropping into a pond. Its rippling effects have touched the shores of Britain. No longer can people choose what's right or wrong. Free will has been given a death sentence even before its appeal can be heard. And a close friend's son, Pelagius has been called a heretic by lesser men. Now the radicals are becoming the orthodox."

The old man turned away for a moment. A cold breeze blew down into the courtyard. The old man looked up and watched the few clinging leaves rattle in the trees. The chill of winter settled in deeper. I shivered.

Noticing this, the duke asked, "Do you want to go in?"

"No, not just yet," I added. "I would like to talk a little more if you don't mind."

With a little smile, he replied, "Sure. That's fine. So what's on your mind?"

As I walked over to the stone bench and sat down, I asked, "So why am I here?"

Casually following my lead, the duke sat down next to me.

"I called you here for two reasons. The first you already answered and the second I have accomplished so far," the old man declared.

"And what would that be?" I asked.

"I have maintained your safety," he answered.

"Huh? What do you mean?" I asked.

"Do you really think that Grallon plans on allowing you to leave the island?" The duke asked.

"I —,"

"You're no longer a boy. Merlinus, you can't afford to be naive. The debt I owe your father for saving my life is paid by saving yours."

His words stung like a dagger. I stood up and stepped away. Turning back, I asked, "What's saying I can trust you?"

"Nothing," he stated.

"What's stopping you from killing me, now that you know what you want to know?"

"Nothing," he added.

"You're not helping me feel at ease," I finished with a half laugh.

"Good."

"Huh?"

"Merlinus, what are you trying to achieve in this life?"

As his words sank in, I could think of nothing. This year had flashed by, though I had been living day-to-day. I hadn't had the luxury of thinking of the future. I had been forced into facing and solving my father's problems.

"You are not your father," the duke declared.

"What?" I asked as I turned and looked at him.

"You are not your father, like I was not mine. We must face our own mistakes just as they did. We must know what our weaknesses are so we can be wiser men. I know you are old enough to know the faults of your father. You have taken on a heavy burden, but I believe you've completely miscalculated how long you are going to have to deal with it. You know it is going to be a lifetime."

I looked down at the grass, knowing he was right. After a laugh, I replied, "Hopefully, I get to carry it until I am old and gray."

"It doesn't matter if the quality isn't there. Merlinus, I promise to do everything in my power to get you back with your family. I will provide an armed escort to Aureliani. This escort is already headed for Armorica."

"Refuse the protection of an armed escort? Who would be so foolish? Not I? When does it leave?" I asked.

"In two days," the duke replied.

"Thanks. I appreciate the help you have given," I replied.

"You're welcome," he finished. "Your father would be proud."

For the first time, those words felt good to hear.

CHAPTER 8

From York, I headed for Aureliani. I wanted to make sure my family was fine and there were no problems with them moving into the villa. I had anticipated problems, but there were none. It was as agreed. I had escorted Ahès and the child back to Armorica; in return, I inherited a villa in between Aureliani and the Loire River.

I arrived at the villa. It was early morning. Following the imperial directions from Aureliani, I approached a fifteen-foot-tall wall that ran east and west for as far as I could see in both directions. Within fifty yards either way, the trees blotted out the view of the wall. Though it had a thick double-door gate, it stood open for anyone to enter. I hesitated as my heart raced. For some reason, I was scared. Building up nerve, I took a step but stopped. My eyes had locked onto the villa's resident plaque. With immaculate craftsmanship, the bronze plate identified me by name as the owner of the estate, Budicius Merlinus Aurelianus.

Suddenly, I thought of Budicius in Barcelona and how the wealth of his villa had impressed me at first and then sickened me by the time I had left. Then, Grallon's words of advice sang in my ears: "Learn from my example, young Merlinus. Use the Empire. Don't fight the system."

I realized that I had done just that, and I felt sick. Though all the distinguished men said I had done my father proud, only shame filled my heart. There was a chance that Ambrosius was already dead. I had no clue anymore and that didn't make me feel good. I had traded my soul for this villa on the Loire River.

"You know you can go in. It is your place," someone remarked in a Gothic tongue. Surprised, I spun around to find my grandmother standing behind me. She had a bright, wide smile as she stared at me. Smiling back, I went to her and wrapped my arms around her. Grandma Sunilda felt tiny in my arms as I hugged her. She had her long silver hair bundled up with a hair pin. Though I could not recall her previous hair color, it seemed whiter than the last time I saw her. She was of average height, hovering just over five feet tall. And though she was in good spirits, Grandma Sunilda seemed so fragile.

"It's good to have you here, finally," my grandmother continued in her native Gothic tongue.

"It is good to be here," I replied in her native tongue. As I still hugged her, I whispered, "Is everything okay?"

"Now it is. Now it is," she added with a brighter smile. "Let me show you around your place."

"Sure, that would be nice," I smiled.

Keeping my arm around her shoulders, I walked next to her through the open gate. Upon entering, I noticed a wooden staircase going up to the elevated walkway that ran along the length of the upper wall. A well-worn dirt path led from the entrance to the start of the long colonnaded portico that joined into the verandah of the winged-corridor villa. As we walked closer, two large oaks stood guard in the front yard in between the main gate and the portico. To my left on the other side of the one oak stood the barn. I heard the horses stirring in the stables. My horses stirring. Chickens and ducks strutting and waddling about were mine. White plaster coated the walls of the various buildings while rusty-red, clay tiles capped the roofs of them.

"You have some horses, but your horses need training," Grandmother remarked as she guided me out around the villa.

"Aren't we going in?" I asked.

"Most of the household still sleeps. We'll go in later," she replied.

"Okay. Sounds good."

Quietly, we walked past the stand-alone kitchen, furnace, and bathhouse. Tall straight trees quickly consumed the otherwise vacant land. We strolled through the loose leaves for quite a distance. The enclosed land ran for a half mile before it terminated at the river. The slope of the bank made it nearly impossible to scale from the river whether the approaching party was swimming or sailing.

We circled back from the river's edge. As we hooked back toward the villa, Grandmother guided me through a small orchard. It was far enough away so people on the river didn't see it but still close enough to bucket water to all the fruit trees without much difficulty.

Returning to the front, we entered the villa. It still slept quietly. We did not wake it. We walked into the audience chamber, which led into the dining room. These two rooms formed the center of the H-shaped villa. The center corridor ran east and west while the long wings went south toward the river and north toward the main gate. Grandmother took me to the southwest wing.

"This is where your quarters are located," she whispered. "It's closest to the library. My room is in the northwest wing so I'm not bothered by the sun and can sleep in."

"Like you did, today?"

"Yes," she replied with her heartwarming smile.

"Thanks," I remarked as I leaned down and kissed the top of her head.

"No, thank you, my sweet Merlin," she replied. Getting up on the tips of her toes, she kissed my cheek and added, "You've done what you have promised. You are a man of your word. Find peace with that."

"I'll try, Grandma. I'll try."

As I stood alone in my own quarters for the first time, I knew I could not find peace here. I didn't deserve this wealth and prestige. I had taken a child from a loving mother.

This imperial estate had turned me into a monster.

CHAPTER 9

Mother treated me as if I was some lord that deserved the utmost respect. It felt unnerving. My conscience would not let me rest. Guilt weighed heavily on me. I didn't want to expose Mother to it. She had too much to deal with already and didn't need more. I had hired some skilled workers for various duties. When I was certain that all would be taken care of, I left them. I could not stay in Aureliani.

I gathered my things and started out for the stables.

"You weren't actually going to leave without saying good-bye?" Called out my grandmother in her native Gothic tongue. Every time she spoke to me, she used her native language. She loved that I had learned it at a very young age. Actually, she could had been the reason I had excelled at languages.

Suddenly, I felt guilty. I turned to her.

"Awh, don't look at me with such a sad face," she said as she raised a thin bony hand to my cheek. Her hand was cold. As I looked down into her warm eyes, I realized that this would be the last time I would see her alive. I wrapped my arms around her and held her tight.

"I'm sorry, Grandma. I know no other way," I whispered in her native tongue.

"Don't worry, my dear. You lead with an honest heart. Don't lose that and you will have no real regrets. You are a strong young man. You have proven that by what you have done. Most would have failed.

"Merlinus, you remind me so much of your father. You have a similar cowlick. When you crop your black hair short the way he liked to keep his, your hair sticks up in the back. Though you don't have a war-tempered physique as he did, you are somewhat taller.

"Your father hoped that you wouldn't have to serve in the imperial legions. He had higher aspirations for you. That's why you had a tutor whenever he could afford one."

Looking up, she added, "You even have his slate-blue eyes, but you are much more than what he had become. He could never say no to women. He bent to their will. Maybe it was my fault, but regardless of the past, don't fall victim to the same.

"He found a good woman in Alicia. I still don't know why your mother waited for my son. She should have found a better man. Or he should have stayed with her when he had first met her. I guess the time wasn't right."

"What are you two doing out this early in the morning? What are you talking about?" Mother called out as she walked up behind us. Mother was only a couple of inches taller than Grandma Sunilda, but she was somewhat heavier. Mother and Julia, my sister, shared many of the same features. Both had light brown hair with dark brown eyes. Each had round chubby cheeks, but they were not ugly, or at least they were not in my eyes. As usual, Mother's hair hung loosely, free of any bows or pins. Her ankle-long tunic wasn't drawn in around her waist.

"Nothing," Grandmother replied in common Latin.

Mother just shook her head. She looked back at me and noticed I was ready to leave.

"Merlinus, what's going on?" Mother asked. "You are going already? You just mentioned it, the other night. I figured that you would give it a little more thought."

"I've been thinking of it since I left for Barcelona," I replied blankly.

A small smile grew on my grandma's face while a frown formed on my mother's.

"Everything shall be fine. I shall go and see the world. I promise to return," I declared.

"You'd better. You'd better," Mother whispered. "You know you should say good-bye to Julia. She would be heartbroken if you didn't."

"Your mother is right, my dear," grandmother said in her native tongue.

"I know. I know," I replied in two different languages.

Both of them smiled.

I wandered the lands of the Roman Empire and beyond. I traveled as far as the eastern ocean, farther than Alexander the Great had ever seen. Searching for enlightenment, I met countless people, both wise and foolish. From a wizard of steel, I learned the secrets of the forge. He showed me how to make swords fit for the God of War. I absorbed all that I could and left nothing of importance behind. There was nothing I didn't want to know, nothing I couldn't learn. Many languages I learned and many secrets I gained. I even spent time with the monks of Egypt before heading for the eastern sea.

Fourteen years later, I longed for the faces of my family. *Would they even be familiar?* I could stay away no longer. As I headed for home, I heard news of all sorts.

By this time, Placidia had become a widow for the second time. Less than a year after I had originally left, Adaulphus had been assassinated in his personal stables by a servant named Dubius. Valia, the new king of the Visigoth, traded Princess Placidia back to the Romans for a large sum of food. Emperor Honorius had then forced Placidia to marry Constantius, a great imperial general. Within five years, though, Constantius had died, but not before siring a daughter named Honoria and a son named Valentinian the third.

Following the death of Constantius, Emperor Honorius pushed his half-sister and her two children into exile. They sought asylum in New Rome. That same year, Emperor Honorius died of dropsy. Factions within the Empire surfaced. Civil chaos followed. The whole chain of command was questioned and challenged. Power struggles ensued between the western military officers and the imperial family. At the regional level, the praetorian prefect of Gaul, Exuperantius of Poitiers was killed by soldiers in Arles. No one was brought to justice for his murder. Joannes the usurper might have secured the support of Gaul against Placidia's claim if Castinus or Aëtius had sought justice. Instead, the military leaders were impotent to the outrageous offense.

So with an army of Alans sent by the Emperor of New Rome, Placidia marched back to Italy and elevated her little boy, Valentinian, up as the Western Emperor. She stood in command as his regent and as Augusta, the Empress of the West.

And now, four years after the civil war, I was home once again.

CHAPTER 10

I returned to my villa south of Aureliani. The silence of night greeted me. Oddly, inside, so did radiating heat. It rose from the hollow floor beneath my feet. Someone had repaired the hypocaust system. It made me smile. This type of heating of a room highlighted Roman civilization. A furnace outside warmed my soles by heating the air under the villa's floor.

A couple of candles still burned. I picked one of them up and carried it with me. I headed for my chambers without announcing my arrival. As I opened the door, an unexpected smell greeted me. It was a sweet soft smell. It wasn't the stale air I had been anticipating. Instead, incense and flowers welcomed me.

Surprise filled me as I neared the bed. A woman lay there, sleeping. The flickering light of the candle showed a face that I never thought I would see again.

It was Ahès. I looked at her silently as she slept. She looked peaceful. I figured she would have looked much older. It appeared that the years had been kind to her.

Why was she here, then? Why was she sleeping in my villa instead of some place in Vorgium? What had happened? It could not be good.

I wanted answers, but I didn't want to wake her. I stood there for a moment. Thoughts from long ago consumed me as I stared at her. I lost myself in the past.

"Who are you?" Called out a young man from behind me. I turned slightly but stopped as I felt the tip of the blade in my back.

"I am the owner of this villa," I declared.

"You lie," the young man answered as the point needled my spine. "Now, who are you?"

"I am —," I started.

"Merlinus," Ahès declared as she sat up in the bed. "Merlinus, is that really you? We thought that you had died. No one has heard from you in many years. Not even a whisper. Where have you been?"

As she spoke, the tip of the sword dropped away. I pivoted slightly so I could see the person standing behind me. He was a tall young man, just shy of my height of six feet. He was much stockier than I. Dark hair covered the top of his head. His dark eyes studied my every movement. He looked familiar. He looked like King Adaulphus. As Ahès leaned against the wall behind her bed, I sat down on the edge.

"Hah, look at you, Merlinus. There's nothing the same about you except your slate-blue eyes. You have eyes like those of Vortimer," Ahès said. Leaning forward, she ran her fingers through my black beard and added, "What is this? You leave with a baby-skin face and return with the waist-long, wild beard of a hermit. Have you been growing that thing since you left fifteen years ago?"

Laughing lightly, I replied, "No, just for the last six."

"So where are the rest of your things? Are they still outside?" she asked.

I lifted the leather sac I had slung over my neck and shoulder. It hung down to the side of my hip. With my right hand, I lifted up my long walking stick.

"These are my sole possessions," I declared. "Well, that is, besides this robe I wear."

"I guess that explains why you brought that sapling into the villa. You didn't want to take the chance of someone stealing it," she finished with a smile. "I would say I like the robe, if it didn't look like you wore it every day since you got it."

I looked down at what I was wearing, and I laughed when I realized that she was right. I had been wearing the same robe since I received it nearly four years ago.

Memories of the last six years of my life washed over me suddenly like the waterfalls of Mount Shaoshi in the Far East. I thought of the old grand master for the first time in months. From all of my teachers over the years, I could easily say that the lessons learned from Dom Fu had been the most valuable. And it was after he taught me the art of the forge that I received this blessed robe.

"Merlinus, are you still with us?" Ahès asked, drawing me back from distant memories.

"Yes, it has been a long time. Too many years. It doesn't seem too much has changed around here," I remarked. "Well, except for the hypocaust system actually working. Who fixed it?"

Even in the darkness shrouding the room, I saw her smile.

"Ambrosius repaired the system last fall," she remarked.

"Ambrosius? You mean . . ." I started and stopped, amazed that he was now a young man instead of the baby with the birthmark that I still pictured.

"Yes," she replied, "he repaired it. Ambrosius is very clever. There are probably a couple of things he could teach you, Merlinus."

"Please, Mother, even a fool can show what not to do," Ambrosius remarked. "Besides, you're making more out of it than what it was. I simply replaced a damaged pipe. The furnace was in good repair already."

Quietly, I listen to him. The baby boy had turned into a young man seemingly overnight. Amazingly, he still lived. And it seemed he'd grown into a good person. I found it difficult to say anything. There was much I wanted to ask, but I didn't know what to say. My thoughts were too guarded, so I said nothing as I studied him.

"It's a pleasure to finally meet you," he began, "I am Ambrosius."

"Hello, young man. It's good to meet you," I replied reaching out to shake his hand.

"Ambrosius, why don't you head back to bed. Everything is all right. The two of you can get better acquainted in the coming days."

"Of course," the young man replied. Turning to me, he added, "Once more sir, it's an honor to meet you. Sorry that it was at the point of my sword, though."

"Forget it. It's completely understandable." I remarked.

With a slight bow, he turned and walked out of the room. He closed the door upon his exit.

Crawling across the bed, Ahès wrapped her arms around me and hugged me tightly. Pulling away, she kissed me on the cheek and hugged me again.

"Oh Merlinus, there is so much we need to talk about. It has been too long and so much has happened since we were last together. Where do I begin?" She asked.

"Fourteen years ago on the shore of Armorica," I replied.

With a light smile, she replied, "Right."

CHAPTER 11

I remained silent as I waited for Ahès to begin her story. Her wild, youthful beauty had been reined in by the years, but she glowed with a refined beauty now. Her dark brown hair showed only a few strands of gray. Within her soft brown eyes, a sadness lingered. Time hadn't made her face or her plump breasts sag. They still enticed my eyes.

"Did you know that Grallon isn't my father? My real father passed away when I was very young. He was such a big man, but gentle. He would toss me up in the air lightly and catch me. For hours it seemed. I would just laugh so hard for so long. He smiled the whole time. He loved me very much," she stated with a bright smile. The warm glow faded when she added, "Everything else is a reflection on a rippling pool.

"Grallon was a young officer under my father. They served Maximus and then Stilicho.

"Father was killed in a battle against the Irish in western Britain. He left Grallon in charge of his affairs in Armorica, at the time. Mother said Father wasn't much of a thinker. He didn't have time for such things. He was too busy making sure imperial plans were put into action. Father was a man of action, while Grallon was a handsome sailing merchant.

"She was candidly honest at the end," Ahès said as her voice trailed off to a sad look of silence.

"My mother relied more and more on Grallon's support as time went by. Through my mother, Grallon became lord of Vorgium. You see, my mother had come from an old, distinguished family," she remarked.

"The Voltinia tribe," I replied.

"Yes," she remarked with a surprised look, "How did you know?"

With a smile, I answered, "I recall the statue overlooking the bay."

She smiled and stated, "Mother's family controlled the salt tanks and garum trade on the Bay of Douarnenez for well over a hundred years."

She added, "Unfortunately, after the death of my father, Mother and I had fallen on hard times. The schools weren't what they once were.

The market hasn't been lucrative in years. Mother spoke of prosperity back when the Empire was still pagan and the worshiped Neptune kept our family strong. Mother watched as her beliefs and family's status became nullified.

"Grallon slithered into her soul and stripped her of what he wanted. At first, it seemed that he cared, but it soon became clear that he was only concerned with my mother's claims to Vorgium. With seven Roman roads radiating from there, Grallon wanted it for his shipping empire along with her family's properties in the ports of the Gallic Sea.

"And after taking claim to everything she had, he humiliated her by having an affair with a Saxon whore. The German slut bore a bastard," she added.

"So, is Vortimer your half-brother, then?" I inquired.

"No, Grallon and my mother had no children. Grallon was previously married. He had three sons from his first marriage. His wife died when she was giving birth to his youngest boy, Paschent. From what I have been told, she died a year before my father. Mother of Mary, so much has happened since we last spoke. Some of it hurts, so please bear with me and I will try to tell you as best as I can."

"Take your time," I replied, "we have all night."

"Hah," she laughed. "It will take longer than that."

"I'm figuring on being around for a while," I answered.

She smiled and pulled up the linen sheets around her. She fell silent as her eyes drifted down from mine. She struggled with something. Something that she wasn't sure that she wanted to tell me.

"I wonder if that statue is still standing," I joked.

"It's hard to say, with it being underwater," she declared.

"What? What happened?"

"A mile inland past the city of Ys has been submerged by seawater for quite some time. One night, the sea gate was unlocked and opened fully. The ocean engulfed everything. It was quite the spectacle."

"How could Grallon let that happen? Didn't he have the only key to the sea gate's lock?"

"Yes," she replied.

"So what happened, did he lose his mind?" I asked.

"You could say that," she mumbled. "In another drunken frenzy, Grallon forcibly took me. Luckily, the last time, his seed did not take."

"What? The child that you took to Barcelona was his?" I asked.

"Well, not really," she replied.

"I don't understand, Ahès, you're not making sense," I remarked.

"The actual child that went with us to Barcelona was the child of Hope, a girl that I knew. She lived in the village southeast of the Bay of Douarnenez. She had become pregnant and I helped her as she helped me. She could not keep her child and I really didn't want to get rid of mine. So before you and I left, the girl and I switched our sons. She tended to Faustus while I brought her sickly child to Barcelona.

"It was Hope's child that laid in that little silver coffin not mine. For the first couple of years, Hope's family cared for Faustus. Without Grallon's knowledge, I paid for the arrangement with coins from his personal coffer. In time, though, Grallon saw me stealing the money and I let him know why I was taking it. He was furious when he found out. He vowed to send the boy away. Fearing the worst for Faustus, I sent a letter for help.

"When Grallon tried to take Faustus, I told him that Bishop Germanus knew and that the bishop was heading for Armorica with a small imperial delegation. The redness in his face boiled past his eyebrows."

"Bishop Germanus?" I cut in. "Hah, it's a wonder he confronted Grallon for you."

"It's strange," she remarked. "It may seem hard to believe, but Germanus seems truly committed to the Faith. Something happened after the episode with the baby Theodosius. A real transformation. He wears a hair shirt now and regrets his part in the conspiracy. Periodically, he drops in to check up on Ambrosius and every time he asks about you.

"Anyway, after I told Grallon, a short while later, Germanus arrived with a delegate of men. He brought charges against Grallon. They were not the charges you would expect; they had nothing to do with Ambrosius or Faustus. Grallon had grown neglectful in his duties to the Empire. The Bishop of Auxerre used my situation to temper the provincial council into righteous action.

"Grallon knew the nature of the charges that were being levied before Germanus publicly announced them. Trying to discredit the bishop, Grallon forced me to take Faustus and sit him on Germanus' lap. I did as Grallon ordered, fearing for my life and that of my son's. At the council meeting, I told the group of clergy and laity that Bishop Germanus was the boy's father.

"Germanus called out, 'Like a true father, I shall care for you, child, and never send you away. This is my promise as father of Armorica's abandoned children. I will show you the world and its heavenly spectacles. It shall be this way unless your father of flesh says otherwise.'"

"Faustus glanced at Germanus and then at Grallon," Ahès said as she continued her story. "While sitting in Bishop Germanus' lap, the four-year-old boy called out to Grallon, 'I go bye-byes? Papa, I go bye-byes?'"

"Grallon stewed as he stared at the boy," Ahès added. "Faustus, then, hugged Germanus. Grallon stood up and stormed out of the hall. Germanus publicly condemned Grallon.

"It wasn't much later that Grallon took me. In a drunken rage, he did it. When Grallon raped me the first time, I swore that if he ever did it again, I would finish him.

"He wasn't gentle with me. The alcohol and the stench of fish from the garum he had consumed seeped from him. It didn't discourage him that I wouldn't let him kiss me on the lips. His slimy tongue licked my cheek.

"I struggled, but he had my arms pinned to the bed. With all my strength, I twisted and thrashed trying to break free. This was to no avail. He lay on top of me. I had trouble breathing from his heavy weight. With his body holding me down, he snatched my wrists in one hand and yanked up my dress with his other."

She stopped. She could not hold back the pain that Grallon forced upon her. Tears streamed down her face as her hands covered her eyes. I went to her. I wrapped my arms around her and tried to comfort her.

"Ahès, you don't have to tell me more," I whispered.

"I know," she said. "I'll be all right. Just give me a moment."

"Of course," I remarked as I wiped away her tears with my thumb.

After a sigh, she continued, "As he was on top and having his way with me, I noticed the key for the sea lock dangling from his neck. And at that moment, I stopped resisting him. Soon after he had soiled in me, he passed out. As he began to snore, I slipped the gold necklace holding the key from his neck. He began to stir and I thought he would wake. Luckily, he did not. He simply rolled on his side, making it easier for me to escape.

"Immediately, I got out of the bed and raced through the villa. I did not stop. Once outside, I ran until I reached the shore. The salt in the air burned the inside of my chest. I stared out across the water. The full moon hovered close to the shimmering surface of the sea. The night seemed so peaceful as I stood at the water's edge.

"After my rapid breathing slowed, I quickly walked toward the sea locks. I went to the dock on the other side of it. Getting into the small boat, I rowed out to the sea gate. I took the key and without hesitation unlocked the chains holding the spoke-wheel crank from lowering or raising the sea gate and I lowered the stone gate. The sea did the rest. It rushed over the edge like a waterfall and pounded the water below. The sea flooded through the opening.

"I heard my name repeatedly called out. Looking toward the villa, I saw a lone man racing along the shore. Slowly my name grew louder and his face became clearer. It was Grallon. I smiled watching him veer to higher ground as the sea swallowed up the land beneath his feet. That was the last time I saw him in Armorica.

"I began to row away from the gate before the sea could pull the boat through it. To this day, I still don't know how I made it to the western shores of Britain in that little boat. I figured the sea would have swallowed me whole. As I grew tired from rowing, I laid in the belly of the boat and hoped the sea would consume me."

She went silent. As her head fell in shame, she stared at her kneading hands. I reached up to comfort her. As my fingers touched her shoulder, her whole body shivered. Breaking her from her past, she turned with a sad smile and said, "I'm sorry. I must be a little cold."

"I can remedy that," I said as I rubbed her shoulders.

CHAPTER 12

After stoking the hypocaust furnace, I returned to Ahès' quarters with a plate of salted pork, cheese, bread, and some wine. She had put on a pullover tunic and placed on her feet some fur-lined slippers. She walked over to the small round table. It sat next to the window. Together, we settled in the chairs by the table.

As I prepared a light meal for us she continued, "After I lowered the gate and flooded the city of Ys, I headed for Britain in search of Ambrosius. Sometime later, I made it to the island. I don't know how long it took. By the time I had reached the shore, I was beyond delirious. Luckily, I was found and cared for by a gentleman named Constantine. He was from the rural districts of Cornovia above the Severn Valley.

"Constantine and his entourage had taken a different route home from the market. They had a good return in wool and had decided to visit kin in Gwent. Traveling the shores of the Severn Sea, he discovered me in my grounded boat. He placed me in one of his covered wagons and nursed me back to health as they made their way to the villa of Honorius in western Britain.

"Emperor Honorius?" I questioned.

"No. He is somehow related, though," she replied. "Constantine and Honorius were high officers on the island. They each commanded a cavalry unit in the island's mobile army. Regrettably, they both retired shortly before the last British revolt by the usurper named Constantine. The two men remained distant from the mounting revolt, having fulfilled their obligation to the army. Neither one of them was naive enough to believe that a usurper worthy only by the name would succeed when they had witnessed a better man fail.

"After regaining my health, I was informed that we had been at Honorius' villa for awhile. It didn't take long for my caretaker to realize who I was. Word of me had already reached the island. His son, Cai, rightfully warned him. Still Constantine assisted me.

"While at the villa in Gwent, Honorius told us how Grallon's honorary titles were confiscated. Germanus returned with imperially endorsed orders and the backing of Agricola, the praetorian prefect of Gaul at the time. Residing in Gaul, Agricola controlled and provided security for the region, and at times, in the northwestern provinces. Grallon could not scoff or ignore this imperial mandate.

"Grallon went to Demetia in western Britain. He hides out now in the mountains of Snowdonia, in the lands that remain under his control. Even in those lands, Grallon falsely lay claim to holding. He gained them from his first marriage. The villa in Gloucester where Vortimer still resides was where his mother was born and raised.

"Now as the High Commander of the British Council, Grallon has hired Saxons to guard the remaining interests of the nobles. And so, the shepherd has the wolves tending the flock."

"What has happen to Agricola's troops? Have they been re-stationed in the East," I inquired. "What happen to him?"

"Agricola died the year after the third consulship of Constantius. That same year, Constantius died. It had been only seven months since Honorius had made the tri-consul a colleague in power," she stated.

"When did you leave the island?" I asked.

"Three years ago," she replied.

"When did you catch up with Ambrosius?" I asked.

"The same year that I flooded the city of Ys was the same year that I met and married Constantine," she added.

"You're married?" I asked between bites of bread and pork.

Sadness returned to her face, the same sadness I saw before she sank into the sea when I sailed away with Ambrosius fourteen years ago.

"Constantine never looked down upon me. He was like you in that aspect. From the day that we shared our vows to the night he died, he loved me as if I was his princess and he were my king.

"When I first made it to the island, I relentlessly searched for Ambrosius. Constantine did as he promised; he helped me find him. Vortimer no longer sheltered the boy. Tired of being used by Grallon, the young nobleman rid himself of his father's unfair burden. Choosing a worthy regent, though, Vortimer sent Ambrosius to stay with a nobleman and his wife in Ribchester on the eastern shores of the Irish Sea.

"At an early age, Ambrosius gained self-reliance and learned horsemanship and hunting. He is quite a remarkable young man. Highly intelligent, but still cordial and polite.

"For Ambrosius' safety, Constantine convinced me to allow the boy to stay in Ribchester," she stated.

Pausing, she asked, "Merlinus, why did you go away for so long?"

Falling silent, I realized that I was holding my breath. I knew the answer and didn't like it. I released the sudden pressure I felt.

"For all the good that I had done them, my family's well-being reminded me of my own wrongdoing. I left everything that I knew and loved behind. I wanted to absolve myself of all my sins," I remarked.

"Don't punish yourself, Merlinus. Though you kidnapped the boy, you saved him. Look what happen to King Adaulphus. They killed the boy's father in his own stables. There was no way that marriage was going to last. It is unfortunate that Ambrosius had to grow up so quickly. But what strife he has encountered has simply made him stronger," she declared. "You gave him a chance, though."

"He is definitely big for his age. I would never have guessed that he was only fifteen years old. He appears just shy of twenty," I remarked. "Nearly a man ready to marry."

"Yes, that's truer than you know," Ahès added. "After staying several years up in northern Britain, Ambrosius came back to Constantine's lands in Cornovia. And for a few years we knew peace. Constantine treated the boy as his own. He taught Ambrosius to be a true man, honorable. And shortly before we were driven out of Britain, Ambrosius met the sweetest girl named Priscilla at a festival sponsored by her grandfather, Honorius of Gwent.

"Even now Ambrosius talks about her. And with the passion of his first love, he swears that he will marry her if he ever sees her again. It's so adorable," she added with a bright, warm smile.

"I'm sure it is, Ahès. You're such a good mother," I teased.

She blushed with guilt.

"I've told him that I am his mother," she remarked. "Was it wrong that I told him I was his mother?"

"What kind of a person he is today is a direct result of your upbringing. That's what a mother does," I remarked.

She looked up and smiled at me.

"Hopefully, he will be able to overcome that," I teased once more.

"Awh," she cried as she swatted at me.

"No. Honestly, it seems like you have done a terrific job. He is well behaved," I declared.

"I cannot claim what I haven't done. He is innately that way," she answered. "This is apparent in how he treats Geraint. He is the son of Constantine and me," she added.

"How old is he?" I asked.

"Geraint is six and a summer's child. He lives without a care in the world. He's only down when he's bored. That one is a handful," she declared. "He idolizes Ambrosius, though. Ambrosius doesn't mind. I think he enjoys teaching Geraint what he can. The boy is attached to his hip when Ambrosius is outside doing something. Only inside does Geraint avoid him. He fears that Ambrosius might try to make him sit still long enough to work on his reading and writing. Geraint does not enjoy the books the way that Ambrosius does. There are times when I swear Ambrosius has left the house, but then I enter another room and find him silently reading near an open window. He can speak a couple languages and read Greek. He speaks highly of Pelagius and warily about Caelestius," she remarked. "You will enjoy speaking with Ambrosius. I guarantee it. Just ask for his opinion on a sinless life.

"One night, after we had been here for a while, he astounded me. He asked, 'If a baptized man and a baptized woman have a child, does the child need to be baptized? And if not, then is there a true need for the Church when the grace of God is given at home?'

"I had no response," she remarked as she shook her head.

The young man had touched on one of the key elements in the heresy surrounding Pelagius. The orthodoxy that the African bishops were preaching held little logic for me. It locked the believer into continuous servitude. A debtor of alms from past generations. No reprieve for self-control and personal actions.

"In truth, Ambrosius is like Geraint's father," she continued, "Unfortunately, Geraint doesn't remember Constantine. It has been two years since Cai was here. That's when Constantine's oldest boy came over from the island to visit and check up on us. He stays in Britain fighting against Grallon.

"After the death of Emperor Honorius, or more important, the deaths of Agricola and Exuperantius, Grallon tightened his grip of power over the British and Armoric provinces. He controlled the Gallic Sea, already. In an effort to consolidate his land holdings on the western side of the isle, Grallon helped his youngest son, Paschent, gain a foothold in Builth. Soon Grallon's raids crossed into the lands of Gwent and into the rural districts of Cornovia. In the southern part of the island, he holds sway in Topsham and Tintagel through his shipping empire.

"Packs of German wolves infest the forests and fords of Britain. Grallon has done little to restrain their growing numbers. In fact, he has encouraged them as they help to consolidate his power.

"It all fell apart three years ago. I still wake up suddenly from dreaming about that night. In those nightmares, just as it happened, Constantine wakes me, saying that the house is on fire. I still hear him clearly. 'Wake, Ahès. Get up! Get up! My love, our home is on fire. Awake!'

"From the dream, I sat up in bed. My heart raced, just as it did that autumn night. Getting out of bed, I picked up Geraint and followed Constantine. Ambrosius followed us as we made our way outside.

"Even if there wasn't a full moon, I would have had no trouble seeing; the long stable stood fully ablaze. Though twenty yards away, the heat of the inferno pressed heavily upon my face. The horses circled restlessly in the corral. Our assailants moved up as we exited the villa. The large group of horsemen walked their mounts forward. As Constantine stepped up, he turned and whispered, 'Run.'

"At that moment, he drew his sword and engaged the horsemen. As I cradled Geraint in one arm, I snatched Ambrosius with my other hand. At first, Ambrosius resisted but stopped when Constantine ordered, 'Go! Go! They cut Constantine down right in front of us. Lifeless, Constantine dropped to his knees, and then fell face forward.

"We would have all perished if Cai and his friends hadn't returned as this happened. Cai had left with them earlier in the week. They had gone on a hunting trip. That night, though, Cai and his friends rushed in on horseback. Four of them threw up interference, while Cai swept up me and Geraint. Cai's friend, Kyle, snatched up Ambrosius.

"I was never so scared for my life as I was then," she whispered.

I poured the last of the wine into her goblet. Without a word, she picked it up and finished it off in a single draw.

"Once they killed Constantine, I brought Ambrosius here. Of course, he wanted to stay, but I would have none of that," she remarked. "For God's sake, he was only twelve years old at the time. There's no way he would have survived. I am not even certain if Cai is still alive. It's been some time since we received a letter from him.

"Here, we have found peace. Britain seems a world away. There's no way we would have made it if it wasn't for the help of your family. Your mother, Alicia, has been incredible. Ambrosius and Geraint adore her or at least her cooking," Ahès finished with a smile.

"Mother is good? What about my little sister, Julia?" I asked.

"She's little no longer. She is engaged to a Roman soldier named Probus. They're supposed to get married this summer. He has family near the Waal River; that's north of the city of Cologne. I believe that they will move there.

"Your mother and sister are simply going to be amazed to see you. It's funny that you've shown up as you did. That's the way they said it would be. No grand, glorious entrance for Merlinus," she replied.

"Well, I'm glad I didn't disappoint them," I replied.

"You must have some stories to tell," she remarked.

"I might have one or two to tell, but not tonight," I added.

"So how did you get here? Did you ride a horse?" She asked.

"No. Not for the last hundred miles. I had to sell the beast because I could not bring myself to eat it," I answered. "Betsy was sold and I was full. Of course, I regretted it when I began walking the final hundred miles nearly a month ago."

"Why didn't you use it for hunting?" she asked.

"The animal had gone lame. Besides, I came upon a town with an empty stomach and smelled roast on a nearby spit. That's all it took," I replied.

"Merlinus, sleep in here for the night. I will take the guest quarters," she replied.

"No, I couldn't," I replied.

"I insist," she added. "I know where everything is. This way the household isn't woken up and you actually get to sleep tonight. Fair enough?"

"Sounds good," I remarked.

As she stood up, I did the same. With a smile, she moved close, kissed me on the cheek, and hugged me tightly.

Letting go and stepping back, she remarked, "It's really good to have you home, Merlinus."

"It's good to be home," I smiled.

CHAPTER 13

I woke with the sudden thought of moving — *wasting daylight. Get moving. Get home.*

I'd been dreaming. With a heavy sigh of relief, I told myself that I was home. I'd been here for a week now. I sat there in my bed letting my surroundings sink in. It felt good to be back. Out in the world, I had to be ready to fight to the death. The cities of men were far more dangerous than the deserts of God.

I got up and went out of the villa and did my daily exercises, which I had learned from Master Dom Fu. Afterwards, I drew some cold, well-water. Surprisingly, I found Mother out near the well. She just stood there, watching the birds flying by singing the song of spring. I viewed her differently after growing up and being away for so long. She seemed so small, so frail. Mother had lost much of her excess weight. I could only assume that the hard work at the villa had worn that away. Her hair had lost its dark brown hue a long time ago. Still, she kept her hair long and loose, though it was now snow white.

"Mother, is everything all right?" I remarked.

She turned with a warm smile, melting away my worries.

"Yes," she said as she walked to me and hugged me tightly. I leaned down and kissed the top of her head as I towered over her.

"I've been thinking that we should have a grand celebration. We shall have it at Easter," she declared.

"Mother, we shouldn't. Times are too tight for some extravagant party," I remarked.

"My baby boy has come back to me. We're celebrating and that's final," she remarked sternly. I smiled, knowing that it was.

I heard a noise and looked toward the gate. In the far distance, a large, impressive train of people, horses, and wagons rolled down the tree-lined lane toward the villa. My heart sank. The fear of losing the villa weighed on me.

I sprinted to the main gate. I quickly shut the large thick wooden doors and barred them, then I climbed the stairs to the wall's elevated walkway. There was no way to defend against this approaching party. The horsemen were four wide and at least ten rows deep as they rode in front of a center wagon while another ten rows guarded the rear. A line of infantry marched single file on both sides of the wagon. The army halted, holding formation. I noticed their standard-bearer. He carried a large wooden pole capped with a X encircled by an O. As the dust settled from the train, my eyes took it all in. It appeared more like an army than a church procession. It left an uneasy feeling within me. I waited, watching from the wall. A man exited from the back of the enclosed wagon. I wondered if it was Germanus.

As he walked closer, I realized that it was. Though he had gray hair and a worn look, I recognized him immediately. Germanus' long narrow face was unmistakable. His short coal-colored hair had smoldered to an ash gray. His beard was fuller and covered more of his face. His hazel eyes were more serene and less scheming. He was less primped but still proper. His attire lacked the pristine condition it had in Barcelona. He wore a off-white tunic with a hair shirt underneath. He sported an old red cloak. It was Bishop Germanus, only older.

What does he want?

"Greetings," he called. "I am Bishop Germa..."

He stopped and stared hard at me as if his eyes were deceiving him. I knew that I didn't look like I did before. The last time he saw me I was only fourteen years old. Now, after nearly fifteen years of growing and minor trimming, my beard covered much of my face and my bones had more stock. I felt like a changed man.

"Merlinus, is that really you? It's been nearly fifteen years since I saw you last! I prayed for your well-being but feared for your health. I'd thought that you were beyond this world," Germanus remarked.

With a smile, I remarked, "I've heard that quite a bit recently. Well, I guess we both know to not believe everything that we hear."

"It's amazing to see you. Whenever I stop here, I ask if anyone has heard from you. I was planning on doing it this time, too," he added.

"One moment, Bishop," I called down, "let me open the door for you and your men." I quickly walked down the stairs and went to the barred gate. Removing the wooden beam, I pushed the door outward.

As I walked toward him, I inquired, "What brings you this way?"

"Anymore, it's never good," he started. "Church business takes me to Britain. With my diocese in northwestern Gaul, I've been selected by Bishop Celestine of Rome to uproot the heresy preached by Pelagius. When Pelagius was alive, he wasn't the problem. He bore all of the fruits of the spirit: charity, gentleness, joy, patience, and good nature. He did not think like a lawyer or a theologian. He was not Caelestius who is still stirring up trouble. Pelagius was concerned about actual events and consequences, not things that could possibly happen and their potential results. It is the implications and ramifications that the Church cannot and will not allow men to preach under the veil of the orthodoxy.

"A while back, a British deputation informed a synod that the heresy thrives on the island. Agricola, son of Bishop Severianus, has corrupted British Christians with his Pelagian beliefs," Germanus remarked.

All of the infantry and troopers remained at least forty yards behind us. As Germanus spoke, a younger man similarly dressed walked up. This man had much thinner features than Germanus. It appeared that this boy of a man had lived his entire life behind the walls of aristocracy. His eyes were a gentle green, not hard and jaded like the majority of the upper class. He had no facial hair, and he kept the brown hair on his head extremely short. There were no streaks of gray, and oil made it slick and wet. His white tunic appeared bleached to a snow white. A red tassel drew the tunic around his narrow waist.

"Ah yes, this is young Lupus. He's the Bishop of Troyes. He was also chosen to go to Britain. Bishop Lupus, this fine gentleman is Merlinus. This incredible villa is his. I hope Merlinus will offer us his hospitality for the day," Germanus remarked as the young man approached.

"It is granted. With it being this early in the morning and no prior notice, however, very little can be offered immediately. It will take time."

"Everything does," Bishop Lupus added. "We must find the patience to deal with it and the wisdom to accept it." Pausing, the young man glanced around and added, "This is a beautiful place, like a temperate Eden. You are a lucky man, Merlinus."

"Thanks. I appreciate this place more and more," I replied.

"Good morning, Bishop Germanus," Ambrosius' voice called out.

Turning, I noticed Ambrosius for the first time. If the bishops had seen him, their body language gave no indication of him. Mother stood near the villa with a worried look on her face. As I smiled to her, she turned and walked away.

"Dear Bishop, what's the need for such an army? I promised that my friends and I wouldn't take anymore of the imperial cattle and we haven't," Ambrosius stated.

"I know, young man. It is true; I haven't heard of any more trouble. I am proud of you, Ambrosius," Germanus remarked with a slight bow. "Besides, this army is not here for you and your friends. We have business in Britain."

"That sets my mind at ease," Ambrosius replied. "At first glance, I thought we were being invaded."

"No. Nothing like that," Bishop Germanus replied. "As I explained to Merlinus, we are heading for Britain. Myself and Bishop Lupus have been sent by Bishop Celestine of Rome. There have been several reports of the Pelagian heresy thriving on the island and word of it has spread to the mainland. It appears that Agricola is the main heretic."

"Hah," Ambrosius laughed. "You make it sound like the plague."

"Well, it is," Bishop Lupus interjected. "It's the plague of the soul."

"Well stated, Lupus," Germanus added. "It's unfortunate that a better Brit wasn't found to fill the see when Bishop Guithelinus died."

"So, are you going to use this army to bleed the heresy out of the island?" Ambrosius asked.

I knew I should correct Ambrosius' tone. I knew why Ambrosius was giving them a hard time, and I felt the same questioning cynicism. They sought to suppress the very beliefs I held high. Their orthodoxy had little regard for individual grace, free will, and self-control. I didn't want to hold back his cutting tongue.

"If need be," Germanus replied.

Germanus' comment convinced me not to correct Ambrosius. Surprise filled Ambrosius' face. He didn't think that the bishop was capable of such extreme measures.

"There's no way that the sword of God would be used against Christians led astray if they reconcile with the orthodoxy. The troopers will be used against the repentless heretics," Lupus declared.

"So are you expecting trouble, then?" I asked.

"In all truth, they are simply the *armati* for the Church," Germanus replied. "Numerous reports tell of a surge in the Saxons numbers, though.

The Saxons have been arriving continually by the boatload. It has alarmed and appalled many people on the island. Grallon has grown less and less receptive to the Council's concerns regarding the Saxons."

"The Council is a bunch of fools for electing Grallon High Commander in the first place," Ambrosius barked.

His sharp, bitter comment seemed to surprise only Bishop Lupus.

"That's beside the point, Ambrosius," Germanus added.

"We must still prepare for the worst-case scenario. I do not foresee a warm reception on the island for us." Bishop Lupus declared.

"How long are you going to spend on the island?" I asked.

"As long as it takes to uproot this heresy," Germanus remarked.

"What about the Saxons? Are you going to do anything about them?" Ambrosius asked.

"They are not our concern," Lupus replied.

"What?" Ambrosius barked. "How can you say that? They are pagans. I thought you stated that you were going to strike down all non-believers with God's sword," Ambrosius remarked in a sharper tone.

"We shall never seek out a fight," Lupus returned strongly. "That's not Christ's way. We shall unleash God's wrath only if we are physically confronted. The blood of the enemy shall only be shed in self-defense."

Ambrosius mumbled something as his foot pawed at the ground. His disposition soured. In these last few days since returning home, I hadn't seen this side of Ambrosius. There was true anger in his eyes. From what Ahès had stated, I didn't fault him for his hatred. Vortigern had killed the only father he had known and driven him out of his home. I would want Vortigern's head on a pike, also. Maybe Lupus was unaware of this. I wondered if Germanus knew the truth.

"Young Ambrosius, I know of the flames that consumed your home and now engulf your heart. Vengeance is not God's way," Germanus remarked.

"But I thought justice was," the young man quickly replied.

Silence fell between us; only the sound of restless horses filled the air. Their hooves shuffled, and the horses sputtered their sighs as the soldiers held their formation.

"There is only a fine line that separates the two when a passionate heart guides the hand of justice," I dropped in.

My comment broke Ambrosius' hold over the silenced bishops.

With a tilted head and a raised eyebrow, he gave me a queer look.

"A very thin one. One that is easily blurred," Germanus remarked.

Once more, silence fell upon us. Once more, I broke it.

"Ambrosius, head back inside and get things started. Have some food prepared for our guests. Start with bread and some cold cider."

As my words sank in, the bitterness in his eyes faded away and he replied, "Yes, sir. Right away."

Ambrosius turned from us and headed back toward the villa.

"Although truly fortuitous, our meeting is very fortunate, Merlinus. Lupus and I are in need of you," Germanus remarked.

"What do you mean?" I questioned. My stomach sank.

"Nepos," Germanus called out. "Keep the men in formation."

"Understood," the man replied in a deep accent. It was hard to tell how tall Nepos was while he sat on his black mount. Nepos appeared to be the size of Ambrosius, but thinner. He sat with ease on his mount. His long, straight blonde hair was held in a ponytail. It was nearly as long as his horse's tail. His natural tan gave an enhanced shine to his light-colored eyes. They were keen as a hawk. He wheeled his mount and called out Germanus' order in an Alan tongue.

Germanus moved closer to the open gate. I drew closer, and he went a little bit further.

"These men you see behind us," Germanus replied in a whisper, "were assigned to us by a decree issued by Bishop Celestine. In the beginning, we had left a council in Arles with a small unit of Alan warriors. Just recently, though, we met up with a large squad of men brought by a man named Carbo. As we travel, all of these men are under the command of this young man behind us named Nepos. He seems to be a reasonable man, but it has been brought to my attention that he ultimately answers to Goar, one of the Alan kings, and his son, Euthar. I don't recall the Celestine's deacon, Palladius, mentioning this. We thought that the Roman named Lucian was the commander of this small unit from Arles, but we were mistaken. Worse yet, Lucian acted as though he never expressed such a suggestion. Though he could fluently speak the Alan's native tongue, he has departed for his homelands in Autun as we traveled north. Shortly after Lucian left for Autun, there was an incident. Some of the Alans from our group raided a villa in the nearby area. When this was brought to my attention and the men were confronted, the Alans argued that there was a misunderstanding. They argued further that there was nothing out of the norm with their behavior. They argued that Euthar and his men engaged in raiding parties when he escorted the Church officials at previous times. Nepos has ensured me that this will not happen again. Still, we are at a tremendous disadvantage. This language barrier is unacceptable. Lives are at stake. I must be assured that my commands are understood and followed. Regrettably, I was going to ask Ahès if I could take Ambrosius with us."

"What? He's just a boy, Germanus," I barked.

"I know. That's why I'm hoping you will go instead," he finished.

His words stopped me in my tracks. It was as if he asked me to walk back to the great eastern sea. As I stewed in silence, I knew I had to go. Either way, Ambrosius would go. At least if I went, I could try to protect him as best as I could.

"You can speak these barbarians' tongue?" Lupus question.

"What was that?" I asked.

"You can speak the Alan's native language, right?" Lupus asked.

"Yes, that's one language I speak fluently," I blankly replied.

"You can speak several languages?"

"Yes."

"Fluently?"

"Yes," I answered. "That's my greatest talent. Latin, Greek, words from the holy lands and phrases from the Orient. Germanic dialects."

"Amazing," the young bishop replied.

"Right, and that's why I'm hoping he will go," Germanus added.

"I will," I whispered.

"Good, young Ambrosius won't have to go," Lupus replied.

I tried not to laugh but struggled to hold it back. A smirk formed on Germanus' face. He knew Ambrosius would still beg to go.

"Why do you feel that comment was funny?" Lupus questioned.

"I do not believe Ambrosius will be turned away from going to Britain. Ambrosius will want to see if he can gain any news of his brother, Cai. I know I lack the will and words to deter him. You may try, but I believe you would be wasting your time," I answered.

"Good. You both shall accompany us to Britain," Germanus said.

CHAPTER 14

We prepared to cross the channel. The weather changed drastically. First, the sky became brooding. Dark thick clouds sank low, touching the churning water in spots. Soon, nothing else could be seen except the pounding sea and the pluming sky.

The crew struggled to keep the ships from capsizing. Germanus and the other priests prayed for our salvation while Ambrosius and I held on to what we could so we weren't thrown into the sea. The elements tore at the sails. Pieces of them flapped loosely, ready to fly off into the wind and never be seen again. Cold saltwater pelted our bodies. I have been on some bad voyages, even run ashore one time, but none seemed as rough as this one. The wind screamed wet stinging words. Its coldness ached within the bone. The ship heaved up and bowed down relentlessly to the mercy of the sea. Germanus tried to assure Ambrosius that he had seen worse.

"Any worse than this and we'll be several leagues under the sea," Ambrosius replied with a grumble.

"Hah," Nepos scoffed as he huddled and shivered by us and then added, "Why should London be any different than Arles? The last time my unit went by sea for the Church, it was like this. We were nearly shipwrecked when we were dispatched from Rome. We should have simply taken the land route to Auxerre."

"You must be beginning to dislike sailing," I remarked in his native tongue.

"An Alan always has a horse underneath them, but I never supposed that it would be sea horses. By Neptune, I pray we make it."

The longer the voyage churned on, the worse everyone felt. The sea made many physically sick. In time, Germanus slipped into a fever-gripped sleep. The morale of the priests fell into a questioning squalor.

"The demons of the sea rage on. They have grown stronger since our brother, Germanus, has slipped into his sickly sleep. What are we to do?"

one of the priests moaned as the gale continued.

In truth, I noticed little change in the weather. The only thing I had noticed was the lack of Germanus' encouraging words. Glancing over to Bishop Lupus huddling with his other brethren, I doubted that Lupus had ever experienced anything comparable to this storm. Then I thought of the constant fear of barbaric raids in his region. It had to wear a person thin, but the whole feeling of being trapped on this boat with nowhere to go except into the sea gave a whole new meaning to hopelessness. Lupus seemed to lack Germanus' ability to inspire others in the moment of physical despair. And with the absence of his inspiration, the sea quickly eroded the brethren's solidarity.

Fearing for their lives, the priests woke up Germanus and begged him to hold a vigil that would break the storm's hold on the sea. Together, they prayed through the last part of the night.

Within a few hours, the first rays of hope broke across the horizon as a new day dawned. The brethren cheered that Germanus had saved the ships and all of the men aboard them from certain death with his chanting and prayers.

Oddly, we went past Thanet without incident. I had assumed that we were going to have problems. Since the time that I'd come home, fears and stories of Saxon raids had been a standard topic of conversation. Grallon allowing them to form a base of operation on the island had pleased no one except the Saxons. And he had solved nothing and only made matters worse.

In time, our ships drifted deeper into the mouth of the Thames River. Even before setting a foot on the welcome shore, throngs of people gathered. It was as if the wind had announced our arrival.

CHAPTER 15

People lined the shore as we sailed past them. They called for us to come ashore. They pleaded. This made some of us leery, myself included. Once adequate space became available, all of the ships dropped anchor and we quickly clambered to shore. All of us, even the crew, were ecstatic to have land under our feet.

"Greetings, people of Britain," Germanus declared in a clear, powerful tone. "We're honored by your welcoming. May God bless you with his everlasting grace."

I still held some bitter memories of Germanus from Barcelona, but I could not deny his talent for talking. Maybe it was his whole attire and attitude. Either way, he cast a spell upon the crowd. People fell silent and stared. They hung upon his words, waiting and wanting more.

"We come with words straight from the Bishop of Rome. It is about the one true God," Germanus stated then paused.

"For the moment, we would appreciate your hospitality. And, a warm meal would do wonders." Bishop Lupus added.

The crowd parted like the Red Sea had for Moses. Bishop Lupus was asking for more than these people could offer. The majority of them wore torn, tattered, or soiled clothes. These people were suffering, landless, and forgotten. Now they clung to the shores, awaiting our arrival. Soon, Germanus saw what I saw. He wasn't blind.

"Or simply a warm fire would do," Germanus chimed in.

"That is not beyond our accommodations," called out a middle-aged man and with this came a flood of people talking.

In a loud, joyous manner, the locals welcomed us as Germanus had the men strike camp. He ordered a grand feast to be prepared from our supplies. Soon, it was ready.

Germanus cleared his throat, raised his cup, and called out, "Eat at my table and you shall not know hunger. I shall fast before I take the bread from your fingertips. Please enjoy the feast."

Only one thing left from the feast early and no one missed it. Hunger had been keeping these unfortunates company for weeks, but left halfway through the long dinner.

The next day, we loaded back onto the ships and finished the rest of the trip to London. In the quiet time that consumed the remainder of the trip, I sat next to Germanus.

"So are you expecting this kind of reception everywhere we go?" I asked him.

"No," he replied flatly.

"What do you expect?" I inquired further.

"It's hard to say. The signs so far don't seem good. So many sad appeals, so soon. And once we reach London we will have to establish our presence there," Germanus answered.

"Why there?"

"I believe that will be our best place to generate a new spring of faith," he added in a matter-of-fact tone.

"So you believe that the brethren there will be of the most assistance?" I asked.

"No," Germanus remarked. "In truth, I am more interested in the town of Verulamium. That's where Alban, a pagan and ex-soldier, sheltered a Christian priest and then was put to death when Alban took the priest's place.

"By centralizing on this local martyr, I'll be able to reach these people. It gives them a focal point of pure Christianity. It's something that will pull them free from the Pelagian heresy that plagues these people."

"Germanus, I don't see the sickness that you speak of in his faith. Pelagius spoke of the love of God, free will, self-control, and the innate ability to feel the grace of God. All else is superficial rhetoric."

Germanus held his tongue. He had a comment he wanted to make but didn't. After a heavy exhale, he drew in air and replied, "There must be social order."

"There would be with self control," Ambrosius replied.

"Hah, that's the one thing lacking in this corrupt, sinful world," Germanus remarked. "Fallen souls can't stand on their own."

"Before God, shouldn't all honorable men kneel?" I mocked.

"Please, Merlinus. Don't play with words. I left the legal courts behind a long time ago," Germanus remarked as he rubbed his forehead.

"Have you?" I questioned. "The setting and circumstances have changed, but the heated rhetoric remains."

He smiled as he listened to my words and saw the logic within them.

"You were always a smart boy," he remarked. "Your father would be extremely proud of what you have achieved and maintained. And in the purest truths, you and Ambrosius are correct. If everyone had self-control, there would be order, but still the hand of the mighty holds the sword of justice instead of the hand of the righteous."

"But the stance taken by the orthodoxy is that man is predestined to fail," I remarked.

"Are we not bound to fail?" Germanus remarked.

"So you will fall from God's grace," I remarked.

"Possibly," he calmly replied. "Even bishops can fall. Just a couple of years ago, the Bishop of Arles, Patroclus, was slain for his sins of simony."

"Then, what is the use of the Church if it is corruptible like everything else is?" I asked.

"Systematic order," Germanus added.

"It seems inhuman," I replied.

"It's a necessary evil," he answered.

"That's debatable," I countered.

"It will have to wait for another day. London is close on the horizon." Germanus declared.

I saw the fairly large walled town sitting on the shores of the Thames. A wooden watchtower greeted our arrival. It sat on the northern shore, forming the most eastern point of the massive wall. On the landward side, sandstone formed the base of the wall. Ragstone framed it. Flint rubble filled its core. London's wall rose up about twenty feet and tapered at the top.

The riverside lacked this imposing wall. Instead, retainer walls and embankments formed its defense. By using the contour of the shoreline, the city seemed open to the riverside but was effectively secure. The first short retainer wall kept the shore from eroding. The second sat further up on the shore, making it much higher than the first. Still, the city was friendly to trade. Wharves lined the thin shoreline of London, waiting for trade ships to drop their loads so the goods could be whisked away. Out of all the pain and suffering, the one grand thing the Romans gave this island was this impressive city.

Through the years, the Empire had its ups and downs. The Empire was in the midst of a major downturn, now. Trade had slumped off. Looking over the city, I saw that several of the Roman buildings were in decay and being demolished. The city had lost its former luster.

CHAPTER 16

In London, the reception was less cordial. Many questioned why we were there. I didn't involve myself with these debates. As anticipated, they centered around what was and was not orthodoxy. Both missed the point of what Christ was and what he stood for. Neither of them were willing to seek a compromise to achieve harmony within the community. And for that, both Germanus and the heretics were wrong.

I did not concern myself with the unanswerable questions of faith, religion, and the Pelagian controversy. I kept close tabs on Ambrosius and what he was doing. As soon as he stepped on land, he spoke to elderly men who he thought might know something, like the one he approached now. The old man stood watching crowds of people. He wore a tan tunic and matching long breeches. A black leather belt drew in his long tunic. A long brown cape hung loosely by his sides. His hood wasn't up.

"Greetings, sir," Ambrosius remarked as he stood next to him.

"Yes, lad," the old man asked.

"May I have a moment of your time?"

"I don't see why not," the old man replied.

"Have you heard any news of Cornovia? That was my home for a long time. It's been several years since I've been there. Any news you could tell me would be good," Ambrosius finished.

"Unfortunately, that's not true," the old man started, "Not all news is good news. Grallon continues to drive people from their homes and off their lands. The self-proclaimed High Commander is consolidating his lands. He has installed his youngest son, Paschent, in Builth. He picked this son over Vortimer for the simple fact that Paschent would look to Grallon for guidance. Vortimer is a seasoned warrior and disagrees with his father on several things. There is no way Vortimer would simply bend to his father's whim. So from the west in Demetia, Grallon pushes his holdings eastward at the expense of others. He has holdings near Exeter but doesn't seem to be stirring up trouble in the southwest.

"In my opinion, Britain would be better served if Vortimer were High Commander of the Council's army instead of Grallon," the old man replied after a quick glance around him.

"What about the resistance? Does no one stand in opposition any longer?" Ambrosius asked as he lowered his voice.

"Yes, there are holdouts, but there seems to be too few to really make a difference. Vortigern has endless supply of soldiers. He simply has more Saxons shipped over to take the place of his fallen dogs."

"Do you know the names of these patriots?" Ambrosius asked.

"There are several, but they are scattered among the provinces. In Cornovia, Gerontius and Cai both lead bands of men and none of them recognize Lord Grallon as High Commander of the Council any longer. Both groups have been officially labeled as outlaws, but only Vortigern and his Saxons would arrest them. Neither group steals from, burns out or kills the country folks. Grallon cannot make such a claim honestly.

"He is a . . ." the old man paused, as he noticed that I had remained in listening distance the whole time. The old man grew leery as he remained silent, studying me.

Noticing the old man's eyes shifting, Ambrosius pivoted as his hand dropped down to the hilt of his sword. Ambrosius released it as he saw only me standing nearby.

"Oh," he remarked. "Don't mind him, sir. He is with me."

The tension in the old man's shoulders melted away. He took a wide scan of the crowd of people gathered to meet the bishops and remarked, "Nowadays, you don't know who might be listening."

"Right," Ambrosius agreed. "Is there anymore that you can tell us?"

"These are tough times we live in. Many enemies want to sink their teeth into this island. The Irish and Picts are just some of the troubles we face. More and more, folks feel that Vortigern and the Council made a bad decision in using the Saxons as auxiliary forces. With their numbers increasing daily, they garrison key points throughout the lower island and parts of the north. The people do appreciate that the Saxons have been able to put Drust and his troublesome Picts in check.

"This is probably one of the few things that can be respected about them. Other than that, the people have grown tired and annoyed with their presence," the old man finished.

"What more can you tell me about Cai and the others like him?" Ambrosius anxiously asked. "They are not stationed at some stronghold, are they?"

"No, they are not that strong. They must stay on the move or Vortigern would simply mount a massive assault against them. Their war bands patrol the highlands, serving the region as protection. The locals there look to Gerontius and Cai for help instead of Lord Grallon. Often, Vortigern's men are the reason the country folk need protection. Besides, some of their sons ride under the banner of the White Boar of Cornovia," the old man added.

"Is there a way to get word to them?" Ambrosius asked. "Is Cai reachable?"

"I'm sure there's a way, but I don't know it," the old man replied as he shifted his weight from his left leg to his right. He looked past us, watching the equipment, horses, and men continue to exit the ships.

"You travel with distinguished guests," the old man remarked as he looked at Ambrosius. "Your friends speak for the Bishop of Rome. Their words carry imperial weight. People bend to them. How do you know them?"

"I am serving as an interpreter for the bishops," I interjected.

"Hah," the old man laughed. "Until now, I wondered if you could even speak."

"He only talks when he has to," Ambrosius joked.

"Thanks for your time, sir. We greatly appreciate it," I added, trying to end the conversation as I pulled Ambrosius so he would walk away.

"Yes, sir," Ambrosius added. "We definitely appreciate it."

"No problem, young lad," the old man replied. "By the way, what happens to be your name?"

"Ambrosius," he answered.

"Ambrosius," the old man repeated. His mind raced behind his squinting eyes as he tried to place the young man's name. Ambrosius' name triggered some memory, but the old man could not place where he had heard it before now.

A look of awe suddenly formed on the man's face as he repeated, "Ambrosius of Cornovia? Son of Constantine and brother to Cai?"

"No," I quickly answered. "Ambrosius of Aureliani."

Surprised by my answer, Ambrosius looked at me but said nothing.

Smiling, the old man replied, "Right. Ambrosius of Aureliani."

"And I am Merlinus. This young man oversees my lands. Maybe in the future, when there is more time, we could talk further. But right now, we must be going."

"Good day to both of you," the old man replied with a nod.

Hesitantly, Ambrosius followed me.

"There was more I could have learned from him," Ambrosius hissed as I led him away from the hordes of people.

Out of listening distance, I replied, "You couldn't have learned as much as he could have. First, you tell him that you are from Cornovia, followed up with your asking about the resistance, and then you finally tell him that you have the same name as a son of a dead Cornovian lord. Did I fail to point out any more of your sheer brilliance? Are you intentionally trying to draw attention to yourself?

"Did you not hear what the old man told you? Your brother, Cai, and others like him, has been driven out and survives only as an outlaw. You must be careful with what you tell strangers, especially when you express sympathies for men labelled as outlaws. Grallon is still recognized as the High Commander of Britain," I preached.

"What does that matter, now? Bishop Germanus is here. If Grallon dares to show his face, the bishops shall have that usurper in shackles," Ambrosius declared in a bitter tone.

"Well, then," I snapped. "Turn around so you can see it happen."

Grallon was there, regally dressed in a purple calico cotton vest with black breeches. He walked up to the bishops as a peer. His hair and beard appeared like snow on his face and his shoulders. The black within it was gone. He looked like Duke Coel. He looked much older, but I knew it was him and I knew what was going to happen.

The throng of people dispersed as Vortigern greeted the bishops. As the people moved about them, they innately formed a wide thick circle around the three important men. The crowd whispered to one another while listening to what the nobles were saying.

"I don't believe it," groaned Ambrosius as he saw them socializing like old friends. The teen just didn't realize that they were old friends or at least old associates. Ahès thought Germanus had changed, but I still saw the same man smiling now as the one I saw in Barcelona. There it was, that self-serving smile of a snake. Or, was I seeing too much into it?

"This is politics, the compromising of principles to achieve one's purpose or plan," I lightly remarked. Ambrosius' hand sank down to the hilt of his sword.

I reached out and grabbed the back of his arm and remarked, "Justice is served little if your head is on a pike."

"What would you have me do, then?" the young man questioned as the tension in his arm faded.

"Do what you set out to do," I replied. "Look for your brother, Cai. We must not stay in London. We shall move out discreetly. Tell no one. I will have the bishops informed of our departure. We will move to the north end of the town. The road that we will take is located there. Okay?"

Ambrosius nodded his head and walked back toward the ships.

CHAPTER 17

What I'd been told and what I'd observed led me to believe that Ambrosius had grown into a highly intelligent, compassionate man. Impatience plagued him at times. For the most part, the young man maintained a positive outlook. Since arriving on the island, he struggled to remain upbeat and cordial. Old painful memories raged in him. He could not hold back the tears as we arrived at his former home in Cornovia, days later.

We reached his old home, or what remained of it. Fire had scorched the walls. The rafters had burned through and caused the roof to cave in. Dried-out vines and brown weeds gave the dilapidated buildings a touch of antiquity; the sadness in Ambrosius' face when he saw it showed a sudden sense of mourning. He refused to set up camp within the protective outer wall of the villa. Instead, Ambrosius rode out alone to the tree line and made camp for that night while we remained near the villa.

He'd been hoping that Cai would have restored the villa, but instead we had found it abandoned. No fires of any type marked the grounds with signs of recent occupancy or activity. So far, Ambrosius' mission had been a complete failure.

We spent the next two days combing the countryside. The last lead regarding Cai faded into the fifth night. With deep reluctance, Ambrosius gave the order to return to Verulamium. Two weeks after arriving in London, we rode into the quiet town where Alban was baptized in the blood of martyrdom.

Word of Germanus' heated debates with Pelagian scions reached us the night before. So did the news of Germanus curing a little girl's blindness. The man telling the story had slurred his words. Either way, her father was a man of high status.

I struggled to accept the miracle. I had seen too much. I was skeptical of all things like that. I wasn't the only one; some of the people that witnessed it firsthand doubted it. Others, like the old toothless drunk, believed it as if it was the Gospel.

So when we arrived, I sought out Germanus' temporary residence set up near the shrine of St. Alban. Ambrosius followed close behind.

I stopped, turned, and faced Ambrosius. He remained silent.

"Allow me to handle the initial talking. Fair enough?" I asked.

Ambrosius nodded his head, too tired to talk. In the last week, we had rode over a hundred miles. Incredibly, only one of our mounts went lame out the group of twelve horses. The Roman roads only went so far and many sections were in disrepair. Stepping in a pothole in the road was what caused the horse to twist its hoof. The fact that there weren't any other problems with the horses attested to the quality of stock maintained in the stables at Aureliani.

Before leaving nearly fifteen years ago, I had hired an old Alan and his son. They were amazing with the horses. The father had passed away a couple of years after I had left. His son, Aspar, remained and still cared for them. Aspar's young son, Velius, helped him with the horses and stables now. My villa had grown into quite the little community during my sabbatical. And Ambrosius had helped its development in the last couple of years.

As we walked closer to Germanus' tent, a man walked toward us. I recognized him. It was Camillus, one of Germanus' assistants. He was tall and thin, almost sickly thin. He had light brown hair and wore a dark brown robe. His short hooked nose gave him a parrot like appearance.

"Greetings. What's the purpose for such a late call?" the young man remarked as we moved in the dark shadows of the night.

"Hello, young Camillus," I called back. "I was hoping to call upon Bishop Germanus, if possible."

As Ambrosius and I stepped into the light of the torches near the tent's entrance, Camillus' stare melted into a friendly smile.

"Oh," he remarked. "Lord Merlinus, I didn't realize it was you."

"No need to be so formal," I replied.

"Can we speak with the bishop?" Ambrosius asked impatiently.

Camillus glanced at me with an inquisitive look. Seeing this, I nodded in agreement.

"I will check if he will see you tonight. It has grown quite late," Camillus replied.

"Understandable. We would have called upon him sooner, but

we just arrived in Verulamium less than an hour ago," I replied.

"Okay," Camillus added. "I will inform Bishop Germanus and see if he can make time for you both."

"That would be great, Camillus," I answered.

"Please wait here," he replied.

"Of course," I added.

Shortly afterwards, Camillus returned. Holding up the flap of the tent, Camillus revealed numerous candles and oil lamps that lit the reception area. Thick drapes divided the large tent into rooms.

"Bishop Germanus will see you. Please come in," he announced.

"Thank you, Camillus," I replied.

Alabaster busts stood in the shadowy corners. As we waited, Ambrosius moved closer and studied the tapestry that had the known world woven into it.

Looking at me, Ambrosius asked, "How far east have you been?"

"I've stood on the shores of the eastern ocean. I mostly walked to the east, but I never felt as sore as I do now," I joked.

He smiled and gave a genuine laugh; it was the first one I heard since we had arrived in Britain.

As we looked at the edge of the world, he shook his head and remarked, "That's amazing. I would love to travel that far east."

"You should. It's a learning experience. This world is incredible. There is so much to it. This map does it little justice. There's a stone wall in the Orient that runs for over five hundred leagues. It completely dwarfs Hadrian's Wall," I replied.

"Weren't you afraid while you traveled alone? That is how you traveled, wasn't it?

"Yes, that's how I mostly traveled. And yes, I was scared at times, but my curiosity superceded my fear," I answered.

With a bright smile, he remarked, "I understand. Do you figure you will return there?"

"It's hard to say," I replied.

"Hopefully, it isn't any time soon," Germanus' voice called out from behind us.

We saw Germanus coming out of a cloth divider held open by Camillus.

"It would be a shame to lose you when you are needed here,"

Germanus announced.

"Well, you don't have to worry. There are no plans to go east of Aureliani any time soon," I replied.

The bishop nodded and added, "Good. Things are becoming more complicated. Any luck in contacting Cai?"

"No," Ambrosius remarked as his eyes dropped from the bishop's.

"We just didn't have enough time to establish contact," I replied in an even tone.

"True," the bishop quickly replied.

Switching the subject, Ambrosius asked, "So is it true? Can you cure the blind? I heard, well, we heard that you healed a little blind girl the other day while in London. Word of you has spread like wildfire. Is it true?"

Germanus remained quiet for a moment. Ambrosius' mouth hung open in anticipation. Germanus' chest drew in as if to speak, but he paused as he glanced at me. I did not look away, but my stare was not stern. I had simply grown used to people's lies and expected the same from Germanus. And for a moment, I saw what seemed like remorse within his eyes, or something like it within his serene look.

"I did all that I could possibly do for that child. Following a short prayer I said for her, I removed the reliquary that I carry everywhere and held it before the open eyes of the child. As the crowd squeezed in on us, I prayed out loud, 'Demons that have stolen the precious sight of this child be gone. By my faith and the true will of God, vision shall no longer be denied this child. If this blindness is the result of divine retribution, the child shall be absolved, and sight shall be restored if it so pleases the Lord. Alleluia.'"

"So what then?" Ambrosius quickly inquired.

"Crackle of thunder and a flash of lightning," I teased.

A young servant smiled as he attended to the couple of candles that had nearly melted away.

"Nothing that spectacular," Germanus smiled.

"So what happened, then?" Ambrosius asked.

"The blank stare of blindness faded from her face and her blinking eyes focused on the reliquary I held in front of her," Germanus answered.

"It was truly a grand moment," Camillus called out from behind us. "When the child turned to her parents and told them she could see them for the first time, the crowd erupted joyously."

Amazement shone in Ambrosius' face. Skepticism clouded my thoughts.

"So the child turned to her parents, and told them that she could see them for the first time ever? How did the little girl recognize them?" I asked.

Silence slipped among us. Realizing my point, Ambrosius' expression grew sharp. Germanus didn't object. He had his own doubts.

"Bishop, do you really think she was blind?" Ambrosius questioned. "Wouldn't you know if you had cured her or not?"

"I only know what she told us. And only through the grace of God could such a thing occur. I am a true man of the cloth and did all I could possibly do," Germanus stated in an even tone. "It is irrelevant what I think. It only matters what God knows and God knows all there is to know. I am not his judge. I am only a guide to those who want to see."

"How does that work when they can't see in the first place?" the young man smirked.

"Ambrosius," I said sharply. I gave him a stern stare.

Smiling, knowing the boy's doubts, Germanus answered, "It was the reliquary. That was the focal point for the little girl. The relics of martyrs drew the darkness from her eyes. I simply held it before her eyes and the relics did the rest."

A bewildered look hung on Ambrosius' face. He didn't know what to say. He looked at me for a word of guidance; I simply shrugged my shoulders. His anticipating stare remained on me. I remained tight-lipped.

"What do you make of it, Merlinus," he asked.

"It's difficult for me," I replied. "I am a man of the here and now. I struggle to accept anything that I do not witness, experience, or believe possible. I have heard too many tall tales to simply accept something without questioning it."

"Only have blind faith in the grace of God, not in the ways of men," Germanus remarked. "The Shroud of God has been soiled by the sins of liars before now. And it will again. Men shall fall, but that doesn't mean you have to, Ambrosius."

I smiled and nodded in agreement. Ambrosius' head lightly bobbed as he glanced at us both and accepted our logic.

"I wish there had been more time, Ambrosius. I wish you would have met up with your brother. There's just no more time. There's whispers of a building revolt. The Saxon dogs of Vortigern grow restless and bloodthirsty," Germanus declared. "Their numbers swell beyond counting. They claim more and more land for their services."

"So what is our next move, Bishop?" Ambrosius asked.

"Home is our destination. We have done what we have set out to do. We have reestablished the Word of God on the isle of Britain once more. The confusing shadow of heresy has been cast away by the all-consuming light of God.

"We leave for London tomorrow. From there, we shall sail home," Germanus remarked.

Ambrosius gave me an odd look.

"There is no need to linger. The heresy has been stamped out, its adherents refuted before the masses, and their books have been confiscated," Camillus remarked. "The Church has won the battle against the Pelagian heretics. This is good news for the Church."

But not for free will.

"That's right," Germanus replied.

"Well, it not good for free will," Ambrosius said, voicing my thoughts.

"Ambrosius, we should make our leave and settle down for the night," I replied as I glanced over him.

He nodded in agreement.

"Thank you for your time, Bishop Germanus," I remarked.

"Good night, my friends," the bishop replied.

CHAPTER 18

The next day, after breaking camp, we rode toward London. With the weather fair and the roads in good repair, we moved fast. Ambrosius and I brought up the rear. We purposely lagged back so we didn't constantly eat the dust kicked up by the horsemen in front of us.

Several hours into the ride, the train had stopped, and we rode up to it. As we approached, I noticed a body on the ground. It was Germanus. He looked unconscious. There was blood on his forehead and his leg didn't appear normal.

His mount thrashed about madly. The horse was seriously injured. It moaned and neighed in agony. One of the troopers pulled out his bow from his nearby mount and shot the maimed animal. Within moments, the beast gave out its last breath and then became motionless.

"What has happened?" Ambrosius asked as we both dismounted.

"Someone constructed a deadfall in the road," Camillus answered while he knelt next to Germanus. "Germanus' horse stepped partially into it and threw him. The bishop jammed and twisted his leg when he hit the ground."

"Can you help him, Merlinus?" Camillus asked.

"I will," I answered. Turning to Ambrosius, I commanded as I held my hands open the length of Germanus' lower leg, "Cut me two thin pieces of oak this long."

"Yes, sir," Ambrosius replied as he went into the woods that lined the road.

I dug into my saddle bags. I brought out a leather sachet of herbs. As I went to Germanus, Camillus moved away to give me room to work. Kneeling next to the bishop, I treated the injury on his forehead. It wasn't much. The little blood was from an abrasion. There was no deep cut. I dressed the wound while I waited for Ambrosius to return.

"Should we try to wake him?" Camillus asked.

"No. We're going to let him rest until Ambrosius returns. I'm certain that the bishop will come to when I secure the braces on his leg. I'll need to tie the straps tight. Can you get me two long strips of strong cloth?" I finished.

"I can do that," Camillus replied.

Shortly thereafter, they returned at the same time. Both brought what I had asked for. Quickly with one stick, I tied a strap to each end. Second, I laid that next to Germanus' leg. Next, I threaded the straps underneath his leg and looped them around the second stick. Looking up, I noticed that a large circle of people surrounded me. Two soldiers stood together watching.

"You two, come here and help," I commanded.

Looking at each other and then me, they asked in unison, "Us?"

"Yes," I confirmed. "Hold the bishop down by his shoulders."

Kneeling next to him, the two large Alans placed their hands on the bishops's shoulders and wrists.

"Ambrosius, kneel down and help me. This is what is going to happen. I am going to twist his leg back to its natural position. Then, you are going to wrap the strap around his leg a couple of times, pull the slack out, and then tie it off. Do it for both straps and do it fast. Are you ready?" I questioned.

"Yes, sir," he replied.

"Now," I said as I lifted and twisted Germanus' leg.

"Awh!" the bishop screamed. He tried desperately to sit up, but the soldiers held him pinned to the ground. Pain dripped from the corners of his eyes.

"Just give me a second, Germanus," I calmly remarked. "I've placed your leg in its most natural position, and Ambrosius is nearly finished tying off the braces. Just try to relax."

With bloodshot eyes, Germanus nodded and then laid his head back and closed his eyes.

"Camillus, have a wagon prepared. For now, just lay down several pillows so he can ride comfortably. We will lift him up and place him inside the covered wagon," I said.

"We should not remain," Nepos added. "We are only a short distance from that village by the creek. We passed it when we were headed the other way."

"Right," remarked one of the troopers holding down the bishop.

"We will seek shelter there. The bishop will recover more quickly remaining still," I added.

Sometime later as dusk settled in, we came upon the village. It was a cluster of sunken huts with thatched roofs. A few folks tended to the chickens and swine.

Our presence quickly gained their attention. With a sharp whistle, more people appeared from within their huts. The town elder, a clean-shaven man with gray receding hair walked out toward us.

"Greetings," he called out clearly.

"Bishop Germanus has been hurt. A few miles back he was thrown from his mount," I declared. "We seek your hospitality."

"Granted," the elder answered.

CHAPTER 19

"We could have been back in London and in better accommodations by now," I told Germanus several hours after his riding accident.

"I can't endure the jarring around in the back of the covered wagon," Bishop Germanus moaned.

With the bishop not wanting to go any farther, we remained in the nearby village. A family who had two huts gave one of them to the bishop. Camillus brought in some of the trappings of his tent to decorate the dreary sunken hut. I had him on a heavy diet of cheese and goat's milk.

It had been several days since Germanus was thrown from his horse and twisted his leg. I woke up early. Ambrosius was up and already outside the tent. He wandered near the fast-moving creek. Ambrosius had grown more restless with each passing day. He didn't notice my approach until I stood next to him. He didn't say anything once he saw me. I remained silent and allowed him his peace. It was obvious that he thought about his brother. It had to be frustrating to be on the island but still unable to make contact with him. I worried that he might do something rash and leave without anyone going with him.

"We could have stayed longer," Ambrosius mumbled.

"I know, but there was no way of knowing that this would have happened," I replied lightly.

"I know," Ambrosius replied as he kicked a small stone into the noisy creek.

"Maybe we can go back for another try," I remarked. "There is nothing saying we can't."

"No," he answered in an empty tone. "Who knows when Germanus will want to leave. As far as I know, it could be today."

I said nothing. He was right. It could go either way.

People flocked to the hut just to get a glimpse of the bishop. To me, Germanus seemed to enjoy the attention, relishing people's whispers of wonder and amazement. Many of them truly believed

Germanus had cured the little blind girl. Maybe if he'd listened to them long enough he would have believed it, too. My doubt still lingered. Ambrosius cared little, either way. He was consumed with finding his brother. Ambrosius was a man of action. Though he excelled at the written word, Ambrosius held it secondary to the merits of one's actions. I could tell that. Good deeds made a person noble, not lands or titles.

His father would have been proud, along with his uncle, Lord Alaric. Adaulphus had no clue that his son had even outlived him. As Adaulphus lay dying in his stables, no hope lived in his heart. His grand Roman-Gothic kingdom had crumbled before his eyes. He would not see his son grow up to be a young, honorable man.

"Ambrosius," I called out as he knelt near the creek. He just stared at it. "I brought over some gold coins."

He turned, looked at me, and smiled. He added, "Are you going to give me a couple coins to cheer me up?"

Laughing, I remarked, "No. I was thinking more along the lines of sending a messenger back to Cornovia. Maybe we can establish a line of communication while we wait for Germanus to recover."

"Really?" he asked, unsure if I was serious or not.

"Yes," I replied.

"Who will you use?" Ambrosius asked.

"I will have Nepos go. I believe he is our best bet. Overall, I trust him to do the task to the best of his ability."

"Do you really think so?" he asked.

"I hope so," I replied.

"It's worth a try," he concurred.

"I will set things in motion," I finished.

Two weeks had passed since I sent Nepos back to Cornovia, and the young soldier still hadn't returned. I grew more and more concerned as the days progressed. I feared the worst for Nepos; maybe another dead fall had been more successful than the one that still had Germanus bedridden.

Ambrosius had written and sealed the letter with the ring of Constantine. Cai would recognize the boar on the shield as Constantine's seal. This was how Ambrosius had arranged it. Now I just hoped Nepos would make it back alive. He should already have returned. His mount was superb, and he was an excellent rider.

As dusk neared, a rider approached. I hoped and prayed that it was the Alan returning.

"Nepos, what news is there?" Ambrosius called out.

The rider didn't break stride and rode through the hamlet quickly. It wasn't anyone I had seen before. It wasn't Nepos. The wind picked up seeming to trail behind the rider. Maybe it had been blowing the whole time, but I hadn't noticed it. The swift gust blew in an irregular pattern. No one else noticed it or cared.

The bivouac glowed ember red as the evening fires were lit. The wind and flames whistled and danced across the logs in their pits. There was a coldness in the air and the fires grew larger. Ambrosius and several of the soldiers had good luck hunting. They took down three good-size boars. The camp and the entire hamlet ate well. And now, some of us sat next to a roaring fire.

"This heat feels great," Ambrosius called as he rubbed his hands and held them out to the fire. "It feels like it is going to be a cold one, tonight."

"Ah yes, young lad. You're right there," Carbo said. He was one of the Alan soldiers. He was an older friend of Nepos. He reminded me of a smaller version of Valerius. His head was round and bald like a melon. But he had a body of a baby bull. He didn't appear the least bit awkward on his horse.

"It had settled in my bones," he said in his heavily accented voice.

"Well, you'd better get closer to the fire," Ambrosius added.

"I'm close enough," Carbo answered. "It's nearly blinding me."

"Well, it's not as bright as their fire over . . ." I stopped, as I realized I wasn't looking at a large camp fire. Instead, it was the roof of a hut on fire. The dry reeds burned hot and high, and the gusts of wind fanned the flames.

"Oh my god," I called out, "some of the huts are on fire. Hurry and get up."

"Help. Help," Camillus called out. "The bishop is in danger. Please help me move him."

As we approached the huts, a shower of hot embers blew toward Germanus' hut. The wind shifted, though, and the hut was spared. Other homes weren't so fortunate. The hungry fire quickly consumed everything in its path. It raced across the roof like an angry will-o'-the-wisp.

One of the campfires must have caused the roof to catch on fire. Terror filled the village.

"Everyone get a bucket and form a line from the creek to the huts," I shouted. "We will bail water onto them that way."

Seeing the logic, people quickly followed my advice. Frantically, we passed the wooden pails back and forth trying hard not to lose any of the water.

It was too late to make a difference. The thatched roofs burned and broke their own supports. The roofs collapsed into the shell of the huts and a fiery cloud of embers bellowed up from each one. Fire prevention was the only recourse. Luckily several of the huts had been spared. No one had to sleep under the stars, but the sleeping space would be tight.

A rider galloped out of the night.

"What happened here?" he called out. I noticed that it was Nepos.

"Has the village been attacked?" he further questioned as the people meandered about the smoldering landscape.

"No, nothing like that. I believe some embers from the fire pits floated up and landed on the thatch roofs. From there, the fires began. The wind has been gusting. The fanned flames turned into short-lived infernos. By the time the village realized what happened, it was too late to save any of the burning huts," I stated.

"I wish I had good news, but I have none. It is the same news that you had before I left. It is as if Cai has gone from Cornovia and hasn't returned in quite some time. From the most reliable sources, he left shortly before you and Ambrosius went to his old estate," Nepos remarked.

"Maybe he has," I remarked. "Maybe the pressure from Grallon's men has made it impossible for him to remain in the area. He is in a constant state of transit."

"Possibly," Nepos replied. "So what's next?"

"Unfortunately," Ambrosius added, "sit and wait. Bishop Germanus is still bedridden."

"I thought so," Nepos remarked. "That would seem to be the only reason the imperial train has remained here. What about the bishop? He didn't get hurt, did he?"

"No. Luckily, the wind shifted and his hut was spared," I stated.

"It was nothing of the sort," chimed in Camillus. "It was a moment of divine intervention. The hands of God shifted the gusting winds away from Bishop Germanus. The grace of God protected him."

"Just as if the Lord Christ and Jupiter Optimus Maximus were one in the same," I remarked with a smile.

"Absolutely not," Camillus barked. Even in the poor light, I could see his disgruntled look. My smile didn't falter. I let the issue drop. Without saying anything else, Camillus turned from our group and walked away from us. He headed for Bishop Germanus' hut.

"I wonder why Camillus didn't like your comparison," Ambrosius smirked.

I laughed lightly, and added, "I can't imagine why. I thought that it was a good one."

"So, do you think I will offend anyone if I made a fire?" Nepos asked. "I'm so cold. I need to get rid of the chill from the ride."

"I doubt that anyone will have a problem with it. I suggest making it in that pit closest to the creek," I remarked.

"Of course," Nepos replied.

"The chill in the air is strong tonight." Ambrosius remarked. "I'll help gather some firewood."

"Thanks," Nepos replied.

After we had the fire blazing in the fieldstone pit, we sat around it. The flames danced wildly for us. Slowly, the small village fell asleep. Still, we stayed up. For the longest time nothing was said, and each of us took turns feeding the fire.

Breaking the silence, I asked, "So what is next for you, Nepos? What will happen when we make it back to Gaul?"

"I imagine that I will escort the bishops back to Auxerre. Once there, I'm not too sure what I will be up to. I know I will have to return to Goar, eventually."

"I've heard his name mentioned before," Ambrosius remarked, "but who is he?"

"He's the king of one of the Alan tribes of Gaul," Nepos answered.

"How is it that you have joined the company of the bishops?" Ambrosius asked.

"This unit, the group I currently command, acts as an armed escort for the Church. We protect the leaders of the Church as they go on their travels west of Milan."

"I see," Ambrosius replied. "So then, you're Goar's right-hand man?"

"Hardly," Nepos replied, as he poked at the coals of the fire with a long thin stick. "He grooms Euthar for that position. I'm not even Euthar's first man. Though Euthar looks like Ambrosius' twin, the young prince behaves like a dog. The privileges of being heir apparent already corrupts Euthar."

"So the two act alike, also," I joked. "Who is this Euthar that you speak so fondly of?"

He said nothing more but laughed lightly as he churned up a cloud of glowing ember.

"Your intent might be to avoid trouble, but you will have it if the villagers see you messing with the fire like that," I remarked.

Nepos slowly glanced toward the cluster of huts. Ambrosius and I could not stop from laughing at his mannerisms. Nepos had forgotten what happened earlier. He meant no malcontent. He gently lobbed the stick into the pit.

"Now everybody can sleep easy," Ambrosius joked.

"Right," Nepos replied with a light laugh. "What's next for you two?"

Home, I hoped, but for Ambrosius' sake I said nothing. I figured if I were to say that, I would be saying that the search for Cai was over. Ambrosius said nothing and glanced at me with a look of uncertainty. Ambrosius shrugged his shoulders and replied, "Home."

"Back —," Nepos began.

"To Aureliani," I finished.

"Right," Ambrosius confirmed.

"So Merlinus, that's your villa where we first met?"

"Correct," I replied. "That little old villa is mine. The back part of the property sits on a high bank overlooking the Loire River."

"It sounds incredible," Nepos replied.

"It is," Ambrosius added. "He has enough land walled in that deer can be taken at the back of his land. He has fruit trees near the river's edge and I've spent several evenings watching deer scale the nearly vertical bank. Hah, they just can't resist those trees."

"There's no wall back there?" Nepos asked.

"Not that runs parallel with the river," Ambrosius clarified.

"Picture the enclosure walls of the estate as a horseshoe instead of a square. The tips of the shoe butt up against the Loire. The land forms a promontory into the river. The animals are so keen that they start upriver to account for the current. They can't fight it and scale the steep bank. A man would have trouble coming to shore from a boat. It would be next to impossible for a person to do while in the water due to the contour of the shore and the depth of the water," Ambrosius added.

"The deer must be using their hooves as picks, sticking them in the rocks and then hoisting themselves up," Nepos remarked as he stood up and put some more wood in the dying fire.

"Exactly," Ambrosius remarked as he mimicked the deer's method of climbing. He grouped his fingers together to form the tip of the hoof and struck at the air several times. I laughed as I saw my old master suddenly before me. Ambrosius' actions mirrored one of Dom Fu's many fighting techniques.

"You don't like my deer-climbing impression," Ambrosius remarked. "I thought I was imitating it rather well. You disagree?"

"That's the whole reason it strikes me as funny. You did it so well," I remarked. "It reminded me of something I learned while in the forests of Mount Shaoshi. A master enlightened me about many things. One of them was fighting techniques based on the movements of animals. He showed how your deer-climbing impression could be turned into sharp precise punching."

Mimicking Ambrosius' motions, I threw a quick punch. The sleeve of my robe snapped in the air from my rapid motion. The two of them just stared at me for a moment.

Laughing a second later, Ambrosius remarked, "That's impressive. But I don't remember the deer making that fancy popping sound like you just did."

"Well, dress them up in a robe and you might," I replied.

Nepos laughed loudly and then asked, "How effective are they? I've heard stories of people fighting that way but never actually saw it demonstrated."

"When performed by a true master, only the hand of God could bring about their defeat," I plainly replied.

"So you are saying that you cannot be defeated in hand-to-hand combat?" Ambrosius remarked.

"I don't ever recall saying that I was a true master," I answered.

"You said that you learned some martial skills. How long does it take to master them?" Ambrosius inquired further.

"A lifetime," I replied. "I was only fortunate to serve under Dom Fu for five years."

"What happen?" Nepos asked. "Did he die?"

"Yes," I replied.

"Did he teach at some sort of school or temple that you attended?" Ambrosius asked.

"No. It wasn't anything like that. I don't know of any place that teaches what he taught me. The man was a visionary. He showed me how to turn simple farming tools or even a walking stick into a deadly weapon. Maybe someday, there will be a temple like that, but I don't foresee that happening any time soon." I replied.

"I still want to see some animal tricks," Ambrosius mocked.

"No tricks," I replied. "They are refined responses to the actions of an attacker."

"I'd still like to see a demonstration," Ambrosius insisted.

"It is getting late and too dark to see anything, anyway," I replied.

"Too late? Do you need a nap? Your deer technique tuckered you out?" he continued.

"No. I was thinking of your safety," I answered. "I didn't want you landing on a jagged rock when you ended up on the ground."

"That's it," Ambrosius said as he stood up. "Now you have to back up your words with actions."

"Why do you think I said it," I replied with a smile and then stood up. Ambrosius stepped farther from the fire and waited for me. I stretched the muscles in my arms, legs, and sides.

"So what critter are you going to unleash on me?" Ambrosius teased.

"Snake," I replied as I closed my eyes and drew in the cool midnight air. Envisioning a serpent, I started to sway and move like one.

"Have you been drinking too much wine again?" Ambrosius asked. "When did you want to begin?"

"I wait for you," I replied as I continued to clear my mind of everything except for the moment and sounds of my surroundings.

"Are you going to open your eyes," Ambrosius asked.

As I kept swaying side to side, I shook my head no. In that moment

Ambrosius dashed toward me. I heard his feet hitting the sand. His breathing grew louder as he rushed me. In perfect timing, I swayed to the right but kept my left foot anchored. Ambrosius tripped and flew face first into the sand.

"What the hell?" Ambrosius grumbled as he spit out bits of sand.

"Is that enough, young lord?" I asked.

"No," Ambrosius barked. I listened to him lumbering to his feet. Unhurt, he still did not sound happy. Recklessly, he charged at me once more.

"That didn't work the last time. Why will it this time?" I asked.

He came at me with his arms open wide as if to bull me over and take me to the ground. I stood still and reared back my fist like a snake's head. With a serpentine jab, I struck Ambrosius squarely on his sternum. He dropped to his knees as I stole away his breath. He gasped for air as he placed his hands on the ground to keep himself from collapsing.

"You will be all right in a moment. Just try to relax," I replied as I knelt down next to him.

Shaking his head, Nepos remarked, "How did you know when to strike with your eyes being closed? That was amazing."

Ambrosius replied, "If you think so, let him demonstrate on you next."

"No thanks," Nepos remarked. "That's not saying that I wouldn't mind learning Merlinus' animals tricks, though."

"Me, too," Ambrosius sputtered.

"Maybe someday, but just not tonight, for it is time for me to retire," I finished.

"Well, then, good night, grand master," Ambrosius said with a smile.

I knew he tried to compliment me. However, I corrected, "Please, do not dishonor the arts by calling me that. A grand master is another level above and several ranks higher than what I have achieved."

"With your teacher gone, can you achieve anything higher?" Nepos questioned.

"Besides showing the Way, Dom Fu allowed me to copy the writings of some Oriental authors. Through him, I obtained precise translations of their works. A couple of years ago, I had shipped the codices to Aureliani. I wonder if they ever made it? I had forgotten about them until now. Ambrosius, remind me to ask Lady Alicia about them when we return home. I had them sent to her."

"If he doesn't, I will," Nepos added. "I am fascinated by the Oriental traditions. It would be an honor to be instructed in their ways by you."

"Don't you think that might be difficult to do while serving Goar, his boy, Euthar, and the Church?" I asked.

"I would think so," Ambrosius remarked. "The Way seems at odds with Christianity."

"Only if you condemn free will," I replied.

"What do you mean?" Ambrosius asked. "Why don't you clarify yourself?"

"One is governed by one's actions," I replied. "Both Buddha and Pelagius would agree with that statement. It's through free will that we can find and follow the Way."

"It is just a guess, but I imagine the Church won't condone that," Ambrosius laughed.

"Nor would Goar, I imagine," Nepos replied. "I wish there could be a way out of my obligations. Lord Merlin, is there anything that can be done? You're familiar with Roman federation laws, are you not? Is there something I can do?"

Walking back by the fire, I sat down. Both Ambrosius and Nepos followed my lead and returned to their seats. I said nothing. Though an Alan by blood, I was only slightly familiar with the laws and customs of the Alans.

"I could only imagine two ways that such a thing could happen legally," I began. "It would take a large sum of gold to compensate Goar and the Church for their loss of manpower, or you would have to do something of extraordinary significance and then you may be able to barter for your freedom."

"Things are looking like they are not going to be changing any time soon," Nepos replied.

"We're not off the island, yet," I replied.

"What does that mean?" Ambrosius asked.

"We haven't been in London for quite some time," I remarked. With a wide slow sweep of my hand, I added, "Even at times of peace, danger lurks in the shadows with greed. Security is an illusion that can only be cautiously trusted. The Empire has shown that, time and time again."

"So are you saying that London may be under siege when we return?" Nepos asked.

"It's possible," I replied. "Anything is."

Ambrosius shook his head and remarked, "I'm too tired to think this deeply."

"It does drain a person," Nepos added. "It feels like I have walked a mile since I've sat down."

"You have," I answered.

"What do you mean?" Nepos followed up.

"I'll save that for another night," I ended.

CHAPTER 20

It was the fourth morning after the fire. I woke early. The sounds of folks moving about kept me from falling back to sleep. Near the back of the tent, Ambrosius remained sleeping. Though Nepos was unsuccessful in making contact with Cai, his efforts had set Ambrosius somewhat at ease. It gave the boy the feeling that he had done everything possible to find Cai. The air inside held a chill. I couldn't see my breath any longer, not like when we first arrived in London over a month ago.

Outside, a bustling world greeted me. The birds breezed by, and people hustled about. They worked on repairing the roofs of the huts. They had almost fixed the damage done by the fire.

Germanus had organized the repair work from where he lay in a nearby hut. He was able to do this by utilizing the manpower from the numerous people that came to visit. Needing to open land for the pilgrims' temporary camps, Germanus directed them to clear an area near the hamlet, which the elders had wanted to slash and burn, but until this point, lacked the manpower to achieve it. By clever insight, the bishop cured two problems with one solution. It seemed impossible to count the earthly miracles the locals applied to Germanus. In no way did he dispel them. If anything, he used the mystique and awe they held for him to keep them enchanted.

As I inspected the final repairs, I noticed Germanus outside. He watched them stand up the wattle for the walls and throw the thatch on the roof's wooden frame.

"Bishop," I called out, surprised to see him walking around without support of any sort.

The bishop's face glowed with a joyous humility. Bishop Lupus stood near him and nodded to me.

"Greetings, Merlinus," Germanus replied in a upbeat tone.

"It's good to see you out and about," I replied.

"The morning air does me good. I have no complaints," he replied.

"There's no pain in the leg?" I asked.

"No. No pain," he replied.

"That's incredible. Has Camillus been helping you walk inside the tent for a while now? You seem to be walking smoothly without the usual tender step that follows an injury like yours," I noted.

"No. This is the first time I tried to walk," he replied.

"Really?"

"Honestly," he answered. "You wouldn't believe me if I were to tell you."

"Try me," I replied.

He remained silent for a moment as he looked at me.

"Okay," he finally answered. "Last night, as I lay on my mat somewhere between wakefulness and a dream, a light began to illuminate the hut wall closest to my toes. The light increasingly poured through it as if a fire grew on the other side of it. A shining figure stepped through the light and into the hut next to where I lay.

"As I looked up, I saw someone that appeared to be a woman. The light and air rippled around the figure, conjuring strange shadows and concealing her features. Her sheer snow-white robe floated as if lighter than air, the same as her flowing locks of silver hair. Her loose, open sleeves, and long train hovered as if suspended by some unfelt wind.

"The energy allowed her to do the seemingly impossible. It was the radiating white light. It felt better than sunlight. It was conscious. Healing. It was God.

"The angel stretched out her open hand and declared, 'Germanus, my loyal son, take my hand and stand. Stand firm, once more, upon your own two feet. From this moment forth, you shall feel no more pain from the fall.'

"As I reached up simply to take the angel's hand, there was a sudden surge of light and then nothing, except the darkness of night. As my eyes adjusted to the little light within the hut, I realized that I was standing. I thought I only touched the fingertips of the figure. I didn't realize that the angel had pulled me to my feet. But at that moment, I was standing and awake.

"I don't feel any pain, not even when I walk heavily upon it. It feels no different from the other one."

"Amazing," I replied.

"Truly," he answered.
"So what is your plan now, Bishop?" I replied.
"To London and then home. How does that sound?"
"Wonderful," I answered.

CHAPTER 21

As we rode down to London, I knew we weren't leaving the island just yet. Countless tents and temporary structures blanketed the grounds outside the city's twenty-foot-high wall. However, it wasn't a siege. People walked freely in and out of London as dusk settled. The gates stood open, or at least the one at Cripplegate did. We went past this entrance.

"We'll enter at Bishopsgate," Germanus remarked.

I noticed that Ambrosius had lagged off to the side of the train. Pulling my mount clear of the slow procession, I worked my way back to the young man. He sat on his mount looking over at one of the camps. Out of the numerous camps flying their family crests, this one had a white running boar upon a black and silver shield. It was the same as a flag that hung in Ambrosius' quarters back in Aureliani.

It couldn't be Cai, could it? What would be the luck of that? It can't be Cai.

"It's Cai," Ambrosius declared as he heeled his mount forward.

"Who could have guessed that. I don't have to give back those solidi, do I?" Nepos asked.

"Sure, you can give the gold coins back if you want," I replied.

"What if I don't want to give them back?" Nepos asked.

I laughed and added, "If you rode to Cornovia looking for Cai, then you did what I paid you to do," I answered.

"I did," Nepos answered.

"Then the gold coins are yours," I replied. "Use them wisely. Don't waste them on women and wine. Save them for what you spoke of the other night. What I gave might not have been much. It is a start, though."

"Okay," Nepos remarked with a light smile followed by a nod. "That was easy money."

"It won't always be that way," I replied.

"Right," Nepos replied.

Nepos and I followed Ambrosius' lead. He dismounted and walked the rest of the way to the front of the dark green tent.

"Cai," Ambrosius called out. "Cai of Cornovia."

"Who asks for him?" grumbled some man from within the tent.

"His brother," Ambrosius answered.

"What? Who?" the voice asked as it grew louder.

The flap of the tent lifted and a man with light-red hair walked out. It flowed down to his shoulders and was all one length. He kept it parted on his right side. His thick moustache hung down past the corners of his lips. He was about an inch taller than Ambrosius and a little more stocky. There was no facial resemblance, but I didn't expect to see any. He looked as if he hadn't slept in days or was simply worn down and sick. As Ambrosius looked upon him, the man's concerned look washed from his face. He replaced it with a bright smile.

"Ambrosius?" the man replied. "What the hell are you doing here?"

"I came to Britain to find you," Ambrosius remarked as he held Cai by the shoulders. Ambrosius looked him up and down, adding as he shook his head, "And it's a good thing I did. You look terrible."

Cai broke free of Ambrosius' grasp. Dropping low, Cai bear-hugged Ambrosius and stood up, holding him like a sack of apples.

"Now what are you going to do, little boy?" Cai barked as he spun in place. Halting, Cai extended his right hand in my direction.

As color returned to Cai's face, he added with a smirk, "Greetings, sir. Sorry about my little brother's manners. Father tried to teach him better. The boy simply neglects what he has been taught."

Cai set Ambrosius on his feet. Dizzy, Ambrosius stutter-stepped. He placed his hand on Cai's shoulder to steady himself.

"I'm Cai, son of Constantine," the red haired man remarked.

Before I could speak, Ambrosius remarked, "This is Nepos and that's Merlinus of Aureliani. He's been everywhere. He has seen the eastern oceans. That's farther than Alexander the Great marched."

The man's light smile faded and he stared straight into my eyes. Without looking away, he added, "And you've been to Barcelona."

"No," Ambrosius jumped in. "Not the shores of Hispania. I said the distant shores of the Orient. What did you call the place, Merlinus? You stayed five years in the forests of Mount Sushi? Wasn't that what you called it."

"Mount Shaoshi. You called it the mountain of raw fish," I replied.

"No," Ambrosius replied. "Cai, it was Mount Shaoshi."

Ambrosius' correction meant nothing as Cai continued to stare at me. I simply nodded my head, knowing he knew what I had done.

"Right," Cai added. "The Orient."

Turning to Ambrosius, Cai said, "I'm sorry, I don't have my head stuck in a book all day long, so I don't always get the names right."

Cai shoved Ambrosius away, and Ambrosius stumbled backwards.

"All joking aside," Cai started, "Why have you come back, Brother? Is Ahès all right?"

"Oh, Mother's fine. It's nothing like that," Ambrosius added. "Bishop Germanus of Auxerre was coming here to preach the orthodoxy as the Roman bishop has ordained it. I saw a simple opportunity to try to track you down. It wasn't that simple. With Merlinus and a few other men, we traveled back to the old villa in Cornovia. I'm not too sure I like what you've done with the place while I've been gone."

"You went back home?" Cai asked with sadness in his eyes.

Ambrosius nodded his head yes, as he lost his jovial smile.

"When?" Cai asked after a long moment of silence.

"Well, it was . . ." Ambrosius paused as he glanced at me.

"It has been nearly a month," I answered.

"Amazing," Cai replied. "We only missed each other by a few days. It was just over a month ago that we headed out for here. Several of the watchtowers on the Saxon Shore have been burned down. Looking back, those watchtowers might be tied into what's happening here," Cai remarked.

"What are you talking about?" I asked.

Glancing at me and then looking back at Ambrosius, he said, "Grallon married Hengist's daughter and Hengist has been given Kent as a wedding gift from Grallon. Hengist has been using his men to forcibly tighten his grip on Kent.

"The Picts that had submitted to the Saxons are also being used against us. There's word of other settlements revolting besides the ones in Kent. The timing seems too precise to be anything other than a staged revolt. The towers were taken out ahead of time to conceal their troop movement. There are reports of countless ships along the Saxon Shore now."

"So what are you doing here?" Ambrosius asked.

"People are calling for the Council to convene. The members of the Council finally see the shortsightedness of Grallon's reasoning. They are calling for a new Vortigern. There must be a new High Commander. Vortimer is the natural choice."

Noticing that his rhetoric was getting loud, Cai fell silent, glanced from side to side, and replied, "Why don't you three come on inside and relax for a moment?"

"Sounds good to me," Ambrosius remarked. "I could use a quick drink. My throat is dry."

"If Cai doesn't have a problem with it, why don't you and Nepos stay here and I'll come back when I have had a chance to speak with Germanus," I remarked. "Unfortunately, we need to stay abreast with what he is doing."

"Oh, right," Ambrosius answered as if he had forgotten, for the moment, who we were traveling with.

"That's fine," Cai remarked. "This way I can make sure Ambrosius stays out of trouble."

"What about the Council? Won't it be convening soon? Shouldn't we attend it?" Ambrosius asked with a raised eyebrow.

I said nothing to question Cai's character but I had my suspicions that Cai was still wanted and would be arrested upon arrival.

Cai chuckled and replied, "Brother, you are still a little naive."

Ambrosius stood silent with a hurt look on his face.

"Oh don't fret, kid. Stay innocent. Don't follow my lead. At times, I have wandered off the right path."

Staring deep into the young man's eyes, Cai added, "Father wouldn't approve of some of the things I have done. My presence at the Council would not be welcomed, unless you think being escorted away in shackles is welcoming."

Looking at me and then at Ambrosius, Cai remarked, "At the time it seemed all right. I wasn't as lucky as some when it comes to crossing a moral line. It just didn't work out as I thought it would."

With a light smirk, I added, "It never does."

Looking back at me, he nodded his head and said, "Right. It never does."

"Then it's settled. I'll catch up with Germanus. Once I know a little more of the situation, I will come back."

"Good," Cai replied.

Turning, I left the tent, mounted up, and went in search of Germanus. I caught up with the bishops' procession as the tail end of it passed through Bishopsgate and made my way to the front of it.

Noticing my approach, Germanus called out, "Where did you disappear to Merlinus? Where's Ambrosius?"

"Ambrosius' brother, Cai, is here. Ambrosius is staying with him," I replied discreetly as I drew up closer to the bishop.

"Really? Well, that must have made young Ambrosius happy," Germanus added.

"Yes, it did," I remarked. "I told Ambrosius that I would touch base with you while he spent time with his brother."

"Right. I'm happy you did. Lupus and I will be heading for the vicar's palace soon," Germanus answered. "I am hoping you will go with us to witness the Council."

"Certainly," I replied.

CHAPTER 22

When we entered the palace, there were numerous men already waiting. A whole gamut of the gentry stood in circles in casual conversations. Some of the faces appeared to be familiar from our time in London, but none of them had I met. Remaining silent, I meandered with the bishops. Germanus drew some of the clergy from the crowd.

"Greetings, Bishop Germanus," remarked a young man who looked like Lupus. He was thin and somewhat tall. He had Lupus' green eyes, short brown hair, and his soft features. He didn't appear sickly like Camillus. "I am Elafius. It is uplifting to have someone such as yourself expressing the orthodoxy so eloquently. Not all here can appreciate it, but I do."

"Thank you, young man. It is good to see eager souls gathering by God's light for His guidance and grace. You were the one that traveled to the synod in Gaul?" Germanus asked.

"That's correct," Elafius remarked.

More people filtered in. The others took little heed of them.

"When will the Council convene?" Lupus remarked.

Glancing around, Germanus and Elafius slowly surveyed the men in the large open room. For the most part, the nobles remained in small groups of four to five men. There were about ten separate clusters.

"Neither Vortimer nor his father are here," the Briton remarked.

"That's right. Nothing will begin until at least one of them arrive," Germanus added.

Two men came in through the side entrance. Other men close by took notice of their presence. Though their hair color and heights were different, the two men appeared related. They had similar facial features. They shared the same nose and the same dimpled chin. The first had black hair with a short-trimmed moustache that only partly covered his upper lip. His hair was kept short. He had oils in it, giving it a slick, wet look. The other had long hair. It was a sandy brown, bushy, and wavy, the opposite of Nepos' thin, straight hair, and it was kept it in a ponytail. They both wore a short tunic drawn in at the waist by a leather belt and trousers. The first had a dark green tunic; the other a tan one. Both wore dark brown trousers.

"Who's this?" I asked as I nodded toward the side door.

"The lead is Vortimer and I believe the one behind him is his brother, Katigern. Don't you recognize Vortimer, Merlinus?" Germanus added.

"Actually, no," I replied. "I never did meet Vortimer."

"Really? Not even when you —," Germanus started.

"No," I added cutting the bishop off.

Following a brief silence in our circle, Elafius added, "Bishop, you are correct. That is Katigern trailing close behind Vortimer."

"Fellow councilmen, may I have a moment of your time?" Vortimer called out as he went to the center of the large rectangular room. All fell silent as the gathered men recognized him.

"I believe it's quite apparent why we are here," Vortimer began in a calm even tone. "Many – myself included -- have grown tired of the Saxon presence on this island. And now, topping all of his many misdeeds, Grallon has given Kent to the Saxons without consulting anyone in this room. I learned of my father's new wife from a servant boy. Maybe, it slipped my father's mind to tell his sons about his marriage to a Saxon. This is unacceptable. There was no council convened. Something must be done. We don't want his leadership or his army of Saxon dogs."

"Before rendering judgment, can I voice my side of the situation?" Grallon called out. The whole room turned toward him. He walked in from the same side entrance his sons had used moments ago. Two young nobles, a few years older than Ambrosius, trailed behind Vortigern.

Staring at Grallon, Vortimer barked, "If your version was worth hearing, then maybe you should have voiced it before taking the vows."

Grallon's smirk vanished. He quickly realized as he glanced around the room of solemn faces that most felt as Vortimer did.

"Well, it seems a little rash to send away the men that have guarded our eastern shores for the last five years," Grallon remarked as he walked closer to the center of the room facing Vortimer and Katigern.

"Well, it seems idiotic to give away the land of a noble that has faithfully served this island longer than you've been High Commander," Vortimer fired back.

Anger burned in Grallon's cheeks. His fists clenched as he came to a halt. Silence filled the room as we waited for Grallon's response.

"So what is it you suggest, oh wise son of mine?" Grallon sneered. "Should we get rid of all of our defenses? You think I am doing something crazy by having barbarians govern our shores. This is standard practice throughout the Empire. Aëtius uses the Huns as we use the Saxons."

"No wonder the Empire is falling to pieces," Vortimer mocked.

"What would you suggest we do?" Grallon barked back.

"These Saxons need to go back to their homeland," Vortimer began. "They've served their purpose. They helped to sustain us in our transition from imperial dependence to true independence. Our people understand the need for protection and have stepped up to provide it."

"I don't believe we have obtained that just yet. I believe we need the Saxons, still. There shall be deadly consequences if they leave prematurely," Grallon retorted.

"I believe we will be worse off if they stay. I do not trust them. They want more and do less," Vortimer quickly added.

"Exactly," a man remarked from the crowd. His words parted the sea of people around him. I had no clue who this man was, but others remained silent as he stepped away from his cohorts. He stood at the same height as Vortimer and had his black hair, but it was much longer. It was thin and hung straight like Nepos' hair. His black hair had receded up his forehead. He had trimmed his goatee short. Glancing at Elafius, I saw a strong resemblance between him and the man speaking. There were several years between the two. Elafius was obviously the younger one.

"I am on the other side of the island in Gloucester, and I am concerned with the growing number of these pagan pigs," the man stated.

"I agree with Eldol," a young man added as he stepped forward. The young man had sandy brown hair and it was shaped like the top of a mushroom. He had a patchy beard and was only a few years older than Ambrosius.

"My brother, Lot, and I have seen firsthand the value of these Saxons are. In the beginning, they served a purpose. It's always better having barbarians killing barbarians. But now it has grown apparent that the Saxons and Picts have banded together in their raids on British lands. We don't want them any longer. Frankly, we don't need them."

"Why did the Saxons have to help if you could handle it?" barked one of the young men with Grallon. He shared facial features with Vortimer and Katigern but had strawberry blonde hair and freckles.

"Paschent," Grallon barked.

"Well, it's taken a little bit of time for my brother to reorganize the defenses. Half of the troops left with Lord Kendel, my father, to protect against the Irish raiding in Demetia, since your father has proven either unable or unwilling to tackle the task."

Paschent went to say something, but Vortigern put his hand up and the young man remained silent.

"I didn't come to bicker, or to get belittled by a boy. It appears to me that the only issue at hand is if the Saxons should stay on your land or mine. This issue is easily resolved. As Vortigern of this council, I decree that each magistrate can decide how to defend their lands. And as a true lord, it's your responsibility to defend the people and the lands of Britain."

"Father, you've heard Urian of Moray and Eldol's opinions. And what about Gorrannus' opinion? I'm sure we all can guess what his is. Or have you once again forgotten about the noble citizen besieged on his own lands by the Saxon enemy," Vortimer candidly remarked. A look of spite and growing hatred hung in the back of his eyes. The young man's stare dropped to the floor and he shook his head. Vortimer seemed ashamed that Grallon was his father. Grallon remained silent.

"Saxons are not the enemy," remarked the other man near Grallon. He didn't share any facial features with Grallon's other sons. He did have greenish blue eyes. His hair was sandy brown like Urian, but his wasn't thick and it was much longer. He kept it pulled back in a ponytail.

"Hah," Urian jumped in. "Ceretic, we should have expected such an answer from the bastard son of a Saxon whore. It's not your fault that Grallon didn't marry your mamma."

"You dare insult my mother. She is a queen," Ceretic remarked as his hand reached for his sword.

"She's the queen of no one on this council. I speak the truth," Urian sneered as his hand rested on the hilt of his sword. "If you feel it's an insult then, take it up with whose fault it is, your parents."

Ceretic went to lunge at Urian but Grallon held him back.

Vortimer stared at Urian and barked, "Watch your tongue, or I'll cut it out as if you were one of Conan's wives."

Young Urian fell silent.

"Like my father, I didn't come here to bicker. I came here to work out real solutions to our mounting problems. We don't want the expense of these Saxons any longer. If you want to maintain them, then, they shall tax your personal funds. No taxes collected through this council shall be used to garrison the Saxons. In the matter of Lord Gorrannus, he must have his lands restored. He should be compensated for what has been unlawfully unleashed upon him."

"It can't be done," Grallon remarked in a dismissing tone.

"It can and it shall be done, either by diplomacy or levied force," Vortimer calmly replied.

"How can you give me an ultimatum? I will not accept such terms. As Vortigern, I do not have to," Grallon mocked.

Almost in a whisper, Vortimer remarked, "I was afraid that you were going to say that."

Grallon smirked as if he thought that he would get what he wanted. Vortimer shook his head slowly in disbelief.

"As a member of this council, I am casting a vote of no confidence in its current High Commander," Urian loudly proclaimed over Vortimer's shoulder.

Vortimer merely shook his head as if he knew exactly how things were about to unfold.

"As a member of this council, you should realize that requires the sealed written intent of any absent noble," Grallon dictated.

"My brother, Lot, personally signed his letter of intent in front of me before I traveled to my father, Kendel, lord of the Powys. Once there, I received my father's sealed intent," Urian remarked as he pulled out the rolled letters from inside his tan leather vest.

"There are others on this council not present besides the members of your troublesome family," Ceretic remarked.

Until now, I hadn't noticed the man as he filtered through the crowd of people. He was a short, stout man with olive skin. Deep but gentle lines of time chiseled his face. Gray sprinkled his black hair. He held two scrolls in his right hand.

"For those here that do not know me, I am Honorius of Gwent," the man said clearly but in a low voice. "I hold the sealed intent of Lord Coel of York and his son, Germanianus of Catterick."

Grallon raised his fingers to his forehead and tried to massage away the mounting migraine. He glanced at Honorius as he held up the letters for all to see. A man standing with Honorius was regally dressed. He wore a woad-dyed tunic with black trousers. A wide black belt drew in his blue shirt. He had black hair, but it was nearly absent on the top of his head. He wore a full beard trimmed short. Though he only had hair from ear to ear on the back of his head, the man didn't appear old. He looked about the age of Elafius, which was no more than ten years older than I.

Grallon called out, "Lord Gorlois, you have not voiced your opinion. What say you?"

"This issue has not directly affected me, so I don't feel it is my place to state my opinion. I do not want my opinion influencing the Council one way or another," Gorlois remarked.

"You're part of this council. It is your responsibility to express your opinion to its members," Grallon ordered. "This is the only way a sound judgment can be issued."

"Well, then," the man began. "I believe your son, Vortimer, has expressed my thoughts on the matter, also. I believe, at this time, we would be better off if we got rid of the Saxon auxiliaries. Since the Empire has cut us loose, we suffered through several bloody years. We have grown strong and no longer need the Saxons' services."

"I believe you're mistaken on this assessment. Therefore, I can not agree to it," Grallon declared.

"In that case, I back the others in their vote of no confidence in you as High Commander," Gorlois replied.

"All of you are sadly mistaken," Grallon remarked. "Who will lead if it isn't me? Urian?"

"I couldn't do any worse than what you have done," Urian barked.

Walking closer to the center of the room, in a low, even tone, Honorius remarked, "I feel that Vortimer should take the position of High Commander."

Honorius' nomination surprised Vortimer. The lord turned toward the elder councilman. A bewildered look hung on his face.

"I don't believe I am the best choice for being the new Vortigern," Vortimer added.

"Vortimer, you have my vote, also," Gorlois added.

"Why?" Vortimer asked. "I want to nominate you, Lord Gorlois."

Gorlois nodded at Vortimer and smiled. Stepping forward, Gorlois added, "I'm not the one on the front line. I'm not the one needing to make decisive decisions without a moment's delay. I have no lands on the east side of the island. Since you reside in London at times, it must be you, Lord Vortimer. Logistically, I can't. There's no time to do what was done when the Kendel clan moved to Powys, while Lot remained near the Wall. And if I know Lord Coel as well as I think I do, I imagine that you were his choice." Shifting his glance to Honorius, Gorlois asked, "Am I correct, dear elder?"

Honorius separated the letters and held one up for all to see. Stepping toward Grallon, the elder remarked, "Here is his sealed intent. If anyone questions Lord Coel's choice, they may read it."

Ceretic reached out and took the letter from Honorius' hand.

"Ceretic, that's not necessary," Grallon remarked as he looked Honorius in the eyes.

"How do you know for certain, Father?" asked Paschent.

Without hesitation, Ceretic broke the seal and unrolled the scroll. His eyes rapidly scanned it line by line.

"Lord Coel speaks of the watchtowers being torched and knocked down. He tells of growing tensions in East Riding. The Saxons are demanding more and doing less," paraphrased Ceretic.

"See. This is proof," Urian declared.

"This is standard rhetoric," Ceretic deemed.

Urian shook his head, put his hand on his hips, and turned away. From my angle, I watched him sputter some slurs.

With an evil grin, Ceretic spouted out, "What do any of these letters matter when we still lack the nobles, Gerontius and Cai. If they still can be considered that. To many they are mere outlaw rabble, but I believe they are still recognized as noblemen of this council. With that being said, they must be present, since this council wasn't convened for the purpose of voting in a new High Commander."

The room fell quiet. They knew that Ceretic quoted their law correctly. Though he obviously twisted it to serve his purpose. I glanced over at Germanus, and he looked away. He knew what I was thinking, but he chose to remain neutral. Ceretic's grin grew as the opposition faded. Honorius simply shook his head and turned away. Gorlois glanced at the others, surprised that no one was voicing a protest.

"Is it really necessary to have Cai and Gerontius present? Their so-called outlaw status is due to their opposition to the Saxon incursion into Cornovia. They were expressing our intent over a year ago in this very room." Urian declared.

"The issue of a new High Commander is crucial. We must follow the laws as they have been agreed upon. The laws have been instilled to protect against the natural anarchy within a council. Like what seems to be developing now." Paschent interjected.

"Then," Vortimer spoke up, "we need only one of them present."

Paschent glanced over at Ceretic and then Grallon.

"Vortimer's correct," Ceretic remarked. "If there's an unannounced call of no confidence, only one noble's opinion may be missing, under the premise that death is always among us."

"No one is greater than the whole. It is that way so civil order can be sustained in troubled times," Vortimer remarked.

I heard people exhaling heavily; that's how quiet everyone remained for a moment.

"You're still lacking them both," Ceretic lightly objected.

The look of defeat sank sadly into Gorlois' face. Still, Germanus remained silent. Gorlois' head dropped down as he turned away.

"Cai of Cornovia can be summoned," I remarked.

All of the eyes in the room shifted and locked upon me. For a moment, I regretted saying a word. Even Germanus stared uncomfortably at me. Hah, like the time in Barcelona. Suddenly, I knew I was doing the right thing.

"What did you say?" Vortimer asked as he stared at me.

"Lord Cai can be summoned to this council and he can express his intent," I blandly replied.

"Besides the fact that you are not part of this council, who are you?" Paschent asked as Ceretic took closer notice of me.

Grallon recognized me and shook his head in disbelief.

"Merlinus, you insist on being my destroyer. I have always provided you with fair dealings and safe passage. In return, you remain like sand in my eye. Since you have crossed my path, I have had nearly all of my estates and titles from Armorica stripped away and now people are trying to dethrone me. How fitting."

"You've brought this on yourself, Lord Grallon," Germanus added.

"It's done," Grallon conceded. "Vortimer is High Commander. The fate of this island lies within his hands, now. You can blame me no longer."

"A notice shall be sent out to the absent nobles informing them of the turn of events," Vortimer declared. "Meanwhile, I shall march out to support Lord Gorrannus and drive the heathens from his lands. Who shall march out with me?"

"I will," called out Lord Eldol.

"As will I," followed Lord Gorlois.

"Good," Vortimer added. "With that settled, only one more matter needs addressing. As High Commander, I deem it necessary to reinstate the Roman register of offices. This will sustain civil order."

"Then what's next, taxes for the boy-emperor Valentinian?" barked Ceretic.

"Hah, that's not what Vortimer is calling for," Honorius sneered. "Maybe you're not old enough, but I remember the time we petitioned the Romans for help. The Empire told us to defend ourselves. Soon after, the Goths sacked Rome.

"As Rome struggled to survive, we sought help elsewhere. We sent an appeal to Agroetius, the usurper Jovinus' head chancellor. We agreed to be governed by Jovinus in exchange for protection. But when this usurper revealed his own lack of power, we expelled Jovinus' magistrates and took steps to govern ourselves.

"Rome's leaders failed us. Roman laws did not. To this day, we utilize their laws to maintain order. If this council I speak at does not have the semblance of the Roman Senate, then where do I find myself at this moment?"

The Council fell silent as Honorius paused. His words caught the nobles off guard. He spoke the truth and his words were sincere. They didn't know how to object. How could they? I watched Ceretic as he stewed in silence. He was trying to think of some objection that he could voice.

"What's stopping any noble from objecting to this sub-Roman standard of government?" Ceretic barked. "What's stopping anyone from appealing directly to an imperial power, possibly General Aëtius?"

"Nothing," Vortimer fired back. "Just as no one stopped some of the nobles from contacting Agricola, consul and prefect of Gaul, nearly ten years ago. I remember when that happened. At least he sent a nominal force to Demetia to protect his family's holdings. It's unfortunate that he died that year. His efforts made a slight difference, but not enough. So a third appeal to Aëtius would have little or no consequence, in my opinion. Honestly, what interest would the general have in this island. We are on the wrong side of the current Roman frontier. Besides, he has no family interest here like Agricola did. Our value to the Empire is nothing compared to Africa or Gaul, for that matter. These lands are not free of trouble and cost more to maintain. Our pleas will be neglected.

"We have been on our own since the sacking of Rome," Honorius added as he stared at Ceretic. "Not all of us have accepted this fact but should."

"So by Vortimer being Vortigern of this council, does that also make him the Vicar of London?" Ceretic questioned.

"No," Vortimer answered. "This city is Augusta on the fringe of the western world. London is an open city for all. I don't believe that can be maintained, if I lead as High Commander of the Council's army and Vicar of London. Besides, the duties of Vortigern mirror those of the Count of Britain."

"Awh, this is outrageous," Paschent cried out loudly. "Next, you'll expect us to address you as the Emperor of the British. We don't need any more political charades."

"No," Vortimer retorted. "That's not what I'm saying."

"Lord Vortimer is not trying to instill something radical here. In my opinion, he behaves in a very rational manner," Lord Honorius added in his slow, dignified manner.

"Right, I'm not suggesting anything radical," Vortimer added. "Lord Coel was Duke of the Northern Front before the collapse of Rome and still he remains there with his son, Germanianus, his heir apparent. As I suggested, I shall be the Count of Britain. By de facto, I am doing this by being High Commander of the Council's mobile army."

"This still leaves two of the major offices empty," Ceretic declared. "Naturally, there is the Vicar of London, but there is also the Count of the Saxon Shore. Who are you going to dictate to these prominent posts?"

"No one," Vortimer fired back. "As I have stated before, Britain is ruled by a council, not a dictator. Leaders are elected based on merit and logic. In accordance, I nominate Katigern to be the Count of the Saxon Shore. Currently, he commands the Saxon fort near Colchester and he has battle-proven skills and handles his army efficiently."

"Well, so what?" Paschent spouted off. "I nominate Ceretic. He controls Portchester."

"With Grallon's help," Urian stated. "Ceretic has not been tested and proved honorable like your older brother has. Unlike Ceretic or yourself, Katigern has traveled to the Northern Front and participated in the major offenses against Drust and his damn Picts."

"Then, who shall be the Vicar of London?" Ceretic questioned. "I nominate Lord Grallon."

"Hah," Urian laughed. "You can't be serious."

"Why not?" Ceretic snapped back.

"When I think of your father controlling London, it doesn't seem as open and free as Vortimer is intending it to be," Urian spouted back.

"Then who?" Paschent jumped in.

"Jonah," Vortimer clearly stated.

"The old Jew?" Paschent scoffed. "Hah, you must be joking."

"I'm not," Vortimer confirmed.

"He's unacceptable," Paschent ranted.

"Why? What legitimate objection is there?" Vortimer stated. "Jonah is an honorable man and has held the respect of this city longer than you have been alive. I stand by my choices. What says this council?"

The room exploded as everyone voiced their opinions at once.

"Silence," Lord Vortimer shouted. A wave of grumbling washed through the room.

"Lord Eldol, are these choices acceptable?" Vortimer asked.

"Yes," the old lord added with a nod.

"And you, Lord Gorlois?" Vortimer continued.

"Jonah is fine," he replied. "And, there could be no better choice than Katigern to be the Count of the Saxon Shore."

"They are both acceptable to me," Honorius added.

"I have my hesitations with the Jew, but none with Katigern or the men that have endorsed them both so far," Urian remarked. "So I support both choices."

"Well, they are unacceptable to me," Paschent barked.

"That doesn't matter," Lord Vortimer remarked. "The majority have consented to my choice. The council has spoken. Your objection has been nullified."

Paschent stewed in silent discontent.

"So Jonah, will you accept this post and serve to maintain order in London on behalf of this council?" Vortimer called out. "A large squad of soldiers will be mandated to assist you in this difficult task."

"On that note, I shall accept the honor that the Council has bestowed upon me," an old man remarked as he stepped forward. This man looked like nothing I had expected. He was shorter and older than I had assumed. He might have been older than both Honorius and Grallon. None of the other prominent men were close to their age except Eldol. Still, Eldol was at least ten years younger than the other three. Jonah was the shortest elder at the council meeting. He had short gray hair parted down the middle. His eyes were like little black berries. Underneath his thick nose, Jonah kept his moustache short. It covered much of his upper lip. He wore a tan tunic with brown trousers.

"Good. Then this matter is settled," Lord Vortimer finished.

As the Council slowly dispersed, I noticed Honorius of Gwent walking toward Lupus, Germanus, and I.

"Greetings, Bishop Germanus," the old noble remarked as he drew within an arm's length of us."

"Hello, Lord Honorius," Bishop Germanus replied with a smile. "It has been too long since we last spoke. How does life treat you?"

"All things considered, I am well," he replied.

"That's good," Germanus remarked. "I will be sure to let Ahès know. She will be glad to hear that."

"I'm also happy to hear that," Honorius added. "In truth, she is the reason I've taken this moment to speak with you. It is my understanding that she currently resides at a villa on the outskirts of Aureliani."

"That is correct," Germanus replied. "She is still there."

"Good," the old noble replied. "Before she left Britain, she had informed me that if I needed to contact her that I should send the message through you."

"Of course, there's no problem with that," the bishop quickly replied. "What message do you need relayed to her?"

"Well, it's not really a message but a request," Honorius started. "I have a granddaughter named Priscilla. She and Ahès like each other and have corresponded more frequently than my purse cares for. And due to the current unrest on the island, I would like you to ask Ahès if Priscilla may stay with her for a while. All cost of accommodations and hospitality shall be well compensated. I hope you would vouch for me."

Smiling and before I could say anything, Germanus remarked, "How quick of a response were you needing, my old friend?"

"The sooner the better. The Irish are raiding on the west side more frequently. I would be crushed if my precious Priscilla was taken and turned into a slave girl, or something worse. It happen to an associate of mine several years ago. Calpornius was so distraught for so long when his sixteen-year-old son was taken and sold into slavery. Luckily, his son escaped and came back to Britain. The boy is actually in the Order as we speak."

"I'm sure Bishop Germanus can give you an answer before this night is through," I jumped in.

Turning to me, he gave me a stern stare and asked, "How is that possible? And who are you? Merlin? Marius? What is your name? Grallon knows you and you know Cai of Cornovia."

"He is Merlinus of Aureliani," Germanus said with a smile. "He owns the villa where Ahès currently resides."

The old man laughed loudly and added, "I feel like a fool."

"No, no. That's my fault, my old friend," Germanus added as he placed his hand on Honorius' shoulder. "I strung you along for fun. I apologize for that. It was poor timing."

"Regardless," I cut in. "Your granddaughter is welcome to visit Ahès at my villa. She can stay as long as you permit. If you so request, I shall put my permission in writing, but I don't believe that will be necessary."

"Thank you, young lord," the old man remarked as he reached out his hand to shake mine. "You cannot imagine the relief you have just provided my old heart."

"Think nothing of it, sir," I added. "Besides being a friend of Bishop Germanus, Ahès has spoke of your kindness. So, as I said, think nothing of it."

"Again, thank you," the old lord finished with a smile.

CHAPTER 23

We didn't march out with Vortimer, the other nobles, and their assembled armies. Instead, Germanus had us remain in London, saying that we would be leaving shortly.

"We are not here for that," Germanus told Ambrosius days later in Germanus' tent.

"I thought we were here to protect the British?" Ambrosius questioned.

"Jonah shall help Vortimer maintain order here in London. We are here to protect them spiritually, not physically," the bishop corrected.

"How can they be taught what is spiritually right if they are physically dead?" Ambrosius questioned.

"What truly matters in this world of flesh and corruption? One must strive for harmony with God. That is the true meaning of life," Germanus remarked.

"How is such a holy balance obtained when one must abandon all sense and logic for blind faith?" Ambrosius asked.

"Not blind faith but reliance on the written words of apostles and prophets," Lupus remarked.

"It appears that the new orthodoxy doesn't matter when its servants do not help the very ones they preach to," Ambrosius added.

Germanus went to say something but stopped when the angry young man marched past him and went outside Germanus' tent. The bishop looked at me for an explanation of Ambrosius' actions. Instead of responding, I remained tight lipped and went after the young man.

The young man stood by himself some distance from any tent. He stared at the western skies.

Hearing my approach, Ambrosius called out, "I cannot believe he will not raise a hand to help these people."

"I can," I replied as I finished walking up to him. "It doesn't serve his purpose. You heard him say that."

"Why doesn't it?" Ambrosius asked.

"It doesn't matter what side he backs. He would be alienating one set of nobles, either way," I stated. "I believe this is the main reason he hasn't picked a side. He is here simply to preach Catholicism as Rome views it. Nothing more."

"So nothing will change his position?" Ambrosius questioned.

"From what I know of him, I doubt it," I remarked. "There is no reason I know of that would make him handle it any other way."

"Doesn't he have any emotional connection with these people, no family, no true British friends besides Grallon?" Ambrosius asked.

"Not that I am aware of," I answered.

"This is unbelievable," Ambrosius grumbled. "Isn't God better served by defending what's right rather than doing nothing?"

"Not always," I answered. "It's never that simple when blood is being drawn."

"So you are saying that we should do nothing?" Ambrosius repeated as his tone grew angry. "Something has happened. It's been happening for several years now. Grallon has been stealing lands and giving them to his Saxon cronies."

"If that's truly the case, why didn't you deal with him when we saw him over a month ago," I remarked. "Why did you let me hold you back?"

When he tried to speak, I interrupted him. "Why didn't you just walk up to him with your boiling rage and cut him down as if he were Julius Caesar? Explain yourself. Are you a coward?"

As my words sank in, he released a heavy sigh. I knew what he felt, but I wasn't trying to make light of what happened to him at the hands of Grallon's men.

I cut him off again when he spoke. "Don't worry too much about what I just said. I only wanted you to think about what you are committing yourself to. Besides, I'm sure you will get your chance to set things right if we stay much longer."

"How do you figure that?" Ambrosius asked.

"It would be extremely difficult not to fight if we are under siege," I remarked.

"Under siege? Here in London? Would they dare?" he asked.

"Yes. The Saxons have to take this city to take the island," I stated.

"They are using Grallon's wedding as provocation for their revolt."

"Merlinus," a loud voice called out from behind us.

Turning, we saw Camillus running toward us. His cheeks were flushed.

"Sorry for the intrusion, sir," Camillus remarked. "Bishop Germanus wanted me to find both of you."

"What's wrong?" I asked.

"The Saxons are marching to raid the Darenth Valley. Bishop Germanus worries that they shall sack and burn all of the villas that remain in the valley. The bishop was hoping you and Ambrosius would ride out with us."

"Ride out?" I questioned.

"Yes," Camillus answered.

"Of course," Ambrosius remarked.

Glancing at him and then looking back at me, Camillus waited for my response.

"We will ride out with the bishop," I remarked.

"Good," Camillus answered.

CHAPTER 24

Night had fallen. A thick chill hung underneath the open starlit sky. Only Nepos and the other Alan troops rode out with us. Cai and his men had rode back to Cornovia to ensure the region stay free of marauders. We had crossed the bridge over the Thames River. Most of the riders carried burning torches as we galloped along the Roman road that ran southeast. We headed for the villa of Evodius.

Before leaving, Germanus stated that this old imperial officer lived by Episford on the Darenth River. Germanus showed concern for this man's well-being. From what I could gather, the bishop had known him for quite some time.

Eventually as the full moon hung low on the open horizon, we approached the large villa of Evodius as it sat on a low terrace cut into the hill near the Darenth River. Smoke bellowed up above it from a chimney hidden mostly from sight. All seemed peaceful and quiet.

Much of the hedged-off fields had lain fallow last year. A circular building stood nearby. Nothing appeared out of order. A steady curl of smoke sailed skyward from the furnace in the building between the villa and small circular building. It reminded me of coming home to Aureliani earlier this year. My heart sank as I suddenly longed to be home.

"Merlinus, tell the squadron to remain here. We will ride ahead and confirm where they can set up camp." Germanus commanded.

"Yes," I replied.

After translating his orders, I rode out the rest of the way to the villa with the bishops. As we were dismounting, a tall, broad-shouldered man walked down the long portico. He had a full head of hair that was cut short of the base of his neck. His black locks curled slightly close to his brow. A thick beard covered his face. The lines along his eyes and cheeks hinted at his old age. He had little gray hair.

He wore Roman robes and sandals and held a burning torch high to cast as much light as possible.

"Greetings, Germanus," the man replied. "It has been too long since we last spoke."

"True enough, Evodius" the bishop replied. "Can we call upon your hospitality for the night?"

"Absolutely," the man answered. "Set up camp near the villa. Avoid the lowlands by the river. They are saturated from heavy spring rains."

Turning to me, Germanus remarked, "Merlinus, tell the men. Afterwards, make your way back to the villa if you so wish. We shall be up talking for a while, I imagine."

"Yes, Bishop," I replied.

After speaking with Nepos, Ambrosius and I made our way back to the villa. A servant boy waited by the front pillars.

"Sir, I'll take you to my master," the boy remarked.

"Thank you," I replied.

The little boy led Ambrosius and me through the east verandah and into the audience chamber. He then led us into a large apsidal room with a domed ceiling that gave much space to the room. The triclinium in the dining room was empty.

I noticed the mosaic. It was superb. A naked woman rode side-saddle on a bull. I would only be guessing, but it appeared to be an image of Jupiter's abduction and rape of Europa. Germanus, Lupus, and Evodius stood to the right in the reception room down the west corridor.

"Ah yes, Merlinus and young Ambrosius," Germanus called out as he noticed me.

The villa's host turned around and faced us.

"Evodius," Germanus remarked. "The lad is the son of Ahès and Constantine of Cornovia. This gentleman is Merlinus of Aureliani. He's serving as our interpreter. He has quite the talent with languages. Besides Latin and Greek, he has mastered a few barbaric tongues, also."

"Really? Which ones?"

"My mother is an Alan. I learned the Gothic tongue from my father's mother. I speak certain Oriental dialect. When I lived in the great forests of Mount Shaoshi, I had met a generous elder who was a master of many arts. I stayed five years under his tutorship," I replied.

"Impressive. It's a pleasure to meet you and your friend," the Roman remarked as he held out his hand. With a firm grip, we shook hands.

"This is a very fine villa," I remarked.

"The finest in the valley," Germanus added.

"That's not saying much anymore," Evodius laughed. "Many of the villas are dilapidated or vacant. They are being stripped of their reusable material like their clay shingles, roof joists, and anything else salvageable."

"Well, Germanus is right, then. That surely makes your villa the best in the valley," Ambrosius joked.

"Right, right," Evodius laughed.

"Merlinus," Germanus remarked, "Evodius has been explaining current affairs to us. Dover and Richborough have been taken. Vortimer and his men have been pushed back west of Canterbury."

"I just received a written dispatch shortly before your arrival," Evodius replied. "It appears that Lord Vortimer is heading back to London. In addition, a large squad of Saxon infantry marched south for Ashford. They are seeking to finish off Gorrannus."

"Will they succeed?" Ambrosius asked.

"There's a good chance that the Saxons have already taken him and are turning north for London," said the host.

"They would not dare such a thing, would they?" Lupus remarked.

Smiling slightly, Evodius observed, "The wolves have grown brave and fearless of the shepherd."

"London must not fall," Ambrosius decreed. His spiritedness surprised even me.

"Indeed," Evodius remarked as his hand palmed his head. "The villas of the Darenth Valley are defenseless. They are outdated and have outlived simpler, safer times."

"You should go with us to London," Germanus declared as he rested his hand on Evodius' shoulder.

With a light laugh, the old host said, "If I were to live my last days in logic I would go to London, but I'm not. This is my home, it may not be much in the grand imperial scheme of things, but I will lawfully hold this villa, just the same. I will not allow it to be taken from me illegally. I will burn it down before I would allow it to be taken. As God as my witness, I swear it shall be done. What will you do, Bishop Germanus?" Evodius asked. "When will you be heading back to London?"

Germanus glanced at Ambrosius, myself, then Lupus and saw the same question on all our faces. The bishop remained silent. He ran his fingertips through his shortly trimmed beard, much of it gray.

"Sides are gathering and boundaries are being defined," Germanus replied. "Wouldn't you agree, Merlinus?"

"That is a fair assessment of the situation," I answered. "It would be good to know all who stood with Vortimer and how they fared at the moment. A truer consensus is needed. Communication is crucial."

"Right," Evodius replied. "If the way stations were securely within Vortimer's command, we could get word to York in half a day. But, it's difficult to say if that's true or not. A rider should be safe until he nears Cambridge. From there to Lincoln, no one is safe except a Saxon. We are left open to these invaders. There are no walls here like in London."

"Being here in the North Downs, the natural terrain acts as somewhat of a deterrent. Besides the headwaters of Darenth, are there any other passages through the North Down?" Germanus asked.

"There's the Stour Valley running south from Canterbury to Ashford and then there is Medway Valley. This valley basically splits the North Downs in half. Hengist will need to at least hold Medway Valley to keep Canterbury secure," the host replied.

"London will be cut off from the south. I doubt that Ceretic will stop the Saxons from driving north," I replied.

In a questioning pause, Germanus glanced at Evodius.

"Yes," the retired officer replied. "There is no doubt what side he is on and the same goes for Paschent."

"They did side with Grallon on every issue," Lupus added.

"Who is this Ceretic?" I asked. "He seemed to be abreast with the laws of the Council."

"His story is hazier than most, I am afraid," Evodius replied. "For what it is worth, I will tell you what is generally accepted. It's said that Ceretic is one of Grallon's many bastard sons. Hah, I think only Kendel of Powys has more. But that's besides the point. Ceretic's mother was one of Grallon's concubines. In time, Grallon treated Ceretic and his mother well, too well for Ahès' mother's liking. Causing unrest between Grallon and her mother while he reigned in Armorica, Grallon sent Ceretic and his mother to reside in Britain. Grallon had lands he gained from former imperial grants. Ceretic grew up in a lifestyle of the privileged. He received a superb education and martial training. Being exiled with his mother, Ceretic retained his mother's tongue and became fluent in several other languages. Grallon uses him as his main translator when dealing with any barbarian embassies."

"Ah," Ambrosius lightly laughed. "Merlinus, you and Ceretic have something in common."

"Hopefully, the ability to talk several languages is all we have in common," I remarked. "Ceretic seems to always be scheming against the Council. To him, the ends justifies the means."

"That's funny," Evodius replied. "That's the same basic impression I had of him. That boy is a weasel."

"They are going to drive at London from three fronts," I remarked. "Push past Rochester, drive down the Darenth, and ride straight up the Roman road from Chichester. They'll burn and scatter all in their path. They'll key on the villas. They'll be the soft . . ." I paused as I realized how candidly I spoke about the looming danger.

"Don't feel guilty, Merlinus," the old man replied. "I've already said the villas are soft targets. You are telling no bad news that I didn't already know of."

"It's just sad how much is lost in wars and can never be regained. Only an ignorant man would burn this villa down," I remarked. "And only a fool would die defending it."

"How could you say such a thing?" Ambrosius remarked.

"This villa is merely a physical structure that can be rebuilt. It is not as though we can be reborn?" I replied.

"Well that depends on who you ask," Evodius replied. "Spiritually speaking, Germanus would disagree. Isn't that correct, Bishop? Never mind, let's not even get started on that subject tonight. The last time we spoke upon it, I swear I heard roosters crowing before we called that conversation finished for the night."

Germanus laughed, held his smile, and added, "That was a good conversation."

"I remembered a lot of wine was consumed," Evodius remarked.

"Indeed, that was a good vintage," Germanus added. "Good times."

A moment of reminiscence hung quietly among us.

"Do you have the men to protect the Darenth headwaters?" Germanus asked.

"I don't have the men to protect this villa, not to mention the valley," Evodius replied.

"Then it is here where we will make a stand against the pagans," Germanus replied.

I said nothing while I looked at Germanus. I wondered if he was simply playing with his words or if he truly meant to fight the Saxons.

"We shall shed the blood of the barbarians before we allow them to bleed this island anymore," Germanus added.

"Thank you, Germanus," Evodius remarked.

"Think nothing of it," the bishop replied. "Tomorrow, I will handpick a squad of light-armed cavalry and patrol the outworks. We shall go up to the headwaters of the Darenth. This is where, I believe, they will come, as Merlinus has pointed out."

"Good. Good." Evodius finished with a relieved look upon his face.

CHAPTER 25

It had been a few days since our night arrival at the villa of Evodius. The bishops and the bulk of the mounted troops rode south toward the headwaters of the Darenth. The rest of the cavalry remained at the villa to keep watch for activity to the west and east of the Darenth.

Ambrosius and I traveled with the bishops to the headwaters. After we returned from the initial tour, Bishop Germanus had his men build a makeshift church out of leafy branches based on a city church. The bishops set up, filled, and blessed a baptizing font. Germanus figured that we would be spending the holiday out in the field. With Easter a day away, it appeared that the bishop was correct in his assumption.

The night passed. The next day Germanus held service and celebrated the solemnities of Easter. Though the Alan troops were mostly pagans, Germanus convinced many warriors of the sincerity of Christianity. Several of them asked the bishop to baptize them, which Germanus did without hesitation.

As I observed the service, I noticed a rider approaching. Though near the camp, the man's horse galloped fast. As discreet as possible, I stood up and walked out and around the group attending the Easter sermon. I quickly recognized the trooper. It was Nepos. He was one of the scouts sent out on patrol.

"Sir, the Saxons are coming. They will be here no later than tomorrow morning," he remarked rapidly in his native tongue.

"How many men do they have?" I asked in Alan.

"Easily a hundred men, but they are all foot soldiers," Nepos reported. After a long pause, he asked, "What did you want to do, sir?"

"First, dismount and take a moment's rest. I will need to discuss this with Bishop Germanus. He has nearly completed his sermon and then I'll speak with him."

"Okay. Don't worry," Nepos added. "Our mounted cavalry can take position on the slopes of the Darenth near its headwaters. We will bring thunder down from the mountain."

I laughed and he joined in. With a smile, he added, "If there is nothing for the moment, I ask to be excused."

"Of course. I will call upon you when I am ready to speak with the bishop," I replied. "There might be something that needs a clearer explanation."

"Yes, sir," Nepos remarked as he turned and walk away. He headed for the wagons. I moved through the crowd back toward the bishops.

Germanus had just finished. He and Lupus walked toward me.

"What did Nepos say? That was him, wasn't it?" Lupus asked.

"Yes. He said the Saxons are on the march and will be here by tomorrow," I replied.

"Come with me, Merlinus," Germanus replied. "I will need you to translate my words to these people. We will need all the help we can get."

Besides the soldiers that had sailed with us from Gaul, others had gathered in our temporary camp. For the most part, these people consisted of desolated country folk. More and more people were being driven from their homes south of London. In addition, a large group of Alans had deserted Grallon's service and Germanus allowed them within our company's ranks. These were the people Germanus wanted to address.

"People, please allow me a moment of your time," Germanus called out loudly.

As Germanus spoke and paused, I translated his words for the Alans.

"Great people of Britain," he continued. "A Saxon army marches as I speak. They come to demand, by force, what does not belong to them. This is unacceptable and must be stopped. These barbarians hold nothing sacred, least of all your lives.

"Shortly, men shall move out against these heathens. At the head of this holy army, I shall ride. We shall take position on the slopes of the valley. From there we shall put the fear of God into these heathens.

"I ask now, those willing to fight on the side of God, please step forward, be baptized by a general of God, and march to smite the Saxons. Alleluia!" Germanus shouted with strong emotion, which I translated and called out with matching conviction.

The ranks of our army swelled. More men fell in line to receive

Germanus' holy blessing. Even the soldiers who had sailed to Britain with us stood in line to be baptized by this self-proclaimed general of God. Like Martin, being a former soldier converted to the holy path, Germanus had great appeal to the Alans. Many of Nepos' men spoke highly of him. Carbo stood in line to be baptized by Bishop Germanus.

With the men still wet from their baptism, the holy army marched out to meet the heathens. Their spirits soared with fervid faith. A wave of hope rolled over me, and I felt invigorated by the bishop's actions.

CHAPTER 26

The Saxon army advanced through the North Downs. We tried to pick the right position to intercept them. Soft-sloped hills enclosed the Darenth's headwaters. Its valley eventually led down to Episford where Evodius' villa overlooked the river's western bank. We had to stop them here to protect him there.

Stationed on both sides of the valley, we waited for the savage army to draw near. Suddenly something broke over the crest of the distant hill. It was the scouts galloping hard toward our position. The Saxon weren't far now. Our stationed men grew restless as they saw the horsemen quickly approaching.

"They'll break the horizon in less than an hour," Nepos remarked a short while later as he brought his galloping horse to a hard halt.

"What is the size of the army?" I asked in the Alan tongue.

"It appears to be a small regiment," the scout who rode with Nepos added. "I believe it is only a portion of the men under Hengist. From what I saw, we have them heavily outnumbered."

I translated the scouts' report to Germanus.

"Good," Germanus remarked. "Tell them to return, have Nepos order the others to pull back and tell them to take position with the eastern unit. Remind them not to engage the enemy. Wait for my call to arms. I will ride back to the right and start the battle cry from over there."

Quickly, I relayed Germanus' instructions as he rode off.

"It shall be done," said Nepos and pulled his horse around and galloped off at a strong pace. The other scout raced back with Nepos and they disappeared into the cover before the top of the hill.

A short time later, the Saxon army appeared on the horizon. They talked loudly amongst themselves. They did not try to hide their presence. They moved more like travelers than warriors. The Saxons clattered and clambered, lugging their equipment and weapons along the path. Step by step, they drew closer and closer.

The spring rain that year had swollen the headwaters of the Darenth, but still they crossed it. We waited until part of their troops had arrived on the opposite side. With an echoing "Alleluia," Germanus' and the army sent a wave of terror through the approaching enemy. Our battle cry soared across the valley like a dragon's roar. On that signal, Nepos' cavalry suddenly surged down into the valley. The Saxons acted as though the very sky was falling upon them. The soldiers in the front turned to cut back across the river while the ones wading midway simply wanted to make it to the shore. In their blind panic, many drowned in the river they had just crossed. The Saxons scattered in all directions, unsure which way was safest.

Our cavalry drove the Saxons back the way they had come and east toward the Medway Valley. I wondered how many recognized the Alan's dragon standard and were thankful for not being skinned alive. The Saxons discarded their shields in an attempt to escape. And through it all, I watched as Ambrosius rode hard against the Saxons. Just revenge was served without striking a blow.

Convinced that the Saxons were in full retreat, Ambrosius rode back with the rest of the cavalry. He wore a bright, proud smile.

"Amazing," he called out as he rode up. "Merlinus, have you ever seen such a thing?"

With a little smirk, I replied, "I have never heard of such a thing."

"That was truly divine," Bishop Lupus remarked. "A defeat of the Saxons with the word of God. Does any nonbeliever need more proof of the power of the Gospel?"

"This holy victory shall be remembered and praised for many lifetimes beyond our's," Camillus replied.

"You really think so?" Ambrosius asked as he dismounted.

"Absolutely," Lupus replied. "This will proudly be featured in the annals of legends."

"As what? The Battle of North Downs?" Ambrosius asked.

"No," Lupus replied. "It's a victory of faith, not force. Alleluia."

"What was that?" Ambrosius asked.

"Praise be to God," Germanus replied and added loudly as he rode toward us, "Alleluia!"

"Alleluia!" roared from the army like a monstrous dragon.

Their unified cheer caught me off guard this time.

The unity of numerous voices gave substance to the word and once more, "Alleluia!" echoed across the valley.

Elated, Germanus dismounted where we stood.

"Could Achilles or Alexander say that they achieved such a victory?" Germanus asked with a proud smile.

"No. No, I don't think that they honestly could say that," I replied. "There is no tall tale or sensational story in the scrolls that match such a divine victory."

Germanus laughed loudly and added, "I think it helped to start the battle cry on the western shore of the Darenth. It carried across the valley like a wave. The chant rolled eastward, driving the frightened Saxons in the direction we wanted them to go."

"What's next?" Lupus asked. "Shall we push them back from here?"

"What do you think, Merlinus," Germanus asked. "What does your keen foresight perceive? Should we be concerned that the Saxons might still try to drive down the Darenth? Should we remain stationed or charge after the heathens and make them submit to our divine authority? Tell us your opinion of the current situation."

How many times have I heard that in my life? For a while, I didn't realize that Father had been the first to ask my opinion. We would sit in the inner courtyard of our villa. He had me reading various military treatises to him. By the age of ten, I had read Julius Caesar's commentary on his Gallic wars to Father. There were several others. Those were all I read to him. He required me to read to him every night when he was home from a campaign. Instead of sending me away to school, he had tutors teach me at the villa. Father feared what was happening to the Empire. He said it was falling apart, rotting away with corruption and ignorance.

After his death and after I left Aureliani, Roman commanders in Persia asked for my opinion. On numerous battlefields I'd witnessed much firsthand, but there had only been a few fights where I was anything more than an advisor. I tried to minimize the guilt I felt from the death I helped to inflict by utilizing battle-proven strategies. I figured by helping to overwhelm an opponent quickly, I was actually saving more lives in the long run. I still hated being a part of the madness. But with barbarian federations as the standard Roman garrison, my skills with languages had become more valuable and easy to profit from.

Still, I spoke what I thought. "I believe we would be best served if we send a report to Evodius. If we pursue the Saxons, we take a chance of having our armies' lines pinched if the heathens circle back or if a separate force drives up through the North Downs in between here and Medway Valley.

"At this point, communication is essential," I continued. "We should maintain the army in this valley, at least for a few days, while sending a messenger back to Evodius to inform him of what has arisen. In doing so, a rider can be sent back here to the valley. By handling it this way, we will not be needlessly moving the army when it is better served remaining here for right now."

"I agree," Germanus replied. "When will you and a squad be leaving?"

"Leaving?" I asked. "You want me to go? You don't feel that it would be best that you go? Do you really think Evodius will accept my word and deal with me?"

"I have no doubt that he will," the bishop remarked. "Besides, I can do more here. These people need my guidance more than ever. Anyway, there is no one else I trust."

"As you wish, Bishop," I replied.

"Take Ambrosius and Nepos with you, also," Germanus added.

"Of course."

CHAPTER 27

Upon returning to Evodius' villa, we found it occupied. We arrived from the southeast. Nothing was smashed, burned, or destroyed. The large amount of rising smoke came from the campfires of the bivouac and from the detached kitchen. It was unclear whose men they were, but it was easy to tell that they were British or at least allies to Evodius.

A small squad of five riders rode hard toward us. Halting, we waited for the riders to finish their approach.

"What business do you have here?" called out the lead rider as he reined in his horse a few feet from us.

"I'm a messenger for Bishop Germanus," I said to the rider.

"Who is that to me," remarked another member of the squadron.

"No one," Ambrosius replied. "But, he is a good friend of Evodius, the master of this villa."

"Oh, I see," remarked the first soldier. "I apologize for the manner of our questioning."

"It is understandable," I replied. "These are dangerous times."

"This is true," said the second soldier. "Let me escort you up to the villa so you have no more delays."

"That would be excellent," I replied.

Only the head mount rode toward the villa. The other four horsemen returned in their original direction. I rode with Ambrosius to the villa.

The head rider remained on his horse as we dismounted.

"Evodius is inside. Best wishes to you, gentlemen," the rider remarked.

Numerous people moved about the villa as we entered. Our presence went unnoticed. Servants passed through the main entrance and the adjacent rooms and hallways. They kept the wine flowing, filling cups as quickly as they could. Some of the noblemen talked amongst themselves while others, drunk from the wine, pawed at the female servants. If I hadn't known better, I would have guessed that we were at a party of some sort, but the conversations lacked the joyful tone created by such events. As we walked, Ambrosius glanced into the various rooms down the hallway. When we neared the dining room, the conversations became nearly deafening. There was nowhere to sit. Only a thin, fluctuating path remained clear for the servants to pass through as they refreshed the noblemen's cups. I struggled to notice anyone that looked familiar. None of these men attended the meeting of the Council.

Before making our way into the crowded room, a servant came to us from the hallway and discreetly remarked, "Lord Merlin, please wait. Let me assist you."

The servant was familiar. He was one of Evodius' closer servants. For some reason, I could not place his name though Evodius addressed the servant by his name. I felt guilty for forgetting it.

"My lord is this way," he remarked. He led us through the crowded hallway heading south. It was near the bath suite. I could hear people talking and water splashing. The quad-chambers consisting of cold, tepid, and hot rooms, with the plunge baths laid on the other side of the wall. In the time spent here in Episford, I hadn't been to this room. It was a small room. Evodius stared at a map of Britain that hung on the wall facing the room's entrance. This was his library. A mounted wooden grid hung on the north wall, with room to house sixteen hundred scrolls. The wooden scroll boxes were made out of forty columns and forty rows. It appeared that each box carried a scroll. The top rows of the wooden grid would require the assistance of the foot stool stashed underneath it. A burning oil lamp hung from a thin stand near every corner. They filled the room with a soft but complete light. As we entered, I drifted toward the scrolls. I wondered which ones I had read. There had to be a couple of them. Were there any I wished I could read? Unfortunately, there was no time for that.

"Dear sir," I remarked lightly. "What's going on? Whose army is this? We didn't leave this many men behind here."

Laughing, the tall veteran turned and asked, "Oh, you noticed the few extra men stationed outside?"

"I would have to say that they caught my attention," I replied.

"Yeah, the bishop shows up and all of a sudden this valley is worth protecting. No, honestly, they won't be here long. In a few days, they are moving out to reinforce Vortimer's position near Rochester. These men are under the command of his brother, Katigern. They've been here since they faced off against Ceretic's men. Ceretic the traitor drove for London. Katigern stopped him," Evodius said.

"So Vortimer couldn't drive past Rochester? What happen to Gorrannus? Is he a prisoner?" I asked.

"He is dead," Evodius lightly replied.

"What?" I questioned.

"He and his family were executed when the Saxons overran Kent," Evodius declared.

"Unbelievable," Ambrosius whispered.

"It is true," Evodius reaffirmed with a short nod.

"So what is next then?" Ambrosius asked as he glanced at Evodius and then at me.

Evodius remained silent with a look of deep concern on his face. At that moment, I saw the age in him. Five years ago, he would not have seemed uncertain and would have offered himself as the protector. Now, age had set in. He lacked his former stern soldier's conviction. Age had stripped him of that. His hand massaged his forehead. All was quiet except for muffled voices in the other parts of the villa. He lost the bravado he had the other night with Germanus.

"Fight," I remarked. "That's all that is left. We must fight these heathens on every front we can."

"Right," Evodius added with a relieved smile. "That's all that we can do. We cannot negotiate with them. How can someone be trusted when they unlawfully strip a nobleman of his titles, lands, and his very life? They do not honor peace, only war."

"So will we ride out with Katigern?" Ambrosius asked.

"Yes," I replied.

"Good," Ambrosius added.

"I agree," Evodius remarked. "So, if that's settled, then, you both might as well enjoy the entertainment and refreshments. Who knows when we will be able to celebrate once more?"

"Hopefully, when Rochester is retaken, we will be able to celebrate the victory," I replied.

"Hopefully," Evodius added with a smile.

"Dear sir, can you send word to Bishop Germanus? None of our horsemen will be able to leave until later. We should send word to let the bishops know of the turn of events," Ambrosius remarked.

A little surprised that young Ambrosius made the suggestion, the old British Roman glanced at me and I nodded my affirmation.

"Of course, that will not be a problem," Evodius answered. "Word shall be sent shortly. I swear it."

"Thank you." Ambrosius finished with a respectful nod.

CHAPTER 28

"We're under attack!"

"It's the Saxons!"

"To arms! It's the Saxons! To arms!"

These screams and many more were heard in the morning hour at Evodius' villa. Smoke hung like fog in the air. People fumbled about the villa. Cries and moans pained my ears. Luckily, the veil of darkness fell from the first blades of the rising sun.

The Saxons had sailed up the Darenth River in several shallow boats and landed at Episford. The granary's roof burned a brilliant red and flickered yellow. Nearly all of their men were ashore. They occupied the riverside in force. The numbers were close, but battle readiness surely went to the Saxons.

"Men," Katigern shouted out. "The enemy is upon us. Rise to arms. Archers fire at will. Take out as many as possible."

Chaos ensued quickly. Many of the servants cowered in fear. Outside, the swords clashed loudly. Men died in agony. A few ran like cowards. Ambrosius, Nepos, and some of the other riders mounted and rode at the Saxon infantry. With spears and long swords, they cut down many pagans. Katigern and most of his men remained on their feet as they hacked and slashed at the enemy. Blood stained the ground. The battle lines fluxed as the tide of the fight flowed back and forth. We held the Saxons at bay. Many men fell on both sides.

Ambrosius charged continually with the mounted Alans against the solid Saxon lines. He fought without hesitation. He used a long spear to wreak death upon the enemy. Ambrosius played his part perfectly in the cavalry's feigned retreat.

Still, Katigern didn't seek a mount. Instead, he charged into the thick of things. He held a short sword in his left hand as he hacked and whacked with a *franciska* in his right hand. His small throwing ax amputated arms as Katigern swung it. I stayed with Katigern and his men.

"Merlinus, grab a sword, protect yourself," Katigern called out as he cut deeper into the Saxons. "Your stick will do us little service, today."

Paying him no heed, I continued to engage the enemy. Empowered by the teachings of Dom Fu, I broke arms with my whirling oak staff. I swept the enemy's legs from underneath them. And I cracked skulls when it was the only way to knock enough sense into them to retreat. Katigern's men roared as they saw me fight.

"Impressive, Merlinus. Fight on," Katigern shouted during his bloody onslaught. The noise of the battlefield grew deafening. The metallic pings pierced my ears, which let in a flood of endless, dying moans. As one faded into oblivion, another took his place in the sickening chorus of fallen soldiers.

Evodius exited the villa. He held a V-shaped shield with his left hand and jabbed with the gladius in his right. I swatted my way to him. I kept a large area clear with the wild wielding of my staff. Evodius only had to worry about the enemy directly in front of him. Though nearly a decade past his prime, Evodius handled his sword with deadly efficiency.

I continued my nonlethal disarmament of the enemy. Swords dropped as I smashed the hands of the Saxons. With broken fingers, they couldn't hold on to the shafts of their spears, either. Some of the Saxons headed back to their boats. Ambrosius, accompanying Nepos and his men, made easy work of them. Our cavalry clipped away the flanks of the Saxons. From the center, Katigern, his men, Evodius, and I pushed toward the river to the east.

In time, a tall, powerful Saxon battled his way to Katigern. Though a well-built man, Katigern looked like a boy standing in front of this Saxon. The Saxon easily stood six and a half feet tall with thick, long black hair and a matching beard. He was much bigger than my father. The man wore a short black bear cape. Its paws hung over the man's shoulders and covered his entire back. He wielded a large two-handed sword.

Without hesitation, Katigern engaged him. The Saxon moved fast for a big man. He brought his sword down on Katigern. Luckily, Katigern caught the thick blade by locking his ax and short sword together. Katigern dropped to one knee from the impact of the Saxon's sword. The Saxon army cheered as the two fought. Skillfully rolling with the blow of the blade, Katigern brought the Saxon's sword down into the ground. Standing and spinning in a wide arc, Katigern swiped his short sword straight across the Saxon. If the Saxon had been shorter, Katigern would have lobbed off the pagan's head. Instead, the bear cape protected the man from the otherwise fatal slice.

Katigern's backside was exposed, and the Saxon easily pushed Katigern down to his hands and knees. The young lord struggled to his feet. As Katigern stood, he stumbled forward. Pulling his sword from the ground, the Saxon reared back to cut Katigern down. Seeing the sword's descent, Katigern rolled to the side. The sword sliced deep into the sod. Letting go of the sword, the Saxon lunged at Katigern as if to rip his arms from his body. The Saxon snatched Katigern's shoulders and drove him back to the ground. Pulling a spear from a dead man's body, the Saxon arched back to slam it through Katigern. As the Saxon brought down the spear, Katigern jammed his sword straight up through the Saxon's belly. The point of the short sword pierced out the Saxon's back, and a strange silence fell over the center of the melee. Two great soldiers reached their end in one fatal moment. Both sides watched their leaders die. The Saxon braced himself with the shaft of the spear as Katigern tried to twist the sword in the Saxon's stomach.

Unaware of the tragedy that had just unfolded, Ambrosius, Nepos, and his cavalry returned in a hell-bent charge, finishing another well-executed, feigned retreat. Ambrosius, Nepos, and the other horsemen sliced through the stunned Saxons. The enemy started to scatter. Confusion crippled them. Their leadership had been gutted.

"Drive the heathens into the river," Evodius screamed over the chaos. Turning from Vortimer's fallen brother, I saw Evodius leading the charge. He had sheathed his sword and armed himself with a long spear. He no longer wielded his shield, either. He speared the Saxons through their backs as if they were fish in the river. He did not stop to gloat over them. Instead, he continued his charge, resolved in his attack.

Men like Evodius were easy to respect. They gave no order that they would not follow or execute themselves. They were honest and congenial while at peace and determined deep in battle. The Empire desperately needed more men like Evodius. Ambrosius could learn several things from a man like Evodius. The old Roman was brilliant in his actions. He exploited the apparent weaknesses in the enemy.

The remaining Saxons clambered aboard their ships. Some of their archers began to provide cover fire for their retreating comrades.

"Evodius, we need to pull the men back. Nothing can be achieved except empty causalities. The victory is ours. It has already cost us dearly," I shouted as I stood near him.

Taking a quick survey of the situation, he shouted, "It is true. The victory is ours, men. Pull out of their archers' range. Let them sail away."

Nepos noticed and followed suit. With a customized call, Nepos signaled to his men and they swung back toward the villa in perfect formation. Only Ambrosius broke formation. Not attuned to the squad commands, the young man failed to notice. Still, though, he looked back and saw Nepos and his men striding up the slope to our position. Bodies littered the ground. Spears and burning arrows stuck out of the corpses. Noticing where one arrow burned at the shaft of a spear, I watched as Ambrosius suddenly yanked it free while still riding.

"No," I shouted. "That idiot is going to get himself killed."

As Ambrosius continued his move, Evodius shook his head and added, "Unfortunately, he's trying real hard."

"Archers," I screamed. "Fall into ranks. Ready and advance immediately."

As they lined up in formation, I commanded further. "Pepper the ships. Shoot long. Don't hit the horse that the jackass is riding."

Our army roared with laughter as the archers provided cover fire for Ambrosius' bravado. The Alan element within our army cheered loudly at his reckless behavior. Nepos called his riders back into action. From my position, Nepos and his men moved like a low-flying flock of birds. They swept back toward the ship like a line of barn swallows. They were twenty yards behind Ambrosius and gaining. Nepos led and Carbo followed straight behind him. As skillful as any Hun, they pulled their bows from the back sides of their saddles and flung arrows over Ambrosius and hammered the heathens sitting in the open ships.

Without breaking stride, Ambrosius raced along the rear of the ship, which was larger than the rest. The flame stood strong at the tip of the spear that Ambrosius carried. With a hunter's balance, Ambrosius heaved the lance at the mast of the ship's sail. The burning spear sank into the wooden pole. The sail caught fire. The Saxons who tried to stop it from burning soon fell victim to the next wave of arrows showering the ship from our archers on the shore. Ambrosius leaned into his mount and raced for our position. Nepos and his men closed in behind him.

"Ambrose! Ambrose!" The army cheered loudly as Ambrosius rode up to us.

"That's crazy," Nepos laughed as he slapped Ambrosius on his back.

"Yeah, that was incredible," Carbo joined in.

"Incredibly stupid," I cut in. The bright wide smile broke from Ambrosius' face as he heard my words.

"What do you mean, word wizard?" Carbo called out as he came up on the other side of Ambrosius and patted him on the back.

"That was an amazing performance, kid. Lord Goar needs to recruit you into our ranks. Besides looking like his son, Euthar, you throw a spear like Euthar. That last shot proved it."

"That showed he should never lead. Not until he grows up," I added. "That last stunt showed that he cared little for the men he rode with. Even after victory had been secured, Ambrosius drew his comrades back into harm's way with his ill-conception of bravery. What did his stunt serve besides to show his pride? Nepos, you or one of your other horsemen could have been maimed or killed."

"And it would have been a good life lived to fall victoriously on this battlefield," Carbo barked. "Word wizard, you say you are an Alan, but Ambrose acts more like us than you do."

"Why die from stupidity when you stand triumphant?" I replied.

Looking back at the river, we watched as the small ships sailed quickly into the distance. The one in the rear meandered along powered only by the current. Lacking a living crew, the ship could not speed its escape like the others.

"Well, at least Lord Evodius can claim a ship and its spoils," Ambrosius said with a smile.

"That's if it doesn't burn and sink. I'm sure he will be thinking of you when boats can't get by to pick up his harvest or deliver his goods." I remarked.

"Young Ambrosius, do not bring me into this," the old Roman remarked as he jabbed the wooden end of his spear into the ground.

"You're not claiming the ship?" Carbo called out excitedly. Evodius stared with intentness and Carbo fell silent.

"The boy is fortunate that I'm not in command here. For if I were, I would have the boy in shackles or flogged," Evodius remarked.

"What? Why?" Nepos questioned.

"That's outrageous," Carbo shouted.

Looking directly at Ambrosius, Evodius declared, "You broke formation and in doing so, disobeyed a direct order from your squad leader. That's why you would be punished."

"Ambrose didn't recognize the call Nepos gave. But, a couple more battles like this one and I'm sure he won't do it again." Carbo called out.

"That's not the truth," Evodius barked. "I watched as the boy looked back before he snatched the spear. He knew what your squad had done."

Ambrosius nudged his horse between the two arguing men.

"What Lord Evodius states is true. In essence, I did disobey an order and jeopardized you and Nepos. I will not consider my actions so lightly again, as I have done here. Please accept my apology."

Evodius nodded. Tight-lipped, Ambrosius pulled away and walked his horse slowly toward the river.

I wanted to say something, but kept silent.

The army slowly dispersed and individuals attended to their less-fortunate comrades. As I broke from the crowd, Evodius walked up to me and remarked, "You did the right thing, Merlinus. The boy will be a great leader if he has the right guidance now."

CHAPTER 29

Defeating the Saxons at Episford had secured the Darenth Valley. Lord Vortimer had taken the Council's army and marched down the Roman road, driving the Saxons into the Gallic Sea. The Saxons sought refuge on Thanet, the island near the mouth of the Thames River. After hearing of the death of Katigern, Vortimer returned to London and it was there that we honored the fallen hero.

At night, we walked out of London's gate carrying Katigern. A tune sang out from the musicians preceding us. It filled the cool night with sadness. Mourners followed close as we headed for the pyre.

Earlier, Ambrosius asked to dig the *bustum*. Vortimer consented to Ambrosius preparing the pit for the funeral pyre. Nepos, Carbo, and I helped him while Germanus washed and anointed Katigern's body.

During our final walk with Katigern, torch bearers and braziers lit our way. Smoke curled up and disappeared into the night. People stood on both sides of our path and respectfully watched the funeral procession. Ambrosius, Carbo, Nepos, and I were just a few of the many pallbearers. All of us wore formal clothing. Ambrosius borrowed his formal wear from Nepos, and a tailor loaned me an ankle-long black tunic. Though enough men carried the funerary bed to make the weight minute, the journey seemed to last an eternity. The path we walked seemed strange, unfamiliar, and foreign, though I had been up it earlier that day.

Finally, we reached the cemetery gates. The bustum we had dug was near the entrance, past the thin stone archway. In a slow, methodical manner we placed Katigern on the pyre as Vortimer and his close friends and family stood nearby. The large group of pallbearers slowly stepped away and stood behind Vortimer. Afterwards, Vortimer stepped forward and stood at the head of the pyre. A deep sadness lingered in his eyes, but there were no tears. The music had faded out. The only sounds were the flapping flags in the steady breeze and the crackling fire from the many braziers. Everyone observed a long moment of silence as Vortimer bowed his head to his fallen brother. Lord Katigern lay cloaked in a black toga with gold trim.

Without a word, Vortimer nodded at Bishop Germanus. Seeing his cue, the bishop slowly walked over by Vortimer. He stepped back and allowed Germanus to stand alone. The bishop glanced back at Vortimer and nodded. Looking back, Germanus raised his arms and the sleeves of his robe slid down.

"Dear God," the bishop called out. "Hear our prayers, oh Lord in heaven who is the creator of all things large and small, from this fallen hero to the distant stars above us. Please keep our departed friend close to your side. Lord Katigern has shown true honor. He has passed from this life in the struggle to turn back the filthy heathens that gnaw at this island. Keep him close until we can see him again.

"So may this man serve as a grand example to us all. Don't let his death be in vain. Rise up as this great hero's soul does," Germanus shouted, then bowed toward Katigern.

Men lowered handheld torches and lit the elevated bier ablaze. Flames roared heavenward. Though the bishop did not want to cremate Katigern, Germanus capitalized on the ceremony. He cast his final spell over the people of Britain. Soon, Germanus would sail back to Gaul.

"That was inspiring, Bishop Germanus," Lord Vortimer stated. "In your honor, I shall restore the churches devastated in the revolt."

"Good," Germanus replied. "You've achieved true peace."

The bishop still pushed Celestine's agenda. His claim was unrealistic. Numerically, we overran the Saxons both times in the valley.

"Merlinus, the Saxons will attack again," Ambrosius voiced as we walked out of the cemetery. "Vortimer needs all of the help he can get."

"Good, you see why you must go back to Gaul." I replied.

"I won't cut and run," he said. "I'll fight for Lord Vortimer."

"So be it. To best serve him, though, you must leave," I replied.

"I don't understand. My emotions make it hard to see clearly."

"Go back to Aureliani and gather more men. Bring them back to help. This is how you will best serve Lord Vortimer. Nepos can suggest men that can be recruited. Maybe you can recruit him," I replied.

A look of surprise sprung on the young man's face. He had not thought of anything like what I had just suggested. Maybe he hoped for an army, but he didn't really think it was plausible. Ambrosius quickly warmed up to the idea. Still, he wore a questioning look.

"Why me, though?" he asked. "Wouldn't it be better if you went since it would be your possessions being sold?"

"No," I laughed. "This way I'm spared the pain of parting with the sold items. Do not provide complete payment to these men under any circumstances. And no payment if possible. They're like dealing with bears and your purse is the hive of honey. Try to hire from the young nobility, they have less wealth and more to prove. This is why you must go. I have been away so long that the ones I would think of are the fathers' of the ones we really need."

"I understand," Ambrosius replied. "Promise them the world."

"Only if they truly believe that you could possibly give it to them," I replied. "Never state something that you couldn't deliver. Some of these men are very shrewd. These are men of actions and don't like being played a fool through half-truths, white lies, and double dealings.

"Maybe you can get away with it for a while, but it always catches up with you. If you do it too many times, you find yourself deserted and thought little of by those you deal with, no matter what you do."

"So I say nothing but the truth?" the young man laughed.

"In your case, yes," I replied in a solemn tone.

"Not even little lies?" he asked. "Isn't diplomacy a form of lying."

"Only with dishonorable men. And no, not even little lies for you."

"Why not me? Is it all right for you to lie?" he asked.

"Some people have a talent for lying, but you are not one of them. You use lies like blunt objects, so leave them to others," I remarked.

"Word wizards," he added, "like you and Bishop Germanus."

"We are in two different classes," I replied. "He dazzles imperial dignitaries and I befuddle tavern folk."

"Equals in my book," he remarked with a smile.

"And I thought you liked me more than that," I joked.

Ambrosius laughed.

In a light tone, the young man remarked, "I will leave with the bishops in the morning. Are you sure you don't want to go?"

"It will be better if I stayed. I will be able to help the nobles. We will save on the cost of crossing twice and most important, you will know that you are expected to come back."

"Right," Ambrosius answered with a smile.

CHAPTER 30

I traveled with Vortimer to survey the damage done by the Saxon insurrection. Vortimer said that we would be back in London before Ambrosius returned from Gaul. I saw no point in not going with him.

The charred gateway of Colchester stood open while the craftsmen repaired it. Though it had been hit hard by seaborne Saxons and raids from the northwest, the streets now overflowed with people. Few people were without smiles in the marketplace at this port city. It had been about a week since the battle of Episford, and a few days since Ambrosius had left with the bishops.

Word arrived that Grallon wanted to meet with Vortimer to parley peace between the Saxons and the Council. It was unclear when Grallon would arrive. In the meanwhile, I wandered through the palace.

I hoped that I had not asked too much from Ambrosius. I had forgotten that Ambrosius was only fifteen years old. Still, I held faith in him. He wanted to do right and had the means and strength to persevere.

"Lord Merlin," called out a little servant boy as he walked quickly toward me. "Vortigern wants you to go to the great hall. He has matters that he needs to discuss with you. I will take you, if you will allow me. Is that okay?"

"Of course, young lad," I replied.

Without a word, the little boy quickly took me to the audience chamber. It was much smaller than the one in London. Still, mine in Aureliani wasn't nearly as large as this one. Upon entering, though, surprise filled me. Grallon stood alone in the empty hall. I turned to the servant boy but he was gone. Grallon still hadn't noticed my presence. His head hung low with his arms behind his back as if shackled. He paced back and forth. I was unsure if I should announce myself.

As I silently debated this, Grallon's head jerked up and faced my direction. His eyes focused and stared at me from a distance. His mouth dropped open as he recognized me.

"Merlinus," he groaned. "What are you doing here?"

As I walked toward him, I remarked, "I was going to ask you the same thing. This isn't Thanet. Are you lost?"

An angry look cut into his face. My comment had angered him. Good.

"Why didn't you leave with the bishops? Haven't you and the other interlopers caused enough trouble already?" Grallon questioned.

"He isn't part of the problem," Vortimer called out as he entered through a side entrance. "You and your associates are the problem. And with him and the bishops' help, we removed the problem from our island."

Grallon fell silent as he turned and faced his approaching son. The old man's posture became rigid. Vortimer's face soured as he stopped in front of his father. There was no love between these two men. If I didn't already know it, their actions wouldn't have told me that they were father and son.

"Did you want me to return later?" I asked Vortimer.

Breaking his stare, Vortimer's eyes shifted to me. For the first time, I noticed how blue his eyes were. There was no guessing if they might be bluish green or possibly bluish gray. They were a sky blue, appearing almost unnatural. In all of my travels, I have noted only a handful of folks with such eyes. He stared straight through me and most of the people he spoke with. His father's lies had worn thin long ago.

"No, Merlinus. You are here because of him," Vortimer replied, then laughed and added, "Hasn't that always been the case?"

Seeing his point about that, I smiled but then asked, "Why am I needed here, though? You both speak the same language. My only real talent is talking."

"And that's why you are here," Vortimer remarked. "If I get too frustrated or angry to speak, then you will do my talking for me."

"This is absurd," Grallon barked. "I don't have time for this. I am here to parley peace between our parties."

As a disgusted look consumed his face, Vortimer barked back, "And what parties do you speak of?"

"You know damn well who I'm speaking of, boy," Grallon snapped back. "The people of Thanet."

"Who? The women and children abandoned by Hengist and his men?" Vortimer fired back.

A surprised look appeared on Grallon's face.

"Their husbands and fathers couldn't care less for the whores and bastards, so why should I give a damn about these people?"

"Abandoned women and children?" Grallon replied blankly.

"Yeah, Hengist and his men sailed off into the night," Vortimer remarked.

"Why didn't you stop him?" Grallon asked.

"Unlike you, Father," Vortimer remarked. "I wanted him to leave."

Grallon didn't know what to say. It was obvious that he didn't know that Hengist and his men had fled in their longships.

"So what is left to parley, Father?" Vortimer questioned. "There will be no problems if they don't return."

In a droning tone, Grallon replied, "What of the women and children? How will they be reunited with their other loved ones?"

"Maybe the cowards should have considered their fates beforehand?" Vortimer answered.

"How can you be so cold and heartless?" Grallon questioned.

"If you care so much for their well-being, then, I will allow you to personally load them in a ship that you furnish and sail them anywhere your damn heart desires, just as long as you and that ship don't dock in a port of Britain."

"Where should I go?" Grallon asked.

"To the bottom of the sea as far as I am concerned," Vortimer answered.

"So this is how it shall remain?" Grallon asked.

"Yes," Vortimer answered. "I suggest that you sell your estates that you have on this island and move back to Gaul. No one honors your presence except the ones you pay or the ones that recently became family. Either way, they are not welcome in Britain."

"Why is that?" Grallon snapped.

"Because they would be Saxons," I answered.

With his mouth ajar, Grallon looked me blankly.

"Thank you," Vortimer replied. "I'm glad someone is thinking besides me."

"Can't this all just be worked out?" called out a lady's voice.

I turned toward the main entrance of the hall. I saw the approaching woman and knew it was Rowan, the Saxon wife of Grallon and the daughter of Hengist. She was prettier than the petals on any mountain ash.

She was all that everyone said she was and more. She appeared on fire as she strutted toward us. She wore a long, sheer red-and-black tunic. Her gown struggled to hold in her voluptuous curves. Silk, cobweb-like red scarves streamed down her arms and out from her wrists as she walked. Long, dark, fiery-red hair flowed behind her. A single spiraling tress hung from each of her temples. As she came toward us, each tress bounced slightly with her large breasts. They were the size of ripe cantaloupes and much more enticing, even more so as I noticed her tweaked nipples. She was more beautiful than Ahès when she was young. Rowan didn't even give me a single glance. Rowan directed all of her charms at Vortimer. With a coy smile, she drew within arm's length.

I had seen women like Rowan wherever I went. These women could move mountains or annihilate nations with the swish of their hair. They wielded sexual power like a sword and that's what the Church feared the most. Ahès never carried herself this way.

"We can work this out, somehow," she said sweetly.

As she neared, an intoxicating perfume poured from her.

"Merlinus speaks for me," Vortimer announced.

She did not see that coming nor did I. She quickly glanced at me but immediately shifted back to Vortimer.

"What do you mean? My lord, you can't be serious. Who is this unkempt man? He has the garb of a beggar," she remarked, as if appalled by my presence.

"He's Merlinus," Grallon groaned.

"There is nothing left to discuss," I replied blandly.

"What?" she remarked in a sharp tone.

"There's nothing left to discuss. The issues have been resolved," I remarked as she now stared at me. Vortimer turned and began to walk away. I followed his lead and turned from the beautiful woman.

"What about my father?" she shouted.

"He's not welcome here," I called out.

"That's not right," she barked as she moved toward us.

Stopping, I turned and replied, "What's not right is your father claiming what doesn't belong to him. He had no problem killing to get what he wanted."

"Kent was given to him by my loving Grallon," she remarked.

"It was wrongly given to him by a man that's no longer Vortigern."

"My husband was High Commander at the time," she barked.

"Yes, he was, and it is because of this unlawful act that he is no longer High Commander of the Council," I added.

"This is unacceptable," she declared.

"Then go back to the heathen lands that spawned you," I replied.

"Grallon, are you just going to let him say that?" Rowan barked.

"And what would you suggest that I do?" Grallon snapped back.

"Stand up for your wife and take control of this situation," she demanded as Vortimer and I neared the exit leading out of the room.

I followed Vortimer out. He stopped and turned when we exited.

"Thank you for handling that. I never can speak to her. I tell myself that I shall not bend to her will. But, I am a pushover for her charms," Vortimer declared.

"Any normal man cannot defend against such charms," I replied.

"Hah," Vortimer laughed. "Does that make you not normal since you defied her?"

"No, that's not it," I added. "You caused her charms to fail by forcing her to talk with me. She had anticipated that you were the only one needing to be wooed and she paid little heed to me. So by the time she realized that she had to deal with me, she wasn't in the right state of mind to charm me. There's no denying that she is a beautiful young woman, but she is just as wicked." I said.

"Wicked as a snake," he replied. As he began to walk once more, Vortimer added, "She has latched on to my father. Her venom has seeped into his soul. There is no logic in lust or love."

"Well said," I replied.

"Once more, I thank you for your assistance," Vortimer remarked as he headed for the outside of the villa.

"It wasn't much, sire," I answered.

Stopping under the portico that faced the empty forum, he replied, "That's what I admire about you, Merlinus. You never seem to be pushing some hidden agenda. Most people do."

Looking down and then glancing back at him, I remarked, "Nothing hidden. My intentions are the old tattered clothes I wear. I seek no riches, but I cannot live without them to a certain extent. Still, I cannot remain silenced to the greed that many have for fortune and power. For it is a small group of people that brings about the poverty of many."

"So if this is the case, what is your open agenda, then?" Vortimer asked.

"I've been in this world for twenty-nine years as best as I can figure. Only one thing has remained consistent over the years and that is my continuous search for knowledge and enlightenment."

"Nearly fifteen years ago when Ambrosius was taken from his true parents and given to you, I thought the boy was going to end up dead. But then, you showed up under my portico with him and I didn't know what to think. Who is he really? I've heard so many stories that I don't know what to believe." Vortimer remarked.

"What does that matter, now?" I asked candidly.

He stared at me for a moment, surprised by my response. He then added, "Just for small talk, I guess."

Laughing lightly, I questioned, "Is there small talk with a lord of London?"

Laughing loudly, Vortimer repeated, "Lord of London, that's a good one. But wouldn't that be old man Jonah's title?"

"Yeah, right," I replied.

He fell silent and walked toward the empty forum. I followed. The evening was nearing its end.

"He's the son of Adaulphus, the dead Gothic king, and Placidia, daughter of Emperor Theodosius and mother of Valentinian the third," I remarked.

Vortimer observed, "That was the prevailing rumor at the time. It just seemed too improbable to be true. To be honest, I believe that whole ordeal has been the undoing of my father. He permanently slipped from honor once he did that."

"Power affects people differently," I remarked. "It didn't show the finer side of your father. My father faltered the same way."

"Honestly, I don't remember your father," Vortimer remarked as his eyes shifted skyward. Already, the stars shined brightly. The night was peaceful and quiet. Only a few people walked the streets.

Breaking the momentary silence, I remarked, "You know he shall return."

"Your father?" he questioned.

Laughing, I replied, "No, I'm sorry. I meant Hengist. Hengist shall return."

"I figured as much," Vortimer replied as his eyes drifted to the stars once more. "Him leaving the women and children on Thanet convinced me of his intentions."

"Exactly," I replied.

"What do you think will happen next?" he asked.

"Hengist is gathering more men and when he figures that he has enough, he will return," I declared.

"If he obtains superior numbers, can he be defeated?" Vortimer said with concern in his eyes.

"Yes," I confidently replied. "You have the will of the people."

"But is that enough against a savage heathen army?" he asked.

"Almost anything can be used as a lethal weapon. You must have the heart or justification to use it," I replied.

"Or simply no heart at all," he added.

"To an extent," I agreed but then rebutted, "If someone passionately fights for what is rightfully his against a heartless interloper, I'm betting on the defender nearly every time."

Smiling, he nodded his head in agreement.

In an instant, his expression shifted to a grave stare. His hand dropped to the hilt of his sword. He wasn't staring at me; he stared past me. I turned and saw someone running toward us carrying a torch. Vortimer stepped up between me and the approaching person, but his hand suddenly left the hilt of his sword, and the tension in his stance faded.

Within the next moment, I recognized the person. He was one of Vortimer's loyal servants. He was a young, well-mannered teen. His hair appeared as a bowl on his head. It sat slightly tilted with the ridge of his hair high on his brow while the other edge of his hair rested on the base of his neck. His thin hair was walnut brown, dark and deep. The limp strands naturally maintained the bowl shape. He wore an ankle-long, off-white tunic. A brown tassel belt brought his tunic in around his waist. He was nearly five feet tall.

"Sorry, my lord," the young man remarked as he handed Vortimer a folded piece of paper. "This just arrived for you."

"Thank you, Aeacus," Vortimer replied.

Vortimer unfolded it and read it silently as he leaned toward his servant. His eyes shifted back and forth rapidly. He looked up with a grave look.

"It's Evodius," Vortimer remarked. "The Saxons have returned, or at least a small band of them has. This letter was dispatched as Evodius was being attacked. I must go to him. I must relieve him."

"No," I replied.

"What? Why not?" he asked.

"I will relieve him," I answered. "Give me a squadron. Tonight, I will take them and we will ride down to Episford. You must follow and take position in London just in case they march or sail to the city. Only you can rally and tap into the emotions of your country men. Jonah can't do that. You must do this to repel the Saxon storm sweeping in from the Gallic Sea. You must convince them to stand united and fight Hengist and his heathen horde. I must leave now. Every moment matters."

"The squadron is yours. May God protect you and help you on your way," he replied.

CHAPTER 31

As I stood in front of the charred, smokeless remains of Evodius' villa, I knew we had been duped. There were burnt bodies, but it was impossible to identify the victims. We made sure there wasn't anyone still in the gutted villa. All of the virid plants throughout the estate no longer remained. The angry fire consumed them along with the silk and cloth curtains and room dividers.

Widening our search, we went through the mausoleum that stood on the terrace behind the main house. No one was hiding. Instead, a dead silence hung over the entire estate. The splendid home had been torched several nights ago, even as far back as the day Vortimer and I had left London for Colchester. Someone held up Evodius' written plea. I suddenly feared for Vortimer's safety.

Shouting to the men that rode with me, I commanded, "We must leave. There is nothing that we can do here. I fear that we have been sent here after the fires consumed the villa and died."

"Why?" Maximus asked. He was the young leader of the squad that Vortimer sent with me to Episford. Maximus was in his twenties, making him at least five years older than Ambrosius, but nowhere near as mature. His hair was brown and stood in short spikes on the top of his head. The hair was nearly shaved off the sides, matching the backside of his head. Most of the men in the squad had matching hair and Roman-style metal-band armor. All of them, including Maximus, wore a dark pine-green tunic with black trousers.

"To divide our forces," I answered as I mounted up.

"Then Vortimer is in danger," answered another trooper.

"We must ride fast before it's too late." I added.

We rode hard for London. An uneasy feeling sat in my belly. I knew we were already too late. As we raced northwest on the Roman road, my suspicion was confirmed when I noticed a large squadron of horsemen heading straight for us. When our two groups approached, their group fanned out to encircle us. We were outnumbered.

"Take evasive actions," Maximus called out.

"No," I commanded.

I pulled the reins up and halted my horse.

"We can't beat these numbers," I observed. "Not here."

"He's right." Maximus remarked.

There were at least five men to our every one. Our squadron of six would have been slaughtered. With a wide circle of men around us, I stared straight into the face of evil.

"Greetings, Ceretic," I remarked. "We would like to pass in peace."

"That's not possible," Ceretic called out. "By sworn order of Vortigern, I hereby charge you, Merlinus of Aureliani, with murder. I am further empowered to arrest you."

"That's absurd," Maximus declared, overtaken by his emotions. "Vortimer would never have you sent to arrest Merlinus for murder."

"We're arresting Merlinus for Vortimer's murder," Ceretic declared.

"That's ludicrous," Maximus interjected. "Vortimer was alive when we left Colchester."

"And dying by all accounts I've heard," Ceretic added, "Merlinus, you poisoned Vortimer while in Colchester the other night. Afterwards, you fled."

"To where? Evodius' villa has been torched. Probably by some of your allies," I barked.

"Maybe it was a careless cook," Ceretic sneered.

"Besides, what do I gain by poisoning Vortimer?" I demanded.

"I'll think of something," Ceretic remarked. "Arrest him."

Four men moved toward me. Maximus and his men went to draw their swords.

"Don't let your men be so foolish, Merlinus," Ceretic called out. "Father wants you brought in alive, but I would rather drag you in dead."

"Hold," I shouted at Maximus and the other four men. "Do not waste your lives on my account. It is me they really want."

Ceretic smiled and nodded his head.

Without incident, we rode back to London.

CHAPTER 32

I paced back and forth in the thatched pen that Ceretic had placed me in after he brought me to London. Though I pondered breaking through one of the walls of the hut, I didn't. I knew that's why Ceretic stuck me in here. He wanted me to try to escape. It would give him an excuse to execute me. There was no way that I was going to make it that easy for Ceretic.

"Lord Merlin," whispered someone just outside the pen. Kneeling near the south side, the boy appeared to be picking something up from the ground.

"Lord Merlin," the teen whispered as he now fussed with his foot.

Staying in the shadow, I replied, "Yes?"

As he glanced at me, I noticed that he was the one that had delivered the letter from Evodius.

"Lord Merlin, I am sorry that I gave you that false message. I thought I was doing a service. I have unknowingly led to the demise of my lord and your imprisonment. Please find a place in your heart to forgive me," he finished.

I laughed.

"Please sir, I beg you for your forgiveness," he implored.

"I would never condemn you for what you've done," I decreed. "You have done nothing wrong as far as I can see. The message was true. Evodius did need our help. We were just late getting it. Tell me this, though. What happen after I left Colchester?"

"Rowan knew she couldn't corrupt Vortimer. So she corrupted his cup bearer. As Vortimer drank a noxious drink, the poison paralyzed him. Having no hope to survive, Lord Vortimer called out for his loyal men. Among those that gathered, I distributed Vortimer's remaining wealth to them as he instructed," the servant declared.

"So was he, at least, honorably buried?" I asked.

"No," he remarked. "Vortimer instructed them to make his tomb on the Isle of Thanet. He wanted his grave marker to ward off any Saxons that dared to cross the sea.

"Instead of doing as he wished, his father had him buried near Colchester."

"What else is there?" I asked. "Jonah isn't still the Vicar of London, is he? Does he still have his small army?"

"Yes, but Grallon says he's the High Commander once more," the servant added. "Jonah only allowed Grallon access to his private villa in the city. Grallon can have no more than ten people with him at a time and Hengist cannot enter at any time. Ceretic was not happy when Jonah stated that you were in his custody since Ceretic had brought you here, to London.

"There was something else, something spectacular. My dying lord spoke of young Ambrosius. He said we should follow Ambrosius. He said you knew why," the young servant remarked.

"Hey you, what are you doing?" shouted a voice. The servant's presence by my pen had attracted the attention of the approaching guard. The man picked up his pace.

The servant adjusted his breeches and stood up. Casually turning toward the guard, he asked, "Is there something wrong?"

"What are you doing? Why are you in front of this pen?" the guard sternly declared.

" My leggings were bothering me so I knelt down to adjust them," the servant declared.

"Well, now, you are done so move on," the other guard replied as they drew closer.

"Yes, of course," the young servant answered and then immediately walked away.

"Stay away from the door," one of the guards ordered me.

As I stepped away from the door, the guard cut the leather straps that held it securing shut.

"All right," the guard commanded. "Come out of there."

Flanking the door, they prodded me forward as I exited the pen.

As I entered the small villa in London, I found Grallon and his wife, Rowan, waiting.

"Are you ready to beg for your life?" Rowan harped.

Laughing, I remarked, "I would never beg for anything from you."

"You dare to make jokes while you stand before me, accused of murdering my first-born son?" Grallon scorned.

"I've been called many things, but they were not all true," I answered.

"So you're saying that you're not a murderer?" Paschent barked loudly as he entered the villa. Rowan smiled at him as the Briton strutted toward her.

"Though I have murdered, it was never your brother. There is no way I would willfully lead Vortimer to his demise. Maybe the murderer does stand amongst us, though. Rest assured that it is not me," I declared.

"You dare accuse one of us?" Rowan crowed.

Making a plain, sweeping motion toward the various servants in the large room, I replied, "Didn't you see these other folks? Possibly being ignorant of the fact, misled, threatened, or even corrupted, one of these servants could have easily poisoned Vortimer."

"Or, this is a futile attempt to transfer your guilt," Paschent countered.

Staring at him for a moment, I shifted my stare to Grallon and remarked, "Grallon, you know that I would never kill Vortimer. You've known me a long time. I haven't changed. My principles have remained the same. I fought side by side with your other son as he fought against your wife's uncle's army. On that day, I witnessed his triumphant struggle against Horsa and Katigern's unfortunate death. Though mortally wounded, Katigern slew the heathen."

As I finished, I shifted my stare to Rowan. Her eyes burned with hatred.

"Hopefully, Hengist can meet the same bloody demise," I added, "when Ambrosius returns with his army."

Rowan lunged at me with her talons extending for my throat. Evil glared from her eyes. She wanted me dead. Grallon and Paschent struggled to restrain her.

"I shall take great pleasure in watching you die," she hissed.

"Did you say the same thing to someone else we all know?" I asked.

"I'm more interested in knowing about this Ambrosius you speak of and his supposed army," someone called out from behind me.

I spun around to find Ceretic an arm's length from me. He gave me a cold, empty feeling of fear. Without blinking, I remained tight-lipped.

"Yes, tell us about the boy's army," Grallon demanded as he still held back Rowan.

Stepping to the side, I pulled myself out of the center of the hostile crowd and remained silent.

"Speak," Rowan hissed.

I said nothing. I refused to speak on her command. Her face grew as red as her hair. She went to say something, but Ceretic interrupted.

"How could a teenager take command of an army without a massive fortune?" the young man questioned. "Are you that rich, Merlinus?"

"Some people are driven by other things besides wealth and power," I replied.

"What else is there?" Paschent asked.

"Honor and principles, not to mention the boy's birthright," I answered.

"Birthright?" Rowan questioned. "What falsehoods do you spread? Servants already whisper similar lies. They say that the blood of kings and emperors flows through Ambrosius' veins. How can you say such lies and have others believe you? They believe you so much that they help you spread these evil rumors. How is this possible?" she questioned. "What power do you hold over them?"

"None. At times, truth is stranger than any tall tale that could be ever told," I replied.

"That's not an answer," she crowed.

"If you are looking for a reason, you need to talk to Grallon," I answered. "It is his fault that Ambrosius holds such conviction for bringing an army to Britain. It was Grallon's men that burned down Ambrosius' home in Cornovia. It was his men that slew the only father Ambrosius knew. Once more, Grallon, you've sowed the seeds of your own destruction."

"Ambrosius' father, Constantine, was no emperor or even a king, for that matter," Paschent remarked.

"Constantine was not his true father. Besides, it wasn't his father that had the imperial blood. It is through his mother that he has the blood of Theodosius in him," I answered.

"How is this possible?" Rowan asked.

"Ask Grallon if I lie," I remarked.

"So you are saying that Ambrosius is the son of Placidia, the current imperial regent and mother of Valentinian? Please! What is your next lie?" Paschent questioned and then added, "She only had two children with Constantius."

"Constantius isn't the boy's father," I stated.

"Then, who is?" Rowan asked. The anger had left her and a look of intrigue hung from her lips.

"Adaulphus," Ceretic answered.

"Who?" Paschent asked.

"Adaulphus, a former king of the Goths," Ceretic clarified. "Before becoming king, Adaulphus served as a general under Lord Alaric. Together, they sacked Rome. The first time this had happened in several hundreds of years. When the Goths took the imperial city, Alaric and Adaulphus took Placidia as a hostage. In time, though, Adaulphus married the imperial princess. Placidia bore Adaulphus a boy who they named Theodosius in honor of her dead father, the great emperor. But it was said that the boy died and was buried in a small silver coffin in Barcelona."

"So you see, Ambrosius cannot be the son of Placidia, then," Rowan chimed in.

"If this is the case, then, why does Grallon remain silent? He knows that I speak the truth," I answered.

As if forgetting about Grallon until that moment, the others glanced at the silent man. Grallon looked old, extremely old. Life was running Vortigern thin. Lines of time plowed deep into his face. He held many secrets and the life of Ambrosius was just one of them.

"So, as the wind casts ill omens upon you once again, Ambrosius heads for Britain as we speak. Know this: the White Boar of Cornovia comes for you all. He is the devourer of evil, the restorer of right. Retreat from London and he shall march upon you and topple your towers," I declared.

"My father shall return with thousands of men to fight you and your boy-leader," Rowan mocked.

"And after Ambrosius slays that heathen, Hengist, Britain shall crown the young lord, master of this island. And though he may be poisoned and disappear from the annals of time, his blood will sustain the fight of right over wrong."

"Get him out of my sight. Tell Jonah that I'm done questioning him," Grallon commanded.

"Kill him, my love, and be done with him," Rowan cooed.

The guards that escorted me from the thatched pen unsheathed their swords.

"No," Grallon ordered. "He is worth more alive than dead, for now."

CHAPTER 33

I wasn't doing well. It wasn't like the time in prison in the Orient when I met Dom Fu. I was the strong one and Dom Fu needed help, or at least my food.

A nagging cough lingered in my chest. The rain dripping into the pen didn't help. I could not avoid it completely. Thick gray clouds blotted out the sun for the second afternoon in a row. I hadn't seen Grallon or his thugs for the same length of time.

Would anyone bring me some food soon? When they had before, I didn't eat much of it, fearing it was poisoned. Right now, I craved anything to cure my hunger, even just a morsel.

Curled up on a wooden bench that kept me off the muddy ground, I slipped into a restless, dreamless sleep.

"Lord Merlin," whispered a voice in the darkness. I blinked and opened my eyes. I struggled to see. It was night. I had slept longer than I thought. Someone was crouched down by the bench outside of the pen. It sounded like Vortimer's servant.

"Lord Merlin, I am going to get you out of there. Grallon and his sons have left London. Jonah has held the city."

He cut the leather strap and swung open the door.

"Are you all right, sir?" the servant asked.

Smiling as the cold rain streamed down my face, I remarked, "I am now. Let's go."

"Yes, sir," the servant replied. "Follow me. I know a safe place for the night."

"Okay," I replied. I was leery about staying in London, but I needed to get out of this cold rain.

As we approached a thatched hut, I could see no safer place while remaining in the walled city of London. We were midway between the northern watchtowers. Smoke twisted upward. The anticipated heat couldn't mirror the actual heat that rolled over me as we entered the hut.

I drew closer to the fire and let it radiate through me. I reached out as if to wrap my arms around the heat and draw it in.

"Do you care for anything to drink or eat?" the servant asked.

"I would not turn away either one and would prefer to have both," I answered. I remained facing the fire. Rain water dripped from my saturated robe.

"That will not be a problem," the young man said. I watched him gather a wooden bowl, a cup, and a spoon.

"What's your name?" I asked as the teen set the items on the table. "I remember you from Colchester and when I was first imprisoned. You spoke to me when I was in the pen. My mind is in a fog at the moment."

He glanced at me as if checking my sincerity. He fell back into his routine of serving a meal. Remaining silent, he poured the wine and placed the clay pitcher on the table.

"My name is Aeacus," he answered as he pulled the chair from the table for me. "I served Lord Vortimer for my entire life up to this unfortunate point. My family have been servants for Vortimer and his mother's family for over a century. With Vortimer's death, I have witnessed the end of a generation with no one to take his place.

"When my lord was dying, he said that you had met my grandfather, Allectus, when you first brought Ambrosius to the island nearly fifteen years ago. Lord Vortimer said you were honorable then as you are now. He said that you could be trusted to do the right thing. The circumstances would have to be extreme for you to behave any other way. Though the situation has become extraordinary, I hope you won't stray from your honorable course."

"Aeacus, at this present moment, your cause will be better served by Ambrosius and his army," I remarked as I felt a lingering chill.

"Yes, an army would be nice," Aeacus remarked as he stood still. "But neither he nor any army has landed on the island yet. None except those of the Saxons."

"Ambrosius hasn't returned?" I asked.

"Unfortunately, he hasn't," Aeacus replied. "Luckily, Jonah has refused to relinquish command of his post. Grallon had no choice but to leave London. He didn't have enough men inside the walls to enforce his point. He left two days ago. When he and his cohorts left, all of the gates were barred. Any officers that remained loyal to Grallon have been detained or sent outside the walls of London." Aeacus replied.

"You said more Saxons have arrived?"

"Yes, several thousand strong," the young man answered. "After Grallon took the crown from his dead son's hands, the corrupt old man sent word for Hengist to return. The Saxon arrived with nearly fifteen ships, or so it has been said. It's an army equipped to conquer the southern half of the island. Tragedy has befallen us.

"On May first, a meeting convened between the Saxons and the British gentry. This took place near Stonehedge. During the parley, Hengist planned an ambush.

"In the moment Hengist shouted 'Saxons, draw your daggers,' many nobles were slaughtered. I'm unsure if we can recover. Our wretched people flee in all directions, burdening Heaven with countless pleas for mercy.

"May our people find justice when Ambrosius returns," Aeacus added. "I hope the people will gather behind him and drive the Saxons back into the sea."

Oddly, I thought of Grallon and his part in this deadly treachery. *Had he finally outlived his usefulness? Could it be that he was simply killed in the chaos? Was he even there?*

"What happen to Grallon? Is he finally dead?" I asked.

"No," the young servant remarked. "He lives. Or he did the last that I knew. When the Council was massacred, Hengist subdued Grallon and kept him from getting harmed. Afterwards, Hengist forced Grallon to give the Saxons everything south of the Thames and east of London. Kent has been given to the heathens. Grallon fled to his stronghold in Snowdonia in disgrace."

"Unbelievable," I said shaking my head. I turned back toward the fire. Though warmed thoroughly, I still felt a deep chill within my heart.

"Dear sir, come from the fire and eat. You will need your strength," the young servant urged.

CHAPTER 34

"He's here. He's here," Aeacus called out the next morning as he swung open the door to the hut and woke me from a dead sleep. I was completely awake.

I found myself where I had lain down last night. I had slept on the floor by the fireplace. I was able to get the chill out of my bones. The embers from the fire fluxed red but grew increasingly gray as the door closed and choked out the breeze feeding them.

"Hengist is here?" I questioned.

"No," he answered. "It's Ambrosius. He has returned with a massive army. They are outside the city's walls. Their ships are drifting in to dock as we speak."

"Really?" I replied.

"Yes," Aeacus added with a bright smile.

"Good," I replied. "I'll meet you outside."

"Okay," Aeacus replied as he turned around and left the hut.

Pulling aside the thick, down-filled quilt, I stood up. Naked as I was, the cool morning air rushed over me. My robe hung in front of the hearth. I found it dry to the touch. After dressing, I picked up the quilt that made up my bedding from the floor, and placed it on the bed that Aeacus slept in last night.

As I exited the hut, the presence of thousands filled my eyes. There was only a thin open walkway between the hut and the lake of gathered people. At first, no one noticed me. The throngs of people faced southward and were too busy talking to take note of me. As I stepped forward, Aeacus spotted me.

"Isn't this incredible?" he called out loudly.

"It's unbelievable," I replied as I tried to take in the spectacle. Words of hope buzzed in the morning air, spreading courage to all. Smiles brightened their faces, glowing with sunshine. It was hard not to sense the joy within the British people.

"The Saxons will not stand against such an army," a man commented as he stood at the back of the crowd along with Aeacus and me.

"The battle has not been fought yet," I whispered, not wanting to fill the crowd with my doubt. Still, the uncertainty of the situation wouldn't allow me to remain silent.

"Why do you say that, Merlinus? Isn't this what you were hoping for? Do you believe the Saxons can conquer Britain, when it is protected by an army such as Ambrosius'?" young Aeacus asked.

"No, not just the Saxons," I answered. "But if they bring Grallon back, they may have a chance."

"Would people follow him, again?" the boy asked.

"Yes," I replied. "That's why Grallon must be dealt with first, before engaging the Saxons. By removing Grallon, we take away the heathen's supposed claim to Kent. Besides, there will be no one of any authority that will argue to keep the heathens on the island. We must consolidate our strength before we face the Saxons."

"I agree," replied a stranger in the crowd.

"Right," agreed another.

Their conviction carried through the crowd. Its loudness swelled and washed across the city, as their calls for justice passed from person to person. Their emotions could not be contained. Everyone from miles around with any British sympathies flocked to see Ambrosius' grand return. Filtering through them, Aeacus took me to greet Ambrosius at the docks.

Several ships carrying hundreds of soldiers sat tied off. Suddenly, I wondered if I had an estate to return to. *How much of it did he have to sell to get an army of this size? What terms did Ambrosius swear to? Who was commanding this army?*

An uneasy feeling sat in my stomach.

As the troops and crew filed off the docks and onto the shore, I spotted Ambrosius within the army. He looked different. He looked mature. A thin, patchy beard covered his face. Although they appeared clean, his clothes were ragged. He spoke with a young nobleman, dressed in furs. The young stranger wore a red Roman cape. They joked as if they were brothers. Oddly, they almost appeared to be brothers, maybe a year separated them in age. They had similar height and build. The other was in better shape. But as the young nobleman glanced forward,

I suddenly wondered if he was Ambrosius. *Were my eyes deceiving me? How could this be possible?* The only real difference between them was their clothing and facial hair. The stranger was richly dressed with a fuller beard and longer brown hair.

"Does Ambrosius have a twin? What's that young man's name?" Aeacus asked.

Before I could answer 'I don't know,' we heard, "Merlinus, over here. Merlinus, you need to meet someone."

I saw Ambrosius and the young man stepping out of ranks as others marched through the city's gate.

"Merlinus, it's great to see you're alive," Ambrosius said as he hugged me. Letting go, he asked, "Is it true about Lord Vortimer? Has someone murdered him?"

Patting his shoulders, I replied, "Unfortunately, it is true. Some coward poisoned him and then blamed the deed upon me."

"Jesus, it's lucky you didn't get locked up," he replied.

"I did," I added as I pointed at Aeacus. "This young lad set me free. This is Aeacus, a loyal servant of Lord Vortimer's. It was Rowan and Grallon's sons that accused and arrested me.

"Worse yet, at a parley convened by Grallon, Hengist, and his men slaughtered numerous nobles. Now the whole southern half of the island is nearly leaderless," I remarked.

"That's not true; Ambrosius has returned," Aeacus said.

"Why do you say that as if that mattered?" Ambrosius replied.

"Before passing on, Lord Vortimer said we should follow you, Ambrosius. You are the one true king, he said," Aeacus added.

I could not believe what Aeacus said. Here was not the place for this discussion. How could Ambrosius be sheltered from it, though? Nearly everyone knew what Vortimer had said. The boy knew no better.

Before I could end the conversation, Aeacus declared, "With Lord Vortimer's dying words, he said Lord Merlinus could best explain why we should follow you."

With a confused look on his face, Ambrosius glanced at me for an answer. I didn't want to say anything. There were too many people listening and too much to explain. More and more eyes looked upon me.

"Is that Ambrosius?" voices questioned.

"No, he's too young to be Ambrosius," others replied.

Glancing around, I pulled Ambrosius away from the growing crowd. The young nobleman and Aeacus tagged along as I drew Ambrosius out of the clustering bystanders.

"What is this about Merlinus?" Ambrosius asked impatiently.

"I'm not totally clear on this myself," I replied. "I wasn't there when Lord Vortimer died. I don't know what he said exactly."

Glancing at me with a surprised look, the young teen turned to Ambrosius and declared, "I swear by Christ and the souls of my family that Lord Vortimer said to follow you. Your parents wore the imperial purple. That is what he said."

"How is that possible?" Ambrosius questioned.

"When I asked the same thing, my lord said that Merlin could explain best," Aeacus looked at me.

I remained silent as Ambrosius and the young stranger next to him stared at me. I wished I knew how this young man fit into the whole mess.

"Lord Euthar," called a voice from outside our small circle. "Lord Euthar, excuse my interruption. You are needed for a moment. Please come with me."

The young nobleman turned and noticed the trooper.

That young nobleman is Euthar? My question consumed me.

"Yes," the young man replied as he pulled away from the circle. "What do you need, soldier?"

The young man walked toward the soldier and spoke with him.

"So your comrade is Euthar?" I asked, trying to switch the subject. "So that's Nepos' superior?"

"Yes," Ambrosius answered.

"Is he your brother?" the young teen asked anxiously as he drew closer.

"No," Ambrosius dryly replied and added in a sharpening tone, "Many have said we are, but we are not even related."

"You could pass for twins," I plainly replied.

"Doesn't that seem a little impossible?" Ambrosius asked.

"Improbable, yes. Impossible, no," I replied and then faded to a mumble, "but that doesn't make sense."

"Neither do you, Merlinus," he added. "Why did Vortimer say I should lead? He didn't even see me fight at Episford. Merlinus, did you have something to do with this? Why didn't he nominate Lord Gorlois or

Eldol? Why me? I am just a son of a dead nobleman, second oldest at that. Why shouldn't Cai lead?"

"Because Cai isn't your brother," I answered.

"What?" Ambrosius remarked.

"The blood of Gothic kings and Roman emperors courses through your veins," I declared.

"That's not possible," Ambrosius countered. "Why are you telling me this now?"

"I am only telling you this because Vortimer and his young faithful servant have forced me to tell you," I replied. "Personally, I see no point in telling you who your parents are."

"What? Why wouldn't you have told me that, anyway?" he asked with anger in his tone.

"What for? What would it accomplish by telling you this? It's not like you had a claim to imperial titles or any privileges associated with them," I answered.

"Why not?" he asked.

"You are supposed to be dead, Ambrosius. Who would believe anyone saying otherwise? Your own mother would not even recognize you as her own. By all accounts, you died fifteen years ago when you were just a newborn," I added. "Ambrosius, I'm not trying to be mean or callus, but you have nothing to prove who you are or, more importantly, who your parents are."

"That's not true," he replied. "I have a birthmark above my right ankle. A loving mother would remember that her first child had a birthmark on his right ankle."

"Supposedly, you died before completing your first year of life," I announced.

As confusion set in, Ambrosius asked, "Who am I, then? It seems like something I should know."

"You are the son of Adaulphus, the dead king of the Visigoths, and Placidia, the current Roman Empress." I added.

"How is that possible? I have lived my entire life in Britain," Ambrosius stated.

"Except when you lived a short while in Barcelona fifteen years ago. That's why Cai asked if I was from Barcelona," I added. "To retain the villa in Aureliani, I took you to Britain for the Empire. The child that Ahès brought on the trip to Barcelona took your place in Placidia's crib. The child grew sickly and died."

"You killed her child?" he questioned.

"No, it was never Ahès' child. Besides, I never killed anyone's child," I answered. "The whole thing was orchestrated by a man named Budicius. He drew Grallon, Germanus, and myself into this imperial conspiracy," I declared.

"Bishop Germanus was a part of this?" Ambrosius asked.

"Yes," a voice called out.

Turning, I saw Bishop Germanus approaching.

"Bishop Germanus, I didn't realize that you had returned," I remarked.

"Yes, I figured Britain could use as much help as possible," the bishop answered.

"So all that Merlinus has said is true?" Ambrosius asked.

"Yes," the bishop confirmed. "I was about the age of Merlinus and he was about your age when this happen. He took over the duties of his dead father."

"I don't understand. Why was this done?" Ambrosius asked.

"Your existence was a threat to the Empire. Adaulphus could have legitimately placed the diadem upon your head since Placidia's blood runs through you.

"In hindsight, I wonder if it would have been better if we would have let that happen. Placidia doesn't have the respect of her most able general, Aëtius, and his Huns. The Western Empire is being torn apart by the bickering and conspiring between Aëtius, Boniface, and Felix. Maybe Valentinian shall grow up and become the restorer of Rome. The Empire needs a strong leader."

"So what are you saying?" Ambrosius asked. "Are you saying that I should march on Rome, right now? And be some grand savior of Rome?"

"Hah. I am suggesting nothing of the sort," Germanus remarked.

"Then, what are you suggesting?" Ambrosius asked.

"Be like Constantine, the first Christian emperor," the bishop declared. "Consolidate your power on the island. After you show how you justly rule, the people will demand that you take the purple for the good of the Empire. That's what I suggest. You shall be crowned emperor of Britain just as Constantine was over a hundred years ago. Instead of York, you shall be crowned in London."

"Don't you think there will be opposition to my elevation by either the nobles or the clergy?" Ambrosius asked.

"No," answered someone else. It was a richly dressed priest who walked up to our small standing circle.

"Greetings," Germanus remarked. "Congratulations, Bishop Elafius for your accession to the see of Gloucester. The Church of Britain is in desperate need of men such as yourself."

"Thank you, Bishop Germanus," the approaching man answered. "I hope your voyage was better than the last time you sailed for our shores."

"Oh yes, definitely," Germanus added.

"It wouldn't take much to do that," Ambrosius joked. "We barely survived the original crossing."

"That's true," the bishop confirmed. "It's a wonder that the mast didn't snap."

"This time was much better," Ambrosius added and then fell silent.

His mind had to be in chaos at that moment. So much to comprehend in such a short period of time. What could he really think? His life had been a lie. My words may have held little weight, but Bishop Germanus was a different story. The bishop had close council with Ambrosius for the last few years. So it was Germanus' admission that gave credence to the truth.

"Young lord," Bishop Germanus began. "No one is saying you have to be Theodosius, son of Adaulphus and Placidia, or anyone else, for that matter. You are who you are. That cannot be changed now. You are, Ambrosius, son of Constantine and Ahès."

"That's correct," Bishop Elafius added. "Nobleman of Cornovia with an innate right to the higher rule."

"What about Lord Gorlois or even your brother, Eldol?" Ambrosius asked.

"I cannot say what Gorlois' reason is for consenting to Vortimer's dying wishes, but I can say for certain what my brother's reason is. He knows what they say about you is true. Besides, he grows weary, and seeks to destroy Hengist's bloodline and nothing more," Bishop Elafius announced. "I know this for certain. I heard him speak these words. After you are confirmed as High Commander, Lord Eldol wants to march out with you and destroy the Saxon threat."

"Grallon must be dealt with first," Ambrosius announced.

"Agreed," Germanus and I said in unison.

"Then, it's settled," Bishop Elafius remarked. "I shall make the final arrangement and, Ambrosius, you shall be nominated High Commander tomorrow morning."

"Okay," Ambrosius remarked.

CHAPTER 35

People gathered and donated the necessary resources to move against Grallon. Any help was welcomed. We had a long campaign on our hands.

Marching northeast on a section of a Roman road, we headed to join forces with Duke Eldol in Gloucester. We passed through the land with no resistance. No one stood with Grallon, no one except the Saxons. Our destination was a stronghold that sat on a hill overlooking the Wye River. Grallon had taken shelter there. A thousand men followed Ambrosius as we went to lay siege upon Grallon.

Various scouts brought word of the heathens' landing near York, more at Kent and closing in on the northern towns of the Wall near the pagan march. I worried that we had left London too unprotected. I hoped Jonah could maintain his effective hold on the city. Yes, we needed to take down Grallon, but not at the expense of London. Before leaving, I helped Ambrosius gather a loyal team of defenders. These men were given specific instructions in assisting Jonah. All city gates remained closed. Country folk were instructed at the forum as to what was going to happen. Access would be limited. That's how we left London.

We received reinforcements as we marched into the western parts of the island. Old Man Kendel and his two sons, Lot and Urian, along with their men, swore allegiance to young Ambrosius. Old Man Kendel had brown hair and a beard with a plait in each. Being long and thick, the braid in his beard hung down to the middle of his chest. The end of his braided ponytail nearly touched the back of his waist. He wore a tunic sewn from a brown bear's pelt. His cloth trousers were colored dark brown like his bearskin shirt. He was shorter and smaller than both of his sons. Urian was the tallest of the three, but Lot was the stockiest and mirrored his father in appearance and wear.

We marched out against Grallon. After our vast army took position nearby, Bishop Germanus and a small envoy rode up to the gateway of

Grallon's last stronghold in Britain. We figured that the bishop could convince Grallon to surrender and avoid further bloodshed. The bishop and his men maintained a vigil outside the tall wooden gate for three days straight.

As the night's black blanket covered the sky, Ambrosius grew impatient and rode up to Germanus. Though not asked, several of us went with him.

"Bishop, order your men back to camp," Ambrosius commanded.

"Give peace more time, lad," Germanus remarked.

"There is no more time," Old Man Kendel remarked. "Each day we wait is more time we give the Saxons to kill more Brits. We cannot sacrifice another British life for Grallon."

"Please give me one more day," Germanus asked as he looked directly at Ambrosius.

"Grallon doesn't deserve another day," Ambrosius declared.

"I do not ask this for him. I ask it for the men regrettably still inside the stronghold. Let me warn them of the pending danger. Your mercy now will better serve peace later," the bishop replied.

Ambrosius struggled with the decision. Glancing from Germanus, his eyes shifted to me.

"One day won't save or sink London. It will drastically effect our standing with the locals, though. By giving them an extra day to evacuate the fort, it shall cement our position with them. Besides, there is no indication from our scouts that the Saxons are near London. To set your mind at ease, why don't you send out a dispatch to London to confirm the city's status," I suggested.

"Do you think that will be enough," Ambrosius asked.

"More than enough," Germanus answered.

"Then, it shall be done," Ambrosius replied. "Merlinus, have riders sent to London. Germanus, send word to have the locals leave Grallon's stronghold or they shall meet the same fate as the traitor."

As promised, Ambrosius commenced his attacks on Grallon's stronghold the following afternoon. It went on this way for several days, but to no avail. The masons had done their work well when building this fort for Grallon. It was nothing like the one that recently collapsed on his builders at a different site. The battering rams did little to the main gate. Luckily, the Saxons hadn't taken advantage of our absence.

Ambrosius maintained a steady correspondence with London, though. He grew impatient with our progress.

As a new day dawned, Ambrosius sought me out. A tired, concerned look consumed his face.

"A young man of your age should not be so weary," I joked.

He ignored my comment and declared, "We must end the siege soon. I refuse to allow Grallon to leave this stronghold alive."

"What do you suggest we do, then?" I asked.

"I am at a loss," Ambrosius remarked as he shook his head. "Is there anything you can suggest? I am open to just about anything."

I studied a couple of the siege machines and then suggested, "Pull back those two machines and we can refit them into catapults. We will rain fire down onto the stronghold."

Working quickly, Ambrosius utilized help from the local blacksmiths and carpenters. The two machines were converted into catapults. As night approached, the machines were ready. Ambrosius ordered the catapults to be loaded and fired immediately.

We filled numerous clay pitchers with a mixture much like Greek fire. Men armed the catapults continuously with this mixture and flung it up and over the walls of the stronghold. Soon, the fort glowed red as the fire inside spread and consumed everything that could be burned. As fire rained down from the heavens, the other siege machines hammered at the walls of the stronghold.

Since the start of the siege, Ambrosius had engineers working on tunnels to undermine the support of the outer walls. As the assault continued late into the night, the sections of the wall over the tunnels toppled down. Immediately, Ambrosius, Eldol and their armies charged through the breech. The capturing of the fort came quickly thereafter. Through the rubble and burnt debris, we searched for the remains of Grallon, but there was none to be found. It was an ugly sight to see, firsthand, the results of our siege on Grallon's stronghold. People lay about dead and burning. My senses were shocked. The flesh of people split as if they were charred swine. It wasn't an enticing scent; it was fire-consumed hair and fabric. The sight of war was unsettling to most. I feared that I had grown detached from the suffering and felt little about the misery surrounding me.

Ambrosius never left my side. I wasn't certain why. If he was just as detached as I was, then that wasn't good. If it was to survey the situation firsthand, then that was good. Though unconfirmed, I hoped it was the latter. He did not act as if he hadn't seen them before. He didn't make vulgar comments. I hadn't seen his demeanor in many men that I had advised over the years. He was handling his command well. It was comforting.

"What is next, Merlinus? Do I waste men and resources chasing a ghost? None of these people appear to be him. So how can I be certain that the threat of Grallon is gone? Isn't his capture the linchpin of my success? How can I secure my authority based on a questionable victory?"

"Ambrosius, if you have any doubt about your victory, simply take a look around. There is no one to rebel. Your word is the authority that rained fire from the heavens. This is as complete of a victory as possible. There is no one to contend it. And if by the off chance Grallon escaped this rain of fire and had the nerve to return, you would destroy him. He has been defeated, or at least his authority has been removed from possible contention. You have done what you set out to do. The Saxons cannot use him as their puppet lord. Grallon has nowhere to hold up in Britain any longer. If he still lives, he will go to Armorica," I finished.

"It's just that this victory doesn't deliver a settling feeling within me," he remarked lowly.

"Most battles don't," I replied. "I have witnessed more than I have wanted. Death in victory and defeat appears the same. You only see it in victory. Take solace in your actions. You have secured your command of the army today. It is time for the next part of the campaign."

CHAPTER 36

The end of the campaign against Grallon had worn Ambrosius thin. At the end, it had even rubbed Germanus raw, rawer than his hair shirt. Though we eliminated the threat of Grallon, it was only half the problem we faced. There was Hengist and his Saxon army.

Now the afternoon rain quickly eroded the morale of the men as evening drew near. I wasn't sure how Ambrosius was going to react to the young soldier's ranting.

"So who is this Ambrosius of Aureliani to me? What has he really done? He has defeated Grallon, the High Commander who cowered behind cobble walls. Is this what is to convince me that he is the son of the World-Restorer? Well, it doesn't," the young soldier said as the rain streamed down him and everyone else.

We walked toward the bonfire. The young soldier stood with his back to us. The eyes of the people near him swelled as we came into view. Without a word, they took a step back from him. The young man's hand fell to the hilt of his sword as if knowing that we were there by the crowd's reaction.

"Please do not insult me further by drawing your sword," Ambrosius called out as the rain pelted us. "If we had a rift between us, I would address you face-to-face," Ambrosius remarked as he moved into view. The young man's mouth hung slightly open from surprise. Our *papilio* had been set up. The wet, angry soldier hadn't expected Ambrosius to come out of our legionary tent with the weather being so terrible. I could not understand why, either. Ambrosius had to drag me into the foul elements to tour the camp. Still, some of Eldol's and Gorlois' men were not set up. They could not. The terrain had made it easier to sleep under the stars. But now, the rain washed away the spiritual strength of the army.

The young man was a prime example of the morale of the camp at the moment. As they stood facing each other, I studied the young man.

He actually looked both older and taller than Ambrosius. Still, Ambrosius did not break his gaze. Ambrosius stood there as if waiting for the young man to repeat himself. The young man's eyes dropped from Ambrosius and he slightly bowed his head.

"Forgive me, gentle sir," the young man replied. "I don't know what has come over me."

With a slight smile, Ambrosius remarked, "Hopefully, just this damn rain."

The crowd laughed and so did Ambrosius, then the young man.

"I am sorry for what I said about you," the young man added.

"Don't apologize for the truth," Ambrosius sternly replied.

There was silence in the crowd. The young man seemed uncertain what Ambrosius meant.

"You are right. Who am I to you?" Ambrosius remarked and then added, "No one. And yes, we have only defeated an old man and the worst is yet to come. But if by chance, fate, or free will, we both make it through this alive, I believe a victory over the Saxons might warrant your respect of my leadership, then."

"Yes, sir," the young man uttered.

The rain continued to pound us all. Ambrosius smiled, nodded, and walked past the fire. I followed and the crowd casually began talking amongst themselves. We approached Eldol's tent, voices echoed within the canvas walls and the rolling of dice could be heard.

"Ah, damn it all," Eldol shouted. "I would be better off standing in the downpour the way these dice are treating me. It would be about the same pleasure. At least, that's free."

We pushed in the flap and looked into the crowded tent. Immediately, we spotted Eldol as he headed to exit the tent.

"Hey, what are you two doing here?" Eldol said with a drunken smile. "Ambrosius, I thought you didn't play and we don't trust Merlinus. He could fix the dice. That's why we don't let him play."

"I don't and you're right about Merlinus. Honestly, I was just wondering if you have some time to talk," Ambrosius called into the tent.

"Sure. Anything is better than losing to these fools," Eldol remarked as he left the shelter of the centurion-size papilio.

"Sweet Mother Mary of God. It's raining hard," Eldol shouted as the water ran through his dry clothes.

We moved underneath a nearby tree to block the rain.

"It's amazing how many men are up braving the rain," Eldol called out as he looked around the camp.

"Well, I guess it's better than sleeping on wet ground since some of them can't set up a tent on this rocky terrain." I added.

"Oh, you're right," Eldol remarked.

"This is not good," Ambrosius remarked.

"No, it is not," Eldol replied. "I didn't realize that it was this bad."

"We need to get out of here. We need to be where the men can set up their tents and get the hell out of this damn rain. Any ideas?" Ambrosius asked.

Eldol paused for a moment and then added, "We are almost to Chester. We have about a day's march left. The Twentieth Legion, Valeria Victrix, was stationed there long ago. There is plenty of room for our army to bivouac there."

"Can we reach it by nightfall?" I asked.

"No," Eldol replied. "Midnight if we marched at double time."

"Then, let's do it," Ambrosius barked.

"What?" both Eldol and I questioned.

"What about the men that already have their tents up?" Eldol questioned further.

"They can bring up the rear," Ambrosius replied. "I doubt that the men who don't have tents up will mind leading the march when they find out they will be able to set up their tents tonight."

"Right," Eldol conceded and then added with a light laugh, "I'll send out the order and get the men moving."

"Good," Ambrosius replied.

We marched hard through the night, but it was well worth the effort. Halfway to Chester, the rain had stopped. On the outskirts of Chester, the ground appeared dry. It took longer than Eldol had anticipated, but the entire army was asleep several hours before the rooster crowed. With his questionable order, Ambrosius had saved the morale of the men and earned even more respect from them, at least the ones that didn't have their tents pitched.

Now the third night in Chester, he cemented his position. We stood at a long row of tables butted up against one another. The tables had a vast assortment of food and drink laid upon them. At one end stood Ambrosius and at the other stood Eldol. Elafius stood by his brother as Germanus and I stood by Ambrosius. Midway between the two, Gorlois stood face-to-face with Euthar. Kendel, Lot, and Urian stood on the same side of the table as Gorlois. To Gorlois' right stood his head commander, Jordan. This man looked similar to Ulfin with his stoic expressions and chiseled chin. Ulfin was Euthar's lead officer. Both lead officers shared physical features. Thin black hair, dark skin, and eyes gave them a strong Hunnish appearance. Jordan had his hair short. Nowhere was it longer than an inch on his head. Though Ulfin kept his face cleanly shaved, he pulled his long black hair into a long, loose ponytail.

To Gorlois' left stood Vitaelis. He was Gorlois' advisor much like I was to Ambrosius. He wore a mustard-colored robe with a wide black cross. The top of it reached the base of Vitaelis' neck and ran down the center of his chest to the bottom seam of his ankle-length tunic. He had black hair and a long wiry beard. His eyes were dark, and he had a long-rippled nose. Nepos, Carbo, and Cai stood near Euthar, helping to fill the ranks. The elite officers from the armies at the table waited as Ambrosius held his mug of ale in a toast.

"It is an honor to stand at this table with such distinguished men. And to be considered its High Commander is beyond belief. But it is effortless to command such noble men as yourselves, for you innately know what needs to be done and do it. It is the common good we seek to sustain. And so we must act accordingly. We have finished the first half of this fight and so we feast in joy for our victory and survival. To our health, gentlemen," Ambrosius shouted as he raised his cup high and took a long drink. We cheered on the young man and drank to everyone's health.

After a heavy draft from his mug, Ambrosius added, "I shall never ask you to do anything I wouldn't do. May the light of the Lord lead our way. Alleluia."

"Alleluia," echoed over the table as it did in the Darenth Valley.

He sat down and began to eat and so everyone else did. The men had recouped their former strength and enhanced it with a deep sense of brotherhood. Joy flowed like wine, and our cups were never empty that night. We lived as if it were our last feast. For some men, it was.

The next day, we marched out against Hengist and his men.

CHAPTER 37

Word reached us that the Saxons had taken position in Conisbrough near the Roman road between Lincoln and York. After the enormous feast on the third night in Chester, we marched east the next morning. Ambrosius planned to intercept the Saxon army or head for York to help uproot the barbaric threat of laying siege to the city. As we pushed forward, our scouting party led the way trying to prevent the Saxons from ambushing us. We reached the western point of Macclesfield. This was not a town but open land that rose up and turned into the Peak District farther east.

At that point, I saw Nepos racing toward us. I rode on Ambrosius left side. As we kept our forward pace, Nepos hooked out to our right and came up along side of Ambrosius without stopping. The young Alan was an amazing rider.

"My lord! My lord," Nepos remarked. "The Saxons are no longer in Conisbrough. They have moved west through the Peak District and down past Kinder Scout. They are positioned at the east end of Macclesfield, a short distance from here."

"Where's the rest of the scouting party?" Ambrosius asked. "Is anyone hurt?"

"No one is hurt," Nepos replied. "The other men are positioned halfway between here and the Saxons."

"Good," Ambrosius answered. "Go back and hold the ground. Have Carbo and the rest of your squadron go with you. I'll have Eldol and Gorlois tell their infantry to pick up the pace. If you come under attack, send someone back."

"Yes, sir," Nepos said and then whistled. Immediately, Carbo and the horsemen broke through the ranks and followed Nepos into a hell-bound gallop.

Two hours later, we teamed up with the Armoric cavalry and the other scouts.

We reached the eastern end of Macclesfield. The Saxons had sunk back into the broad foothills. Bogs and brush clogged the wide-open path and forced us to shrink our man-per-line formation.

"They are trying to take away the advantage from our cavalry. It will be harder for us to sweep out and around their flanks," I called out.

"We need to get moving, then," Ambrosius replied in the Alan tongue. "If they make it to Kinder Scout before we can attack them, then our advantage will be gone. Nepos, form a row of riders as wide as you can. Move them up at a fast, steady pace. Not too fast, the infantry needs to keep up."

"Right," Nepos answered and then once more whistled out a command. His men responded immediately.

"Eldol, let's send up two units marching at double time. They will engage the enemy and hold it stationary while the bulk of the army has time to catch up," Ambrosius added.

"Good thought," Eldol replied. "Marcellus, you heard the High Commander. Make it happen."

"Yes, my lord," Marcellus replied.

The old soldier wore a transverse crest helmet like that of a Roman centurion. His cheek and brow were scarred from prior battles. Marcellus was a good warrior and disciplined in the Roman ways of war. Lord Eldol, and in fact Lord Gorlois, had maintained the Roman military structure for their armies. It would seem that the Roman legions of long ago had made a lasting impression on both leaders and their men. Eldol led the Valeria Victrix while Gorlois headed the Second Augusta. A black boar on a red sheet flapped wildly in the wind as Eldol's standard. Gorlois' standard-bearer carried a red flag with a charging black goat.

Marcellus pulled away from our head group and drifted back to the infantry units. Within moments, a sharp report called out from the trumpeter, instructing the men what to do. Our group swept to the side to let the two units by. These men moved quickly toward the crest that Nepos and his cavalry had passed over. In time as the soldiers in the two units dropped from our line of sight, a rider broke over the horizon coming toward us. It was Nepos returning.

"My lord, the Saxon army are positioned on the next moorish plateau. They appear ready to fight," Nepos reported to Ambrosius.

"Good," Euthar called out.

"What's the terrain like?" Ambrosius questioned.

"It's an open tract of land a mile long. Thin woods enclose the field. The closer hills to the north are on the left-hand side as we approach," Nepos finished.

"Return to the group. Tell them to hold their position. One last thing, how many units could march side by side?"

"Honestly, only two," Nepos replied. "If you went three, the men at the ends would almost be in the woods. Even with their tight twenty-men-line formation, I doubt that sixty men can stand side by side on the narrow plateau."

"All right," Ambrosius acknowledged.

Ambrosius looked at the various units within the army that he commanded. This wasn't one massive uniformed army. Only the men of Eldol and Gorlois mirrored the Roman martial discipline. Old Kendel and his two sons, Lot and Urian, each commanded seasoned warriors that formed large war parties. In addition, three cavalry units heeded Ambrose's commands. Besides Nepos' squad, Euthar and Cai led the other two. And though at times more of a hazard than a help, there was the mob squad that had attached itself to the army. This group included the volunteers picked up through the course of the campaign. Many of them had been utilized in nonmilitary tasks, but still a large group remained restlessly waiting instructions. These were common folk ready to take matters in hand. Somehow, the fifteen-year-old Ambrosius kept the various parties in check. It amazed me how well he handled his power.

"This is what I suggest," Ambrosius declared. "Kendel and Urian's units will move into the northern woods. Kendel will circle up onto the closest hillside while Urian's men remain in the woods below you. Nepos and Euthar's cavalry units will form the outer lines of our attack. Eldol and Gorlois will march along side the riders. Our volunteers will form the center."

"What?" said several leaders in the group.

With a light laugh, Euthar remarked, "Don't get me wrong, I think everyone should do their fair share of fighting, but don't you think the freemen will be overwhelmed?"

"Slaughtered, if they don't retreat," Ambrosius quickly answered. "The volunteers are simply there in the center to get the Saxons to fully commit their forces. As the center retreats and the enemy races after them,

Eldol's and Gorlois' units will hold their position. By doing so, they will have the Saxons flanked. While Kendel and Urian circle to the north, Lot and his men will take the southern woods. If all fares well, we will have the Saxons trapped and unable to retreat. Cai and the rear guard will contain the center rush of the Saxons as the freemen retreat."

"That's a good plan. It will work well with the terrain," Eldol replied as he nodded, smiled, and then patted Ambrosius on the shoulder. The others also nodded in agreement.

Kendel and his sons went into the northern and southern woods before crossing the crest to the next plateau. Euthar and Nepos split and swung their men out to the flanks as all of us climbed to the higher ground. Reaching the level land of the plateau, we saw the true extent of the Saxon army for the first time. The motley group stood in no rank and file. They simply waited for our approach. Our center core had a similar appearance.

After explaining the plan several times, the mob squad realized the logic of Ambrosius' thinking and no longer felt insulted or sacrificed by his plan. As I saw the size of the Saxon army, I wondered if we had enough men to contain them. We would know soon enough. Ambrosius' plan quickly took shape. The infantry and cavalry lines slowly inched forward, giving time to Kendel and his sons to get in position. They would cap the trap if all went well.

Waiting no longer, the Saxons charged our position. As anticipated, they blew through the center core of freemen. The mob squad suffered from the Saxons' swords. Their retreat came quickly, but still drew the enemy in as planned. Gorlois' and Eldol's men stood steady behind their long shields. Their strength channeled the enemy deep along their ranks. Half of the enemy was surrounded as they chased after the retreating freemen. Cai brought the rear guard up into position as the running freemen had cleared the ranks of our army in the backfield. The Saxons had begun to move their reserve warriors into the center, but before Hengist had completely committed them, Urian and his men broke their cover and charged the field. Realizing he was trapped and already outflanked, the Saxon sounded a massive retreat. We tried to drive the enemy down, but they scattered into the cover of the Peak District. We had lost our chance to finish off the Saxon threat.

The commanders of the various units regrouped at the eastern end of the plateau. A disgusted look was cemented on Ambrosius' face.

Others didn't look so disappointed.

"We'll camp here for the night," Ambrosius announced as he turned his horse from the group and added, "We will pursue them at first light."

"No," Urian shouted. "We need to pursue them now and finish this, today."

I wasn't sure if anyone else noticed what I had. Ambrosius was reaching his boiling point. His hand clenched the horse reins into a fist. How Ambrosius reacted to this situation would shape how effectively he could govern the British Council.

True to character, Ambrosius tried to maintain his composure. He looked down at his fist and relaxed his grip as he drew in and released a heavy sigh. Everyone remained silent, even Euthar. The Alan prince simply shook his head. Others looked away as Urian scanned the group of leaders looking for support of more action. His father and older brother shook their heads in disagreement.

"Come on," Urian shouted. "The Saxons are on their last leg."

Ambrosius could not hold back any longer.

"Please do us all a favor and shut up," Ambrosius commanded as he glared at Urian.

"What did you say to me?" Urian questioned.

"I said shut up and think before you do anything," Ambrosius ordered. "It is your fault, may it be incompetence or arrogance, but your actions have led to them still having a leg to stand on. We had the bastards trapped. If you would have followed the agreed plan of attack, the Saxons would have been completely outflanked and annihilated by now.

"Instead, you want us to charge out into the night in unfamiliar territory. To do what? Most likely, we would get ambushed by Hengist's men. Go right ahead if you think that is the best plan of attack since you sure the hell don't want to follow my orders. Take your unit of men and march out after the Saxons. I no longer want you in this army. If you remain under my command and disobey another direct order, I will have you bound and flogged."

"And I would do it for the High Commander," Old Man Kendel barked. "That's so I could bleed out the disgrace from my clan."

Uncertainty washed over Urian's face as he took a second look at his father. There was anger in the old man's eyes. Urian's eyes fell to the ground as he remained silent.

Looking up at Ambrosius, Urian replied in an even tone, "I will inform my men to set up camp for the night."

"Good," Ambrosius answered.

Urian walked away without another word. Ambrosius looked over at Old Man Kendel and gave a nod of thanks to him. The old warrior reciprocated the gesture.

Evodius would be proud at how quickly Ambrosius had matured.

CHAPTER 38

We gave chase to the Saxons as the darkness faded from the eastern sky. The Saxons made no attempt to conceal their line of retreat. They headed in a northeastern direction. Nepos and his cavalry trailed the Saxons across Whaley's Bridge. The Saxons took the southern route around Kinder Scout and avoided its higher ground. At this point the Saxons cut due north on the southeastern fringe of Kinder Scout.

From there we gazed across the vast moorish saddle.

Eldol called out, "Hengist will head for Oughtibridge as he makes his way for Conisbrough."

"Why there?" I asked. "Why not a more direct route to York?"

"Conisbrough is a Saxon watchtower on the road to York. He could regroup and possibly repel a siege there," Lot answered. "This is how the safety of the island has been comprised. They garrison points on key roads and waterways for Grallon and simply switched their sworn allegiance to Hengist."

"Then, we must push these Saxons harder. Cai, Euthar, and Nepos will ride out to engage the enemy. Do not stop until you either confront the enemy or reach the Roman road, tonight. Is this understood?"

"Yes," the three answered in unison.

"Good. Understand this, also," Ambrosius added as he looked at Euthar. "The job of the cavalry is to hinder the retreat of these sea dogs, not to sweep in and annihilate them."

"Why not?" Euthar asked in a light tone.

"Because even the infantry has earned the right to help send these Saxons to hell," Eldol barked out.

"Alleluia," cried out the armies.

On we marched. Well-conditioned, Eldol's and Gorlois' units moved quickly across the rugged terrain. Kendel and his sons made up the midsection of the martial train while the mob squad filled the position of the rear guard.

By midafternoon, the rear guard had crossed Oughtibridge. Not much after that, one of our riders returned, reporting that the three cavalry units had engaged the Saxon army, or at least its rear guard. Reaching Ecclesfield, we were offered nearly the same open battlefield as at Macclesfield.

"Instead of the mob squad in the center, they will take the wings as the Armoric cavalry did in the first battle. Eldol and Gorlois will serve the first charge as the strong center. Kendel and Lot will give the first reserves. Urian, maintain the rear guard."

The infantry units marched into position and prepared themselves for the next battle charge. Noticing our arrival, Nepos and Cai's units disengaged and swept back behind the front lines of our infantry units. Euthar and his horsemen held the Saxons so they could not even think about retreating. With an ear-piercing whistle from Euthar, he and his men raced to the side of the field and out of the center of the battle as the two enemy lines of infantry clashed for the first time that day.

Slaughter filled the ranks as the opposing fronts slammed into each other. Neither pagan nor Christian, nor British nor barbarian were spared the spear. Blood ran like rain from the wounds. The tide of the battle surged forward and rolled back between the two sides. Our grim determination broke through their lines and sent them into retreat. We gave chase and continued to engage the enemy.

Men died that day without any mourning. Many fathers and sons had no funeral rites. Dead Christians lay on dead pagans. I saw no angels carrying souls to heaven. I saw no golden chariots carrying away the pagans to their hallowed halls. The grass drank itself red. Crimson covered its emerald blades. Men struggled to charge forward. Bodies layered the field. Only the crows were happy. They flocked to the bodies and picked pieces of flesh from them as the battle raged on.

Our lines began to falter. Ambrosius called the rear cavalry out of the reserves and pushed them into action.

"Nepos, we must hurry our forces forward or today shall be lost," Ambrosius shouted as he heeled his mount into a strong charge. A wall of galloping flesh, we entered the battle.

With an echoing battle cry, Euthar and his Armoric cavalry followed our lead. Along the front lines, we laid waste to any enemy in the way. Saxons' swords raised to strike down our comrades fell as we sliced away the arms and hands holding their weapons.

Duke Eldol, Gorlois, and their men lumbered forward as we swept by. They gave strength and solidarity to our charge. They hammered a wedge through the enemy lines.

Duke Eldol killed his way toward Hengist. Though Hengist nearly looked identical to his brother, Horsa, with his black hair and beard, there seemed to be a few years that separated the two Saxons. Hengist appeared to be the elder, but he looked younger than the British lord he now engaged. Hengist wore a gray wolf cape instead of the black bear cape Horsa wore. Eldol and Hengist stood eye to eye.

Sparks flew freely from their swords as they rained blows down upon each other. Seeing the courageous confrontation, Duke Gorlois pushed his men to help reinforce Eldol's position. Feeling his support, the Duke of Gloucester snatched ahold of the tall, powerful Saxon and dragged him back into our line. As chaos continued, the Armoric cavalry turned the tide of the battle. Large sections of the enemy retreated, leaving Hengist to meet his fate, alone.

CHAPTER 39

Captured alive, we hauled Hengist through the streets of Conisbrough. If this was a Saxon town, it was that no more. Townspeople cheered wildly as they saw the chained Saxon. People threw stones, mud, and anything they could at the hated heathen. Already he bled from a cut to his forehead from a tossed stone. The ox-drawn wagon carried him to the small forum as more and more people gathered to catch a glimpse of the evil man.

"Stop," Ambrosius shouted as he climbed up on the wagon. "God has saw it fit to judge him before the Council and this is how it shall be."

Words murmured through the crowd but fell silent as Ambrosius glared at them. Soldiers stepped up to enforce his orders. He hopped down from the open-ended wagon.

"Pull this to the portico at the end of the forum. We will use one of the shops to sort this out," Ambrosius ordered. He used his army of men to create a wall between the Saxon and the gathering townspeople.

As the evening laid the sun to rest, lit torches spread through the town. Even if this council of men debated Hengist's fate all night, the gathered crowd would have held a vigil until we concluded. The wood-burning braziers stood watch on the towers and at the gateway, casting a revealing light upon the crowd. Surprisingly, the people remained restrained. For now.

Inside the shop was a different matter. The leaders of the armies stood around Hengist.

"Why is this animal still alive?" Bishop Elafius called out as he pointed at Hengist. Looking at him closely for the first time, I saw the man that killed Lord Katigern at Episford. Even in shackles, the Saxon's sheer size was intimidating. If the bishop wasn't careful, Hengist might wrap those chains around his neck and tear the bishop's head off. Regrettably, I had seen it done, and the man that had performed it had the same look in his eyes as Hengist.

"He might be more valuable alive than dead," Gorlois remarked. "The Saxons have overrun York. Though Coel had died in his sleep before this happened, the bishop was killed when York fell. Maybe we can regain York by bartering."

"Would they honor any deal?" Euthar questioned.

"There is no honor among heathens. This man before us personally has made too many mothers childless and too many wives widows. This moment is not here before us to judge what should be done, but to witness what will be done. I shall hack this heathen into pieces as Samuel struck down the king of Amalek."

Instantly, Hengist lunged at Bishop Elafius. Before he reached the ranting bishop, the hilt of Ambrosius' sword jolted Hengist in the cheek. Blood poured from Hengist's face as the pointed end pierced his flesh. Hengist dropped to his knees.

"Take him to the center of the forum and execute him," Ambrosius calmly as he sheathed his sword.

"I swear it shall be done," Duke Eldol replied.

By sword point, the Duke of Gloucester led Hengist out to the center of the crowded market square.

"On your knees," the duke ordered.

Refusing, Hengist remained standing. With the hilt of his sword, Eldol brought it down hard on the Saxon's shoulder. The giant of a man dropped to his knees. Without hesitation, Eldol hacked off the heathen's head.

CHAPTER 40

Two days after Hengist's execution, Ambrosius and the army headed for York. Ambrosius sought to completely uproot the Saxon threat. A few days later, Ambrosius and his men surrounded the city of York.

"Move the siege machines into position," Ambrosius shouted.

"Do you think that is a good idea?" I questioned. "Don't you think we should try to negotiate with them?"

"That is not an option I am offering. I will not give the people of Britain false hope, only to be stabbed in the back by these heathens," Ambrosius barked. Turning away from me, he shouted even louder, "Load the catapults and then wait for my command to fire."

Listening to his orders, they armed the siege machines and stood prepared to fire. Noticing that they were ready, Ambrosius slowly raised his arm up. Already, the death from the battles sickened me. I didn't have the stomach for more bloodshed. As I stared at York for only the second time in my life, I dreaded the thought of watching it burn. The landscape around the walled city had been scarred enough. Ambrosius reared back his hand behind his head. As he did, I saw the gateway door opening.

"Don't fire," I shouted as loud as I could. "Don't!"

"What?" Ambrosius questioned.

"They are opening the gate," I replied.

"What?" Ambrosius asked and then looked at the gate.

A small group of five Saxons walked out of the walled city of York. Oddly, though, the lead man carried in his outstretched hands a long length of chain. The other men all appeared to be unarmed.

"What trickery is this?" Duke Eldol called out.

"I'm not certain," Ambrosius replied.

"There's only one way to find out, Lord Eldol." I called out.

Ambrosius, myself, the Duke of Gloucester, Bishop Elafius, and Bishop Germanus walked out to meet the small group of Saxons. With ten feet between us, the man carrying the chain stopped. He looked like Hengist but not as tall and intimidating. He looked like the Saxon's son.

"The day has come and I've seen my gods fail to deliver victory to my people. I can only assume my father, Hengist, has gone to them. Death stands ready to greet my people and death has sent your army as its messenger. If there's no mercy within your hearts to spare myself and my people, my father has bound us with this chain. So, do to us what you will for this is the last act of Octa, son of Hengist," he ended.

I translated his honorable words. Silence fell between us after I finished. None of us expected this. Octa continued to hold the chain out for Ambrosius to take. As Octa stared into Ambrosius' eyes, I saw none of the malice that had filled his father's eyes. He was different from his father, smaller in stature and filled with less rage. Octa had his father's black hair, but sported no beard or fur cape. Instead he wore legionary-style, metal-band armor over his dark green tunic. His outfit reminded me of what Maximus and his squadron wore the night I was arrested by Ceretic. He even wore black trousers.

"Upon your word, I bind you to these terms as if by this long length of chain," Ambrosius replied. "So, keep your chain as a reminder of your promise. Know this as my pledge to you. If you break your word and cause treachery like your father, I shall exact this justice."

Staring at each of the Saxon delegates, Ambrosius received their strict attention and then continued, "Octa, son of Hengist, I shall execute every single one of these men that gather in council with you, either personally or by my directive. Then, I shall systematically decimate your people. All the while, you, Octa, the son of Hengist shall bear witness to the senseless destruction of your people. And when you beg for death to escape the pain you've caused, I shall give you only more pain. I shall inflict injuries that would draw you near death. Only Christ has felt more pain, but you shall have no chance for martyrdom, for my powerful physician shall draw you back to your living hell."

Ambrosius paused for a moment as he motioned in my direction.

"This is my pledge to you that I swear to fulfill, this being witnessed by a prince of Gaul and a lord of God," Ambrosius finished.

Silence consumed the morning air. Not even a songbird sang. Ambrosius' conviction stunned everyone standing near him. The weight of Ambrosius' words made Octa hesitate in responding.

With a hard swallow, the young Saxon replied, "By my own free will,

I accept this pact of peace. I ask only one other thing. Is there somewhere on this island that my people can call home?" Octa asked.

Ambrosius remained silent. Germanus drew in a breath as if to say something, but Ambrosius raised his hand and silenced him. Octa's eyes squinted as if unsure if this was a good sign.

"What you ask for cannot be decided until further debate. I must convene a council to give you an answer to your question," Ambrosius replied.

"I expected nothing to the contrary from an honorable man such as yourself," Octa remarked.

"Until a decision has been made, you and your people will be kept and treated as if you were the closest of allies," Ambrosius stated.

The sincerity of the teenager's words gave an undeniable strength to Ambrosius' promise of mercy. As if Ambrosius' words rendered them crippled, the small group of Saxons dropped to their knees in submission.

"Being your hostages, prisoners of war," Octa rose to his feet and added, "I stand ready to bear your decree."

"Then, you shall have your answer by nightfall," Ambrosius replied with a slight bow. Turning to me, he added, "Merlinus, gather the rest of the nobles so the Council can be convened."

"It shall happen," I replied and stepped away from the group. I was enthused by the idea of no more bloodshed between these two peoples, even if it was just for a while. Ambrosius had offered an honorable parley. He took another step toward being a good leader.

Once more, I stood in the courtyard of York. This time, there was no tranquil silence. Loud bickering filled the evening air. At least forty loud, angry men were shouting at one another. Duke Coel wasn't here. He had died in his sleep before the Saxons stormed York.

"Why is there even a discussion regarding these Saxons," Urian remarked as he stepped in the space between the two sides. "The son of Hengist should have been taken to the city forum and executed just like his father. End of problem. No more Saxon."

"I wish it were that easy," Gorlois replied as he sat on a stone bench between the two sides. "Octa's people aren't the only Saxons."

"Lord Gorlois is right. There will be more," Eldol replied.

"This is even more of a reason to execute them. Purge this island of the pagans," Urian quickly added.

Standing up, Bishop Elafius called out, "Their leader, in council, has come before us to beseech our mercy. As honorable Christians, can we be any less merciful than the Hebrews were to the Gibeonites that lived some six miles from Jerusalem. We are too few to govern the entire island effectively. Hengist had succeeded in that. So why don't we establish Octa and his people near Hadrian's Wall, giving them a vested interest in the security of the island. And if they become traitors, we shall nail their heathen hides to the Wall."

Silence fell as Bishop Elafius finished speaking. Only the flickering of the flames from the standing torches nearby could be heard. Ambrosius surveyed the sides with a simple shift of his eyes. He watched as Bishop Elafius' words settled in. He didn't want to influence the Council's sentiment. Seeing an honorable closure to the conflict, I hoped Ambrosius would endorse it.

"So be it," Ambrosius decreed. "If no one disagrees and can offer other feasible terms to this treaty, then it shall be so deemed. Octa and his people shall hold the land near the Wall, willfully subjugated by the rule of the Council."

The terms of the treaty were sworn to and Octa prepared to take his people north. Urian would govern the transition. Lord Eldol agreed to accompany them to ensure the integrity of the Council.

Elated by a final bloodless victory, Bishop Germanus prepared to set sail for Gaul with Euthar while Ambrosius and I remained.

"Bishop Germanus, I would like to have a letter delivered to Aureliani. I need to get word to both Ahès and my mother. It's bad enough that we are not returning with you to Gaul, but if I did not send any news to Aureliani, nothing could protect me from the wrath of those women," I told him.

"Ah, right," the bishop replied with a smile. "A woman's scorn is more terrifying than any barbarian horde. No worries. It shall be done."

"Thank you, Bishop Germanus," I finished.

CHAPTER 41

Two years ago, Ambrosius and I had watched Euthar and Germanus as they cast off from the docks of York. They had wide smiles on their faces as they drifted out to sea. The bishop had used the British victories to promote his agenda. Euthar liked the chance to seize land. For his serve to the Council, Euthar received a parcel near Winchester. At times, I didn't hold the same principles as them. Still, I considered them close comrades. I didn't think that would cause a conflict between us.

Now, Bishop Germanus and Euthar stood next to each other on the approaching ship. This time it was on the west side of the island. Before, they came to support the Roman Church against the British Pelagians, and now they came to do battle against the heathens of Ireland. Bishop Celestine had sent numerous letters hounding Ambrosius for support. Ambrosius consented to allowing Palladius to layover in a British port. He was the deacon to the Bishop of Rome. Palladius' father was a consul sixteen years ago. Though Britain stood outside the Empire, it and Ireland still fell under the celestial sway of Bishop Celestine, or so he thought.

The Church paid extremely well. It reminded me of the blood money that Dom Fu refused. If I knew that I would lose the honor and friendship of the old master, I wouldn't have taken the money. I wouldn't have left the forest of Mount Shaoshi, either. It felt like a lifetime ago, and now the first bishop of the Irish Christians was coming ashore.

"Back again," Ambrosius called as he stood by me.

"Ah, yes, our grand comrades," the bishop called out.

A young priest named Docco came with us. He had joined the order at a young age. He wore a white habit with a brown stripe that ran from his collar bone to the bottom of his ankle-length robe. He had no facial hair and his brown hair was tonsured. He had gentle brown eyes and carried a cordial smile. He was excited to meet the other church officials.

Docco called out, "It's an honor to finally met you, Bishop. You've enlightened my path. Did Bishop Palladius come? Are you going to Ireland in his stead?"

"Heavens no," Germanus replied. "Heretics are bad enough. I don't have the strength to convert a whole island of heathens. That will take a special man of faith to achieve such a feat."

"Well, hopefully, Bishop Palladius is that man. And just maybe, a peace by Christians can be shared between the Isles," Docco added.

Bishop Germanus remained silent. I expected him to say something, but he said nothing. His silence choked the moment. Bishop Germanus showed no emotions.

Finally, the silence was broken.

"Greetings, people of Britain," a young man called from the ship as he walked toward the boarding plank.

He reminded me of Bishop Lupus. *Was he Palladius?* The Roman priest wore a deep-blue tunic. The wide white cross centered on his chest went the length of his gown and across his shoulders. He wore a white skull cap. His brown hair poured out from its edges. Behind him came another even more richly adorned. His smug face revealed the high gaze of aristocracy. This priest wore a snow-white robe with a wide blue cross. A thin gold cross overlapped the center. He wore a gold skull cap. A short, matching blue cape hung from his shoulders fastened by a golden brooch. The cape glittered in the sun from its golden seams. Others lingered behind him as he stepped onto the shore.

A young boy moved directly behind him and jumped to the shore from the boarding planks, too impatient to wait his turn to leave the boat. The boy appeared to be a few years younger than Vortimer's servant, Aeacus. But this boy was no servant and didn't appear destined for the Church. Instead, the boy sported a short white tunic with a red cape flapping behind him as he rapidly moved about. He wore black trousers and form-fitting boots made of black leather. He didn't appear related to any of them. He had his black hair pulled back in a braided tail. He lacked their soft features. Already the boy had a chiseled chin with a wide jawline. He was stocky for his age but not chubby from lazy, luxurious living.

"Agricola, behave or you will feel the switch again," the announcer hissed lowly at the boy. The boy Agricola stopped and stood still. He had felt the switch and knew not to push his luck with this man. Regaining his placid demeanor, the announcer added, "It is my honor to introduce the imperial deacon of Rome. The Bishop of the Eternal City, Celestine has sent his deacon to be the first Bishop of Ireland. You are in the presence of Palladius," the young priest declared with a hand gesture to the smug man.

Palladius was about the same height as Germanus, but had no facial hair. His hair was as gray as Germanus', though he looked younger. He held his hands up, leery of touching anything that would soil him or his clothing. He glanced around as if expecting more. What was this man going to do in Ireland? Germanus' manner made sense now. Major affairs were at work. Germanus' silence showed that he was subservient to this deacon. Ironically, the deacon and his entourage's manner appeared like the Pelagian crowd Germanus confronted two years ago in London.

"Where is this Lord Ambrosius?" Palladius called out. "Why has he sent a herdsman and a young cohort to greet someone such as I."

I remained tight-lipped. Ambrosius looked at me in disbelief.

"Your eminence," Bishop Germanus dryly said. "This is Lord Ambrosius."

"Oh, I see," Palladius replied. "My apologies are forthcoming regarding your apparent poverty. I meant no offense."

"Of course," Ambrosius remarked as he reached out to shake the deacon's hand. The stranger simply nodded his head.

"It is good to meet you," Palladius added with a glassy smile.

"Likewise," Ambrosius added. "When were you wanting to sail to your new diocese? All preparations have been made."

"That is splendid. The sooner the pagan temples are brought down, the sooner I can return triumphantly to Rome as God has intended," Palladius stated in a lofty tone. "I shall convert these pagans immediately."

"It's good to have a plan," I replied.

"Yes," he continued as he walked beyond us. "We shall sail to the island and lay claim to the land Niall granted the Church. Years ago, within the treaty between Niall and Stilicho, the Roman Church had given a substantial gift to the Irish lord while he was alive. In return, Niall donated land so a Christian see could be established in Ireland."

"Where exactly are these lands located?" Ambrosius asked.

Palladius looked at the young man who had introduced the deacon and remarked, "Where did you say it was, Solinus?"

"It's at the north end of the Wicklow Mountains. Though in Leinster, the lord of Connacht holds sway in the region. His name is Nathan. He is said to be a pagan." Solinus stated.

"Such silliness shall soon be snuffed out," the deacon remarked.

"Success shall be through God," Germanus added and then casually meandered away from us. Without drawing attention, I followed.

"Is everything okay? Are the claims by the Church true?" I asked.

"That shall be determined soon enough," Germanus added.

CHAPTER 42

I felt sick as I watched the shores of Ireland grow larger on the horizon. This had nothing to do with the ship. We traveled with a master of the sea, Gillian. Old Man Gillian wasn't much taller than Jonah. He wore a short tunic made from leather that was thoroughly conditioned with lanolin. He belted up a matching pair of leather breeches. His thick bushy gray beard crept up high on his cheeks and his hair hung to his shoulders. With his short neck, his head looked like a melon ball of gray hair sitting on his shoulders from the back. He sported a dudeen, though it wasn't always lit and smoking. Only the captain's ears and around his eyes were dark tan from the sun and sea. His small chubby hands were tanned dark, also. He commanded his ship well. Old Man Gillian was one of the many Irish who had migrated to the western shores of Britain. He had made an honest living through the shipping trade. The Irishman's ship was at least ninety feet long and about fifteen feet wide. It had a shallow draught and a flat bottom. Three light Roman galleys followed us. Each had a crew of thirty oarsmen.

"Lord Merlin, are you all right?" Nepos asked as he drew up next to me. "You look as gray as the overcast sky. Why didn't you stay in Britain with Germanus?"

"I wish I had," I whispered as I looked down and watched the waves repeatedly slap the hull of the boat.

"Why didn't you?" he asked.

"Standard answer," I replied.

"What's that?" Nepos asked.

"The common good. Whatever that may mean anymore," I added.

"I don't understand," Nepos replied.

Switching to the Alan's tongue, I remarked, "Pay no heed to me. My mind is foul. I should've told Ambrosius, from the beginning, that he shouldn't involve himself in the Church's affairs. Any support has been one-sided. I am convinced of that."

"I still don't see your problem with the Church," Nepos remarked. "The Church pays really good."

"You still serve its purpose. Stop doing what they need and then tell me how much support the Church will provide."

"Ah, the whispers of palace intrigue," Euthar loudly joined in as he slapped our backs with his large hands. Standing between us with his arms around our shoulders, he added, "Though I'm Nepos' commanding officer, he goes to you more frequently for advice."

"A man shouldn't be faulted for a good sense of direction," I plainly replied.

Euthar laughed loudly. The entire ship heard him and at the very least the boat directly behind us. He did it purposely. He wanted the attention, and he got it. All eyes glanced in our direction.

"You are unique, Merlin," Euthar uttered. "You speak your thoughts freely with no concern of the context or consequences. Most take greater care with their lives."

"No need to sacrifice one's principles for something that will eventually be stripped away, no matter what is done," I answered.

Nepos looked away as he held back his laughter. He could not hide his smile from me, though. Euthar laughed loudly once more and slapped our backs again.

"It sounds like you three are having too much fun," Ambrosius added in the Alan tongue. Though Ambrosius struggled with some of the words, the three of us understood him. He had even learned some of the Saxon dialect. He handled the British dialects fluently. Living on the northwest end of the island exposed him to the Irish and Picts words.

"Only Euthar seems overjoyed with the present adventure," I replied.

"Oh, that's not true," Euthar replied. "Nepos has been looking forward to this, also. He was truly disappointed when this expedition was put on hold last year because of the siege of Hippo. It seems that the Church can only afford one crisis per year. Well, it didn't help Augustine. The old bastard died during the siege. He picked the wrong Arian to annoy. Gaiseric is not someone to deal with. That Vandal always ends up with the upper hand."

"What does the Church expect to achieve in Ireland?" I asked.

"Who cares? Just as long as we all get paid, right Nepos?" Euthar remarked as he shook Nepos.

"Yes, sir," Nepos replied. "It is good to be paid for the work completed."

"I don't believe this. I have my arms around the walking dead," Euthar called out. "Ambrosius, save me from their clutches."

"Save yourself," I dryly replied. "And, let go of us."

He laughed, shook his head, and stepped back from us. Looking over at Ambrosius, Euthar added, "These two have no sense of humor."

With a light smile, Ambrosius replied, "You're right about Merlinus. I know he thinks he is funny, but he isn't. Nepos is not that bad. He has something funny to say at least once a day. With Merlinus, he's more monthly."

"Hah, monthly like a woman," Euthar shouted.

"It's better that than to fight like one," I replied.

"What are you saying, I fight like a girl?" Euthar roared. His tone shifted from merry to menacing in a single moment. "Watch your tongue. You're not the only one that knows the eastern ways of war. Besides, you got to be twenty years my elder. That makes you an old man so I'll give you one more warning. I've cut down bigger men for lesser reasons."

I remained facing away from him. His hand had dropped down to the hilt of his sword. I heard the clink of his ring against the metal-tipped handle. He wanted this confrontation. He wanted to establish the pecking order. He wanted me to know that I should fear him and therefore respect him, but I felt neither. Slowly, I turned. He stared hard. His manner amused me. I smiled.

"This is not the ideal time or location to come to a better understanding between us. Don't get me wrong, young Euthar, I do see that it is necessary that we settle any differences between us, but for the sake of this mission and the stability of your command, I advise against it at this time. I suggest we resolve our differences on British soil, instead of Irish soil," I finished.

"Come on, Euthar," Ambrosius cut in with a light tone. "Let it go. How do you expect to win an argument with someone who speaks the truth in twenty different tongues?"

"Or twenty different ways to say a lie," Euthar snipped.

"That's better," Ambrosius replied as he wrapped his arm around Euthar's shoulder. "Honestly, what's this mission about? Though Germanus eagerly sought my assistance, he has failed to provide details to this operation, and states that he's unable to go at the last moment."

"Ah, don't concern yourself, my friend," Euthar mumbled. "The papacy seeks more souls, that's all. The one presbyter, Solinus, speaks of the British Church sending missionary men to Ireland. The Romans figure that if the British somehow secure the Irish, the British might be strong enough to secure a toehold in Gaul. It is just empty words, words that only mean a damn to men like Merlin."

"I'm not too certain about that," Ambrosius answered. "So, you and I are here to protect the mission while the bishop converts more people into becoming Christians? Nothing more?"

"There's a little more to it," Euthar remarked.

"Why doesn't that surprise me?" I muttered loudly enough for Euthar to hear and look at me.

"What else is there?" Ambrosius quickly asked.

"There is a large stone ring near Niall's land grant. Palladius wants us to take the pagan stone down. They want to eliminate any source of religious conflict," Euthar remarked.

"Don't you think it will create conflict by destroying their monument," Ambrosius remarked. "I've been told of the significance of this ring. It's said that an Irish man that controls the land that can be seen through the Ring commands the island. I think there will be major trouble if the Irish learn of the Church's plan."

"Now you know why the Church is paying so well," I remarked to Nepos. "You should barter for your soul while you still have one."

Nepos frowned but said nothing as he scratched his head.

We neared the shore but did not dock. Instead, we ran up the coast to the river that wound back inland to Almu. Skillfully, Old Man Gillian navigated through the shallows as the three galleys followed.

"So we will reach Almu by night," I called out to Gillian.

"I suggest we take to the shore soon. Camp for the night. Then at first light, we should sail for Almu," the old man replied as he handled the rudder and continuously eyed the waters and the course of the ship.

"Is it that far to Almu?" I asked as I drew closer and lowered my voice.

"No. That's not the issue," the old man stated. "I don't think we should begin the hardest part of the journey this late in the day. We won't receive a warm welcome here."

"Are you certain of that?" Ambrosius asked as he drew closer, also.

The old man ran his hand through his beard, looked up at the waning sun, and remarked, "Yes, my lord. This is what I advise. Nathan, lord of the Connacht, is a cunning man and shouldn't be taken lightly."

"That is what I've been told repeatedly," Euthar called out. "Where is this Almu? Will we be there soon? We must push on. Palladius will not accept a camp on this barren shore."

Looking at me and then Ambrosius, the old captain remarked, "What is your decision, my lord?"

"Unfortunately, this is not my mission, my friend," Ambrosius remarked. "This operation is being led by Euthar and his men."

"As you wish, my lord," Gillian remarked. "Men, tighten the sail and put the oars in the water."

Glancing at Ambrosius, the old man added, "We will be at the mouth of the river within an hour."

"Good," Euthar answered in his stead.

CHAPTER 43

"You are not welcome here," a young man shouted in a thick accent from the shores of Ireland. I barely understood him. Ambrosius had taught me much about the various Brythonic dialects in the last couple of years in Britain, but I struggled with this Irishman's words. He had brown hair, was beardless, and stood in front of a much taller man with thick red hair and a beard that was parted into two long braids. That man had eyes as sharp as Hengist.

"I speak on behalf of the lord of Connacht. You are ordered to turn your boats around and head back to Britain or wherever you came from." the young man continued.

"I knew this would happen," Gillian whispered.

"Keep going," Euthar ordered.

In a single-file formation, we sailed on the river.

"Gillian, tell your people that Lord Nathan is not in good humor. He does not like the rumors he has heard about your people and the Giant's Ring of Ireland. Either way, turn back and trouble won't ensue. Your god is not welcomed here," remarked the young, beardless Irishman.

"I am not here to trifle over phantoms and spirits," Euthar called out loudly. "I am here to enforce a lawfully drafted contract between the Roman general, Stilicho, and the Irish lord, Niall."

"You're joking, right?" the taller Irish man interjected. "Both of those men have been dead for nearly twenty-five years. And since that time, I've ruled these lands and will continue to govern them."

"We do not seek to dispute that or even to trespass upon your land," I called out calmly. "This is why we sail upon the river, grand lord. We do not want to dishonor you in such a manner."

"Wouldn't a river such as this that runs deep inland naturally fall under the rule of a great leader such as myself?" Lord Nathan questioned.

"Normally," I remarked in an even tone. As Euthar remained tight-lipped, I added, "But not in this case."

"And why is that?" Nathan's young spokesman asked.

"Bishop Palladius holds the land where the headwaters of this river flow from. Right now, we float on the water that came from the land that Lord Niall granted the Church."

Nathan laughed loudly like Euthar, but his laughter had a sincere tone. He was humored by my response. I hoped that was a good thing and would help work past this tense situation.

Looking directly at me as we sailed closer to his position, Lord Nathan spoke, "If you were to have someone other than Old Man Gillian at the helm, I would assume you were a true moron and I would smite you down. This world suffers too much from the follies of fools. This isn't the case, though. So under his guidance, it is possible for your ships to travel only on the water coming directly from the Church's parcel of land. And as such, I shall not overstep my bounds, but do not see this moment of leniency as anything else. My loyal man, Donald, has spoken the truth. You are not welcome here nor is your one Christian god. Step ashore before reaching Almu and you shall find no mercy. You shall feel the entire brunt of my army. Do not test me. You shall not like the results."

"Your words shall be honored. We shall not dock until we reach the shores of Almu," I answered.

"Then pass and be gone," Lord Nathan called out, then turned away and walked from the shore.

Silence consumed us except for the low waves hitting the side of the boats as we rowed inland. The land was barren of people and still lacked any noticeable structures. Evening crept in while the sun sank lower into the island. We continued on.

With night nearly complete, we reached the shores of Almu. Due to the late arrival, we unloaded the ships and set up a temporary camp nearby for the night.

"Today won't be the end of our troubles," Old Man Gillian remarked.

CHAPTER 44

It was just before the next sunrise when Gillian was proven correct. The situation was critical even before I left my tent with my walking stick. Several swords had been drawn already and Ambrosius' sword was one of them. That made me nervous. To no surprise, Euthar stood up front arguing. Ambrosius held Euthar back with his left hand as Ambrosius held his sword in his right at guard. Nepos and Carbo were on the right and left side of Ambrosius. Moving slowly, I walked up to them through the crowd.

Facing my comrades stood three large men and another man behind them. All of them were bigger than any of us, but still none of them were as large as Hengist, or even Nathan. The one standing closest to Ambrosius and Euthar had red hair pulled back in a braid. His patchy beard made him look young. His eyes were stern with anger. It would only take a few more words to push him to blows. To his right, and a couple of steps back stood a man with brown hair cropped off at his shoulders and parted on the right side. He had a thick, shortly-trimmed moustache that ran the length of his upper lip. Back to that man's left and several feet directly behind the red-haired man, a blonde-haired man waited anxiously. His eyes bounced between the front man, Ambrosius, and Euthar. The fourth man had his arms crossed. With no nervous twitches or jerks, this brown-haired man who had his long locks in a loose ponytail simply surveyed the situation.

The three front Irish men had their swords drawn. The fourth sneered as tempers continued to boil. He waited for a reason to unleash his three thugs.

"Load up and leave the same way you came," commanded the red-haired warrior.

"We have a binding contract," Euthar barked.

"Let me handle this, Euthar," I calmly replied.

"Hah, Merlinus, you must be joking or still sleeping. This is where

I earn my keep," Euthar remarked.

"Humor me for a moment, young lord. Let me work through this and possibly resolve a pending issue between you and I all at the same time," I remarked.

Euthar paused as he looked at me oddly. He tried to read me, but I gave him no more.

"This can't be worked out," the fourth man called out. "Angus has given the terms. Leave now or there will be trouble."

"How much trouble?" I asked as I drew to the front. Both Ambrosius and Euthar parted to allow me through. As my comrades stepped back from the Irish men, the three warriors stutter-stepped while glancing back at the fourth. The fourth ran his fingers through his closely trimmed goatee and moustache. He looked puzzled as he stared at me.

"There is always trouble in life. There is sweat and sacrifice in honest labor, but there is suffering and slavery in strife," I replied.

"Spare me your words. They do nothing for me. Besides, it's your friend that started this argument," the fourth remarked. "Leave or Angus, Colin, and Banning will show you what trouble is."

"So, if they give me no trouble," I started as I took a closer stance between Angus and the brown-haired man, Colin, "does that mean our troubles would be over?"

The fourth paused and then added, "For now, maybe."

"I see," I replied. "I knew we could work through this. Now, no one has to leave."

"Enough," commanded the fourth. "Take him."

Angus moved at me first. Loosely holding the staff, I slid it straight toward his face. With blinding accuracy, the tip of the staff whacked the red-haired man between the eyes. He dropped to his knees with his hands covering his face. Blood streamed through his fingers. With a sweeping arc to my left, I clubbed Colin's sword out of his hand when I cracked his right wrist. Sweeping to the right, I disarmed the third. Banning pressed his intent with a charge and I knocked it out of him as I drew back and jabbed the end of my staff into his belly.

More than thirty people stood around us. A strange silence hung like morning fog, so thick that it was impossible to tell if the sun had breached the horizon. The fourth Irish man stared at me with a stunned and worried look on his face. Each eye was the size of a *solidus*. He was unsure if I was going to come after him. I knew this from the shifting of his feet as if he was ready to run or cower.

I stared into his eyes and asked, "Will we have any more trouble?"

Too scared to speak, he slowly shook his head no.

"Good," I answered. Looking back at Euthar, I asked, "And have we resolved the issues between us?"

Thoroughly impressed, Euthar had a wide smirk on his face. Without a word, he nodded his head.

"Good," I added, with a little smile. As I turned completely from the four Irish men, the crowd erupted into conversation. Nepos and Ambrosius drew in closer as the others did.

"That was incredible," Carbo remarked as he slapped my back. I kept walking to bust free of the crowd. People trailed behind me.

"Ambrosius, we need to keep this moving," I remarked back to him at a discreet level.

"Right. That man, Galloway, the one you spared, will gather more men. I guarantee that," Ambrosius replied. As he walked up along side of me, Ambrosius glanced around as if looking for someone.

"Where's Gillian?" I asked.

"I don't know. That's who I was looking for," Ambrosius remarked as he continued to scan the crowd.

"He's looking for a guide," Nepos added.

"Good," I replied. "Everyone is seeing this for what it is."

"Where is Palladius and his entourage?" Ambrosius asked. Instantly, we all stopped and scanned the crowd as we stood forty feet from where the altercation occurred.

"I don't see any of them. I haven't even seen little Agricola," Nepos replied.

"Nor I," Euthar and Ambrosius said in unison. I chuckled as the two of them mirrored each others' words as they did their appearances. I hadn't thought about it for quite some time, but with them side by side it seemed hauntingly apparent that they might be twins.

Not allowing myself to be distracted, I asked, "Are they still sleeping? Has anyone seen them leave their tents yet?"

Ambrosius and Nepos smiled and shook their heads no. As if on cue, Solinus came out of the tent a few moments later.

"Euthar, go talk with him and express the urgency of the situation.

Let him know that we need to go," Ambrosius declared. "Nepos, track down Old Man Gillian so he can get us out of here."

"Yes, sir," they both answered.

CHAPTER 45

After much arguing with Palladius, most of us rode out of Almu on horses nearly two hours later.

Riding at a slow pace next to me, Nepos asked, "Do you think there will be more trouble?"

"Yes, there will be more," Ambrosius replied as his eyes continued to scan the surroundings.

"Hah," Nepos remarked. "Is that why Old Man Gillian didn't ride out with us?"

"Maybe," Ambrosius smiled. "No, Old Man Gillian took the ship farther upstream."

"Don't get me wrong. I don't mind riding, but why didn't we all load back up onto the boats?" Nepos questioned.

"Besides it taking longer by boat, Gillian didn't want to take a chance of the ships bottoming out from the weight. He's been told that the water's depth decreases farther upstream." Ambrosius added.

"So why are Palladius and his entourage on the boats?" he remarked.

"Holy shit isn't that heavy," Ambrosius replied with a smile.

Nepos and I laughed.

Looking forward as we slowly rode up into the Wicklow Mountains, I spotted a column of riders approaching at a steady gallop.

"I wonder what they want," Nepos remarked.

"I doubt that they are coming to welcome us," Ambrosius remarked.

As he spoke, they broke their column formation and fanned out in a ten-men line and they were at least two horses deep. The riders whipped their mounts into a hell-bent gallop.

"Take action, men," Ambrosius called out.

All unsheathed their swords.

"Split and sweep out wide to clip their wings," Ambrosius added to his order. "Merlinus and I are the center riders."

I swung to the right while his group went to the left. The Irish didn't expect our maneuver and could not adjust to its sudden execution. I clubbed two riders clear from their horses. Their horses scattered in opposite directions. My comrades were even more deadly with their swords. In the first charge, we wiped out over half of their riders. Carbo and Euthar were cut. However, both continued to fight. Their rage numbed their minds to the pain. Hopefully, that would last the length of the battle.

Bodies littered the open field that laid across the rising foot hills. One of the riders I had hit was still alive, but his legs seemed broken. At that moment, I wondered if my form of attack was less humane than the others, for this man would linger in a miserable, crippled life while his cohorts maintained their dignity in death. The man struggled to drag himself clear of the path of the battle as we came charging back with a second run. Galloway rode at the opposite side of the crippled Irish man.

"Swing left, then hook back hard right," I loudly commanded in the Alan's tongue. Our horses veered hard into Galloway's side. Somehow, he avoided being beheaded, but his upper arm bled. The other riders weren't as lucky. We were not finished, though. Hooking immediately, we came up on the back side of the right flank of their cavalry. We weeded out several more of the Irish. As we did, the rest scattered in all directions, except for the direction of the Giant's Ring.

"Is everyone all right? Do we need to remain here any longer?" I called out.

"I'll survive," Carbo called out.

"Damn it," Euthar barked as he looked down at his arm. "I'm bleeding like a stuck pig. I need to at least wrap this damn thing."

I rode up next to him to take a closer look. Blood flowed hard from his left arm. The long deep slice went from the center of his biceps to the side.

"Can you move your fingers?" I asked.

He did with no problem.

"Amazing, I would have thought you would have lost movement. That needs to be stitched up. Don't move your arm," I added.

"How do you expect me to get down?" Euthar remarked.

"Nepos and Ambrosius, help him," I commanded.

I worked quickly. Going into my saddle bags, I pulled out a needle and a long thread of catgut. Euthar endured the pain well as I ran it through his flesh numerous times. He gritted his teeth, but he didn't jerk from the stitches. Although he needed many more, I stopped after running a wide stitch pattern that cut off the flowing blood.

"That should suffice. We need to keep moving," I remarked.

Euthar nodded his head in agreement. After helping him back onto his horse, Ambrosius and I mounted up and we rode up higher into the Wicklow Mountains. The river drew closer on our left as we approached from the west. For the first time, I saw the Giant's Ring. It looked like a stone wheel with no spokes standing on its side, ready to roll downhill. There was a stone jam in front of it and behind it, as if to keep it from going down the mountain. As I looked at it, I wanted no part in tearing it down, but I already knew I would. So I tried to think of a way to protect it or somehow preserve it.

"There it is," Ambrosius called out.

"We've gone through these scrapes for that?" Carbo barked. "What kind of weak preacher is this Palladius that he fears a stone ring? No wonder Bishop Germanus stayed in Britain."

"Hah, it makes you wonder," Ambrosius remarked.

As we remained there waiting, I remarked, "Do we really need to take it down?"

"Of course," some man called out.

We all turned to see the bishops, their entourage, Gillian, and his men approaching.

"I will not preach the word of God within sight of such a pagan eyesore," Palladius called out as he rode up on a white horse.

"How can you be certain that this is a pagan monolith?" I asked.

"If you are so fond of it, take it back to Britain when you leave. You've done what you have been hired to do, once that God forsaken ring is out of my sight," Palladius remarked as he rode up closer.

"Good. Then, I will take it with us when we leave," I declared.

Everyone laughed except Old Man Gillian and Nepos.

"Come on, Merlinus," Ambrosius remarked. "Have you lost your mind? How do you figure to take it anywhere?"

"Very carefully," I added.

"Impossible," several people said.

"Only to those that think it," I replied. "Watch a dreamer at work."

Quickly, I organized the manpower and directed it into the various tasks. Long straight trees were chopped and rolled down the hill, and then bound together as a raft. Four of them were constructed. Extremely long ropes were ran through the Ring and fastened to the trees standing on both sides of the path, which headed down to the river. All the while, men dug a shallow trench as wide as the stone. They ran it down the mountain. Soon, the necessary preparations were complete. I walked up to the Giant's Ring with a large mallet. All eyes were upon me.

"So who's honor is it? Who wants to be considered the conqueror of Ireland by taking possession of the Giant's Ring?" I called out.

"Euthar, it is his honor," Ambrosius declared.

"Here you go, Euthar. Slam out the stone wedge and the ropes and trench will do the rest," I finished. "Be careful. Don't tear your stitches."

Euthar whacked it a few times. After the third hit from the war mallet, a crack split through the rock and chips flew as the Ring rolled over the broken wedge and down the hill. The long ropes allowed it to roll only so far while the shallow ditch guided it on its way. The trees bowed from the weight of the Ring. As the taut ropes were continuously loosened and retied, the Ring rolled farther and farther down to the river. Before nightfall on the second day in Ireland, the Giant's Ring lay safely on a raft of logs, ready to be towed to Britain.

It was well into the night when the ships reached the open sea. The sky was bright even with no moon. Like countless grains of glowing sand, the stars illuminated our way. I stood at the bow of the boat. Being in the lead ship, nothing obstructed my view. Britain appeared as a black mass that grew on the horizon. The colors transgressed from black to blue. Sky blue had been replaced with the deepest royal blue. I fed on the raw beauty and felt exhilarated by the view and the feat we had accomplished.

"Nights like this one convinced me that I wanted to be a sailor," Old Man Gillian called out lightly.

I turned. He was a short distance from me. Preoccupied, I hadn't heard him walk up the center planks that ran the length of the boat.

"Hello, sir," I replied. "Grand night. Much better than the time I came to Britain two years ago. I thought the ship would surely sink."

After a light laugh and a quick intake of breath, he exhaled from his dudeen. A plume of smoke filled the air. As he pulled the short-stem clay pipe from his mouth, the captain remarked, "I've had a few of those trips myself. You never get use to them, lad. You just got to ride them out."

He fell silent, but steadily hit his dudeen. Smoke curled up from it and streamed out of his mouth in giant clouds that swirled then faded in the breeze. As we stood there in silence, I suddenly felt silly and a little embarrassed that I had this old sea captain towing a huge stone ring back to Britain.

I laughed lightly. "Thanks."

"Why do you say that, young man? I don't understand. What do you mean?" he added.

"I appreciate your towing the Giant's Ring back to Britain," I replied and then added, "I'm not too sure what I'll do with it once we get there."

The old man laughed and added, "I'm sure you will think of something. You always do. I must admit that I'm quite amazed by your various talents. At first, I thought the Giant's Ring couldn't be moved, but then you did it. I've never seen anything like this done and probably won't even hear of such a thing again. You give people the feeling of being part of something grander than themselves. Besides, the astonished look on that pompous priest's face made it worth the trouble. I just hope the rafts hold together."

"It would be a shame to lose it now," I added.

"I agree. It is a true tragedy that the stone had to be removed, but what you have done so far has preserved it. I hope you keep the circle unbroken," the captain finished. Turning toward the stern of the ship, he added, "Farewell, young man."

"As you, sir. As do you," I added.

We had the Giant's Ring towed to Winchester and hauled it by water as far as we could. It drew the curiosity of all who saw it. The crew and passengers were in good spirits and good health as we docked in Winchester.

"So what now? I've done all I can for you, lad," Old Man Gillian remarked with a toothless smile. "It's yours, now. Good luck, because I haven't a clue what you can do with it. You have any ideas yet?"

"I'm thinking we can still use the logs. We'll take long ropes, lasso the logs, and tie them to several teams of oxen and roll the Ring ashore. Hopefully, we can keep the logs together while we move the stone on the land."

"So once we finally get it to Winchester, what do you want me to do with it then?" I don't really want to keep it. There's nothing I can do with it," Euthar said while standing by Gillian and me.

At that moment, I saw no real use for it. Still, I felt proud that the ring remained intact. *No cracks. A circle of grand tradition remained unbroken. United.*

Then, a vision rolled over me like a warm wave from some southern sea. It was the future, a future where a hundred noblemen sat at this table in peace and celebration.

"Give it to Ambrosius and he can make it the council table," I remarked.

"What was that?" the three of them asked.

"Whenever you call a council meeting in Winchester have the councilmen gather around it. And at this round table, all men are equal. There is no head of this table. For the High Commander of the Council is still only one voice at this table of many," I remarked.

"Yes," Ambrosius remarked. "I see it. I like it. What do you think, Euthar? With your help, it will be so."

"Have it. It's yours. Just as long as I still have my claim to Ireland," Euthar added.

"Of course," Ambrosius answered.

With a bright smile, Euthar added, "Then, there's no problem with me."

Glancing over at Gillian as he drew on his dudeen, I asked, "So what do you think, Captain?"

He smiled brightly, nodded, and added, "I like it. I knew you would think of something. Now, we just have to drag it to Winchester and we will be set.

"Yep," I added. "Just like that."

All four of us laughed.

CHAPTER 46

"What's next, Merlinus," Ambrosius asked a year later. We were living temporarily in Winchester.

"What do you mean?" I replied.

"What do I do now? I have defeated or subdued nearly every known enemy. Only Paschent and Ceretic remain. They haven't been heard from in quite some time," Ambrosius remarked.

"It has been said that they withdrew to Gaul," I replied.

"Right," he replied. "Are they stirring up trouble?"

"It must be assumed that they are," I answered.

"So, what should I do, then?" Ambrosius asked once more.

"Remain High Commander and live your life," I replied.

"What do you mean?" He asked.

"Lead by example," I added.

His eyes narrowed at my terse advice.

"These are troubled times that we live in, my young lord. At this point, there is no safer place than Britain. You and the Council have united the lands south of the wall and some north of it. Euthar's campaign in Ireland served two good purposes. By escorting Bishop Palladius on behalf of the Bishop of Rome and dismantling the Giant's Ring, you gained imperial favor and helped secure the western shores. Hopefully, you can remain in the good graces of the papacy and not get drawn into future Church affairs."

Pausing, I turned and glanced at him. He turned to me, wondering why I had paused.

"The Roman general, Boniface, has been recalled back from Africa. Soon, he and Aëtius shall battle for supremacy while the Empire suffers. The Vandals have free reign in Africa. Carthage will be sacked and Rome shall starve. This island has little concern with this. You're the reason for that. You're the High Commander of the Council's army; you personally observe and uphold the Council's laws. With imperial generals killing imperial generals to secure their position with Empress Placidia, Rome seems severely flawed in comparison.

"If what you see on the island is what you want, then take steps to maintain it. For the next eight seasons, maintain a strong mobile army. Continue the repairs and modifications to the Saxon forts on the eastern shores that you have begun. This will help set your mind at ease regarding Paschent and Ceretic. Truly, the destiny of Britain rests in your hands."

He continued to look at me with a solemn look on his face. He had a familiar look, the loss of innocence. He was just a young man with the weight of the Giant's Ring on his shoulders. Though he would disagree, there wasn't a person I would rather have had in his position. He had matured so quickly since we had met a few years ago at my villa. Ambrosius had maintained his principles and had become a true Roman gentleman.

"It can't be that easy," he remarked.

"It isn't," I replied. "It's always easier said than done. Everything takes time and effort, and usually takes more than you expect for, either. But you have many factors in place already."

"Was I not too young to be elected High Commander?" he asked.

"That's one of the things you have in your favor," I replied. "Many will not confront you directly. Your diplomacy will be tested to the limit."

"How do you figure this?" he asked.

"With your youth, some will try to manipulate you. They will figure you're inexperienced, while others simply will not want to test your youthful vigor," I finished.

Accepting my logic, he nodded. He then shook his head and remarked, "Never did I expect to go so far."

I laughed, knowing how he legitimately deserved much more.

"Why do you laugh?" he asked.

"Because you deserve so much more," I replied.

"I don't want any more," he quickly replied. "I'm not even sure I want what I already have."

"Why is that?" I asked.

"I no longer have the freedom of choice. It's no longer about my life, my dreams. I must consider the welfare of people I've never met," he remarked.

"You don't want to remain as High Commander?" I asked.

"I really don't know," he answered. "Everything has been happening so fast. All that I have done is react to everything that has happened. There's been no time to think things through completely."

"Well, what you've done so far as High Commander has been good," I reassured him.

"Well, in these moments of leisure, I have more time to stew in self-doubt," he replied.

"You shouldn't," I replied. "To be honest I cannot provide an instance when I truly disagreed with your decisions. Young Ambrose, you are not alone in feeling overwhelmed by leadership. The Theban historian, Olympiodorus, noted that Constantius regretted the emperorship he held for only seven months. And that was over ten years ago."

"Yes, but that's the weight of the Roman Empire," Ambrosius replied.

"Please do not take this the wrong way. I do not mean to be pretentious when I say that I have endured many battles. The point of declaring this is to give weight to my words."

"How many leaders have you advised?" he asked.

"On which continent?" I joked, but as I did the visions of death on the battlefields soured my smile and sank like lead in my stomach. Shaking my head, I added, "After these battles in Britain with you, I have fought against more races of people than the great Alexander of Macedonia. From the northwestern seas to the grand eastern ocean, I have killed or facilitated the defeat of thousands of men. I am not proud of this. It just seems to be the only good talent that I have retained through the years. I can speak enough languages that I can survive in any large city from here to the islands of Asia.

"I have known many evil men. There were only a few good ones and one of them is you. I tell you these things to gain nothing. I am not with you for that. I have already lived like a prince and do not wish to remain that way. Blood money leaves a bitter taste in my mouth. I no longer have the stomach for it. I should've retired to Aureliani long ago."

"So, why are you here?" he asked.

"*Romanitas*," I replied.

"What?" he questioned. "The Roman way of life?"

"I interpret it more as its civilization or civil mentality. Though you may formally know little of it, you innately revere it. Your actions have maintained its good repair on the island. They will remember your noble feats for years to come.

"Paulus Orosius from Gallaecia said your father wanted to restore the glory of Rome. Your father was assassinated before his Gothic vigor could do that. You are the son of the World-Restorer. I hope to witness its glorious return. A Gothic phoenix rising from the Roman ashes of anarchy. You're a true Roman even though you were born after the sacking of Rome. Resurrect *Romanitas*."

"So shall I rule as an emperor in Rome?" he asked.

"No," I replied. "Rule as you do, through the Council. Roman imperialism shall fail. It's just a matter of time. Any slave-based society does. It will occur most likely in either in Armorica or in Hispania, on the fringes of the Empire far from Rome's militant hand."

"Have you heard dissent on the island?" he inquired.

"Only what has washed ashore," I replied. "These words of revolt have traveled here on the trade ships as it seems to be the habit of any plague, whether flesh or spirit. People here do not want unrest. The raids and revolts still rage within their dreams. They don't want the siege of Hippo or the hordes of Huns. You have shown them new respect based on old principles."

"Isn't the Council the same as the Roman Senate?" he questioned.

"Maybe the Senate from the Old Republic, but surely not the present-day one. Its positions aren't earned by merits. Its honors are sold to the highest bidder.

"Don't worry. You will do fine, but you should think possibly of marrying one of your noblemen's daughters."

"There once was a girl I cared deeply for. I don't even know if she's alive. I had met her before Mother and I fled the island. Her name was Priscilla. Since my return, I've been unable to find her," he finished.

"Priscilla of Gwent?" I replied.

"Yes," he said with a vexed look on his face and then added, "How do you know her?"

"I only know of her," I replied. "But, I do know where she is."

"Huh? How's that?" Ambrosius sputtered.

"I spoke with her grandfather, Honorius of Gwent. Just," I paused as I thought of how long ago I spoke with him last. Then, I whispered, "My god."

"What's wrong?" Ambrosius asked.

"It's been three years since I've been home. It was the night Vortimer became the High Commander of the Council. It was the night we caught up with Cai in London," I stated.

"Right, I remember," Ambrosius replied. "But, where's Priscilla, right now?"

"It's just so crazy how fast the years have gone by. The first year was the Saxon Revolt, the second was the parading of the Council's army through the provinces," I remarked.

"You said that was a great idea," he remarked defensively.

"I did and I still stand by it. You have given presence to a name, authority to words. It has give the people of Britain solidarity," I remarked.

"*Romanitas*," he added.

"Right," I agreed. "It has taken more time than I had thought it would. The campaign across the Irish Sea is what complicated matters."

"You were just saying how it was a good thing. That's another thing you backed," Ambrosius added with a smirk.

"It still has complicated things," I added as I shook my head. "There is too much politics being played out between the Roman and British churches. They are polar opposites on the issues of spiritualism. A slave and born with sin or free to willfully serve, these are your choices."

"How about this?" Ambrosius remarked. "Why don't you just tell me what Priscilla's grandfather told you?"

"Well, he really didn't tell me anything about her. It was more of a request for her," I stated.

He closed his eyes and shook his head. He wasn't humored by my responses.

"Okay, okay. I'll stop," I added with a laugh. "The last time I knew, Priscilla was staying at the villa with Ahès."

"What? When?" he anxiously asked.

"Like I said, I spoke with Honorius about three years ago. At the time, he asked if Priscilla could stay at the villa with Ahès for a while. He worried for her safety. I don't know for certain, but I believe that she is still there," I answered.

"Really?" he questioned.

"Yes," I confirmed.

"Then, why didn't I see her when I returned to Aureliani to gather an army to fight Grallon and his Saxons?" he asked.

"My first guess would be that you two might have passed each other in transit," I replied. "Like what happen with Cai and us."

"I can't believe that's she's in Aureliani," he sputtered.

"What's wrong with that?" I asked. "She must be safe or we would have heard something."

"She's there and I'm here," Ambrosius replied.

"There's nothing saying you can't return to Aureliani," I replied.

"Really?" he remarked as if thinking it was simply out of the question.

"Yes, really," I replied. "you are not physically bound to Britain."

"What about my responsibilities? Won't I be missed?" Ambrosius replied.

"Hah," I joked. "Euthar could take your place and you could go back to Gaul and bring Priscilla and your family back to Britain and no one would know the difference."

"Or I could just let Euthar be High Commander," Ambrosius said as he turned to me with a solemn look on his face.

"No," I barked. "You can't give that title away. It is a position gained through the Council. Besides, you are the perfect commander. Educated, powerful, merciful. You are the one needed at the helm."

"What does it matter?" Ambrosius questioned. "People will think Euthar is me. You, yourself, say that Euthar and I could pass as twins."

"Only on the outside," I added. "Send out word that you will have the Council here in Winchester on Whitsun. Have a grand party to celebrate your leadership and commemorate your victory over Grallon. Afterwards, travel to Gaul so you can marry Priscilla."

"I will," Ambrosius answered.

CHAPTER 47

Dusk stood nearly complete when I saw a rider galloping down the roadway to the villa near Winchester. The news could not be good by the way the young man was riding. I walked outside to greet him. As I made my way to the front entrance, I saw Ambrosius.

"A rider approaches," I remarked.

Saying nothing, he walked outside with me. As we walked down the long portico, the rider dismounted.

"Greetings," he called out. "I have an urgent message for Lord Ambrose."

"I am him," Ambrosius replied.

The young rider pulled a sealed letter from a saddle bag. Walking toward us, he held the letter out for Ambrosius. He broke it open and began to read it. A worried look formed on his face.

"What's wrong?" I asked.

"The Irish have landed in Demetia and marched inland, plundering as they go," he declared.

"Who did the letter come from?" I asked.

"Lord Eldol. He asks for me to send troops." Ambrosius stated.

"Will you?" the rider asked.

"Yes," Ambrosius replied. "Before carrying my response back, stay for dinner. It's nearly finished."

"I cannot. I must return with your answer as soon as possible," the young man replied.

"It is because of this that you must stay," Ambrosius remarked. "Merlinus must have some time to draft the letters that you will deliver to the towns as you ride back. This way men can be organized more effectively. As I approach the various towns, the men will be ready to ride."

"I see your point," the young man replied.

"I will give you a fresh horse to travel with. Your mount appears to be completely spent. I will provide you with fresh horses at each stop you make. This way you will travel as fast as you can ride."

"I would rather stay with my mount. It is a good horse and I really would rather not part with it," the rider said.

"I see that it's a good horse and that's why I am hoping you will accept what I offer. I fear that you may ride her lame.

"Shortly, after I have marched to Lord Eldol with as many men as I can muster, you will have your mount back in pristine form. I shall personally deliver the mare to you," Ambrosius replied.

"How could I refuse such an honorable man?" the rider remarked. "I accept."

"Good," Ambrosius remarked. "You will stop at the first crossroad on the way. You will deliver three letters to Flaccus, the officer of the way station. One will go northeast to Silchester and the other two will go southwest to Old Sarum on the low road and the high road to Exeter. This way Gorlois is notified of the situation. Simply continue northwest to Cirencester. There, give the letter to Marcellus; he is a high officer in the area."

"I know who Marcellus is. I have delivered other correspondence to him. He already knows of the situation," the young man replied.

"Good," Ambrosius added with a small smile. "Rest for now. Enjoy the refreshments that this villa has to offer."

"I could definitely use something to drink," the young man replied.

As he motioned for the rider to go down the walkway, Ambrosius glanced at me.

"I'll take care of the letters," I answered with a nod.

"Thank you," Ambrosius added. "Also, summon Euthar."

"It shall be done," I replied.

CHAPTER 48

Before the expected arrival of Euthar, another rider approached from the south. Though not even noon, the villa buzzed with activity. Calming his mount to a halt, he scanned the hordes of people busily moving about him and his horse. The young man struggled with his bearings. Ambrosius and I walked in his direction to greet the young horseman.

The rider had a familiar face. I couldn't place his name, but I had met him a few times before. He worked for Decentius; I believed he was one of his sons, but not his eldest. The teen wore a long tan tunic. A black tassel drew in the garment around his narrow waist. His light brown hair matched his eyes. He wasn't big but handled the horse well.

"Lord Ambrose," the young man called out when he spotted us approaching. He dismounted from his horse and jogged toward us.

"Lord Ambrose," he added. "Forgive me, my lord, for I bring you ill news."

"Worry not, young Julius," Ambrosius remarked. "I would never feel ill of you."

"You haven't heard it yet," the boy added as his head lowered. "It's news from Gaul."

As Julius' words reached me, my heart sank.

"What could be so pressing there?" Ambrosius joked.

"It's news from Lord Merlin's villa," Julius replied as he looked straight at me.

The color drained from Ambrosius' face. He looked as ill as I felt. *Someone had died. Who was it?*

"Your mother, Ahès, is severely ill," Julius stated. "They do not think that she will live."

"What about my mother?" I asked.

"I'm sorry," the young man added as his eyes dropped from mine. "The letter stated that Lady Alicia had passed on several weeks back."

"Was there anything said about Priscilla?" Ambrosius asked.

"She is the one who wrote the letter," Julius answered.

"Did she say anything else? Do you have the letter?" Ambrosius asked.

"Yes, I did bring the letter. She hoped that you would return to Aureliani for your mother's sake. My lord, you wouldn't leave us, would you? We would be lost without you," Julius finished as he handed the opened letter to Ambrosius.

Without a word, he took the letter. Ambrosius' eyes scanned it. His face held the gray tint in his cheeks. He looked as though he might physically be sick.

"I am truly sorry, my lord," the young man added.

Ambrosius' stare didn't break from the letter. I was unsure if he even heard Julius.

"I . . ." he began, once more.

"It's all right," I replied to Julius. I turned him from Ambrosius and escorted him back toward his horse.

"You've done well, young Julius," I remarked as I patted the young man on his shoulder and added, "let your father, Decentius, know that Lord Ambrosius appreciates the prompt delivery of this letter."

"Yes, sir," Julius replied lowly.

"Does your mount need anything?" I asked and then added, "If so, stop at the stables and have one of the workers handle it for you."

"Yes, sir," he replied as he mounted his horse. "Lord Merlin, should my father have a ship waiting to sail?"

"Yes."

"It shall be ready," Julius replied as he pulled his horse around and galloped off in the direction from which he came.

CHAPTER 49

"Where is Ambrose?" Euthar called out as he dismounted.

"Lord Ambrosius is ill," I replied as I walked up to Euthar.

A grave look captured his face. His concern surprised me.

"Is he going to be all right?" the young lord asked.

"Eventually, he should be fine," I replied.

"Will he be marching out with us?" Euthar asked.

Not knowing the answer, I replied, "Let me escort you to his quarters. He wanted to speak with you as soon as you arrived. There were some issues that he wanted to discuss with you."

"Of course," Euthar remarked as he handed the reins of his black horse to Ulfin who had ridden up with him. The rest of his men stayed a short distance outside the villa's walls.

"Ulfin, take command of my horse while I meet with Ambrose," Euthar remarked.

"Yes, my lord," the young man answered as he took hold of the horse's reins and led the horse outside the villa's walls.

"Why doesn't he stay in the palace at London or Cirencester? That's where the High Commander of Britain should reside. He lives too humbly," Euthar declared as I guide him to Ambrosius' chambers.

"These are his lands," I remarked. "The Council gave these lands at no charge. Ambrosius doesn't have the wealth to acquire residence in London or Cirencester. Eventually, he will build a palace. What do you want him to do? Increase taxes to do it sooner?"

"He could," Euthar declared.

"He doesn't want to," I stated. "Won't others follow his example?"

"To a certain extent," Euthar added. "Men of high standing follow men that convey the most power."

"So why do you follow him?" I asked.

"Because I am a noble man," he replied.

"To a certain extent," I answered and stopped.

As he stopped, he looked at me with an odd expression as if unsure how to take my statement.

Before he could say another word, I remarked, "We are here."

He laughed as I swung open the thick wooden door and walked in. Ambrosius sat by a table while a young noble girl, Sevira, read to him. The teenage girl had black hair that hung like a silk curtain. She was a pretty girl with a chalky complexion and wore a long white tunic with gold trim at the collar and bottom seam.

"You are a true wizard of words. A Cicero for our time," Euthar remarked with a wide, gregarious smile.

"What sickens you?" Euthar called out in a loud, thick tone as he saw Ambrosius' depressed state.

Remaining silent, Sevira stood up and drifted away from the table. Ambrosius gazed out the window and turned away from it. His face hung low. Dark sacks of ash sagged under his eyes.

"Ah, Euthar, you brighten my day," Ambrosius called out.

"Why does your wizard make you suffer?" Euthar barked as he gave me a light jab with his elbow. "If he didn't speak twenty languages or couldn't twirl his walking stick, Merlinus wouldn't be worth a damn."

Holding Priscilla's letter once more, Ambrosius shook it as if it had leeched upon his hand. He then added, "My heart fails me. Only a cold, callous man is shielded from what afflicts me. The woman that raised me as if I was her own son may soon die. The only girl I have ever loved suffers from the same sickness."

"Ah, I can only imagine your pain," Euthar replied. "I'm cold and callous as Merlinus. Though the son of a king, I'm as alone as an orphan. It's been many moons since I saw Father. I am detached from his world."

"Maybe a king should be aloft and unbiased," Ambrosius added.

"To a certain extent," I quickly added.

"Is that all you say," Euthar chuckled.

"Do I need to say more? Do I need to say that a king must have some type of connection with whom he governs? He must treat them well or there shall always loom civil chaos," I stated. "Then, he is ruling a prison, not a kingdom."

Ambrosius nodded his head in agreement.

"So where do things stand with Lord Eldol? How many men does he really need? How many does he already have?" Euthar asked.

"Honestly, I can only guess how many he really needs," Ambrosius replied. "As many as possible, I would imagine. Paschent has allied some Saxons with the Irish. I imagine the Irish are being led by Galloway. Five hundred men would help to defeat such an alliance."

"How many can you muster up?" Euthar inquired further.

"I should be able to gather a hundred, maybe two," Ambrosius answered. "Word has already been sent to gather in Cirencester and then march to Gloucester."

"Why do you need to go, then?" Euthar asked. "Go to Gaul. Settle your affairs in Aureliani and return reinvigorated and ready to rule with your little queen by your side.

"If you allow me, I shall lead your men into battle and decimate these barbarians once and for all. I should have killed that damn Irishman when we went with that Roman deacon, Palladius."

Amazingly, I watched as color returned to Ambrosius' face. I saw that Euthar had already convinced him. Ambrosius simply struggled with finding a reason to accept Euthar's suggestion.

"I could not rightfully request such service from you, Euthar," Ambrosius replied.

"You didn't. I offered." Euthar replied.

That was enough for Ambrosius.

"That is true," Ambrosius responded. "Besides, in my present condition, I could place our warriors in harm's way with some poor choice. A distracted mind is fatal on a battlefield."

"Then," Euthar added. "I shall lead the men in your name. Merlinus shall march with me to provide his priceless wisdom. We shall be victorious."

"Will the Council follow Euthar?" I asked. "Unfortunately, I have my doubts, especially without some formal notice ahead of time."

"Then we won't tell them," Ambrosius added.

"What?" Euthar and I called out.

"We won't tell them. Merlinus, you are always saying that Euthar and I could easily pass as brothers. Twins, you've said."

"It's not a good idea," I remarked. "Besides, Euthar has a full beard."

"I'll shave it," Euthar said with a wide smile.

"I'll give him my wardrobe if it will help," Ambrosius remarked.

"Right," Euthar replied.

"This is not a good idea," Sevira remarked from the shadows in the back of the room. I had forgotten that she was in the room.

She was a nobleman's daughter, and extremely intelligent, but still only a young girl. She had been babying Ambrosius' every need since Julius delivered the letter. Ambrosius had no clue how she clung quietly by his side, waiting to serve him.

"And who are you, child," Euthar asked.

"Sevira," she answered.

"Well, at this time, Sevira, we don't need a child's opinion," Euthar said sharply.

"I beg to disagree with you," I remarked, "since she is the only one speaking any kind of sense here besides me."

"Oh, come on, Merlinus," Ambrosius remarked. "Don't you think that you are making more out of this than you should."

"No."

"Okay," Euthar remarked. "This is what we will do. I will change my appearance to mirror Ambrosius, but I shall march out as Pendragon. To the ones of any importance, Merlin and I will explain the situation to them. But for the army, we will let them assume I am Ambrosius."

"This is something Grallon would try to pull," Sevira remarked. Euthar gave her another sharp stare.

"I doubt that Eldol or Gorlois will be fooled by this," I added.

"Right," Euthar answered. "I figured we could make Eldol understand the situation. I'll take the letter. Besides, he's the only one we'd have trouble with. Gorlois will accept whatever we tell him."

"This could work," Ambrosius remarked.

Sevira shook her head in disagreement.

"Sevira's right," I added. "Grallon would do something like this."

"It is, isn't it?" Ambrosius remarked.

"It is," I reaffirmed.

"I can't do this," Ambrosius stated. "Euthar, I'll just have you lead my men until I return with Priscilla."

"Okay," Euthar replied. "Merlinus, you must stay to ensure my command is not questioned."

"There are a few more things you need to settle before you go," I stated. "There are a couple of sees that are vacant, Ambrosius.

The town folk of York and the City of Legions seek your approval in their choice in bishops."

"Do you know of their choices?" Ambrosius asked.

"Yes," I stated. "They have nominated Samson for the bishopric of York and Docco for the City of the Legions. The choices seem to be good ones. You met Docco. He came with us to meet Germanus when we escorted Palladius to Ireland. Remember?"

"Right, I remember him," Ambrosius replied. "Okay, send my approval. Anything else?"

"What about Nepos?" I asked.

"What about him?" Ambrosius and Euthar said in unison. Smiling, I shook my head.

Looking at Euthar, I remarked, "Nepos is a good man and has faithfully served you numerous years now. He has only voiced the innate desire that everyone has -- the desire to be free. I hope you will either set him free or transfer his servitude to Ambrosius or myself."

Euthar laughed a hearty tone. He smiled brightly and added, "Hell, I thought he was your man, already. If it's up to me, he's free or whatever you see best. He's a good warrior. Not my best but still a good fighter. Anything else? Hell, you know if you take Nepos, you're going to be stuck with Carbo. Are you still sure you want Nepos freed?"

Ambrosius, Euthar, and I laughed. Sevira remained silent.

"That's a tough call," Ambrosius said with a smile. "Is Nepos worth the headache of Carbo?"

"Not hardly," I said.

"Too late," Euthar added. "It's a done deal."

"All right. All right," I stated. "But it might cost you later."

"Fair enough," Euthar finished.

CHAPTER 50

The morning after our meeting in Winchester, Euthar emerged a changed man. He went far to mirror Ambrosius' appearance and hauntingly achieved it. He shaved off his beard and cropped much of his hair. He was Ambrosius. The similarities between Euthar and Ambrosius remained uncanny. Though he did not call himself Ambrosius, Euthar never corrected the many people that mistakenly called him Ambrosius.

Before that morning, Ambrosius sailed for Armorica. Sevira went with him. They rode through the night to make it to Decentius' place where a boat waited for them.

More could be said about what I personally witnessed with Euthar, but that will be done in another tale. For now, let it be sufficient to say that Lord Euthar defeated the foreign armies that had landed on the western shores of Britain. He returned to Winchester victorious and emerged as Pendragon, neither Ambrosius nor Euthar.

As soon as I could excuse my presence, I sailed for Gaul. Once we reached the shores of Gaul, myself, Nepos, and a handful of his men rode for Aureliani. As we traveled, I felt anxiety growing amongst us. Arson had charred much of the fields. Hardship gripped the land. Dangerous looking folks lingered on the roads. They appeared to be brigands. I feared for our safety for the first time in a long time. In accordance, we shifted our travel patterns. We eliminated our open afternoon travel to riding hard in the evening and morning. We moved in the shadows to shroud our presence. We didn't linger anywhere too long.

We arrived at my villa late one night. It had been several weeks since we left Britain. Luckily, there hadn't been any confrontations the entire journey. The gate stood closed, though.

"Do we set up camp for the night?" Nepos asked as he rode his horse up next to mine.

"Yes, that would be best. There's no need to startle the household.

We are here and we are safe. We will set camp a short distance from the wall. That way Ambrosius will notice our presence in the morning," I stated.

"Yes, sir," Nepos remarked. Pulling his horse away, he heeled the mount into a steady walk.

"Men," Nepos called out. "We are setting camp up over there, off the road."

Without hesitation, the men wheeled their horses off the road and dismounted by the small clearing. The camp quickly took shape and a fire was started.

It felt good to be home. This time was even better than when I first met Ambrosius. Several times recently, I had wondered if I would ever see this place again. It still appeared well-kept in the moonlight.

My only regret was not being here before Mother passed. We never did have that Easter celebration. For Ambrosius' sake, I hoped Ahès was well or Ambrosius got to say his last good-byes before she passed. I didn't want him to have the same empty feeling I did.

The others settled in for the night. I stayed up and stared into the fire. Red and yellow flames mingled. I kept them fed as the flames entertained me with their burning song and dance.

Still, sadness filled me. I thought more of Mother. I thought of the time we stood outside the villa when Germanus arrived as he headed for Britain. I remembered holding her, hugging her tight. I towered over her small frame. What would I have said or done differently if I were to know that was the last time I would ever speak with her face-to-face? I felt empty of any real memory of her except saying good-bye. This shamed me and regret churned in my stomach like a hunger that could not be satisfied. We should have stayed for the party she was planning. That was all she talked about; that was all she asked. She was heartbroken when Ambrosius and I left with Germanus shortly thereafter.

I stood up and walked away from the fire. The cool evening air rushed over me. I drew it in deep. It slowed my racing emotions, but did little to take away the pain. Knowing that there wasn't anything I could do, I tried to shake off the chill of regret, gave thanks to God for the moments we did share, and released a heavy sigh of relief knowing that our paths would cross once more in the hereafter.

I wondered if Ahès was even alive. I returned to camp and rolled out my bedding. And then, I whispered a prayer for Ahès.

CHAPTER 51

The next morning I awoke to find Ambrosius standing in the camp. A bright smile sat on his face as he towered over me. He was a completely changed man. There was no gray in his cheeks like the last time I saw him. I had not seen him this happy before now. It wasn't even a half a year since I saw him last. Spiritually, he was a different man.

"So what warrants such a great honor of having an appearance from Merlinus the wise?" Ambrosius called out as he poked at me with the tip of his sword.

Smiling, I replied, "I thought I was returning to my home."

Laughing lightly, he remarked, "Oh really? I was told that the former owner abandoned this villa in search of titles and treasures abroad. Do you have anything to substantiate these wild claims of yours?"

"Only my word," I replied.

"I don't believe that is going to be enough," he replied as he held out his hand for me. Taking hold of my hand, he helped me to my feet. Hugging me tightly, he released me and then patted my shoulders.

"It's really good to see you, sir," he said smiling.

"Not as good as being home," I replied. "I've been waiting for this moment since I left five years ago. God, it's great to be home."

With his arm around my shoulder, Ambrose added, "It sure has taken you a long time to make it."

My loud laughter woke the rest of the men in the camp. Although startled, the men quickly settled down as they saw Ambrosius.

"Lord Ambrose, it is good to see you," Nepos called out joyfully.

"There are no nobles here, only good, hard-working folk," Ambrosius replied with a smile.

Immediately, Ambrosius answered many things with that one comment. He had no intention of returning to Britain. He had forsaken his command and lands for love. I knew it without asking. I knew if I was only to offer him room and board for his services he would accept it if Priscilla remained. A happiness filled his eyes, which I had painfully watched fade away day by day while he was High Commander of Britain. I was glad to see the glow in his eyes had returned, but also sad knowing what was being sacrificed.

Not sensing his intent, Nepos asked, "Lord Ambrose, why haven't you returned to Britain yet? Will you soon?"

Still smiling, Ambrosius simply shook his head no. He had liberated himself from the chains of leadership. It explained much about his current demeanor.

"Your brothers wonder when you will return. The councilmen ask for you. The Council is not the same without your leadership. Sir, why don't you return?" Nepos asked.

"I do not desire it when I have everything I need here. Come inside and I shall show you the true source of my happiness. Let me introduce you to Priscilla, the keeper of my heart. Soon she will be my wife. All of you must stay for the wedding. I insist," Ambrosius commanded.

"Insist all you want, but you are their commander no longer. You just said that," I joked.

I broke his smile for a moment and then he laughed loudly.

"Turning my own words against me, already. Oh hell, there goes the peace," Ambrosius remarked as he slapped my shoulder. "If you're staying then I'm leaving."

Nepos, Carbo, and the others laughed as they followed Ambrosius and me toward the long colonnaded portico. Quickly, people gathered as we walked forward. Some of the faces looked familiar, but many I had never seen before now. An unknown person walked straight toward us. I assumed it was Priscilla from the fact that Ambrosius suddenly picked up his pace, and he raised his arms up to greet her.

As he lightly kissed her cheek, Ambrosius turned to us and said, "This beautiful woman is Priscilla of Gwent."

"Greetings, dear lady," I replied.

"The pleasure to finally meet you is mine. Even though I've never met you, I owe you many thanks. Most of all for reuniting Ambrosius and me," she replied as she kissed me.

She was a tiny, black-haired angel. She hovered near five feet tall. Her black locks hung past her shoulders. A light, thin dress covered her slender curves. Her skin glowed with a deep tan. A soft, gentle brown filled her eyes. Silver hoops through her ear lobes were her only jewelry. A natural, dark rose made her plump lips even more enticing. Her firm small breasts pointed outward in the cool morning air.

"Women like Priscilla bring back the faith in humanity for me," I replied.

"Why do you say that?" Ambrosius asked.

"Because if a beautiful lady as Priscilla can love someone with as many shortcomings as you, then there are still miracles in this world," I stated.

She giggled as the others and I laughed. Ambrosius shook his head and continued to walk toward the entrance.

Their wedding would be a spectacular event.

"Ahès must be ecstatic," I remarked. "Is she still inside planning?"

As if I had suddenly slapped them both, a hurt look swelled upon their faces. Priscilla looked away and Ambrosius stepped up.

"Mother died shortly after we received the letter from Priscilla," he remarked lowly.

"I'm sorry, Ambrosius. I wish you would have had one last chance to speak with her," I remarked.

"Oh, I did. I did," he said with a slight smile, though sadness lingered in his eyes. Shaking his head, though, Ambrosius added, "She didn't last much past my return."

"I hope she didn't suffer too much," I added.

"She wished the best for you and thought the world of you. You do know that, right, Merlinus?" Ambrosius finished as he pulled me away from Priscilla and the others.

"She had a large place in her heart for you," he added lowly.

"There's no need to tell me these things, Ambrosius. I know," I stated.

"I have to," Ambrosius added as he placed his arm on my shoulder. "Mother made me promise her that I would. She knew that you would say that, and I had to promise to say, 'Shut up and listen.'"

I just shook my head, knowing that she truly told him to say that.

"You gave her hope when she had none. You showed what a true friend means and what they are willing to do for one another. Repeatedly, you had supported her and asked for nothing in return. She loved you for that."

"Thanks. That really means a lot. Ahès was a special woman.

It's unfortunate that she will not see you marry Priscilla. She would have been glowing with joy."

Ambrosius smiled and said, "She told me I would be silly if I didn't marry Priscilla. I was already convinced of that."

I reached up and patted him on his back and added, "I am truly happy for you."

"Thanks," Ambrosius finished with a brilliant smile.

CHAPTER 52

Various groups of people arrived at Aureliani for the wedding of Ambrosius and Priscilla. Surprisingly, Bishop Germanus and his retinue were some of the first to appear. His presence noticeably lowered Priscilla's anxiety level. Though she knew that he would show, she had been nervous about something going wrong. Her mood and manner became upbeat upon the bishop's arrival.

The same could not be said about Ambrosius. He waited anxiously for Euthar. Previously, Euthar had sent a letter stating that he would attend, but it now was the day before the wedding and Euthar still hadn't arrived.

Going outside that morning, I saw Ambrosius and Germanus walking toward the closed front gate. I quickly caught up to them before they started up the stairs that led to the top of the perimeter wall.

"Greetings, Merlinus," Germanus called out as I approached. Ambrosius simply nodded his head toward me. Concern held his lips closed.

I nodded at Ambrosius and added, "Hello, Bishop. I'm not interrupting anything, am I?"

"Oh no," Germanus replied as he followed Ambrosius up the steps.

"The bishop is just trying to pacify me. I've been whining to him about Euthar not showing up yet." Ambrosius added.

"Oh, you're making more out of it than what it really is," Bishop Germanus said with a smile.

"It would mean a lot to have Euthar here. You want him to take part in this splendid moment. That's all." Bishop Germanus added.

"There's still time," I added.

"Right," Ambrosius replied sarcastically.

"Never give up hope. That's essential in everything, my son," Germanus added sincerely.

"I know, sir," Ambrosius added. He shook his head and looked out over the wall. The wind picked up and filled the silence between us.

Ambrosius yearned for Euthar's arrival as a brother would. His arrival seemed more important than Cai's. Ambrosius remained tight-lipped and stared into the woods. Within a short distance, they consumed the view of the road to Aureliani. Still, Ambrosius watched the slender trunks of the tall trees swaying in the breeze. It did little to alleviate the anxiety that soured his face.

"Well, if Euthar doesn't show up, you will be able to catch up with him when you go back to Britain," Germanus replied.

"Go back to Britain?" Ambrosius replied as his head jerked towards Germanus. "Who said anything about going back to Britain?"

A surprised look formed on the bishop's face.

"What about your place at the head of the British Council? Are you not still High Commander?" Bishop Germanus added. "When was the last time you were in Britain?"

"I haven't been in Britain for two years," Ambrosius added.

"What? Really?" Germanus questioned.

"Euthar has been acting as High Commander. I have been debating about abdicating my command, permanently," Ambrosius added.

"Amazing. Very few would have given up such martial power," the bishop answered.

"You did when you became a bishop," Ambrose added.

"Not willingly," Germanus responded.

"What?" Ambrosius and I muttered in unison. His answer had surprised both of us.

Germanus smiled and then added, "I was conscripted into becoming the Bishop of Auxerre."

"Really? How did that happen?" Ambrosius asked.

"It's a long story," the bishop added.

"I have time," Ambrosius added with a smile. "It's still early."

Germanus laughed but fell silent. He seemed reluctant to elaborate on it. Ambrosius and I didn't pry.

"It has been years since I have thought of those days. I was a different man, then," the bishop added and then fell silent. He meandered away from us. Ambrosius glanced at him, but then turned back toward the road, once more, looking for Euthar. In the silence, Germanus seemed miles away as he peered off into the distance. Sensing my inquisitive eyes upon him, the bishop glanced at me. I looked away.

"Two years prior to my becoming a bishop, six men portrayed themselves as Roman emperors," Germanus began. "At that time, I was the Duke of Farther Gaul and had been for the last few years. Following the murder of Stilicho and the defection of many military leaders in the area is when I received promotion. Though I had little involvement in martial affairs prior to this, all of that quickly changed. The ever-present barbarian tribes made certain of that. I found myself involved in organizing the local civil defenses. There was no one else doing it. Greed and dissension kept the imperial government in chaos. Verbal allegiances sickened the Empire. And when the circumstances became extreme and Rome failed to provide the protection I continuously requested, I sought to secure ties with the usurper, Jovinus. He had the support of the Burgundians and Alan tribes. With their martial strength, the usurper seized several prime towns in northern Gaul. With a rapid transfer of control, his rise to power seemed secure. It was only momentary, though. The new regime failed to form durable treaties with the other factions. Most important, he failed to obtain peace with your father and his Goths.

Though appearing not to be listening, Ambrosius was now looking at Germanus. He waited for the bishop to continue.

"Why couldn't Jovinus make a pact with him?" Ambrosius asked.

"At least two reasons can be given," Germanus replied. The bishop fell silent once more. It reminded me of how he behaved when he traveled with Palladius to Britain. He was reserved and said very little.

"What happen?" Ambrosius asked as Germanus remained tight-lipped. I shook my head, trying silently to tell Ambrosius not to pry.

"I would," Germanus began but paused as he noticed my gesture. Following a light laugh, he added, "Oh, it's all right, Merlinus. It just hard to put all of the events in order. And as I had said, it has been so long since I really thought about the times before becoming bishop.

"I was not and have not become privy to all of the dealings of Adaulphus, but I do know some things and one was his troubles with a man named Sarus.

"At that time, there was a violent blood feud between them. Many Goths considered Sarus a traitor. He and his brother, Ammius, had attacked Hermanaric, driving a sword into the Gothic king's side. Sarus and his brother argued that they were avenging the brutal death of their sister, Sunilda."

"Hah, that was my grandmother's name," I candidly replied.

"Luckily, she wasn't the sister of Sarus and Ammius. The Gothic woman was drawn and quartered by wild horses," Germanus added as he glanced at us.

"What warranted such treatment of a woman?" Ambrosius asked.

"Supposedly, it was punishment for the treachery of her husband," Germanus replied. "King Hermanaric had the woman executed. The animosity within the Gothic tribes had been festering and, at this point, boiled into a blood feud.

"So years later, when Jovinus the usurper retained Sarus for the Goth's military services, Jovinus secured an enemy in your father. Adaulphus served Emperor Honorius by hunting down Sarus and his men and overwhelming them with his superior numbers. After the death of Sarus, there might have been a chance that Jovinus could have secured his tyranny with your father's help, but Jovinus further complicated matters by elevating his brother, Sebastian, instead of Attalus who your father supported. That's when Jovinus' administration began to fall apart and with it my honorary title of duke.

"Luckily for me, I was one of the few magistrates of Jovinus who didn't lose his head. Still, though, my own staff had turned against me. Left with no other option, I allowed the divine authorities to conscript me into priesthood and make me the Bishop of Auxerre. At first, I had lost everything except my life. Through my family ties and profitable behavior, I gained favorable view from imperial powers in Ravenna. Soon, I was offered a deal to retain my former lands and possessions. All I had to do was facilitate your kidnapping. So, I agreed. If it hadn't been through the grace of God by providing the admirable example of a fourteen-year-old boy, I would be no better than Patroclus of Arles and back living in my sinful ways.

"Can you picture it, Ambrosius? Against the odds, you have this young man put into a position of caring for a newborn and somehow safely transports him across hostile and rugged terrain," Germanus finished as he looked at me with a placid expression.

"I don't believe it," Ambrosius called out.

With a surprised look on his face, the bishop turned to Ambrosius and added, "Why do you think that?"

"No, no. That's not what I was referring to. Sorry, look who's here,"

Ambrosius remarked as he pointed toward the road.

Surprised, I spotted the steady train of trotting horsemen for the first time. They had made it midway down the visible section of the road. The four standard-bearers rode in two pairs in front of the main formation of riders and wagons. The streaming-dragon standard of Euthar ran front with the white boar of Cai riding next to it while the black boar of Eldol flowed behind them and kept company with the black goat of Gorlois. The British nobles had finally arrived in grand fashion. The four leaders rode side by side forming the head of the train.

Seeing Euthar once more, I suddenly wondered if Ambrosius was still standing by my side. It looked like he was now riding toward me with a bright smile on his face. I glanced in the direction of where Ambrosius last stood and found him there still. I turned my glance so I could see them both at the same time. I watched as a bright smile crept over Ambrosius' face. I tried to compare the two to dispel the illusion of them looking alike. Their resemblance was undeniable. Matching dimples pitted their cheeks in exactly the same way. Their hair held the same walnut hue.

As Bishop Germanus stood next to me, he whispered, "Amazing."

With a slight laugh, I added, "It's just the Brits."

Ambrosius laughed and turned toward the stairs.

"Oh, right," Germanus replied. "I was just marveling at how Euthar looks so much like Ambrosius."

"I know, I know," Ambrosius replied in a dry monotone. "We could pass as brothers."

"More like twins," I added as Ambrosius continued down the stairs to the barred gate.

"How is that even possible?" the bishop asked with a glance.

"It's not," Ambrosius shouted back as he lifted the wooden beam that kept the gate closed.

"Logic tells me to agree with you, young Ambrose, but my eyes tell me to reconsider," Germanus remarked.

"Exactly," I added.

Ambrosius pushed open the gate and walked out to the bridge that spanned the deep ditch. He paid us no further heed.

"Thank you, Merlinus," Germanus added.

"For what?" I questioned.

"For this moment," Germanus quickly added. "If you hadn't cared for

Ambrosius when you did so many things would be different. I shudder at the thought of what kind of person I would be. I am thrilled that I do not have to face such a fate. But I would be a shallow man if I did not ask for your forgiveness. I willfully placed you in harm's way and you handled it honorably."

"That was years ago and only for a moment," I added.

"But it saved many lives from a world of hurt," the bishop added. "That's why it's more of a reason to ask you for forgiveness. In truth, it's disgraceful to have waited this long to ask for it."

Suddenly, a heavy rusty anchor sat in my belly. It was all of the angst and bitterness that I had carried for the bishop over the years. I walked toward the steps but found I could not move. The weight of the moment kept my feet cemented still. With words whispered from the past, I heard Ahès say, "See, Germanus has really changed." Unlike the last time, I agreed with her words now.

"Let it trouble you no further," I replied and then started for the steps.

"Thank you, Merlinus" Germanus added and followed my lead.

CHAPTER 53

Later that night after dinner, we stood outside the villa enjoying the evening air. A blazing pyre soared skyward. Its light cast shadows out of the front part of the courtyard as the guests moved about, talking, drinking, and dancing.

Others from Britain had arrived after the group traveling with Cai and Euthar. Priscilla's grandfather, Honorius of Gwent, was one of these late arrivals. Silently, I walked with Bishop Germanus and Priscilla to his covered wagon parked inside and near the perimeter wall.

I entered the wagon, seeing Honorius for the first time in several years. He looked extremely frail. He had ridden in comfort, though. His covered wagon was furnished with a long couch that could easily be used as a bed. Pillows and thick blankets covered it. Priscilla and Germanus sat on a shorter bench that faced Honorius. I knelt inside; too tall to stand upright in the wagon.

"I'm so glad you made it, Grandfather," Priscilla whispered as she leaned closer to him.

"Me, too, my child. Me, too," Honorius remarked. After releasing a heavy sigh, the old man shifted and propped himself on pillows. Looking at me, he added, "I am indebted to you, Lord Merlinus. You have kept my dear, sweet Priscilla safe and in sound spirits. Thank you."

With a smile, I added, "Think nothing of it."

"And, it's good to see you also, Bishop," Honorius added.

"Likewise, my friend. Likewise," Bishop Germanus replied.

Glancing at Priscilla, I interjected, "Sorry, my lord, for not giving her better sense in picking a man, though."

Priscilla smiled and shook her head while the other two laughed lightly.

"She could have done much worse," the old Brit remarked. "She could have married the self-proclaimed Pendragon."

"Oh, Grandfather, Euthar is not that bad," Priscilla remarked.

"He's not," Honorius remarked in a sharp pitch. Suddenly, a coughing fit gripped him. Harshly, he hacked.

"Grandfather, settle down. Don't get yourself worked up over nothing," Priscilla added as she stood up and sat down on the corner of the couch next to him. With her left hand, she slowly rubbed his back while she rested her right hand on his arm.

"Young lady, don't you worry about me. You should be only concerned for your soon-to-be husband. He needs to return to Britain before there is nothing there to return for. Euthar does the name of Ambrosius an injustice. Many are confused by the close resemblance between your fiancé and the self-proclaimed Pendragon. Euthar tarnishes the respect due Ambrosius," Honorius said lowly.

"What do you mean by that, Grandfather," Priscilla questioned. "Is Euthar stirring up trouble?"

"No," the old Brit added. "But, Euthar does little to stop those close to him from wreaking havoc on the countryside. If I didn't know better, I would swear that Grallon had returned to power."

"It can't be that bad, old friend," Germanus added.

"You saw that I wasn't the only noble from Britain to come for the wedding. Eldol came for answers. He does not accept the answers Euthar has been offering. Frankly, my patience wears thin like the rest of the Council. When shall Ambrosius return to take command of the Council's army? We assumed that his absence was merely temporary."

"I don't mean to make light of the situation but are you serious?" Germanus remarked. "I don't believe he has any intentions of returning to Britain."

"Really?" the old Brit asked.

"That is the truth," the bishop remarked and then added as he looked at Priscilla and then at me. "Is it not?"

I remained tight-lipped. Priscilla looked at me and then shrugged her shoulders.

"He never said anything about going back to Britain. Honestly, it seems like any time Britain is brought up, Ambrosius switches the subject," Priscilla added. "Has he said anything to you, Merlinus?"

"When I had first returned home, a couple of months ago, he expressed that he had no intention in returning to Britain to command the Council's army. And earlier today, he conveyed the same sentiment," I answered.

"Why would Euthar continually state that Ambrosius might return at any moment? Hell, that's the only reason I never gave a vote of no-confidence in Euthar's leadership." Honorius remarked.

With a light laugh, I replied, "I think you just answered your own question, sir."

Honorius paused, then slowly nodded his head and added, "You might be right, young lord. By repeatedly stating that Ambrosius was due to return soon, Euthar has been able to maintain his position as High Commander, indefinitely."

"Bishop, do you think Euthar would do such a thing?" Priscilla asked.

"I wouldn't put it past him," Honorius jumped in. Priscilla patted her grandfather's hand and then looked back at Bishop Germanus.

"Unfortunately, I have heard of worst ways of men trying to keep their positions of power," the bishop remarked.

"What do you think, Merlinus?" Priscilla asked.

"I don't know," I replied. "Why don't I just ask?"

"You can't do that," Priscilla exclaimed.

"Why not?" I answered in unison with Germanus and Honorius and then added, "It's not like I have confronted Euthar about it. All I have to do is ask Ambrosius in the presence of the other British nobles."

"Would you do that?" Honorius asked.

"Why not?" I replied.

"I would be indebted to you, once more, if you did," the old noble replied.

"Think nothing of it," I said as I started out of the wagon.

"Merlinus," Priscilla called out as she quickly followed me outside. "What are you going to do?"

"Nothing but talk," I replied with a slight smile.

"Oh, great. That doesn't set my heart at ease. Not at all," Priscilla snipped. "Please, Merlinus, don't make a scene."

I stopped as I heard her soft plead. I saw a scared look in her eyes. Tomorrow was her wedding.

"Please, Merlinus. Everyone has been drinking heavily. I'm afraid nothing will be settled and prides will be bruised."

How could I resist her? I couldn't.

"I'll make a deal with you, young lady," I smiled. "I will not bring up the subject until two nights from tonight, but if it is brought up and freely discussed, I can join in."

She laughed lightly and then added, "Why does it feel like I'm dealing with a devil?"

"Ah, that hurts, Priscilla," I replied.

"Oh, you're not that bad. It just feels like I'm going to regret agreeing with you," she added.

"All right, all right," I added. "Come with me so you can keep me out of trouble."

"Okay," she replied with a bright smile.

Together, we walked back toward the huge pyre in the front courtyard. Ambrosius stood by Euthar as he spoke with the other nobles.

"Finally, Lady Priscilla has arrived," Lord Cai called out. "Maybe, now, we can get a straight answer."

As she looked at me and then back at Cai, she gingerly asked, "To what?"

"When will you and Ambrosius be returning to Britain?" Eldol butted in.

She glanced back at me with a horrified look on her face. I could not help but shake my head.

"Well, I don't really know," she replied. "We really haven't discussed it."

"Well, we're discussing it now," Eldol added. "What's keeping you and Ambrosius here?"

Blank looks appeared on both of their faces. Neither Ambrosius or Priscilla said anything.

"What's the reason to head back to Britain?" I asked.

"He's the High Commander of the Council's army. He is needed on the island. You should know that, Merlinus" Cai added.

"I thought Euthar was handling that," I quickly added before Euthar could say anything.

"That was meant to be only temporary," Vitaelis bluntly remarked. Gorlois was unable to make the wedding. His advisor, Vitaelis, had come instead.

"Why can't it be permanent?" I asked.

"Because the Council never voted on that," Eldol quickly replied. "So, the question remains. When do you think you will be returning to Britain, Ambrosius?"

A concerned look remained on Ambrosius' face as he looked at me. All eyes were upon him as he stood silent. I nodded to him with encouragement. He glanced at Priscilla, and she smiled.

Following a heavy sigh, Ambrosius announced, "I have no intentions on returning to Britain. This can be seen as my final abdication of command."

"You can't make Euthar the High Commander," Eldol remarked.

"I'm not. I leave that up to the Council. If the Council has issues with Euthar's leadership, then the Council should be gathered and the issue should be addressed at that time. British affairs should not be resolved in Gaul. We are here for a wedding."

CHAPTER 54

I wasn't wrong when I predicted that Ambrosius and Priscilla would have a wonderful wedding. Unfortunately, the outside world refused to honor their peace and happiness for long. During the following spring, bad news flooded the villa like a heavy winter thaw.

"Merlinus," Ambrosius began one afternoon. "I've received word that the Romans have finally made peace with Gaiseric and the Vandals."

A cold chill slithered through me as I heard his words.

"What's wrong, Merlinus?" Ambrosius asked. "Is this not good? The Romans can concentrate more on Gaul, now."

"It's only good if you are Gaiseric," I answered. "The Vandals have seized the granary of the Empire. Nothing good can come from this. They control the prime provinces of Africa. Gaiseric is not finished. He will not stop until he has taken Carthage. Not even Rome will be safe from him. I warned you that this would happen when we were in Britain."

"Don't you think Aëtius will establish Rome's presence in Africa, once more?" Ambrosius countered.

"No," I retorted.

"How can you give a simple answer to such a question?" he asked.

"Aëtius has too many enemies and too many dangerous allies," I answered. "He relies too heavily on the Huns. Attila is as ruthless and nearly as cunning as Gaiseric. Aëtius has no real, powerful Roman allies. His wife has made sure of that. This is how I can say that Aëtius will not reconquer Africa. So Gaiseric now securely holds the bread basket of the Empire."

"Won't Emperor Theodosius send another army to Africa to deal with the Vandals?" Ambrosius asked.

"Not while Aspar, the High Commander of the Eastern Army, remains in control. It is said that he has a secret pact with Gaiseric," I replied.

"So many double dealings going on," Ambrosius muttered.

"Unfortunately, that always seems to be the case," I remarked.

"Too bad more do not rule as you did."

"Hah," Ambrosius replied. "You speak as if I had done something special. I only did what I said I would, protect and uphold the Council's laws. Besides, all is not lost. There is still Euthar on the island."

"Hah," I mocked. "The self-proclaimed Pendragon himself."

"Do you doubt his leadership on the battlefield?" Ambrosius asked.

"Not in the least bit. In fact, he can deal with the sheer reckless abandonment of human life much better than you can. That much is clear," I remarked.

"Well, I'm glad you think that," he added.

"But this trait does not serve peace and prosperity well," I added. "There is more to ruling than just being victorious on the battlefield. You, of all people, should realize that."

He stewed in silence for a moment.

"If this wasn't enough, we have received letters from various magistrates from northern Gaul," Ambrosius added.

"What are they calling for?" I asked.

"Many officials are seeking an alliance with Gundahar and his people. They speak of publicly breaking free from the Romans and trying to establish the Gallic Empire. Many of the officials are gathering later this year in Trier. Unwisely, I agreed to go," Ambrosius finished.

"What? Why?" I questioned.

"At the time, I figured it would be good to check all of our options," Ambrosius answered.

In a whisper, I added, "Great, I hope it doesn't get worse?"

"It has," Ambrosius added.

Turning, I asked, "What do you mean?"

"The underclass grows restless. Tales of servants murdering their masters have multiplied. Runaway slaves are banding together. These revolts rear up like Hydra. Their leaders are many. More and more of them speak of an organizer named Tibatto," Ambrosius clarified.

"I've heard whispers of his name since coming home," I interjected.

"It's reaching a roar in some crowds. Passive Pelagianism has died a heretic's death. Still, people are not completely blind. The imperial servitude becomes more intolerable by the day.

"In no way do I support civil chaos, but I'm a little surprised that there hasn't been a full-blown revolt yet," Ambrosius remarked. "People see how the Empire has turned Christianity into holy slavery by inventing predestination. Its development and ultimate acceptance, I believe, is a result of Rome being sacked by the Goths. Now civil disobedience is certain damnation. And with predestination, it is a sin to be born. No pure infant shall be born, they say."

"They have turned spiritualism into imperial bureaucracy," I added.

"Because most men need things spelled out for them," a sweet female voice added.

I knew it was Priscilla before I even turned. Her voice turned her words into honey when she spoke. In picking the perfect princess, Ambrosius couldn't have found another to pale Priscilla. Even in the cool morning air, her beauty glowed like the rising sun.

"Greetings, Merlinus," she said with a sweet smile.

With a light hug and a small kiss to her cheek, I replied, "Good morning, my lady. You have picked the perfect morning to rise early. The gold from the sun melts across the horizon coating the clouds in a royal red frosting."

"So why do you two ruin the sweet moment with the sour talk of politics?" she smiled.

"I have no idea," I replied with a shake of my head.

"Because not everything is a pretty sunset," Ambrosius spouted out.

"This is a sunrise, my dear," Priscilla said as she wrapped her arms around him and kissed him.

"Well, it's easy to see who should do the thinking for you two," I added.

Ambrosius just shook his head in light disgust but remained in her hold.

"We're just teasing you, my love," she added.

"We were?" I questioned. "Oh right. Yes, we were just teasing you."

"So who holds the discussion hostage, the Vandals, the Huns, or possibly someone closer like Gundahar?" she asked.

"Well, we have already covered their misdeeds. We have moved on to someone else," I replied.

"Oh really? Who?" she asked.

"A man named Tibatto," Ambrosius answered.

"Tibatto?" she questioned with a concerned look on her face.

"Yes, Tibatto. He's organizing the underclass," Ambrosius added.

"If it was the same man, he was here last week to speak with you while you and Merlinus were gone to the forum in Aureliani," Priscilla declared.

"What?" Ambrosius questioned.

"Yes, a man stating his name as Tibatto was here last week. He asked to speak to you. I told him that you were unavailable. He asked if it would be all right to return at a later date, and I told him that would be fine.

"Honestly, I thought he would have returned by now," she added. "I apologize for not telling you. At the time, I thought nothing of it. He didn't seem to stress the importance of meeting with you. I am truly sorry."

"No worries, my love," Ambrosius replied. "Nothing hurt."

"That's right," I added. "We will simply have to wait to see what this man named Tibatto wants."

"Right," Ambrosius stated.

CHAPTER 55

At the villa, it was nearly evening when a few men appeared and rushed the western corner of the perimeter wall. I thought we were being raided. I had been sitting on the western wall watching the sunset. I was glad we had been in the habit of keeping the gate closed and barred. The men seemed surprised that no easy entrance stood open to them. As I walked slowly on top of the foot-wide wall toward the main gate, the men noticed me. Giving them no regard, I kept walking.

"Where is your master?" the man barked at me.

"There are no masters here," I replied.

"Then, fetch the man they call Ambrosius Aurelianus," he ordered. "Someone needs to speak with him."

Neglecting a response, I kept walking. Approaching the far corner, the man below lagged behind me. He didn't realize until late that I wasn't doing what he had instructed me to do.

"Where are you going?" the man remarked. "I'm talking to you. Hey, where are you going?"

I didn't have to say anything to Ambrosius. He was at the gate before I had even reached the corner. He waited on lifting the wooden bar that held the doors closed. I slowed my pace as I saw the small group of men gathering outside the entrance to the villa.

"Greetings, my friend. How goes it? Is this not nearly a perfect evening?" one of the other men called out with a fake smile. He hadn't bathed in weeks and appeared to have slept in the same clothes since then. He had on a long off-white tunic. Stains and mud marred it in several spots. A black belt brought in his tunic around his waist and held his sheath at his hip. Though he had a shaved head, peach fuzz covered the top and back of it. He had dark foreboding eyes. His smile lacked teeth to make it complete. There was something I didn't like about him and it had nothing to do with his appearance.

"You have misstated yourself," I said in a dry monotone.

"What do you mean? The evening air is cool and refreshing," he remarked as he glanced around as if a person could see it if they looked.

In the same tone, I added, "How can we be friends if I have no clue who you are?"

Glancing into the villa's courtyard, I saw Ambrosius smile and shake his head as I gave the man a hard time.

"Please, young man, time is of the essence for me," another man remarked.

As the group parted, the man stepped forward. He had flowing gray curly hair that came down to his shoulders. He appeared refined compared to the man in front of him. His brown tunic and matching breeches were clean and not tattered. He appeared more as a scholar than as a soldier or servant. He didn't garnish a weapon like all of the other men accompanying him.

"Please, can you fetch your master," he added in a gentle tone.

"As I told your man, there are no masters here," I replied.

Frustrated by my answer, his head dropped for a moment. After lightly shaking his head, the old man looked back up at me and added, "Well, can I speak with the owner of this villa?"

"You are," I replied.

My answer surprised him. With a confused look he glanced at the men with him. Remaining silent, they simply shrugged their shoulders.

The middle-aged man looked at me and asked, "Doesn't Lord Ambrosius reside here? Is this not his villa?"

"Yes. No." I replied.

An even more confused look consumed his face.

"Yes, he lives here. No, this is not his villa," I clarified. "Look at the plaque. This is the villa of Budicius Merlinus Aurelianus."

"Oh, I see," the man replied. "My apologies to you. I had been wrongly informed."

"There's no need for an apology," I answered.

"So, is Lord Ambrosius available to speak with me?" he asked. "Can we come inside?"

"Yes. No." I answered, once more.

His eyes squinted as he tried to grasp my meaning.

"Yes, he is here. No, your men cannot enter," I answered.

"This is outrageous," called the one man that I had left standing on the other side of the villa. He now stood with the others in front of the main gate.

"Silence, Brutus," the gray-haired man barked. "I'm handling this."

Looking up at me, he added, "I am in dire need of speaking with him. How can this be arranged?"

I glanced down at Ambrosius, he nodded yes to me.

"Have your men pull back from the wall and you can enter alone," I said.

"That's unacceptable," Brutus shouted.

The old man glared at Brutus as if he would tear out his tongue if the man said another word.

"Pull all the men back to that point of the road on the far side of the villa's shallow ditch," the gray-haired man stated as he pointed with his left finger. His men immediately obeyed his command. Within moments, they stood on the other side of the ditch.

"Ambrosius, open the gate," I shouted down to him.

Removing the long wooden beam from the back of the double door, Ambrosius and Velius each manned a door and allowed the old man in. Afterwards, they immediately sealed the doors and barred them shut.

"Velius, come up here," I remarked.

"Yes, sir," Velius called out as he sprinted toward the stairs leading up to the wooden walkway that I stood on. Velius looked as though he was related to Nepos. He was tall, thin, and had wheat-colored hair. Velius kept his hair at shoulder length, though. He had maintained my stables in pristine condition even after his father, Aspar, died from a head injury he received when thrown from a horse he was breaking.

As we approached each other, I remarked lowly, "Give a loud shout if they rush for the villa's walls."

"Yes, sir," he whispered as he stepped aside to allow me down the stairs.

Going past him, I walked to the villa's courtyard. The old man remained silent as I approached.

With a short bow and a slight wave of his open palm, the man remarked, "Greetings, I am Tibatto."

"This is Ambrosius," I said as I pointed and added, "I am Merlinus."

With a bow, he added, "It is good to make your acquaintance."

"Would you care for something to drink?" Ambrosius asked.

"Yes, that would be greatly appreciated," Tibatto remarked.

"Do you also want to go inside so we can talk privately?" I asked.

"Honestly, I would rather speak out in the open. I would feel more at ease," he replied.

With a light smile, I remarked, "That's understandable."

"I will have some wine brought out," Ambrosius added.

As Priscilla quietly approached, Ambrosius remarked, "My dear, please bring out some wine."

"As you wish," she answered and then headed back to the villa.

"I apologize for my cohorts' manners. They are not the most cultured individuals," Tibatto replied as he looked at me.

"There's no need for that," I answered.

"I am a little surprised why you are calling upon me, though," Ambrosius replied as he raised his open hand up to guide Tibatto in the direction of the small stone table set up underneath the large oak tree.

As we walked toward the wide oak, he enquired, "Do you know who I am?"

"Both Merlinus and I have heard of you. It's said that you are organizing the underclass."

"Yes. This is correct," the old man replied.

As we sat down on the stone benches near the round stone table, Ambrosius asked, "So why are you seeking me out?" Glancing side to side, he added, "I am not oppressed and there is no one oppressed here."

Laughing lightly, Tibatto remarked, "I am not here to set you free. I'm here because I've been told by many less-fortunate that you are a righteous man and a great man of war. I am in need of someone like you."

"Hah, you are in need of a lot more than that if you are seeking to free the slaves of the Empire," Ambrosius remarked.

"This isn't a laughing matter," Tibatto hissed. "I am here for the salvation of thousands."

"You're here talking about the slaughter of slaves if you are suggesting an armed revolt," I declared.

"I am here for their freedom," the man snapped.

"What do you think will happen when the slaves revolt?" Ambrosius asked. "Do you think the Empire will do nothing? The Empire is a slave-based state. It's not like they are going to say that they have been wrong for the last five hundred years of servitude. Aëtius will send a legion to smite your revolt."

"I realize that," the man remarked. "That's why I'm here asking for help."

"You will need a true act of God to defeat a Roman legion," Ambrosius added.

"And you don't believe that God is on our side?" Tibatto asked.

"Not when the blood of the innocent is spilt," I remarked.

"There is nothing innocent about the Empire," Tibatto shouted.

In an even tone, I added, "I'm not talking about the Imperial Army. I'm talking about the farmsteads and villas that will be pillaged and burned by you and the Romans when you are hard pressed for food and supplies. What happens to the farmers that simply don't have enough to help?"

"I promise —," he began.

"You can promise what you want, but that does little to stop a swinging blade," Ambrosius added. "Honestly, I believe you waste your time here. I do not want to involve myself, my family, or this villa into any action against the stability of the Empire."

"Stability? What stability? How can the Empire protect itself from the barbarians when it has the barbarians guarding it? It cares little if it can continue to collect taxes for its coffer. How can you support such a system?"

"And after you tear down the old, what, pray tell, will be the new system?" Ambrosius replied as Priscilla poured wine in the cups she had brought. A concerned look hung on her face. Ambrosius looked up and caught her glance. With a small smile, he broke the ice from her lips and she returned his smile, then finished passing the cups and left. She was a good woman. She knew when it wasn't good to stay. Ambrosius would tell her everything later that night. He told her everything. He always did. She made me envious of him.

In all of my years, I have failed to find a woman that could enrapture my heart like she did his. Love filled every moment that they were together, no matter the company. He loved her so much that it made him sick when he wasn't with her. I saw that when we were in Winchester. And after meeting Priscilla, it seemed simple to see why.

"It would be on true Christian beliefs," Tibatto stated with an eloquence reminiscent of Germanus' oration. He added, "All men would share in the burden to sustain society. No man would be the property of another man. Free will shall reign."

"Who will enforce it?" Ambrosius asked.

"It was my sincere hope that someone like you would," Tibatto said as he raised his cup to Ambrosius.

"Or possibly Brutus," I remarked.

My comment paused him and shattered his glass smile. Ambrosius glanced at me and smiled, seeing Tibatto squirm from my comment.

"Sometimes Brutus' methods serve a purpose," he remarked.

"Are we still talking of a true Christian purpose? For some reason, I struggle with the thought of Brutus being a true Christian," I added.

His eyes dropped from mine, and his head lightly bobbed forward. He picked up his cup and finished off his wine.

Setting it down, he remarked, "That's some good wine." The man stood up and added, "I wish I could convince you of the significance of our cause. It's hard to make someone sacrifice for something they already have."

"Not when you convince them that they might lose it," Ambrosius added.

"Right," the old man added with a short grin. "I apologize for wasting your time."

"You don't need to apologize," Ambrosius responded. "It is better to sort out our differences now, and not when matters are much more dire. I fear greatly what your actions shall unleash upon the land. I ask that you avoid the land around this villa."

"I'll try," he said as he turned to walk away.

"And we will try to forget that you were here. Never can tell who might ask," I replied as I stood up to show him outside the walls of the villa.

After letting him out and placing the bar back in place, I returned to the table where Ambrosius had remained sitting.

"What do you think? I didn't say anything you didn't agree with, did I?" asked Ambrosius.

"If you would have, I would have said something," I replied as I sat down.

"Well, I'm glad that is over," Priscilla remarked as she returned and sat down at the table.

"I'm afraid that this matter is far from over," I replied.

"What do you mean?" she asked.

"His revolt hasn't begun, yet." Ambrosius stated.

"Exactly," I remarked.

"Do you think they will return? Will they cause trouble?" she asked.

"It's hard to say. It will depend on how hard-pressed they are by the Romans."

CHAPTER 56

A couple months later, a messenger from Trier arrived. I expected it to be from some Gallic official. Instead, he carried a letter from my sister, Julia. She had a home north of Cologne on the river Waal. Several years ago, shortly after Julia had married Probus, an imperial officer, she moved there to be close to his family. In the letter, Julia asked if she could come and visit for a while. She wanted to bring her three children. Though she didn't bluntly state it, she feared the trouble brewing.

"Merlinus, we must do something. We must, at least, go and escort Julia back to Aureliani," Ambrosius stated when I told him of the letter.

"I know that," I replied. "I just worry that our presence may be misconstrued. Were you still wanting to go to the gathering in Trier?"

"Well, we can handle it one of two ways. When we are in the area, we can hear what is being said and, more importantly, who is saying it. Or let things unfold and simply react to events as they happen. I think the choice is obvious," remarked Ambrosius.

"Right," I replied. "Stay neutral. React to things as they happen."

"Hah," Ambrosius laughed as he shook his head and added, "That's not the choice I was going to make. We must be proactive in our own defense. We are foolish if we rely on Aëtius or anyone in Rome for our protection. You said it yourself: Aëtius has few friends. This is why we must be open to what the magistrates and Gundahar have to say. Tibatto and his men are doomed to fail; that's why they are not an option."

"But out of the two revolts, isn't the peasant revolt the more justifiable cause?" I questioned. Though we both knew that I was right morally, I still knew that he was right about the futility of Tibatto's uprising. Ambrosius turned away from the impasse we faced.

"This is why we must wait and react as things happen," I added. "Besides, this villa and all of my lands will be confiscated if Rome got word of my involvement."

"What involvement? It's a meeting," Ambrosius remarked.

"A gathering of treasonous conspirators," I replied.

"How can you say that?" Ambrosius shouted.

"What else can you call them? They conspire to betray the state," I calmly observed.

"And what state is that, Merlinus? Rome falters. Day by day, that becomes more obvious. I'm not sure it can shake out of its current social slump like it has done in the past. The hope and splendor that once was Rome is now no more. Emperors are not even safe to stay in the Eternal City. Instead, they rule over a city of swamps."

Rome's leaders have failed us, not her laws. Though I said nothing, I could not help but laugh lightly. I shook my head and smiled. The thought reminded me of Honorius of Gwent. It was the first time in a long time. He said the same thing to the British Council over five years ago.

"What's so funny? It's true what I say," Ambrosius remarked in a sharpened tone.

"I know," I replied to his own statement. "There's only a thin tolerance for treason. That's what worries me."

"So is that your answer? You're not going with me to get Julia and her children?" Ambrosius asked.

"No, that's not my answer. We just need to proceed with extreme caution. That's what I'm saying. I have too much to lose," I replied.

"Right," Ambrosius sneered. "I doubt that you can trade me in for another villa like you did before."

"So cold, but true as the northern winds," I replied.

Ambrosius remained silent. There was a growing bitterness in his eyes. His spirit was restless and mine sought tranquility.

"We will travel on the Roman road that runs northeast through the city of Rheims. If we keep going, it will eventually lead us to Cologne," I replied.

"You do realize that Cologne is over a hundred leagues from here, right?" Ambrosius asked.

"Unfortunately, yes," I answered. "That detail only enhances my anxiety. If war breaks out, the roads will be one of the first things locked down and guarded by both the Romans and the Gauls."

"When should we leave?" he asked.

"In the morning," I answered. "The sooner we have Julia and her children back here in Aureliani the happier I will feel."

"My sentiments exactly," Ambrosius replied.

I thought of something offhanded and laughed.

"What's so funny?" Ambrosius asked.

"How many usurpers have been crowned in Trier?" I remarked.

"There has been quite a few of them, especially if you count the ones that resided in Trier," Ambrosius remarked.

"Maybe that's part of the reason the Romans moved the capital of Gaul to Arles. I'm afraid they may ultimately lose Gaul due to it," I added.

"The borders of the Empire are shrinking," Ambrosius added.

"Yes, they are," I confirmed. "What happened in Britain is happening here, now."

We brought extra horses so we could switch out our mounts for quicker travel. Carbo and Nepos came with us. Priscilla and Sevira remained at the villa.

As planned, we passed through Rheims and continued our northeasterly direction. We talked very little, even less in the towns we passed through heading for Cologne.

CHAPTER 57

As we made it to Cologne and crossed the Rhine, the lands opened up to a wide valley. The Waal River ran east to west in the distance. We rode in closer to follow the river farther east. Reaching a third of the way into the valley, a squadron of riders appeared on the near horizon. Due to the slight slope of the land, they had remained out of sight on their approach. We were outnumbered and left trapped on the open plain. We couldn't retreat out of the valley to higher ground before being overcome by the opposing riders. They had already picked up their pace to engage us. We simply maintained our course, but readied ourselves for death. Weapons stood half-drawn as the group grew closer.

The four of us – Ambrosius, Carbo, Nepos, and I – halted. The squadron of nine charged our position. They broke their line formation and encircled us. A Roman officer commanded a group of Huns. This could not be good. Nepos and Carbo pivoted their horses slightly so they faced the riders behind Ambrosius and myself.

Standard legionary body armor protected the officer. The Roman wore a red tunic underneath his armor and a short, red cape fastened to his shoulder with golden brooches. The metal bands appeared to be bronze. He had receding short black hair and olive-tan skin. His eyes were black pits, lacking all emotion.

"What business do you have here?" the Roman questioned.

"We head for a place just east of here," I replied.

"What business do you have there?" the Roman questioned further.

"Our own business," Carbo barked.

As he did, the Hun behind the Roman grew restless in his position. The Hun sidestepped his horse so he had a clear line of sight. Carbo's horse stirred behind me and the Hun followed the movement. His small eyes above his flat nose missed nothing. He had long black hair and a thin goatee. The Hun sat low on his horse. Though short, he had a broad chest and a massive head. His dark, swarthy complexion told of his years of riding under the open sun.

The Roman's stare shifted to Carbo, but came back as I replied, "We go to meet someone."

"Oh really? And who may that be?" the Roman continued in an arrogant tone.

"What authority do you have to make these inquires?" Ambrosius barked back.

"You dare question my authority, boy? I could have you and friends executed for such insolence. I am Vitalinus, field officer to Avitus of Auvergne and the Imperial Army. I am here to reinstate the respect that Roman laws deserve and root out any rabble-rousers. The Empire will not tolerate such an element within its midst."

"Well, that makes me feel safer," Carbo remarked.

Either understanding Carbo or not appreciating his tone, the Hun directly behind Vitalinus drew his sword.

"Attila. Sheath your sword," the Roman commanded in the heathen's tongue. The Hun's eyes sharpened as they shifted from us to Vitalinus. It was obvious that Attila didn't appreciate being told what to do. Still, though, the Hun followed the Roman's command and slid his sword back down in its sheath.

"Good," Ambrosius replied. "Now that this is cleared up, we can be on our way."

"Hah, this is far from cleared up." Vitalinus remarked. "I'm not convinced that you're not part of the trouble brewing in this part of Gaul."

"Well, I'm not convinced you're a field commander for Avitus," Carbo remarked.

"Enough Carbo," I barked. Still, the Huns tightened the circle around us. I knew that Ambrosius, Carbo, and Nepos were ready to counter any attack from the Huns. I didn't want that.

"We travel to visit my sister, Livia," I lied.

"Why are the others with you? Are you related?" he asked.

"None of us are related," I answered.

"I find it hard to believe that you are going on a causal visit to your sister's," Vitalinus replied.

"We are not just going for a causal visit," I added. "We are going to escort her and her children back to my villa, which is south of here."

"I'm still not convinced of your intentions," the Roman replied.

"I cannot help that," I replied. "I have told you the truth."

"How can I be certain of that?" the Roman declared.

"The only suggestion I can make is that you travel with us and I'll introduce you to my sister and this matter can be resolved."

"Oh yes. You're going back with us. In shackles," Vitalinus barked. "Attila."

For a moment, the Hun and his men hesitated at the Roman's command. We did not. Nepos, Carbo, and I drew swords and charged through the ranks. Both Carbo and Nepos pulled their cavalry sword and gladius from their sheathes. Each sliced through the bellies of the riders on both sides of them. Ambrosius shot straight for the Roman. With my sword drawn, I raced for the two Huns nearest Ambrosius which was the opposite side of Attila. With my left hand, I drew the sword sheathed on the right side of the horse. Swiping hard right to left, I hacked off the head of the first rider. The follow-through finished off the second rider as I drove between them. I turned to Ambrosius; he had Vitalinus off his horse and down on the ground with a dagger needling the Roman's throat. I charged toward the others to help Nepos and Carbo corral in Attila and the other Hun. Catching them off guard in that one moment, we now had the upper hand.

"For some reason, you've instigated this quarrel. In doing so, you forced us to subdue your unwarranted aggression. Now that we have walloped your pompous ass in this pretty, little river valley, what do you think your options are?" Ambrosius asked.

"Not good," Vitalinus replied.

As Carbo laughed, Ambrosius added, "Things are not that gloomy, Roman. We just need to clear this up so we don't have any more misunderstandings. This is what I have to offer you. Worst case scenario, we finish what we have started and end your life along with the other two. But, I fear that would cause future trouble that my friends and I don't want. Next, there is a possibility of dragging you to Cologne. Or, I could honor your word that we won't have any trouble from you or your men on our way to Cologne and your group can travel as our accompaniments and not our prisoners."

I translated Ambrosius' words into the native tongue of the Huns.

"You have our word," Attila called out.

"And mine," Vitalinus replied as he laid motionless on the ground.

"All is good," Ambrosius said as he stood up and then helped the Roman to his feet.

Unfortunately, Julia had to wait. This matter had to be cleared up as soon as possible. I had no doubt that Vitalinus was a Roman officer. He acted as if the war had begun. If possible, I had to get this officially resolved and avoid being labeled an enemy of the state.

We went to Cologne without further incident. Arriving at night, I sought out Avitus. I left Vitalinus and the Huns under Ambrosius' care. There was no way I was going to take Vitalinus to Avitus in bondage. I wanted to avoid any chance of situation spiralling out of control. I wanted to plea my version of the events to Avitus of Auvergne.

The issues were sorted out, and the quarrel between Ambrosius and Vitalinus was resolved. Luckily, Probus served under Avitus before Julia's husband had died. As the distinguished Roman explained, the veteran Probus honored Avitus' command though Avitus had gained his post through nepotism. So when Julia and her children came to Cologne fearing for their safety and the Roman became aware of their plight, Avitus had them escorted to Aureliani by a detachment he personally picked.

So after many thanks to Avitus, we left Cologne and headed west on the road going to Rheims. From there, we rode hard for Aureliani hoping to stay out of the war between the Romans and the Burgundians.

Reaching home, we found Julia and her children waiting for us. Her light brown hair had faded mostly to gray. She had retained extra weight, and her dark brown eyes had a sadness lingering in them. She looked like Mother.

This was the first time I had met her children. Her oldest was a boy named Probus. He was six years old. By Julia's accounts, the boy looked like his father. He had brown hair cropped short. He was thin and not that tall. Her middle child was named after our mother, Alicia. She reminded me of Julia when she was a girl, a little chubby but still cute, with long, light-brown hair. Allain was Julia's youngest and still a baby. Unfortunately, Julia's husband was killed about a year ago, shortly after their third child was born.

It was good to meet them, finally, and even better to have everyone safely at Aureliani.

CHAPTER 58

In late spring following the defeat of King Gundahar, news of Litorius marching into Armorica arrived. The reports of the size of his army told me that the Romans were not taking the revolt lightly. By all accounts, the army was much larger than the one Ambrosius amassed on the island. This left no doubt in my mind what the Romans planned for the rebels.

Days after the first messenger, a small group of travelers arrived. Surprise filled me as I saw who was traveling in it.

"Greetings, Merlinus," Germanus called out as he slowly dismounted from his horse. As Velius steadied the bishop's horse, Germanus added, "Thank you, young man."

"It was nothing, Bishop," Velius replied lowly.

"Bishop Germanus, what do we owe for this surprise visit?" I remarked.

"Hopefully, you will still offer your hospitality after I tell you what brings me," replied the bishop.

"I doubt that it is as dire as you make it out to be," I added.

"The Romans march here," the bishop stated in a solemn tone as he walked up to me.

"And I should be concerned?" I asked.

"Yes, they march for this villa," he replied as placing his hand on my shoulder. "They believe that Tibatto has safe refuge here."

"What?" I remarked. "How's that possible?"

"People have said that you made a deal with him and that's why you haven't suffered from his raids," the bishop remarked.

"Where were these liars when his men raided and took a quarter of my livestock?" I replied to Germanus without looking away. Realizing that I had raised my voice, I added, "I apologize, Bishop. I've been carried away by my emotions and have forgotten my manners. Come in, rest and refresh yourself. Your people are welcome."

Smiling, he remarked, "I was hoping for no more."

"And I'll give no less. It's good to see you, Germanus," I replied as I walked with him to the inside of the villa. "I believe the last time you were here was when you wedded Ambrosius and Priscilla."

"Yes," Germanus said with a frown. "Unfortunately, my duties detain me from visiting people on a causal basis anymore."

"Just another day in the great Bishop Germanus' life," I joked.

"Thanks for your sarcastic sympathy. I expect nothing less from you. Maybe that's why I like coming here," the bishop remarked.

"Really?" I replied.

"No," the bishop plainly replied.

Both of us erupted into laughter. We sat down on the couch in the villa. The bishop settled in and relaxed.

"So why would the folks figure that you have any dealings with Tibatto?" the bishop asked.

"Tibatto has been here," I remarked.

"But that was nearly two years ago," Ambrosius added as he walked into the leisure room. "We fought a band of his men more recently, though. Like Merlinus said, they raided the cattle. They drove off or killed nearly a quarter of our stock. Some of us ended up with some nasty scars from it. By the grace of God, no one was killed."

Ambrosius approached us and the bishop smiled brightly. Germanus looked like a father happy to see his son after he had returned from a long trip abroad, and he stood up and hugged Ambrosius.

"It's good to see you, my son," the bishop replied.

"Likewise," Ambrosius added. "What brings you around?"

"Unfortunately, the news isn't good," Germanus replied as he returned to the couch. "The Imperial Army led by Litorius heads here. He is the top lieutenant of Aëtius."

"Right," Ambrosius replied. "Still, I don't understand why they march here. They believe that we're harboring Tibatto?"

"Unfortunately, yes," the bishop replied.

"That just doesn't make sense," Ambrosius added. "When Tibatto came here nearly two years ago, Merlinus and I told him that we would have no part in his uprising and that we would not shelter his people."

"I wouldn't worry too much," Germanus added. "I have had dealings with Litorius before now. A little brash and a Roman pagan, he is still a reasonable man. We can clear this matter up when his army arrives."

"Good," Ambrosius added. "That is what I was hoping for."

"I know, my son. Your heart is true." After a pause, the bishop added, "When I have doubts, I come talk to you. There have been many moments when your and Merlinus' opinions have served me well. I do not search for an agreeing answer, and you do not always offer it. You offer your truest thoughts and that's invaluable in a world of white lies and black truths."

"So well put as always, Bishop," Priscilla remarked.

"Ah, dear lady, you brighten our existence with your presence," Germanus remarked as he stood up from the couch.

"It's good to see you, Bishop Germanus," she added. "You appear in good spirits."

"I have no complaints that I haven't caused," Germanus smiled.

She laughed lightly. Followed in by Sevira and Julia, both of them placed their serving trays on the table. Quietly, Sevira filled the cups with wine. Politely, she handed them to the bishop, Ambrosius, myself, and then to Priscilla and Julia.

"Thank you, young lady," the bishop replied to Sevira.

"You're welcome, Bishop," she replied with a nod and then left.

After sipping his wine, Ambrosius asked, "When do you think we can expect Litorius' arrival?"

As he held his cup with both hands, the bishop remarked, "I believe it will be less than a week before the arrival of his army."

"Should we ride out to meet him?" Ambrosius asked.

"No," Germanus quickly added. "There is too much of a chance of something going wrong."

"Then, we will wait for him," I answered.

CHAPTER 59

Two days later we heard the marching legion. They trekked through the countryside like a grand Persian army with their infamous droning kettle drums. The instruments served as an effective form of mental warfare. Germanus assured us that we had nothing to worry about. I felt anxious from the Romans' anticipated arrival, and so did everyone else.

The Roman presence became known while I was holding class. I had been holding an informal school ever since Julia came back to Aureliani with her three children – Probus, Alicia, and Allain. Numerous children attended, some even from the city of Aureliani itself. Their appearances had only occurred in recent months.

Today, though, the drums echoed in the distance and fear contorted the children's faces. They looked as though they wanted to run but didn't know which way to go. As I taught them underneath the large oak tree, some of the children stood up.

"Settle down my children," I cooed. "We know who is coming. The Empire has arrived sooner than expected, that's all."

"What should we do?" said Silius, the oldest child of Velius. He looked like his father. He had fine wheat-colored hair and was thin but tall for his young age. The scared look in his small brown eyes mirrored the nine other children. He was only five years old, but he was still the spokesperson for the class. Anxiously, they waited for my response.

"What we were doing before," I stated.

"And what was that?" Silius asked.

"Learning, for some of us," Sylvia said. She was Silius' younger sister. A year separated the two, but the way Sylvia behaved, one would guess that she was the older sibling. She was a petite, blonde-haired angel with a little devil's wit. Priscilla said I was a bad influence on her. I told Sylvia to think without restraint. Priscilla said I shouldn't teach her such things. It was extremely dangerous for her. Sylvia thought like a man. Priscilla worried that Sylvia would eventually get hurt for speaking her mind. Priscilla was unfortunately right.

I could not help myself, though. Sylvia was my little protégée. By the age of two, she followed me throughout the villa from sun up to sun down. Though the daughter of Velius and his wife, Roma, Sylvia acted as an orphan and looked to me as her gracious caregiver. Now, at the age of four, she spoke complete thoughts with a biting wit.

I smiled and struggled to hold back a light laugh. Sitting nearby, Priscilla gave me a judgmental shake of her head. I dropped my smile and tried to regain my teaching composure.

Looking back at Sylvia, Silius remarked, "And what are you learning while the Romans are marching toward us?"

"Acoustics," Ambrosius called out as he walked up to the class.

"Acoustics? What do you mean, Lord Ambrose?" Sylvia replied. "Do you mean, what song they march to? Can you tell the makeup of the army by their marching music?"

"Well, maybe," Ambrosius replied, "but not really."

Her smile vanished.

"What do you mean, then?" Sylvia remarked in a hurt tone because she was not aware of the answer.

"He speaks of the actual sound, itself," I remarked.

Ambrosius nodded his affirmation.

"By listening carefully to the drums, an approximate guess can be made about the distance between us and the Romans. Though we hear them faintly now, soon the sound shall disappear as if they were never there." I finished.

"How is that?" Sylvia asked.

"Because the men are down in the far valley. The hills swallow up the sound, silly," Silius remarked.

Sylvia looked at me with a questioning look. I agreed with a nod.

"So then," Sylvia quickly added, "when we hear them again, they will be much louder because they are much closer."

"That's correct," Ambrosius added.

"What else can you learn from acoustics?" Sylvia asked.

"Acoustics could always help when searching for thunderstone," I remarked.

"Thunderstone?" Ambrosius asked in unison with all of the children as they moved closer to me. Priscilla, Julia, and Sevira smiled as Ambrosius and the children clung to my words. Sitting by the three women, Germanus laughed loudly and slowly stood up with his ever-present staff.

"Why do you laugh, Bishop Germanus?" Sylvia said in her soft angelic voice. "Do you know what thunderstone is? Do you have some? What is it?"

Germanus smiled as he approached the cluster of kids. He stood on the path between the children and the large oak.

"Thunderstone," he bellowed. "That's rock struck by lightning."

"Does it have magic, then?" Silius called out.

"Can it shoot thunderbolts?" called out Scipio, the miller's eldest boy.

Laughing, I interjected, "No, it doesn't have magic, but the stone will never be the same. Just like the person who purposely searches for thunderstone will not be the same if they are able to find it."

"Why's that?" Sylvia asked. "How will you be changed if there is no magic?"

"Because you must learn more about acoustics to find where the lightning hits," Germanus added.

"But how do you do that?" Silius asked.

"By counting the moments after the flash of lightning. The sooner the sound of thunder, the closer the lightning hit," Sylvia responded.

With a look of complete surprise, Germanus added, "That's right."

Riding hard through the open gate, Nepos and Velius returned from scouting. Ambrosius walked in their direction as soon as he noticed their arrival. Germanus and I stood between them and the children. Curious, their little heads tilted to the side, but we blocked their view of the riders by shifting our stances.

"All right. All right. All right. That covers the lessons for the day. Children, return to your homes. Except for Evelyn, Scipio, and Simon. I will have Nepos ride with you," I called out.

Evelyn, Scipio, and Simon simply nodded their heads in agreement. It was easy to see that they were related. They all had black hair, dark eyes, and thin features. Evelyn was the oldest and tallest, then came Scipio, and finally Simon at the age of four. A year separated each one, making Evelyn six. Being the children of Scrofa, the miller, they lived between the villa and the Romans. Sylvia and Julia's children drew closer. Sylvia stood by me, but I had to grab hold of Silius' shoulder so he didn't go to his father.

"Come with me, children," Priscilla called out. She corralled them in the opposite direction and as she did Germanus and I headed in the same direction as Ambrosius. Nepos and Velius had dismounted and they were telling Ambrosius something.

"They are in the second valley not the first," Nepos remarked. "It is a huge army. I haven't seen its equal. It dwarfs the armies that battled in Britain. It engulfs the valley side to side all at the same time."

"It is as he says," Velius added.

CHAPTER 60

Within the hour, a small detachment arrived. Well-equipped and regally dressed, an imperial officer rode through the open gate at the front of four other horsemen. The Roman had black hair and was taller than the four Huns he rode in with, but still short in stature. Though stocky, he didn't appear awkward on the back of his horse. He wore the standard, Roman-style armor and his tunic was a cardinal red along with the cape fastened to his shoulders. His dark eyes were piercing. He seemed like a man that wasn't easily duped.

Four riders followed this imperial group. They appeared to be men of the cloth and were familiar. The man I assumed to be Litorius seemed irritated by their presence. His henchmen circled in position kicking up a cloud of dust that kept the men in white linen at a distance. They coughed and choked as it rolled over them.

The man remained mounted while his horse took a couple steps toward us.

"I am searching for a man by the name of Ambrosius. Is he here? It's said that this is his villa," the man remarked.

"Yes and no," Ambrosius answered.

"What?" Litorius bellowed.

A worried look formed on the face of Priscilla. She didn't like the way Ambrosius answered the man. And as the large man shifted in his saddle and rested his hand on the hilt of his sword, I wondered if it was the best possible wording at that moment. Still, I held back a smile as I thought of the time I responded to Tibatto.

"I am Ambrosius," he added. "And no, this isn't my villa."

His four horsemen fanned out into a line. The man's eyes scanned our group. Litorius sized up Nepos and Ambrosius, mostly. His eyes glanced across Bishop Germanus, but they returned as he recognized Germanus. He relaxed his posture.

He laughed and asked in Hunnish, "Is that Bishop Germanus."

"Yes," answered the rider right behind him.

Still smiling, the Roman called out in Latin, "How is it that every time there is a disturbance in this area and I am called in, you are there? How do you explain that, Bishop?"

Stepping forward, Germanus lightly bowed toward the younger man. Though he had easily twenty years seniority on the lieutenant, Bishop Germanus still showed his respect to him.

"I am shepherd of the meek and the weak," Germanus answered. "And, you are the protector of them."

"It's hard to protect them from themselves," Litorius barked.

"And that's why I am here. In these troubled times, a person in my position is in perpetual motion serving the suffering and confused," Germanus answered.

"There's no question on what you preach, Bishop Germanus," one of the men in the second group called out. "What is being taught here? It has been stated that this school fosters profane thinking. Who is the ordained man that preaches and what doctrine does he truly follow?"

"Huh?" I remarked.

The man looked like the Bishop of Aureliani. He wore an ankle-length tunic that was chalk white with a red cross in the center. His skull cap was also red. There was a strong presence of gray in his black hair. From the lines of aging on his face, the man of the cloth appeared old, older than Germanus. One of the riders looked like Natalis, the city prefect of Aureliani. He was a thin man dressed a red silky tunic and had gray hair with a receding hairline. The other men looked familiar but I couldn't be certain if I had seen them before now.

"It's said Merlinus is a Pelagian and preaches the ways of the Orient. Is this true?" another added.

"Silence," Litorius commanded. "We are not here for that."

"But —," the Bishop of Aureliani said.

"Silence," the Imperial Lieutenant ordered.

After a long moment of silence, the Roman added, "It has been stated that you have had dealings with a fugitive slave, an enemy of the state. A man that goes by the name Tibatto."

Ambrosius stepped around Germanus and remarked, "Yes, this man has stood within these walls. He even spoke of words of rebellion, but not once did we offer or give support to him or his cause."

"It's said that you are a great battle lord. It has been said that Tibatto paid dearly for your services," Litorius stated.

"I have fought in some truly grave battles and one of them was against Tibatto's own men. They raided the surrounding lands," Ambrosius declared. "This happened over a year ago."

Litorius remained silent as he tried to surmise the situation. Reacting to the sound of a galloping horse, Litorius' head jerked as a rider raced into the villa's courtyard. Noticing that it was one of his men, he relaxed. The rider quickly stated something to one of Litorius' henchmen. Breaking ranks, this rider walked his black horse up next to Litorius and whispered something to him.

"Good," Litorius said. In Hunnish, he ordered, "Tell the men to move on Tibatto's position. Go with them and take command of the situation. I will rendezvous with you as soon as possible."

The horseman pulled away and rode off with the other rider that had brought the scouting report.

"Now, where were we?" Litorius asked in Latin.

"Sending the men to capture Tibatto," I replied in the Hunnish tongue.

While others had blank looks on their faces in regard to what I said, the lieutenant took a long, hard look at me but then laughed loudly. Pulling his horse away from us, he called, "We're done here."

Without a word more, the Roman officer rode out of the villa's courtyard. His Hunnish guards rode out with him. The other group lingered for a moment, but followed suit. For some reason, their questioning worried me more than Litorius' did. The various local officials didn't like my little school. Until now, this was something I was unaware of.

CHAPTER 61

Several weeks had passed. Litorius had captured Tibatto. Now, it was just before Eastertide.

"When was the last time you heard from Euthar, Merlinus?" Ambrosius asked.

I just shook my head no, having no idea when it was.

"I told you that the Council had voted to keep Euthar as the High Commander. He just returned from capturing Octa after the Saxon had rebelled in northern Britain," Priscilla added. "He sent us an invitation to his Eastertide gathering in Winchester. Now that the trouble has subsided here as well, are we going?"

Ambrosius fell silent. She obviously wanted to go.

"I forgot due to all of the recent trouble. Things went well for the Romans, though," Ambrosius remarked. "They annihilated any threat of another Gallic Empire with the death of Gundahar and the majority of his army. They have quelled the peasant revolt. Was I wrong about the Empire? What do you think, Merlinus? Is the Empire recovering?"

"You won't, mister, if you try to dodge my question," Priscilla scorned. "I want an answer on why we are not going. Euthar made it to our wedding when he had every legitimate reason to miss it. Why do you suddenly not care to see him? You don't make any sense, sometimes."

Ambrosius said nothing, but he shifted his stance. He grew anxious. His eyes darted about. His mouth opened as to say something but didn't. Instead, Ambrosius ran his hand through his hair and gave out a heavy sigh. For a moment, he had the look of an old man. I saw the same doubt in Evodius' eyes when I realized he needed protecting.

"Maybe he just can't visit Euthar where he is at," I observed.

"Merlinus, don't give him any excuses," Priscilla sternly stated.

Ambrosius remarked, "Honestly Priscilla, I really can't, can I? Euthar took my place as Pendragon. How would that look if I show up at the Council?" Ambrosius remarked.

"Please, they would be honored by your presence. It's not like you have to hide from the British," she remarked. "Everyone knows that Euthar took your place."

"Do they? So why do I still hear stories of Ambrosius fighting in Britain?" he asked. "Priscilla, as odd as it may sound, I don't want to step on that island ever again. I have more bad memories than good ones associated with that place. I feel if I go back I'll never return."

"You can't be serious?"

"Yes, I am" he simply replied.

Her left eye squinted lightly as she studied him and then glanced at me to see if Ambrosius was simply teasing her.

"You're serious?" she asked.

"Yes," he confirmed with a somber look on his face.

"So you're saying that you're never going back?" she asked.

"What for?" he replied. "There is nothing there for me. I have no family left on the island except Cai and Geraint."

"Well, don't you want to —," she started.

"I don't want to go back to the island. I didn't even go when Geraint sailed to stay with Cai," he said cutting her off.

A sad look melted down over her face. Although he didn't mean to hurt her, his words did just that. Without a word, she turned from us. As she did, he knew what he had done. She began to walk away. He went to her and gently grabbed her arm.

"Oh Priscilla, I'm sorry," he stated. "I didn't mean to be so short and cold with you. It's just . . ."

A couple of tears trickled down her cheeks. Ambrosius fell silent and wiped them away with his hand.

"I'm sorry. I didn't mean to make you cry," he announced. "You still can go if you want."

"I can't go by myself," she stated.

"I would never let you do that," Ambrosius added. "Merlinus can escort you to Winchester."

"What?" Priscilla and I said in sync.

Ambrosius laughed and added, "What's wrong with that idea?"

"I am needed here at the villa," I remarked.

"Says who?" Ambrosius remarked. "No one believes that this is your villa, anyway. Besides, what can you do that I can't handle?

I'm sure I can teach your class something while you're gone."

I remained silent, knowing that he was right. There really wasn't anything that I could do that he couldn't do.

"Oh, never mind," she added. "It's too late to make it there in time."

"Not if we leave tonight," I answered.

"Are you serious, Merlinus? Would you go with me?" she replied.

"Sure," I answered. "What's the worst that could happen?"

Ambrosius said nothing but shook his head in disbelief. After I did, I hated that I said it. I suddenly realized that I had tempted fate. The last time I was in Britain during Eastertide, I stayed for nearly five years.

"This will be wonderful, Merlinus," Priscilla said. "I've heard from various friends. They all hoped that I would go to Winchester. It's been years since I've been home. I'm so glad we're going . . ."

She glanced at Ambrosius and her smile vanished. Ambrosius smiled, wrapped his arms around her, and held her tight.

Kissing the top of her head, he added with a whisper, "Don't think twice about going. You know you will enjoy yourself. That's why you have to go. Just don't be too disappointed when you find out that Merlinus can't dance."

"What?" she said as she pulled away. Turning to me, she added, "Is that true, Merlinus?"

"Just because I refuse to dance with Ambrosius doesn't mean that I don't dance," I added. "Don't worry, Priscilla, we will have a grand time. Just don't let me drink too much."

"Sounds like you should be concerned, my dear," she said as she looked up at Ambrosius.

"I'll take my chances," Ambrosius replied as he kissed her.

Priscilla, her entourage, and I set off for Britain. We took the Roman road north through Chartres and Evereux to the Seine River. Times before, we had dealt with a man by the name of Gallus. He handled good solid boats. He handled everything for Germanus when he went to Britain. It had been through Germanus that Ambrosius met Gallus. And it was through him that they shipped Euthar's army to the island.

Things had changed and Gallus was dead. We had to seek assistance from other sources. Nepos had ridden ahead to try to make arrangements that would be ready upon our arrival.

Nearing the docks, Nepos shook his head when he spotted us. With a loud shout, he called out, "You won't believe this."

I rode up closer so he didn't have to shout out our business.

"What happened?" I asked. "Are the boats not ready?"

"No, that's not the reason the trip is off," Nepos remarked.

"What? Why do you say that, Nepos?" Priscilla asked.

"Civil war has broken out in Winchester," Nepos called out.

"Oh my god," Priscilla and I said in unison.

"Have Octa and Eosa escaped?" I asked.

"No," Nepos stated. "It's even worse. Duke Gorlois left. And now, Euthar has marched out against Gorlois. The duke is entrenched on the outskirts of Winchester on the western side of a stream running through the nearby valley."

"What? How's this possible?" I remarked. "I have a hard a time picturing all of this. What happened?"

"There was a quarrel with Vitaelis. Vitaelis is the close advisor of Gorlois. He went on the campaign against Grallon and the Saxons. Long black beard. Kind of looks like you. Remember him? Anyway, Oswald, the Saxon that has taken over Gallus' operation here on the river, said Vitaelis quarrelled with Ambrosius. It appears that the people still haven't realized that Euthar is Pendragon," Nepos stated. "Euthar made several blatant advances on Ygerna, Gorlois' wife. Vitaelis pointed them out. There was a quarrel and the duke, then, withdrew from court."

"What a mess," I remarked. "I guess we might as well turn around and head back to Aureliani."

"Right," Priscilla replied. "There's no sense in going, now."

"Wrong," Nepos replied. "Oswald received the letter from Pendragon addressed to you, Lord Merlin. He got it yesterday, but didn't have a reliable rider to deliver the letter. His seal on the letter would seem to confirm the quarrel between the two lords. Lord Euthar wants you to sail for Portchester and rendezvous with him at Wallop."

"What for?" I asked.

"Euthar hopes you will help," Nepos replied.

Emptiness left a cold feeling in me. I shook my head in disbelief. I had no desire in assisting Euthar. *How could I get out of going?*

"What are you going to do?" Priscilla remarked.

"I don't know," I remarked.

"Lord Euthar has made arrangements to sail you to the island," Oswald remarked as he walked up to us. "All is paid in full and ready to go."

I didn't know what to say. There was no way I wanted to be tied up in any civil war over a woman.

Not even if it was Priscilla?

I glanced at her. She had a deeply concerned look on her face. Even as the worries of war troubled her, she still appeared beautiful as ever. Ambrosius was a lucky man. He had found his soul mate; he had found his one true love.

Had Euthar?

"You know Ambrosius would want you to go," Priscilla remarked lowly. "He would want you to get a status of the situation, firsthand. If Euthar needs Ambrosius, I'm sure he will sail to Britain."

She was right. He would want me to go. Ambrosius would sail to Britain if Euthar needed him.

"She is right," Carbo replied, having been silent up to this point. He had come with Nepos and a few other men. They had accompanied us to ensure Priscilla's safety.

"She's always right," I said with a light smile. My comment broke her look of concern for a moment, but then her smile faded.

"I will send word to Ambrosius of what has happened. He will either come and get you personally or most likely send Velius to bring you home. I will sail to Britain," I added.

"A couple of us could remain behind and escort her back safely," Nepos replied.

"Impossible, all of you will be needed to ensure that I make it home safely," I added. "I don't know about the rest of you, but I'm starting to agree with Ambrosius about not wanting to go to Britain."

Priscilla and the others laughed lightly. Though I joked about it, I was beginning to think it was true.

CHAPTER 62

I stayed much longer in Britain than I had intended. I had done many things that I was already beginning to regret. The seeds of treachery had been sowed and would soon trouble tomorrow. I had helped the High Commander betray the Council, simply for his heart's desire. Euthar told me that he now had found his true love. He needed Ygerna. Euthar had to have her; his means to this end sickened me. And as I witnessed the collapse of the Council, I knew that the state I had helped build was gone now.

Hope was gone from the island. The illusion of Pendragon being Ambrosius was no more. I saw it vanish like morning mist under a strong rising sun. The moment of realization came when we rode with Euthar through the British countryside last year. On a clear, sunny day, I watched as townspeople went inside their houses to avoid dealing with or paying homage to Pendragon. They closed and barred their windows and doors as if we would ravage them like some cold winter wind. This compared poorly to the time riding with Ambrosius a year after Bishop Germanus first went to Britain. People ran out into the cold pouring rain to greet us and walk with us as we rode through their town.

Euthar had only a few good men. His closest advisor was Ulfin of Ribchester. Loth of Lodonesia was a good leader and even a better battle lord but still loyal to Pendragon. These two men and Marcellus of Cirencester formed the core of Euthar's power on the island. Those that had reluctantly recognized his high lordship, now, only nominally observed him. Descent didn't disappear when his army defeated Duke Gorlois. It simply lost its recognized leader.

Still, Lord Euthar already had an heir to his lands. Pendragon and Ygerna named their baby boy Artorius, in honor of the legendary British commander, Lucius Artorius Castus. Both Euthar and Ygerna had ties to this legendary figure. Euthar grew up hearing the stories about the men who followed him in northern Britain. Some Alans served under Artorius while he was the prefect of Ribchester, and when he was elevated to an imperial duke. In the distant past, Artorius protected Ygerna's family in Ribchester and her family had prospered ever since.

Euthar's rule was severely flawed. He had done Duke Gorlois completely wrong. There was no other way to look at it. The duke was a good man, stern but fair. His only bias was for the truth. Lord Gorlois had lacked the prowess or the ambition to be High Commander, but had the humility to be a loyal noble. That's until he was slighted beyond reconciliation by Euthar's advances toward Ygerna.

As we stepped onto the shores of the Seine, Nepos remarked, "I don't ever want to go back to Britain."

"Nor do I," I replied.

We traveled south on the Roman roads. There was a hundred miles between us and home. We rode hard to make it to Chartres by late nightfall. We made incredible time. At Evereux, we traded in our horses for fresh ones before the noon hour and then continued riding hard for Chartres. Though extremely tired, we knew that we would be at my villa soon. We were over halfway home when we reached Chartres. We didn't linger, though. We left Chartres before the sun heard the rooster crow.

In the evening as we approached my villa, concern tightly gripped my heart. The door appeared charred from an old fire and open to anyone wishing to enter.

"By the gods, what has happened, Lord Merlin?" Nepos remarked.

"There is no telling," I whispered, and then heeled the horse into a harder gallop. The villa's courtyard felt abandoned. There was no livestock needing tending. The chickens that once were, were no more. What happened here? Whatever it was, it wasn't good. As we all dismounted, Nepos unsheathed his gladius. Though here, I didn't feel at home.

"Spread out men and find out who remains. This is not good," I commanded.

"There's no need for that, hero," remarked a familiar voice. "No need to try to save anyone now."

Turning, I found Ambrosius standing under the portico. He looked sick, sicker than I had ever seen him. Gray tinted his face. Black bags hung under his eyes. He looked like he hadn't slept in days.

Like a zombie, he walked toward me. He didn't say anything more.

"What happened? Was the villa attacked?" I asked.

"Where have you been, Merlinus?" Ambrosius asked as he stood in front of me on the edge of tears. "Where have you been?" He repeated with emotions choking out the clarity of his words.

"Huh?" I remarked. "You didn't get my letters? I got your letters. The ones I'd received from you expressed no urgency in my return."

Ambrosius snatched hold of my tunic, shook me hard, and shouted, "That's a lie! That's a lie! I wrote to you, pleading for your return. I pleaded with you to come back and care for Priscilla during her difficult pregnancy."

He shook me harder and added, "Priscilla is dead because of you."

"What? Impossible. Never would I hurt that child," I answered.

"When you didn't return and she tried to give birth to my son, there were complications and you took them both away from me."

"Oh my god," I whispered. My heart dropped to the ground. It hurt to think that she was gone. It hurt even more to think that it was also true of his future son.

Blinded by emotion, Ambrosius swung wildly at me.

"Stop," shouted Nepos. "Lord Merlin had nothing to do with their death. You know that, Ambrose."

Evading his fists, I drew close to Ambrosius and wrapped my arms around him. He struggled, at first. I held him tighter, trying to calm him. With his head buried in my shoulder, Ambrosius cried painfully.

"She's gone, Merlinus. She's gone," he cried.

I could not console him. I could only support him from falling. As I held him, Sevira walked toward us along the colonnaded portico.

"I am sorry, Merlinus. I know you would never intentionally hurt Priscilla," Ambrosius moaned.

"Just let it all go, my friend. Don't keep that bitterness inside. It will do you no good. I swear to you that I didn't know about Priscilla's pregnancy. And if I would have even sensed the slightest sign of trouble with her term, I would have come immediately. It's like I was given a second set of letters without any mention of Priscilla being with child."

"Maybe you were," Nepos remarked at a low level.

Euthar's name wasn't mentioned, but I had a sudden nagging suspicion that his hand had a play in this. Ambrosius pulled away from my hold and looked at Nepos. The soldier didn't look away as Ambrosius gauged the man's words. Ambrosius said nothing, though. He let it go. Nothing was bringing Priscilla back now. There was no denying it.

"Some of Tibatto's men still linger in the area," Sevira announced. "Nearly a week ago, they attacked the villa. They torched the gate. It still shuts, but it must be braced. Velius and a few other men were killed. Roma has taken their children and headed for Tours. They have family there. Julia and her children went with them. Carbo went with them."

Though Velius was dead and my sister gone, I felt more sadness knowing that Sylvia was gone. I couldn't see how far Sylvia had progressed. I had figured that she would be unbelievable. I had been hoping to get back to teaching. I figured it would help to bring back some normalcy to my life, but that was gone just as my star pupil was. What I had been anticipating was nothing but memories, now. The security that had once made this place great was gone. Uncertainty hung over the villa. No one knew what the future would bring.

CHAPTER 63

These were the lowest days of Ambrosius' life and they weren't much better for Aureliani. Outlaws ravaged the villas between the Seine and Loire. The rebelling elements of society had reduced the villas to self-sustaining farmsteads, geared for survival instead of prosperity. Nepos and I restored the defenses to the villa. We were not going to fall prey to the brigands.

Ambrosius did nothing except stay out of everyone's way. He was a living ghost for two years. If Sevira had not been there, Ambrosius would have starved himself to death. She made sure he ate at least once a day and kept him clean. He hardly spoke. It had been months since I had held a conversation with him. I had stopped trying. I understood his pain and didn't push the issue. Something or someone would come along that would pull him out of his emotional stupor.

Being a few miles southeast of Aureliani along the Loire, we received a high share of travelers before they reached Aureliani. So a man, woman, and two children did little to hold my attention as I continued performing long-needed repairs. In fact, they had passed my detection until Sevira personally sought me out and notified me of their arrival.

"Lord Merlin," she called out as I hauled fieldstones from the back of an open wagon. "There are some people here."

Resting my hand on the wagon, I wiped my brow with the other. Looking at them in the distance by the gate, I glanced at Sevira and remarked, "Feed them if they are hungry and guide them to the city if needed."

"They are here for you or more specifically Ambrosius. The man asked to speak with Ambrosius but then asked for you, also. So, I came and got you first. I hope you don't mind," Sevira remarked.

"Did he say anything more?" I asked.

"No. He does look familiar. He might be from Britain," she said.

"Okay. Thank you," I added.

For some reason, I thought of Ulfin, Euthar's next in command, but dismissed this notion because it seemed unlikely. Even if Euthar wasn't with him, I would have expected the arrival of a larger party than this.

As Sevira walked toward the villa, I called out, "Sevira, please bring some chilled wine, cold cheese, and sliced bread."

She turned, smiled, and said, "I will make sure that it's done."

"Thank you," I replied.

As I turned to face the couple and the two boys, I noticed that the man slowly walked toward me. Heading in his direction, I met him halfway between the portico and the main gate. I recognized him right away. It was Ulfin of Ribchester. He appeared haggard and old beyond my years even though he was actually as young as Euthar and Ambrosius. Gray cropped up throughout his head of hair. Small gashes and scars marred his otherwise chiseled face. The lady with him had straw-colored hair. It was chopped short like a man. She did not look like a man, though. Her soft cheeks and small nose gave it away. She had dark sad eyes. The horrors of life had ripped the innocence from them. She looked like the mother of the little blond-haired boy, but not of the other. In that boy as I looked at him, I suddenly saw Euthar.

"Greetings, Lord Merlin," Ulfin remarked with his hand extended.

"Though I'm surprised, it is good to see you," I replied as I grasped and shook his hand. A small smile broke across his marble face.

"Thanks. Thank you," he said as he grasped my hand with both of his. "It has been a hard journey, Lord Merlin."

"Come out of the sun. Bring your wife and children under the shade of my oak," I replied as I motioned for the lady to come toward us. Smiling widely, she walked to us, holding the boys' little hands.

"Cora is not my wife and Artorius and Marcellus are not my boys, but we will take what you offer," Ulfin replied with a light smile.

"So what's the reason for the long trip?" I candidly asked.

"I have a lot to explain," he answered.

All of us, including Sevira gathered, under the old oak tree. Sevira set the serving tray on the stone table. She had chunks of white and orange cheese cut into bite-size bits. One couldn't have asked for a better day. The light breeze carried the soothing songs of the birds nearby.

"May I have a piece of your cheese, Madame," the little brown-haired boy remarked in a formal tone.

Sevira and I were both a little surprised by his proper, precocious manners. He had features reminiscent of Ambrosius and Euthar: straight brown hair, dark eyes, short nose, and a narrow but soft face. The other boy, quiet and reserved, had blond hair and blue eyes. They were about the same height, which was about three feet tall.

"Why, of course you can, little man," Sevira replied in a sweet tone. She lifted the small silver platter of cheese to allow the young boy to pick the piece he wanted.

"Well, thank you," the boy replied as his eyes scanned the chunks of cheese. Finding the one he wanted, his small fingers plucked it.

"You're welcome," Sevira answered.

The boy swallowed the chunk of cheese. Immediately following, the boy shouted, "Papa! Papa! You're here, You're here. How is that possible? Papa, you're here. Papa, how is that possible?"

Instantly, the boy sprinted past us. Turning around to see where the boy was heading, I saw him shooting straight for Ambrosius, who had silently walked up behind us. A surprised, confused look formed on Ambrosius' face as the little boy rapidly approached him. Nearly on top of him, the boy wasn't slowing down. In an instant, the boy sprung up at Ambrosius when the boy was two steps from him. Naturally, Ambrosius caught the child and carried the boy back toward the table.

As he did, Ambrosius replied, "To tell you the truth, little man, I don't know how it's possible since I don't know who you are."

"Oh Papa, why do you tease me?" the little boy said sadly. "Aren't you happy to see me? When did you leave Britain."

As Ambrosius looked right at me, he asked, "Merlinus, what's this all about? Who is this little... Ulfin? Is that you? What are you doing here? Where's Euthar?"

"Papa, you were fighting the Saxons. Right, Papa?" the boy remarked. Ambrosius just looked at the boy, unsure what to think.

"Arthur," Ulfin called out. As the boy turned to Ulfin, he added, "That's not Papa."

"What? He looks just like Papa. He even talks like Papa. Are you sure that he's not Papa?" the boy replied. Turning in Ambrosius' arms to look at him, he asked Ambrosius, "You're not Papa?"

"No, I'm not that lucky," Ambrosius replied with a light smile.

"Wow," the boy replied. "I ... I ... I thought you were Papa.

Well, it's nice to meet you," the boy remarked as he hugged Ambrosius around his neck.

I watched as a wave of emotion washed over Ambrosius' face as he held the boy. He had to set the boy down. The emotion hurt more than he could bear. Struggling to hold back the tears, Ambrosius ruffled up the boy's hair with his right hand. The boy frowned but said nothing. Kneeling down eye level with the boy, Ambrosius added, "I'm glad to finally meet you, also."

Ambrosius hugged the little boy and patted him on his small back. Standing up, Ambrosius glanced toward Ulfin with a smile, but it faded as he saw the sadness in Ulfin's eyes.

Seeing this also, Sevira remarked, "Arthur, will you and your friend help me? I still need to feed the chickens. If you do, you can have two more chunks of cheese."

"I would help for free," he remarked. As they started to walk away together, the boy stopped and asked, "Can I still have the cheese when we're done? Can Marcellus have some, also?"

"Yes, you both can," Sevira replied with a smile.

Arthur and Marcellus reached up for her small hand and together they walked away from us. I could not help but laugh at the boy.

"Is Euthar still alive?" Ambrosius bluntly asked.

"Yes," Cora quickly answered.

Ambrosius' stiff posture relaxed as he heard her response.

"But he is not well, my lord," Ulfin added. "A sickness lingers within him. It has been like that for the last year. Most speak of curses. I figured it was poison. No one liked him after he killed Gorlois and took Ygerna. People simply respect his power and nothing more.

"He knows that the end is near. That's why we're here, my lord. He has already given the army to Loth of Lodonesia. Euthar's baby daughter, Anna has been given to Loth's son, Budicius. And I've been instructed to give Artorius to you. If this is not an option, I swore I'd raise the boy as if he was my own."

"The boy shall never need as long as we live," I answered.

"Right," Ambrosius added with a heavy nod.

"He shall have an education fit for an emperor," I remarked.

"Hah, finally," Ambrosius laughed loudly. "A protégé has returned. The master shall no longer sulk for a star student. Ever since little Sylvia left, Merlinus hasn't been the same. Now Merlinus can stop moping around the villa."

Everyone except Ulfin and Cora laughed at his comment. The darkness shrouding Ambrosius broke. I felt hope at the villa for the first time since the death of Priscilla.

"You all can stay, Ulfin," I added.

"I must return to Britain and inform Euthar, first," Ulfin replied. "I would like to return, though."

"Of course. That's fine," I answered.

"Were Cora and young Marcellus staying here to wait for your return? They are more than welcome to remain."

"No. No, they're going with me," Ulfin replied. "They came to help with Arthur. We figured his best friend might make the trip easier."

"Right," I answered. "I see your point. The way the two carry on together, it appears to have been a good assumption."

With a light smile, the warrior added, "It seems so."

"Well, safe travels and a speedy return," I replied.

"Thank you, sir," Ulfin remarked with open hand. "You have lifted a heavy worry from my king's thoughts and mine."

Shaking his hand, I added, "Think nothing of it."

Eventually, after several months, Ulfin returned. He arrived late at night, and I was the only one up. After letting him in and giving him food and drink, we spoke.

"I fail to bring good news. Euthar was buried before I set foot on the island. What will we tell Artorius?" Ulfin asked.

"What do you mean?" I replied. "We have to tell him the truth."

"I just fear that the news will put him into an ill-tempted mood that he might not grow out of," he stated. "Let me tell him that the last time I saw his father, Euthar was still alive."

In silence, I accepted Ulfin's suggestion.

And so for two years, we lived peacefully at the villa getting to know little Artorius and helping Ambrosius cast aside his dead, heavy heart. All the while, the Empire struggled to survive and continued to sacrifice prime land in Gaul to its greedy German garrisons.

CHAPTER 64

The scene reminded me of London, thirteen years ago the night Vortimer became High Commander of the Council's army. This time though, everyone talked all at once and nothing intelligent could be heard. Personally, I didn't see what the debate was this time, here in Aureliani.

As before, the argument centered around the use of barbarian garrisons. The local magnates were against Aëtius parceling off land to the barbarians. They would arrive soon to claim their promised property. These foolish nobles overestimated their manpower and martial skills. The enemy was the Alans instead of the Saxons, this time. Instead of defying an impotent commander, the nobles planned to disobey an imperial decree being enforced by Aëtius. Maybe if this was thirteen years ago, Ambrosius could once again rally the righteous to victory. Not now, though; I feared Ambrosius had passed his prime. Most important, he lacked the conviction for such a feat. Little Arthur had done wonders for Ambrosius' spirit, but Ambrosius' heart would never be whole again.

As I looked around the room filled with pompous people, I wanted to laugh. There was no one present that was ready to undertake the task at hand. Only the men that traveled with me to Aureliani had any clue of what was being contemplated at this meeting in the city's amphitheater.

"We must tend to our defenses," one of them remarked.

Another spouted, "We shall drive these heathens from our lands."

I laughed and turned away from the group of gathered magnates. Without a word, Ambrosius followed my lead. Our departure drew the attention of most of the men.

"Where do you go, Ambrosius?" a councilman called out.

"We haven't made our decision, yet," remarked another.

Turning and facing the large group of prominent men from Aureliani, I remarked, "I've made my decision. I shall simply comply with Aëtius' orders."

"What?" many shouted. "What about you, Ambrosius?"

"Don't you have a spine?" shouted others.

"Yes and a mind," Ambrosius stated. "It tells me not to commit suicide. There will be no victory, only annihilation by defying the emperor's decree."

"Thanks for the vote of confidence," remarked Natalis, the city's prefect, as he came to the front of the group. He wore a toga, or maybe the toga wore him. He struggled to handle the excess material as he tried to state his case. Beads of sweat appeared on his high forehead, where his gray hair had receded past the top of his head. His eyes showed fear in the council meeting. I laughed, imagining him on a battlefield.

"If I were to imply something else, I would be lying," Ambrosius added. "We don't have the men to break free from the Empire right now. Only arrogance and stupidity would entertain the notion of possible victory. Look what happen to Gundahar and his people during the consulship of Isidorus and Senator. They were wiped out by the Romans. That was less than ten years ago and they were better equipped."

"So are you calling us idiots, then?" Natalis questioned.

"Only if you defy the emperor's orders," I stated.

"I figured that you would take the least to convince," Natalis added.

"Regrettably, you have figured wrong," I replied.

"Unbelievable," others remarked.

The rumbling of voices rolled on. We walked out to our horses.

"Do you think that we made the right decision?" Ambrosius asked.

"Absolutely," I replied. "Besides the fact that the Empire hasn't done anything illegal, there isn't more than five men in that group of fifty that can effectively wield a sword. We would be slaughtered."

As we mounted up, Ambrosius replied, "I didn't realize you had trouble dying for a cause."

"I do when the cause is stupid," I snapped.

Ambrosius laughed and asked, "So what will happen?"

"This is going to unfold one of three ways," I stated as I heeled my horse into a walk. "First, Natalis will officially defy the Empire with a written response. Or, they will wait until the arrival of the Alans to express their discontent. The third alternative would be that they come to their senses when they see what they are up against."

"So, which one do you think it will be?" Ambrosius asked

as he trailed behind me.

Laughing, I replied, "Do you really need to ask? I know it isn't going to be the last one. Actually, I figure that it's going to be the second one. The magistrates shall keep the status quo, but when Goar and his people arrive, the magistrates will resist."

"Hopefully, their arrogance doesn't blind them too much or for too long," Ambrosius remarked. "You Alans are not known for mercy, especially for the weak or old."

Nepos laughed lightly and Ambrosius smiled back at him.

"Right," I added. "I think if anyone there that had any sense it was the priest named Annianus."

"But he didn't say anything," Ambrosius remarked.

"Exactly," I laughed.

Ambrosius smiled lightly but then added, "Don't you think he should have said something?"

"Maybe," I replied. "But a person shouldn't argue with idiots because observers might not be smart enough to tell the difference."

Ambrosius snickered, shook his head, and replied, "Ah yes. The true brilliance of Merlinus shining through to enlighten us, once more."

"Oh yes. Oh yes," I added. "I take the role of the palace scholar with great honor."

"I was thinking palace jester," Ambrosius stated with a dry laugh.

"So was I," Nepos added.

"For all the years of advice I have given both of you, this is the thanks I get?" I snipped.

"You're lucky that I have never given you my gladius for all that you've taken me through," Ambrosius barked as he moved his hand onto the hilt of sword.

"See how good my wisdom is?" I declared. "If I hadn't been advising you, just imagine where you would be."

"Dust and bones in a little silver coffin," Ambrosius declared in a serene monotone.

It spun my head as I thought about all the time I actually did spend with Ambrosius. It was as if I were his father and mother at times. Conceived in darkness, I delivered him from civil chaos. Right. I kept trying to believe that lie.

"It is a wonder that you never ran your blade through my belly,"

I added. "It's not like I never gave you a reason to do it. Although I'm glad you didn't, I'd understand if you did."

Laughing, he shook his head and added, "Don't think I never thought of doing it, because I have. You're just lucky that I'm a gentleman."

"I do have the strangest luck," I replied. "I have been truly fortunate to be a part of your life. In your twenty-some-odd-years, you have lived several lifetimes."

"Hah," he scoffed. "Now, that's why I have so many issues in my little old world. It all makes sense now. You are a genius, Merlinus."

I laughed with him and then we fell silent as we rode east toward the villa. Though he joked about it, I sensed spite in his words.

CHAPTER 65

It didn't take long to find out the magnates' plan of action. Shortly after Goar's arrival, there was trouble. Within a week of the conflict, locals showed up at the villa's gates. I stood at the gate, stopping one of the larger groups from entering. The one that led the people was the priest, Annianus.

"Greetings," I called out as they stood before me.

"Dear sir, I am Annianus," the priest replied, stepping forward.

"I know who you are," I remarked. "You went to the meeting at the amphitheater in Aureliani. If you and these people are on a pilgrimage to Tours, you are headed in the wrong direction. Don't worry, a lot of folks do that. For some reason it's easy to get turned around in the woods here."

"I wish we were lost but that is not the case," the priest remarked. "Goar and his people have arrived and the displacement has begun."

"Right," I replied. "We have already been visited by some of the earlier victims. Unfortunately, it is as I had expected."

With a slight frown and a light nod, the priest conceded, "Yes, unfortunately, you were correct. Why didn't they listen to you?"

"Arrogance is the only reason I can see," I replied.

He shook his head in agreement.

"Have you seen many refugees?" the priest asked.

"Including the group you have with you now, I would say we have seen nearly two hundred people that have been driven out of their homes and off their lands."

"This is not good," the priest remarked.

"Not at all," I added. "So what are these people going to do?"

"I was hoping you may have a suggestion," the priest added. "Any help you can provide shall be repaid sevenfold in heaven."

"Can you guarantee that rate? I'm sure more would invest if such a return truly existed," I remarked sarcastically. "Honestly, I'm not sure what I can really offer, though. We are already stretched thin."

I don't know why I was refusing to help. It wasn't just one thing, it was many things. Already there was no room within the walls of my villa. More people slept in my barn than livestock. With overcrowding, there would be food shortages. And if any of these people were fugitives, there would be more trouble that I didn't want or need.

He didn't seem convinced. He looked around the courtyard. There was a lot of space with only a few tents up.

"Couldn't more tents be put up?" the priest asked.

"Yes, but there are too many people to feed," I replied.

"This place appears nearly deserted," the priest replied with a sharpened tone.

"Just about everyone is out gathering food and other supplies," I added. "That is, what food remains to be found."

"What am I supposed to do?" the priest asked.

"I don't know," I answered with a shrug of my shoulders. "Return to Aureliani and work out a deal with the Alans?"

"They are barbarians," he barked.

"Yes and they are fierce fighters," I stated. "And they have the backing of the Empire."

"I can't believe you are turning away these helpless people. How can you live with yourself?" the priest ranted.

"Before you excommunicate me and condemn me to hell, take a look behind you," I ordered. "I've already promised to help those people."

As he turned around, I pointed past the people he came with here. A large group moved toward us. Ambrosius was returning. The amount of people outnumbered the ones with Annianus. A look of disbelief overcame the priest. He shook his head.

"This is a disaster," he whispered.

"I couldn't agree with you more," I replied. "The magnates have forsaken these people by defying Aëtius and the Empire. These same nobles could not adequately defend against the peasant revolt. How did they expect to defeat a well-trained army like the one that Goar leads? Such foolish arrogance. It shall cost these people dearly. It already has."

Ambrosius had rode ahead of his group of walking people. He halted his horse next to us.

Looking at the priest, Ambrosius remarked, "Greetings."

"Hello, young lord," the priest replied.

"What brings you to our neck of the woods?" Ambrosius asked. "If you folks are heading for Tours, you're going the wrong way."

"No," the priest answered. "These people have been driven from their lands by Goar and his evil men. We came here seeking refuge."

"Sure. Whatever we have to offer, you folks can have it," Ambrosius remarked without any hesitation.

With a surprised look, the priest glanced at me then back at Ambrosius and added, "Lord Merlinus stated that there is nothing to be offered."

"We don't have enough for the people we are sheltering now," I answered. "There's no way we could also support these people."

A questioning look formed on Ambrosius' face and he added, "We can't just turn these people away, can we?"

"Yes, we can and we should," I remarked. "What happens when the food runs out? What then?"

"We deal with it when it happens," Ambrosius answered.

I turned away from them. This wasn't what I wanted. Where was my peace? Didn't I deserve some for all that I had done for people? Where was my happiness? There was always some tragedy, some crisis. Why was it my concern to care for every charity case? It left me feeling empty. Worse yet, I didn't want to do it because of the guilt I felt. The bad emotion ate hard at my insides.

"If your people need to set up a temporary camp, they can set something up outside the walls of the villa. This is the best that I can offer. And if we are attacked, your people can come within the walls, then."

"But what about their belongings? What little they have left would surely be lost," the priest explained.

"Then go somewhere else and leave me alone," I snapped at the priest and then stumped off. I left Ambrosius with the priest.

I heard Ambrosius tell the priest, "Please forgive him, dear priest. I'm not sure what troubles him."

"It can't be that everyone has their hand out," I sputtered under my breath. I kept walking and went around the villa to the other side of it.

The moments drifted away. Without an entrance on this side, it was the quietest place I could find still within the walls but still near the villa. I tried to let it go. I tried to not think of walking into the deep forest and never returning. I was close to the point of living as a hermit. One more thing was all it would take.

"Lord Merlin," Sevira called out as she approached from behind me a little while later. "You're needed at the main gate."

"I'm through speaking with the priest," I barked.

"It's not Annianus, my lord," she added lowly. "It's a Roman representative and he has a squadron of Alans with him."

My heart sank into my stomach. The end was near. I turned and followed her back to the gate. A short distance from the main entrance just outside the walls, Annianus and his people were setting up their temporary camp. I could see him looking this way.

The Roman stood in front of me and Ambrosius. Behind him stood five tall, sword-wielding warriors. They wore silver chain armor while the imperial official wore a white linen toga with his cingulum. A scarlet stripe ran along the straight edge of his toga. He skillfully draped the cloth as he slowly walked. He could show Natalis how to strut like a true pompous imperial ass. He was a young magistrate. He was well-kept. With nothing out of place, the Roman looked more like a statue than a man posing for one. He was cleanly shaved. His black hair was short and slick. His high bangs were oiled and drawn straight down on his forehead. He wore his cologne like a whore. He had dark beady eyes and held a scroll in his hand.

"Greetings, citizen of Rome," the stranger declared. "I am Eugenius and I bring an official decree from the Emperor Valentinian the Third. It has been deemed in the best interest of the Empire to settle several Alan federations in the Aureliani area. All landholders must comply. A portion of the land must be given in trust to these imperial allies."

As the Roman spoke, one of the five warriors listened closely to what we were being told. The man appeared a little bit older than the others. He also looked stronger than the rest or at least bigger than the other four. Oddly, he looked familiar, not so much as I might know him, but I had seen him before now. I remembered his face. His high cheeks, chubby nose, and long ears quickly took me back many years. I struggled to think of where I had seen him. He was so much older than when I first saw him. If he would have had any facial hair, I would have never recognized him. Who was he with that I also remembered? Where did we all meet?

"Who is this man?" the Alan asked in his native tongue. The Roman ignored him as if he had said nothing at all.

"We have a map of this area. It includes the lands that you occupy," the Roman continued.

Looking at me, the Alan remarked in Gaulish, "Who are you?"

"I need you to review this map so we can handle this matter properly," the Roman stated as he continued to ignore the Alan talking.

When did I met a high-ranking Alan recently? No, it was long ago. He was a boy that lived north of Barcelona. That's where I knew him.

"Alaigne," I whispered. "Draco."

"That's it. That's me," the Alan remarked excitedly in his native tongue as he glanced back at the other four warriors. "Alaigne is where I have seen this man before now. But that was nearly thirty years ago. He was a boy at the time."

"Why don't you and your headman come in and we can settle this matter in a more relaxing environment," I stated. With a bright smile, the Roman nodded in agreement.

"Stay here, Draco. He hates Alans," the Roman remarked in the Alan's tongue as he turned toward him.

"Why is that?" the head warrior remarked.

"His mother was murdered by your kind," the Roman lied.

He turned and smiled at me, not realizing that I understood every word he had just said. Without hesitation, I snatched the Roman by his throat. Not expecting it, he stared bug-eyed. The Roman's face swelled red as he struggled to breathe. The four rear guards went for their swords. Draco studied me. I could have easily torn out his windpipe. I had the right grip. All I had to do was clench my hand and yank. I had seen it done.

I released the Roman. Staring at the Roman as he gasped for air, I barked in the Alan's native language, "If you ever tell another lie about me or anyone I know, I shall tear your throat out. Do you understand? Or do I need to tell you in Latin, also, so there's no misunderstanding?"

As the men continued to draw their weapons, Draco raised his arm and held back his advancing men.

Looking at Draco, I continued in his native tongue, "I instructed this man to tell you to come inside the villa so that this matter can be resolved. My intent is to comply with the imperial decree. I just want to retain my fair share of my imperial honors. I have imperial documentation inside the villa. These lands were granted to my family by Emperor Honorius twenty-eight years ago."

Turning to his men, Draco said, "Stay here. Eugenius and I shall go inside to review his documents. It shouldn't take long."

I nodded to him, turned, and led the man through the main entrance. The Roman followed us in.

Knowing that this day was soon to come, I had previously gotten my papers in order. They were in the same place they had been for more than twenty years. They were in the villa's library, sitting securely in a stone box sunk into the stone floor. Hopefully all I had to do was let them review the paperwork, compare it to their imperial register, and settle on what they felt they were entitled to allocate to the Alans.

Walking down the long colonnaded portico, Sevira carried some papers in her hands. She smiled at me as she approached. Without a word, she handed the papers to me.

"Thank you," I remarked as I took them from her. I turned and suggested, "We can review these papers underneath the shade of the oak over there."

"Sure. That's fine," Draco remarked.

I had reviewed the documents several times over the years. I always marveled at the craftsmanship that went into the papers. But I also wondered what would happen if their authenticity was questioned. Did Germanus still have his copy of the transaction? I had no real way to refute it if he didn't. And that's what made me nervous now.

Carefully, I rolled the papers out onto the stone table. As I stepped back, the Roman moved in for a closer inspection of the documents. A look of awe draped his face.

"These are amazing. They were actually endorsed by Emperor Honorius," the Roman remarked.

"The endorsed documents were triplicated. You are viewing one copy, another is under the care of Bishop Germanus of Auxerre and the last copy should be in Ravenna," I declared.

"Right," the Roman replied. "You must have done something extraordinary to obtain such imperial honors."

"What did you do in Barcelona? Valerius was the man that you were traveling with when I first met you. My father didn't like that man, though my father had to do business with him. I remember you were traveling with a girl and a child. Did it have something to do with them? My father said it had something to do with Empress Placidia. Did it?" Draco asked.

The Roman's eyes grew sharp as he waited for my response.

"Even though some of the parties involved have died, it's not good to reveal details of a private deal," I replied plainly.

Saying nothing, Draco simply shook his head in agreement.

"Honestly, there is nothing that we can do here," the imperial official declared. "There is a clause personally initialed and stamped by the Emperor Honorius' secretaries. It states that these lands are exempt to federations."

"What?" Draco remarked as he glanced over at the papers.

"Yes, it's right here," the Roman pointed out.

Though I was well aware of this clause, I didn't expect it to be honored.

"With that being duly noted," I remarked. "I am willing to allow river access on my lands outside the walls. This way the Alans can maintain their nomadic habits. Is that acceptable?"

"I cannot say it is set in stone," Draco remarked, "I would say that it nearly is, though. I will return to Aureliani and discuss this matter with Lord Goar."

"That is all I ask," I replied.

"I shall return with his answer in a few days," Draco replied.

I shook his hand and then escorted them out through the open gate.

CHAPTER 66

This was the third morning after the visit from the Roman and his squadron of Alans. Still, we hadn't heard a response to my offer. I wasn't sure what to expect. The possibilities were numerous and it made my stomach sour thinking about them.

Silently, I broke bread from the loaf and passed it on. Ambrosius took it and did the same. Annianus sat at the breakfast table along with Sevira, Nepos, Ulfin, and Artorius. Although I usually enjoyed silence, it seemed eerie at that moment. Right then, I didn't want to be left to my own thoughts. None of them were comforting. We should have heard back from Goar. And I didn't like what I was starting to hear whispered around the villa. The camp was being infiltrated by rabble-rousers. And that's why we hadn't heard back from the Alans. They waited for someone to step out of line so they would have a reason to confiscate the land. Treason or a blatant disregard of imperial decrees were the only ways my claim to the lands were null and void.

"Why haven't we heard back from Goar or any of his Alans?" Annianus asked.

I didn't want to answer.

"I wish I knew for certain," Ambrosius remarked. "What do you think, Merlinus?"

I didn't answer.

"Merlinus?" Ambrosius asked as he glanced at me.

Still, I didn't answer. I didn't want to share my poisoned thoughts.

"Merlinus," Ambrosius added a little louder. "Why do you think the Alans haven't returned?"

"They are waiting for us to step out of line. Then, they will sweep in and wipe us out," I bluntly remarked.

"Just like the Huns?" Artorius called out excitedly.

"Artorius, don't interrupt," Sevira remarked.

"Yes, just like the Huns, Arthur," I replied. "The Alans are infamous for skinning their enemies alive."

"Wow," the little boy replied. "Uncle Nepos, you never told me that."

"Merlinus, don't tell the boy such things," Sevira remarked.

"Yes, Arthur, they are fiercer than the Huns," I replied. "Isn't that right, Nepos?"

"Why do you say that?" the boy quickly asked.

"They are the real power in New Rome. General Aspar controls the armies of Theodosius as if they were his own," Ambrosius explained to the boy.

Dio rushed into the dining room. He was one of the unfortunates. He had short scraggly brown hair and was skin and bones. A thick tunic that Ambrosius gave him hid much of the vicious truth, but the lean look of hunger still lingered in the boy's face.

"Lord Merlin, an army stands outside the villa," the young man replied. "It appears that they are about to move on the people's camp."

"Why would they do that?" Sevira asked. "They haven't done anything wrong, have they?"

I didn't say anything but only looked at Annianus.

"Is there anything we should know, Priest?" Ambrosius asked.

A frown formed on Annianus' face. Leaving them behind, I headed for the outside. The others followed. Once there, I went into a light jog to the outer wall. Climbing up to the elevated walkway, I saw Goar's army for the first time. His cavalry lined up six riders wide with at least ten sets deep. This didn't include the miscellaneous riders and other military personnel, such as the standard-bearers, scouts, several Roman advisors, and a massive bodyguard unit.

In comparison, the peasants fell into uneven lines facing the imperial squadron. A chaos of commands confused the ranks of the refugees. They couldn't organize their lines. They would be slaughtered.

My presence had drawn the Alans' attention. One of Goar's bodyguard made a beeline for my position next to the main gate. As he rapidly approached, I saw that it was Draco. I had hoped my straight dealings with him had had a positive effect on him.

"Greetings, Lord Merlin," Draco called out in the Gallic tongue.

"Greetings," I replied in his Alan tongue. "How goes it? How may I be of service to your lordship?"

"What did Merlinus say?" Artorius asked.

"Shh," Sevira remarked.

"I'm sorry, I just want to know what Merlinus said. Nepos, can you translate for me? I struggle with the words of your people. I'll have to try harder to learn it," the boy remarked as he followed everyone out of the villa.

"For right now, why don't you go inside and work on some of your Greek studies," Ambrosius replied. "Do this for me. Okay, Arthur?"

"Sure, Uncle. I'll do that," the boy remarked. "You just give me a shout if you need my help."

"Of course I will, my little king," Ambrosius remarked. "Now, run along and do what I ask."

"Yes, sir," the boy replied and complied.

As Arthur ran off, Ambrosius came up on the wall beside me and surveyed the scene.

"One of Goar's villa was attacked and it's said that some are in this camp outside your walls. My lord wants to know why this camp remains on your land. Are you raising some kind of army?" Draco called up to me.

"No," I remarked in his native tongue. "I have no affiliation with this refugee camp except for allowing them to maintain it temporarily. They were driven off the lands they once maintained. This happened when their landlords resisted the imperial decree that you are here to enforce. How can this matter be resolved without innocent bloodshed?"

"My lord had initially accepted your holdings and your offer of free access to the river. But after the raid, more questions have been asked and more seem to be required."

"Voice your complaints and conditions and they shall be addressed," I declared. "I have presented myself only in a lawful manner. It is my intent to continue this. I offer myself as a mediator between the two parties on this field today. I do not harbor criminals of the state nor will I ever. This is my solemn oath. Yes, there may be a bad seed within this camp, but it must be weeded out. The whole crowd is not corrupt."

"I will carry your words to my lord," Draco called out as he pulled his horse in the direction of the army. With a couple quick jabs of his heels, Draco kicked his horse into a hard gallop. Even before he reached his lord, the peasants rushed at the Alans' position.

With an instant response, the Alan horsemen moved like a swarm of angry hornets and engulfed the peasant army from all angles, obliterating what little cohesion it had.

Draco halted mid field, debating if he should join the fray or not.

"Come on," I whispered. "Keep going to your king."

As if breaking his stalemate, Draco continued to his lord's position. Back in the thick of the fight, I saw the peasant standard-bearer change to a large white rag. Soon all of the peasant standard-bearers followed suit. Still the Alans hammered the mob.

"Are the Alans going to quit?" Annianus asked.

"They should," Ambrosius remarked. "The warriors must see that the peasants are trying to surrender."

"The horsemen will not stop," Nepos replied.

"This is unacceptable," Ambrosius added. "We must do something."

"We will die if we try to intervene at this point," I replied. "It would be best if we remained here."

"And if this is how you feel then," Ambrosius replied. "I believe we shall soon part ways, permanently."

"One man cannot make a difference, not even ten. That is certain death waiting to greet you out there," I declared.

"There's no sense in loosing one's principles by trying to avoid what comes to us all," he declared.

I hesitated.

"So be it," Ambrosius remarked as he ran down the stairs from the elevated walkway. As he reached the courtyard, he turned and declared, "Live as a coward while I'll die as a man."

Nepos and Ulfin followed Ambrosius' lead. Annianus opened the gate for them. Afterwards, the men rode hard for the fight. With swords, spears, and axes in hand, Ambrosius and his men immediately altered the tide of the battle. They halted the unhampered destruction of the peasants. The Alans had to organize a defense against Ambrosius' strong aggressive flank attack. Goar sent in a small squadron of reserves. There were fifteen men in it.

As I came down the steps to the courtyard, Sevira and Annianus gathered near me.

"Grab horses and swords," I commanded.

The three of us rode out from the walled courtyard. I drew my sword and raced for Draco's position. As we closed in undetected, I screamed out a loud battle-cry. Joining my call, we drew the attention of some of the fighting Alans. Part of them pulled out of the main conflict to counter our sudden rush. We reached Goar's and Draco's position well before they were able to intercept us.

Instantly gaining his attention, I commanded, "Stop this madness. The peasants are beaten."

"You have fortified their position," Draco replied.

"No, I have not. Ambrose joined the battle because of the disgraceful slaughter. These are not soldiers, Lord Goar. There is no honor gained in the Alans slaughtering these people," I declared.

"They are lawbreakers," the old warrior king insisted in his native tongue.

I fell silent as he spoke. I studied him for a moment. Looking at the Alan for the first time, I saw Nepos within his features. The warrior king had straw-colored hair, which was thin and straight. It was pulled back in a ponytail. He wore a silver conical helmet. The shiny silver matched his long shirt of scale armor. He had strong piercing eyes.

"Maybe some of them, but definitely not all of them. Call an end to this mindless massacre. Let's resolve this in a civilized manner." I added in the Alan tongue.

King Goar did nothing but nod to Draco. The Alan warrior broke from the group and whistled out a command. Immediately, the Alan cavalry responded and ended their attack on the peasants.

As this happened, I noticed a rider coming from the villa. It was a small rider. It could only be Arthur. Euthar would be proud of how the boy handled the horse and recklessly raced onto the battlefield. Ambrosius would have his hide when he found out what the boy had done.

Arthur gave a loud, clear battle cry as he approached with a drawn sword. He was a miniature horseman.

Halting his horse, Arthur shouted, "Which one is mine, Merlin?"

Both sides couldn't help but laugh at his courageous mannerisms.

"Ah," the old king remarked. "Finally, a warrior worth facing."

The Alan reached behind his back, drew out one of his two sheathed swords, and then added, "Before we battle to the death, do me the honor of telling me your name, little warrior king."

"I am Artorius, son of Euthar Pendragon, lord of Britain," the boy responded as he removed his oversized helmet.

King Goar fell silent. He looked like he had seen a ghost. It was strange to see his demeanor. He lowered his sword and nudged his horse up to the boy. The king shook his head in disbelief.

"You are the son of Euthar and just as bold," King Goar whispered.

"Arthur, what are you doing out here?" Ambrosius shouted from a distance. He rode hard to our position.

"Euthar? It can't be you," the warrior king mumbled. "What trickery is this?"

In an instant, the old warrior king withdrew his other sword from behind his back. And as he did, his cavalry unit of bodyguards encircled us with their weapons drawn and ready to attack.

Arthur laughed for a moment but fell silent when the old warrior-king's look grew stern.

"When I first got here two years ago," Arthur quickly added in a calm tone, "I thought that he was my father, too."

"There is no trickery here, great warrior king," I remarked. "This man is Ambrosius."

Interrupting, one of Goar's men called out, "My lord, do we finish them?"

"No," I commanded.

"Why not?" Goar replied. "What is stopping you from stirring up more trouble? I want promises and I want hostages to guarantee your promises," Glancing at Artorius, the warrior king commanded, "I want the boy."

"No," Ambrosius exclaimed.

"Then finish off the peasants. Starting with him," Goar commanded as he pointed at me.

"Okay," Ambrosius conceded. "Then you have me, if you are taking the boy."

"Done," Goar quickly remarked with a bright smile.

"No," I objected.

"Too late. The deal is done," the Alan warrior king stated. "Your life and lands are spared if you can remain loyal."

CHAPTER 67

It had been less than a week since Ambrosius and Artorius left as hostages. I decided that I would personally go to Auxerre. If anyone could set things right with the Empire, it would be Bishop Germanus. With Ambrosius and Artorius in trouble, Germanus' cooperation was nearly certain. I just hoped other emergencies didn't have the good bishop detained.

As I gathered a few belongings and supplies, I headed for the stables. It being early in the morning, I hoped to leave without any farewells. It was always easier that way. I left letters of instructions and best wishes, but it wouldn't be that simple. Nepos sat waiting. He stood as soon as he saw me approaching.

"I saddled two horses. I'm ready to go," Nepos replied lightly as if he didn't want to disturb the sleeping dew.

"Aren't you always," I replied. Pausing my step, I asked, "Why is that? Haven't you grown tired of being drawn into these messes? You have faithfully stayed by both Ambrosius and I since we faced off against Grallon and the Saxons. Why is that? You could have easily found better people to serve."

"Lord Merlin, I highly doubt that," Nepos said solemnly. "For the last thirteen years, I have served an empress' son and his wise wizard. I see no better circle to stand in. I have been blessed with the chance to be with true legends, my lord."

Falling silent, he slightly bowed his head.

Laughing, I remarked, "Please Nepos. I'm afraid that you sleepwalk. It's time for you to wake up."

The stoic stare didn't crumble as I joked.

"Regardless, if that's the truth or not," Nepos remarked. "I'm ready to ride out to get Ambrose and little Arthur back. That is what you are doing, isn't it?"

"Basically," I answered. "First, I am heading for Auxerre. I am going to try to get Germanus involved. Although you may have high regards for myself, I have my doubts about my clout."

"Good thinking," Nepos remarked. "So what are we waiting for?"

With a light smile, I shook my head no and added, "Not this time, Nepos. You're needed here. Ulfin will need your assistance in protecting Sevira and this place."

"But —," Nepos began.

"Not this time," I cut him off. "I need you to protect what little possessions I have left. I want you to know that if I don't come back that I have given the villa to you. It's in writing. Sevira knows about it."

"No, my lord. I can't," Nepos declared.

"You must. It's what you rightfully deserve. There is no time to discuss this any further. I must be on my way. Please do this last thing for me," I remarked.

"Yes, my lord," Nepos conceded. "I'll get your horse."

After bringing out the horse and while I mounted up, Nepos removed the long oak bar from the gate.

"May you have the speed of Mercury, my lord," Nepos shouted.

"And with it, I won't be long," I replied.

As I rode hard for Auxerre, I hoped that I hadn't used up all my blessings. Little Artorius and Ambrosius needed them more than ever.

I had never been to Bishop Germanus' residence, but I had no trouble locating it. I rode through the open gate at his in-town villa. It stood unattended. Dismounting, I glanced around, but didn't see anyone outside the villa. Looking back at it, I noticed some elderly man making his way down the colonnaded portico.

"Can I help you?" He called out as he drew closer.

"I would like a moment of the bishop's time. I know that it is impolite to drop in unannounced, but this is a dire matter. Is he available?"

"I am afraid he is not in Gaul. Matters abroad delay his return," the old servant replied.

At that moment, I felt as though I might collapse. Exhaustion from the ride or the failure to find Germanus – pick the reason, whichever it was – hit me at once and I felt weak in the knees.

"Are you all right, sir? Do you need to sit?" The servant stated.

"I'll be fine," I replied. "Could I leave a message for him?"

"Of course," the old man remarked. "What is your name?"

"Merlinus," I started.

"Merlinus?" the old man questioned.

"Yes," I confirmed.

"Merlinus of Aureliani?" the old man inquired further.

I nodded yes, unsure if it was a good thing that he knew me.

He smiled and replied, "Oh sir, you must come in. Let me get you something to drink, anything. The bishop wills it. He stated that if you ever graced his home with a visit that you should be treated as if you were him. Please, please, come in and tell me your message while you rest."

At that moment, something to eat and drink would do me just fine. My stomach growled that it was empty. The bloating hunger came on suddenly, and I replied, "How could I refuse such an offer?"

He took me into the luxurious villa. Germanus had mosaics of various events taken from Genesis and laid into the floor. The main entrance opened up with Adam and Eve standing near the tree of knowledge. The serpent coiled around the base of the tree.

Stopping in front of a couch, the old man turned and replied, "Please take a seat. I shall return with food and drink."

I did as he suggested. The soft seat felt good on my sore bottom. Suddenly, I felt as though I was back in Britain at Evodius' villa. The two men had similar tastes. It was unfortunate what happened to his home. I hoped his death was painless.

A short while later, the servant returned with a young man carrying a small table. The boy placed the table by me, and the old man sat a wide silver tray upon it. It had sliced bread, salami, cheese, and wine. The old man poured a glass and handed it to me.

Allowing me to take a long drink, he waited and then asked, "Is there anything else you would care for at this moment?"

"Absolutely nothing," I remarked. "Well, except to have the bishop arrive sooner rather than later."

Laughing, the old man replied, "Sorry, but I can't fill that request. It's unfortunate. I had hoped that the bishop would have returned from Britain by now."

"He's in London, again?" I asked.

"No, not this time," the old man replied. "He's on the west side of the island. He corresponds regularly with the Bishop of Gloucester."

"Is Elafius still the bishop?" I asked.

"Yes. His brother died a few years back," he answered.

"Death visits us all eventually," I replied.

"For some of us, it's sooner rather than later," called out a familiar voice.

"My lord," the old man called out as he looked past me. "You have returned home safely, once more!"

"Yes, I have, but who has not? For there's no other reason that this honorable man would visit my home," Germanus called.

I stood and turned toward the bishop's voice. Instead of seeing the man that I remembered, I saw an old feeble man. So frail that he might break if I were to assist him to the couch. Still, I helped him sit down.

"Don't look at me like that, Merlinus. Don't clam up on me when I ask you what you need help with. You would never come here unless you desperately needed something right away. Where is Ambrosius?"

My head dropped low.

"And little Artorius?" the bishop inquired further.

My head dropped lower.

"What happened?" asked Germanus as a grave look consumed him.

"Goar, lord of the Alans, has taken them as hostages. Trouble erupted between his people and the magistrates of Aureliani," I stated.

"It's not just Aureliani, my lords," the old servant added. "All of Armorica is in chaos. The Romans have abandoned us to the wolves."

"What was your plan of action, Merlinus?" the bishop asked as he helped himself to some of the food on the tray.

"I hoped to travel to Goar and try to parley their release. That's as far as I have gotten with it," I answered.

Struggling to his feet, Germanus smiled and replied, "No sense in unpacking. We should just get moving."

Bishop Germanus and I rode north. Within days, we reached the Seine River. As we did, we encountered a scouting party of five riders.

"What business do you have on these imperial roads?" the head scout questioned. I assumed he was an Alan due to the language he used.

"We are on official business," I replied in his native tongue.

"Tell him that we come to speak with his king," Germanus replied.

Relaying his message, I stated to the Alan, "The imperial Bishop Germanus wishes to speak with the great warrior king, Goar."

"Lord Goar has no time for such trivial things," the scout remarked.

"The bishop has no time for such talk, either. He serves Rome with the grace of God. He seeks no trouble with your king. Instead, he seeks to remove a thorn from Goar's side. The bishop seeks order and balance. Please give him a moment to speak with your king."

The scout looked at his comrades; they shrugged their shoulders.

"Ride with us back about one league. There is a field there. You can wait there for my lord's procession. He marches to meet up with Aëtius. I will tell him that you wish to speak with him. If he chooses to speak with you, he will. This is the best that I can offer you."

"The bishop appreciates this chance and accepts your terms and conditions," I replied.

Immediately, the group split in two. The scout I spoke with, and one other, rode back with us. The other three went in the direction of Auxerre. We were guided to the middle of a large open field and instructed to wait. Afterwards, the two Alans scouts continued riding farther east in the direction of the king's procession.

While we waited, Germanus had his tent canopy set up to shield us from the sun. Within an hour of their departure, I spotted Goar's army entering the field. His iron-armed cavalry rode straight for us. His army filled the road. I spotted the head scout who had guided us to this field. He broke ranks and rode up to us.

"I have told my lord that you wanted to speak to him, but he is in no mood for talking," the scout replied.

"Tell him that it would stop unnecessary bloodshed," I replied.

"He stated that he had written orders that could not be superceded," the scout remarked. "Aëtius the Magnificent has instructed my lord to subdue the rebellious element rooted in Armorica."

I just shook my head and replied, "Very well."

"What's wrong," Bishop Germanus remarked. "Why isn't Goar's train stopping?"

"He has direct orders from Aëtius to subdue Armorica," I stated.

"This is absurd," the bishop declared. "Come with me and translate everything I say."

Germanus walked up to the road that the army was marching on. I repeated everything he said.

"Great king of the Alans, I beseech a moment of your time," I began

Germanus' translation. "I do not confront your command. I only want to save the surrounding communities from any further calamities."

One of his bodyguards replied, "Keep your distance."

Germanus looked at me for an interpretation. I just shook my head no. As the king continued by us, Germanus walked parallel with him down the side of the road. Germanus motioned for me to follow.

I repeated what he said, "There must be some common ground that can be reached so there is no further bloodshed."

I shouted Germanus' translated words, but the king acted as though I'd said nothing. Looking at Germanus, I shrugged my shoulders.

Suddenly, without hesitation, Germanus walked up and seized ahold of the warrior-king's bridle. The large horse halted. And with it, the entire Alan army stopped. Instantly, Goar's men drew their swords and had Germanus and me surrounded. A raising of Goar's hand kept Germanus from being struck down. The old warrior king stared at the bishop. Germanus didn't look away; he simply released his hold on the warrior-king's reins.

"Dear king, we only seek to stay your wrath from smiting the innocent. We support justice, and honor the Empire as you have for over twenty years," I remarked.

The old warrior king glanced at me, looked back at the bishop, but then, looked back at me. His eyes studied me.

"Why are you here? You have caused me nothing but trouble," the warrior king remarked as he continued to stare at me.

Germanus glanced at me with a nervous look and asked, "What's wrong? Why is he staring at you? What is he saying?"

"He recognizes me," I told Germanus.

Turning back to the Alan king, I remarked, "You have two people that are very dear to me. That's why I am here. I want them back."

The king laughed loudly and smiled. His bodyguards had odd looks on their faces as if they never before heard their king's thick hearty laugh.

Dismounting, King Goar walked with us to our open tent. After drinking the wine we offered, the old warrior king remarked, "I stop, but this doesn't change anything. I must campaign in Armorica. Rome has ordered this. The lords of Armorica have forced my hand."

I translated the king's words.

"We shall obtain a pardon for Armorica," Germanus replied.

"Impossible," Goar grumbled.

"It will be done. We just need time to obtain it. Please. We implore you to give us a chance," I pleaded.

"This is what I will do. I shall allow you your chance. I will have a few of my men accompany you to Italy. Then, we shall both find out how much sway your priest really has. And maybe, he can save Ambrosius and little Artorius."

"What do you mean by that?" I asked. "They're not with you? Where are they?"

"Is everything all right?" Germanus asked in a concerned tone.

"They were taken into custody by a Roman official. They are being taken to Ravenna," the warrior king stated.

"What? Why?" I questioned.

"Because of you," Goar replied.

"Me? How do you figure that?" I asked.

"The Roman named Eugenius has them," the warrior king added.

My heart sank and I whispered, "I've got to get them back."

"I'll help you as best I can," Goar added.

"Thank you," I replied and he nodded.

"In the meanwhile," the old king remarked in the Gothic tongue, "let us speak briefly and privately. You do still understand me, yes?"

I simply nodded my head in agreement.

"Good." he continued in the Gothic tongue.

"What's he saying?" Germanus asked. "Is he speaking in Goth?"

"We do not have time for idle translations," the old king commanded. "Soon, Ambrosius and my little warrior king shall have no time left, so we will need to part ways very soon."

"Lord, I know that you are the great king of the Alans," I began in the Gothic tongue.

"Hah," King Goar cut in. "I've never been the great king. That's why I have kept my head and I'm still alive. The line between Burgundian nobles and Gallic aristocrats was nearly blurred out of recognition. That's why the Romans killed King Gundahar. It was good that his and my people parted ways."

I could not stop from smiling. I wanted to laugh, but I held it back. The old king smiled.

"It seems that we share something in common. At one time, we were regents to Roman emperors and Gothic kings. And how is it that you raised the better of the two?"

"Euthar and Ambrosius were twins? I knew it," I remarked. "How?"

"I have asked that question myself, several times this past week," the king remarked. "It's strange how things worked out. It is a story no less fantastic than any epic by Homer or a tale about Troy."

"What do you mean by that?" I asked.

"Those were crazy times. I still don't know how I kept my head. After the execution of Jovinus in the year of Senator Lucius' consulship, I figured I would be hunted down and executed. Luckily for me, the Empire is always in need of fighting men, especially ones that don't think too much. This is why I do not speak Latin. I appear less competent that way.

"Anyway, in time, after the execution of Jovinus, I was called upon by the Gothic king, Adaulphus. I was surprised by the reason King Adaulphus requested my presence. We had dealings before and maintained good formal relations between our two people, but because of the bad blood between him and Jovinus' general, Sarus, I never expected what he asked of me.

"After much delay and reassurance of friendly intentions, we met. This was shortly after Empress Placidia had given birth.

"The meeting was to cement an alliance between his and my people, as he put it. King Adaulphus offered his newborn son as a hostage. This was the youngest of the twins, Euthar. Though terrified by the offer, I could not refuse without causing an unbridgeable rift between us."

"So this is how Euthar ended up in your care?" I asked.

"Yes," the old warrior king answered. "In return, I gave Adaulphus one of my daughters. She was promised to be Euthar's bride. My daughter was executed with Adaulphus' other children after his own death."

"Forgive me," I remarked.

"There's no need for that," King Goar replied.

"So you knew of Ambrosius back then," I remarked.

"Only as Theodosius. I thought the boy was dead. But after Euthar had gone to Britain to battle Grallon and the Saxons, I began to hear that there was a man that looked remarkably like Euthar," the king said. "Adaulphus kept the birth of Euthar a secret. Empress Placidia didn't know that she had given birth to twins. To this day, I don't think she knows the whole truth."

"Why would King Adaulphus keep such a secret?" I asked.

"Besides fearing for the children's well-being, he didn't want the twins being pitted against each other when they came of age. He didn't want a Gothic version of Romulus and Remus. King Adaulphus saw too much of a chance of palace intrigue. He didn't want them falling victim to it."

"Right," I replied. "There was enough of that with his marriage."

"Yes, you see things well. You've helped Ambrosius and my little warrior king to see well, also," the king added with a nod. "You need to get them back."

"I will," I replied.

CHAPTER 68

We traveled south for Autun and met up with Germanus' old friend, Senator. The man gave letters of support to Bishop Germanus to help secure peace with the Romans.

People flocked to us or, at least, to Bishop Germanus. His name drew respect like Martin of Tours. People purposely sought him out.

We didn't linger anywhere we went. We trekked after Eugenius and his entourage. They moved fast to make it through the mountain passes before snow choked them closed. We had to do the same. The bishop was getting old, so we couldn't move as quickly as I wanted. The journey through the mountains was treacherous. Still, Germanus saved an elderly man from drowning in a deep swift stream running through a mountain gorge.

By the midyear, we went through Milan and neared Ravenna. Through our entire journey, the bishop tried to maintain a low profile. Germanus didn't care so much that people knew about him. He and I were concerned for Ambrosius and Artorius. We didn't want Eugenius tipped off that we trailed him to Ravenna. We didn't want him changing his present course. We wanted him to go there, if we couldn't intercept them en route. If Eugenius wanted Ambrosius and little Artorius dead, they would be. For now, they seemed to still be alive.

We planned to enter Ravenna at night. We wanted to be unnoticed. We would seek simple accommodations in a local inn. And then, discreetly, we would gather what we could about Eugenius and his plans for Ambrosius and little Artorius. Many things remained a mystery with this man. How much power did he wield, or did he have powerful friends? I had overreacted when Eugenius came to the villa with Draco and his Alan squadron. Now Ambrosius and Arthur were paying the price.

We approached the imperial capital from the west. The dense massive swamps kept the roads narrow and, at times, nearly inaccessible. The scent of salt passed over us when the wind blew strong toward the west.

We drew closer to the Adriatic Sea, which was six miles east of the city. Ravenna stood among the tributaries of the river Po. At its third-mile mark, we crossed the bridge spanning the Candidianus River.

"Why does this man ride relentlessly for Ravenna?" Germanus asked.

"I've asked myself the same thing several times and come up with one thing," I declared. "He's coming here to see what he can find out about me, the villa, and the imperial family. I do not know if he seeks to harm me or somehow further himself by obtaining privy information. Based on what I did, my guess is with the first one."

"Right. I understand," Germanus replied. "Don't blame yourself for what has happened."

"Who should I blame then?" I remarked. "There is no one else to blame. This trouble is solely upon my shoulders, Bishop."

"Keep your wits about you, my friend. The only guilt that you should feel is the aggression you showed Eugenius in your first meeting. Any pain and suffering he inflicts is what he must account for. It does not fall upon you to answer for his sins," Germanus replied.

Within the range of the city's walls, we dismounted from our horses and walked the remaining way to the main gate to give a passive impression to the guard. Given how badly the bugs bit us, I wished we had simply ridden the rest of the way to the gate. Torches and braziers on the walls and tower flared up as we approached.

"State your business. Why such a late arrival?" the guard questioned from behind the gate.

"I am a servant of God," Germanus called out as we stood in front of the gate. "I am here to speak with Peter, the bishop of this fair city. I apologize for the hour but I could not rest another moment knowing that I was near the imperial city. We seek simple accommodations at a nearby inn for the night."

The sentinels opened the double-door gate. A third sentinel stood directly behind them. He was the one that spoke. The three guards all wore legionary-style armor. The metal bands were buffed silver. The third guard rested his hand on the hilt of his gladius. We did not put the Roman on edge; it was the time of our arrival that did.

"Is there a place in Ravenna that will understand and accommodate such a late arrival from poor planners?" Germanus requested.

"There is a place that caters to such travelers, but the social climate might not be to your liking," the Roman guard remarked.

"If there are private chambers for lodging, then I would be interested in knowing its locale," the bishop added.

"Then this place will suffice for the night. Take this road the whole way. You will travel some distance, though. After passing several blocks of housing, you will reach the main square. It is wide. You will continue to the far side of it along this road. Travel quietly or you will be harassed by the prisoners in the gaol. Once you pass the gaol, you will see the inn that I speak of. Safe stay, Bishop Germanus."

"Thank you," Germanus stated without another word.

Out of hearing distance of the gate, I inquired. "How did he know who you were?"

"I don't know," Germanus replied. "Hopefully, we will know more in the morning."

CHAPTER 69

It was a short first night of rest in Ravenna. Neither Germanus or I slept past the first rooster's crow. Soon after that there was a knock on the door. Bishop Germanus turned to me with a grave look upon his face. I walked to the door.

"Who is it?" I asked.

"Victorius, a servant of the imperial household. I come bearing welcome and gifts," the young male voice called out.

With a bewildered look, Germanus shrugged his shoulders, unable to offer a reason not to let the man in. Opening the door, I stepped away from the threshold. A very young man stood in front of the entrance. His features were soft and refined. His clothing was immaculate. His long tunic was snow white and drawn in around the boy's thin waist by a golden rope belt. Gold embroidery decorated the cuffs of his long white sleeves. He had short black hair and light hazel eyes. He carried nothing, though.

A large man behind Victorius held a large silver tray on his shoulder. This man had a smoothly shaved head, black eyebrows that nearly touched in the middle, and dark eyes. He wore a mustard-color tunic with a crimson cloth belt. Though his face was mute, the man's massive limbs expressed who he was or at least what he could do. He appeared to be a eunuch.

Victorius bowed to us.

"Please come in," Germanus replied.

The young Roman walked into the room followed by the man with the silver tray. The large platter held many kinds of delicious food. They all lacked any type of meat. There were fruits, nuts, cheeses, and bread. The man sat the tray on the small table near the door.

"I don't know what to say," Bishop Germanus replied. "This is a pleasant but unexpected surprise. 'Thank you' seems to be obvious and plain, but for the moment, it is all that comes to mind. What warrants such treatment? Do all guests receive such things?"

Laughing lightly, Victorius added, "Not hardly. This place usually shelters the somewhat infamous, not the renowned like you."

"Please do not think this odd, but who do you think I am?" the old bishop asked.

"You are Bishop Germanus of Auxerre, are you not?" the young man asked.

"Yes, I am. But how did you know that I was here, when I arrived just last night and sent no word ahead that I was coming?" Bishop Germanus asked.

"I see your point," the young Roman remarked. "This city holds no secrets. The night sentinel must have been instructed to announce your arrival. Word of you heading for here came from Milan. It reached here nearly a week ago. The revered empress ordered that I have this silver platter delivered this morning."

"She is too gracious. I gladly accept the gift," Germanus replied.

Bowing his head, Victorius turned and walked for the door. Opening it and exiting, the eunuch followed without even a sigh. We looked at each other with stunned expressions.

Germanus then asked, "What do you make of it?"

"We must move much faster than I had previously anticipated. Things were already in motion before we arrived. We can only hope that the separate factions do not have access to the same informant. We are truly foolish if we assume that. We must find Ambrosius and little Artorius today, preferably this morning."

Nodding his head, Bishop Germanus replied, "Are you ready to go?"

With a smile and a nod, I followed him out of the room and then out of the inn. He headed for the forum to get his bearing and move from there. We did not even reach it before Bishop Germanus stopped. I nearly walked into him as he stood in front of the gaol. It was Artorius and he was looking at us from behind the black, wrought-iron bars. I could not believe they had the four-year-old boy in the pin. Seeing and recognizing us, he smiled, remained still, and said nothing.

"Your eyes do not deceive you unless mine fool me," I whispered to the bishop.

"Blessings be to God. He lives, but where is Ambrosius? Is that him laying down?" the bishop asked.

Ambrosius' head raised up from the bench next to little Artorius. They were the only prisoners in the gaol. Before sitting upright, Ambrosius' eyes scanned the area to see if there was anyone else around us. There wasn't. The city streets stood bare as a starving man's cupboard. Only keepers were awake and busily opening their shops. Ambrosius casually got to his feet and stretched the sleep from his body.

"Glad to see you finally decided to come," Ambrosius said with a light smile. "I was beginning to think you didn't care."

"Right," I replied. "It must feel like an eternity behind those bars."

"It's not that bad," little Artorius whispered.

"For now," Ambrosius added.

"Right," Germanus replied with a faint smile. "We will get you both out of there as quick as possible."

"How do you figure on doing that?" Ambrosius asked.

"Not sure just yet," I added.

"You could always bust us out of here," little Artorius replied as he slowly glanced from side to side.

Everyone laughed.

"Only problem with that is that Merlinus and I would end up in there with you and your uncle," the bishop replied as he leaned forward on his long walking staff.

Our presence quickly drew the attention of the Roman guard on the other side of the gaol. As the watchman walked around the pen of iron bars, he called out, "What are you two doing? These criminals aren't allowed visitors."

"We are not speaking with criminals. We are talking with these two that have been wrongfully imprisoned," Bishop Germanus replied with a sweeping hand gesture.

"That might be your opinion, but it surely isn't the warden's opinion," the guard said as he now stood next to us. He rested his hand on the hilt of his gladius. He had a broad chest and big arms, but he was still smaller than the eunuch from just a while ago. The guard wore a helmet, but I still noticed that he had black hair. Short stubble showed that he hadn't shaved recently. He had a light complexion as if he didn't see the sun.

"Well, I would like to speak with the warden so this matter can be resolved," Bishop Germanus replied. "Could you ask him when I may speak with him?"

I remained mute as the guard looked at me and then back at Germanus. Nodding his head, the Roman replied, "I will check."

"Thank you," Germanus quickly added.

A short while later, the Roman returned and replied, "The warden will see you. He will be out in a few moments."

"Okay. Thank you. God bless you, my son," Germanus replied and the guard lightly cracked a smile and nodded. The guard succumbed to Germanus' polite charm. I realized the difference between him and the priest Annianus. Germanus delivered all of his words with a genuine sincerity. Annianus' words lacked that depth; they were shallow. This was Germanus' talent; he was able to capture and deliver his emotions through words he spoke.

"I guess we can only wait," I replied.

It quickly became apparent that the warden wasn't coming to speak with the bishop. Noticing that we were still patiently waiting, the guard went back inside and then returned more quickly than the first time. The guard wore a bewildered look upon his face.

"He's gone," the guard called out. "The warden must have left out the back entrance."

"Is there someone else I can speak with regarding this matter?" the bishop asked.

"No," he replied with a shake of his head. "Unless you are friends of the imperial family. These two prisoners were placed in the gaol by a palace official named Eugenius. He gave strict orders that the prisoners must remain here and not be transferred without his being present. I'm sorry."

The guard turned, lowered his head, and walked away. He went inside the warden's office and disappeared for a while. Bishop Germanus looked at the door where the guard went, then at the forum and then down the roads as if looking for the warden. Already, though, numerous people filtered through the area. Even if we saw the warden before, we could have lost him in the groups moving about the market square. The bishop went to the iron gate of the gaol. A long, thick-linked chain locked the gate. The bishop slowly sank to his knees as he stared at the gate. He bowed and prayed to it while mumbling words I barely heard. For a long time, he did this.

Some time later, the guard came outside the warden's office.

As he came to the front of gaol where the bishop still prayed, I asked, "What's their crime?"

I could see that my question was going to get a sharp response, but the guard spotted Germanus in prayer. The Roman paused and then lost the anger that gripped his face. He just shook his head in disbelief.

"Honestly," the guard remarked as he put his fingers up to his forehead. "I'm not sure what they are being held for. The warden doesn't know either. These two are a mystery. Everyone has their guess but no one really knows. Actually, guys are betting on it. Eugenius said that it was of the highest matter, state security."

"Hah, a matter of state security," I scoffed. "That little man is tough and at time mean as a little bear, but I don't think he has killed a senator, yet."

With a light laugh, the guard asked, "How old is the boy?"

"He turned four earlier, at the end of spring," I answered. "I struggle to see what risk he has to the security of the Roman Empire."

"So do I, among other things," remarked someone behind us. "There must be some kind of reason for doing something as profane as imprisoning a child."

Turning, I saw young Victorius and his eunuch. They stood next to a man that could pass as the boy's father. He had a sharp calculating stare, always looking for the inside information to exploit. This was something the boy had not acquired yet.

"When a man of reason comes face-to-face with the acts of stupidity, he naturally tries to apply the one thing that is always lacking," I replied.

"What's that?" Victorius inquired.

"Logic," his companion replied as he looked more shrewdly at me.

"Exactly," I confirmed with a light smile.

"Guard," the man called out and my heart sank.

As if suddenly recognizing who the man with young Victorius was, the guard snapped to attention and replied, "Yes, Secretary Volusianus."

"Who did you say told you that this boy was a threat to the state?"

"Well ... Well," the guard stuttered. "I ... I ... I heard it from the warden. He ... He ... He said that Eugenius, the imperial notary and cousin to the Bishop of Ravenna, said the boy was."

"The archbishop would tell you that they are fourth cousins through marriage," Volusianus replied.

With a light laugh as if he already knew that, the guard replied, "Yes, sir."

"Well, go get the keys and unlock the gate so I can get some questions answered," Volusianus ordered.

The guard's head dropped in dismay and replied, "I can't, sir. The warden left and took the keys with him."

"That's absurd. Where's the logic in that?" the angry Roman secretary sputtered.

I bit my lip but failed to hide my smirk from the hard glance of Volusianus. It broke the anger in his eyes and he laughed.

"Don't try to apply logic to lunacy," he added with a smile.

"Exactly," I replied.

"Now what? Any suggestions?" the Roman asked me.

"One," I replied. "Victorius, can I borrow your man?"

"Sure," the boy replied, though he wore a bewildered look. "Samson is strong, but he can't break chains. Not even if he had hair. Right, Samson?"

The eunuch nodded his head yes.

"I don't want him to break the chains. I just want him to open the door," I replied with a smile.

"But how?" the boy questioned.

"Samson, please come forward," I said as I went to the gate.

The man went to the gate and stood next to me. I had noticed a design flaw in the gate. The pins attached to the door sat down in the hinge. There was no metal above the pins to keep them securely in the hinges. Pointing at the crossbar in the gate near the pin, I said, "Lift up on this bar as hard as you can, Samson."

Hesitating at my order, the eunuch looked back at Volusianus and then the Roman secretary nodded his head yes. Samson yanked on the door and easily popped it free of the hinges. The gate hung loosely, being kept from the ground only by the locked chain after Samson let go of it.

"Amazing," young Victorius called out.

Ambrosius and little Artorius did not move. They simply looked at the Roman secretary.

"Please, please come out," Volusianus remarked.

"Thank you. We are indebted to your pity," the bishop replied as he suddenly stopped praying and lumbered to his feet. Stumbling slightly,

Samson steadied Germanus.

The Roman secretary looked at Germanus and remarked, "Consider it a fair exchange if you will only come and see my dear boy. He burns with a terrible fever. It melts away my boy's strength. The physicians give his mother and I no hope. We are left only with mourning. Please tend to my boy."

"Of course," the bishop replied. "Lead the way, Secretary Volusianus."

CHAPTER 70

Numerous nobles called upon Bishop Germanus while in Ravenna. Bishops, an imperial chamberlain, and the patrician's secretary coveted his attention. Germanus willfully accommodated them. Each time, he went to them.

One day, while still in Ravenna, there came a knock on the door of Volusianus' estate where we now stayed. I opened the door. I found Empress Placidia standing near the threshold. Her presence stunned me. Since our arrival, I had seen her several times from a distance, but now she stood right in front of me. She was with two other woman servants. They looked older than Placidia and did not speak. Though over fifty years old, Placidia was still beautiful. She had few lines on her face. Gray highlighted her dark hair. Her outfit was nothing extraordinary. In fact, it was homely. She wore a white linen tunic and no eye-catching jewelry. I knew that she didn't want people to know she was there.

I last saw her thirty years ago. She had changed very little. Her one eye slightly squinted as she studied me. I had shaved off my customary long beard and cropped my hair, different from when I was younger. There was a chance that she could recognize me, but the chances were extremely slim.

"I am here to see Bishop Germanus," Empress Placidia stated in a refined tone.

"Please come in," I remarked.

She moved in a slow, graceful, dignified manner. After she and her handmaids had walked through the threshold, I closed the door.

Turning to them, I replied, "It will be just a moment. I will get the bishop for you."

"Thank you," the Empress replied.

Returning with him, I smiled at her and left the room. I didn't go far, though. I wanted to hear what was said. I sat on a lounge couch and acted as though I were reading.

"Greetings, my dear empress," the bishop replied, slowly strolling in. "This is a blessed day when you visit. Thanks for honoring me with your presence. I am somewhat surprised, though. I highly doubt that I merit such a guest and gifts as you have given."

"Contrary to what you may think," she began. "I believe you warrant such attention. Seeing you brings back many good memories from a lifetime ago."

"Thank you for the praise," the bishop replied with a light nod.

"There's no need for that," she replied. "I am curious because of the prisoners you had released. Does it have anything to do with the gentleman that showed us in? For some reason, he looks familiar."

"Yes, he has some connection to this," the bishop replied. "But there is someone else I would like to introduce to you."

"Really?" she remarked. "Who is that?"

"Please follow me," Bishop Germanus remarked.

Taking no heed of my presence, Germanus led Placidia and her companions outside to the garden behind Volusianus' villa. After a moment, Germanus came back inside.

"Could you please go and get Ambrosius and Artorius?" the bishop asked.

"Are you sure you want to do that?" I asked.

He didn't say anything. He just looked at me. I stood up and did what he asked. They followed me out to the garden. As Empress Placidia saw Ambrosius for the first time, she appeared truly surprised. Her mouth hung open. Her handmaids seemed indifferent with him. Empress Placidia immediately drew close to Ambrosius. She appeared as if she might cry, not in pain but from joy. She fought to hold back her tears. Her eyes danced back and forth from Ambrosius to Germanus.

Smiling, she reached out her hands and remarked, "You cannot imagine how much you remind me of someone I used to know."

"I hope he was not a foe or fool," Ambrosius replied with a smile.

With a light laugh, she added, "No. Far from it, I would say."

"That is good," he replied.

"Where are you from?" she asked candidly.

"Originally?" Ambrosius replied. "If the stories are correct, I was born near Barcelona."

She turned pale, but then asked, "Did your parents tell you this?"

"I truly don't know. I never knew my real parents. Before I was even a year old, I was taken from my parents and raised in Britain," Ambrosius replied. "My father died when I was a baby, as I have been told."

"That is awful. Why would anyone do such a thing?" she replied.

"I've been told that it was in the best interest to handle things that way," Ambrosius replied.

"Do you believe that?" she asked.

"Actually, under the circumstances, I do," he added plainly.

"Really?" she replied with a tone of surprise and slight.

"Oddly enough, yes," Ambrosius confirmed.

"And so, what is the story with this young man next to you?" the Empress asked, as she looked at Artorius. "How old is your son?"

Laughing lightly, Ambrosius added, "This young man isn't my son."

"What?" she replied. "That's hard to believe. He looks so much like you."

"I am his uncle," Ambrosius added with a warm smile.

"Really? The two of you look like you could be father and son," she replied.

"He and the boy's father were twins," Germanus said.

She couldn't hide her surprise. She glanced at Ambrosius and then looked at Bishop Germanus. Bishop Germanus nodded his head yes.

"So then, what is your name, young man?" she asked.

"Marcellus," Artorius lied.

"Oh, I see," she replied.

"Dear lady, since you are a guest here," the bishop remarked, "I would hope you would allow me the honor of treating you as Our Lord, Jesus Christ, treated his last dinner guests. Please allow me to cleanse your feet as you sit."

"I would be honored."

Already prepared, the bishop stood up slowly, picked up a large bowl, and draped a cloth over his arm. He lifted a clay pitcher with his other hand and knelt before her.

"Please, everyone sit down and remove your footwear," Germanus remarked. Ambrosius sat next to the Empress on her right. He removed his sandals. As he did, she watched him. She stared at his right foot. At first, I didn't know why, but as I looked where she was looking, I knew. I spotted Ambrosius' hairy birthmark just above his right ankle. As she looked at the birthmark, he noticed her.

"Oh, what happened?" she asked. "Were you burned somehow?"

"Oh, this?" he asked as he pointed to the birthmark.

"Yes."

"No," he remarked. "That's my birthmark. I've had it since I was born."

"Interesting," she replied.

"Not really," he said with a smile.

She laughed as she slipped off her sandals. Quietly, the bishop went through the Christian ritual. The bishop, with great care, handled her feet. After soaking the cloth, Germanus ran it gently over each foot. He continually dipped the cloth to ensure that it was saturated with water. For each person, even the two handmaids, Bishop Germanus repeated the ritual. Afterwards, we enjoyed a light dinner with the Empress and her servants.

As the supper drew to a close, the Empress remarked, "Ladies, please return to the palace, gather the gifts that I have in my quarters, and return with them."

"Yes, my lady," they remarked and then left quickly.

CHAPTER 71

Empress Placidia sat silently. For a woman who had been through so much in her life, she still looked surprised.

"Dear Germanus, is this some kind of witchery?" She questioned. "I've heard tales of one of your present companions. They say that he is a true wizard, a master of many things."

"People say many things and do even worse, but I swear on everything I hold true that this is not some diabolical deed," Germanus declared. "I am here to give back what I had wrongfully taken away so long ago."

"What do you mean?" she replied.

"I think you know what I mean," the bishop remarked as he glanced at Ambrosius.

"How is such a thing possible?" she questioned with pain in her face. "I still wake at times with a vision of the tiny silver coffin in my mind. I cannot shake those troubling thoughts."

"It is my fault if it's his fault," I added. I didn't know why I spoke. I shouldn't have, but I continued. "There was a girl, Ahès. She had a child out of wedlock. Her boy was born during the consulship of Constantius and Constans."

"That's when my baby, Theodosius, was born," she whispered.

"Paid well, I took Ahès and the child she cared for to Barcelona," I added. "By the time we had made it there, the child was ill."

"Through imperial instructions," Bishop Germanus added, "her baby was switched with your child. Your brother, Emperor Honorius mandated this to happen. If we hadn't, someone else would have carried out your brother's orders. Even though you and Adaulphus had united the two kingdoms, there would have been no future heirs."

"So, you are telling me that my son, Theodosius, lives and he sits next to me?" she remarked as she looked at Ambrosius.

"What does your heart tell you? What do your eyes tell you?

Does he not look like Lord Adaulphus," Germanus declared.

"That's not enough," she snapped. She was being defensive. She didn't want her hope to hurt her once more.

I didn't want to hurt her once more but added, "And the birthmark?"

She turned to me with tears welling up in her eyes. I saw her sitting in that little church near Barcelona. Once more, Adaulphus sat next to her. He had a strange, confused look on his face this time. He wanted to comfort her, hold her, but Ambrosius didn't even know her. Instead of placing his hands on her shoulder, Ambrosius turned away from her. His eyes scanned the luscious lawn and hedges. His eyes met my eyes as I watched him. With a stern look, he stared and then his eyes dropped away. They fell to the ground, remaining there until the Empress looked over at him.

"And what do you make of the situation?" she asked him.

With a light laugh followed by a shake of his head, Ambrosius remarked, "At this point in my life, I have known this longer than I have not and yet still I don't know what to believe."

"So why are you here telling me this?" she asked as she suddenly stood up, took several steps away from us, and then turned toward us.

Though Germanus and I stood, Ambrosius remained seated. With his forearms resting on his thighs, Ambrosius looked up at Placidia and remarked, "Honestly, I don't know why the great bishop has told you. I thought we remained here to parley peace for Armorica so Lord Goar does not decimate our countrymen."

"So what do you plan, Bishop Germanus? Some glorious coup?" she questioned.

"No. I am a part of the old guard. My life in this world is limited. As I dreamt of traveling recently, I questioned why I had to go. The Lord told me in my dream, 'Do not be afraid. I do not ask you to travel out but to finally journey home. There, peace shall comfort your eternal rest.' "

Germanus paused but then continued, "I am no Querolus. I do not want to change my life. I am satisfied with who I am. But I cannot envision eternal peace if I did not tell you the truth. And now, I ask for forgiveness before the eyes of God, from the last person that I had transgressed upon. Please find mercy for my soul."

She said nothing. She held back her emotion. What was she feeling? Betrayal? Deceit? What would she do to us? There's nothing sanctifying in my part of the kidnapping, so I remained motionless.

"And why are you here?" she asked me suddenly as she glanced in my direction.

"No reason," I replied, "Other than I wanted to mend old friendships. The civil storms of recent years have done much damage to them. I fear that they may already be beyond repair.

"Many times, I have felt like a father to Ambrosius. It hasn't been until these last few years that I learned that I am the child needing guidance in order to reach proper manhood. I failed the common folk in the face of oppression. Ambrosius championed their defense. I wallowed in wanting while he became a hostage to safeguard his brother's boy. Some could even say that I'm worse yet; I had convinced him to put his faith in what Pelagius preached and follow me into heresy. There is more, but I'll neither bore you nor damn myself any further."

She said nothing. She gauged my words like Thoth might weigh an Egyptian's heart upon death. Her eyes made me want to tremble. She had power still. It would take very little for her to have me executed. They would only hesitate with Bishop Germanus. The rest of us would not even raise a concern.

"Dearest Augusta," Ambrosius remarked as he remained seated. "I have set aside a British crown. I do not look to pick up the Roman diadem. I look to gain nothing more than knowing that I have spoken with my mother."

As Ambrosius spoke, Empress Placidia's smile beamed with a proud maternal glow. She returned to his side and sat down next to him.

She took his hand into hers and spoke. "When I first saw you, I thought that I saw the young Gothic king that I had married so long ago. You are Adaulphus' son. There is little of the Roman features within you. Hah, your father would be happy with that."

"He does have your eyes, Your Highness," I added.

"That is true," Germans admitted.

"He's distinguished by beauty of face and form. Ambrosius is taller or possibly the weight of the world has simply made me shorter," Placidia added in a sweet tone.

She fell silent, once more. She squeezed Ambrosius hands, raised them up and then kissed them. Tears welled up in her eyes. Ambrosius released her hand and wiped the tears from the corner of her eyes.

"Please, my lady, you must let me brush away your emotions. Your maidens shall be returning soon. What would they think of our hospitality if they return to see you crying?" Ambrosius remarked.

She smiled as more tears welled up in her eyes. Standing, she wiped away the rest of the tears with the back of her hands. She lightly tugged at her tunic, straightening it. Slowly, she paced about the garden, regaining her passive demeanor.

"Dear Bishop Germanus, you have given me so much unsuspected joy," she remarked as she turned and faced us. "Name what you want and I promise it shall be yours."

"There is nothing more than forgiveness that I ask," the old bishop remarked with tears in his eyes.

"Even as saintly as you are, there must be something I can give or grant you," she added with a smile.

"There is but one thing a dying traveler asks for," the old bishop requested. "Please take me home so I may be laid to rest on my native land."

Years showed their stress and wear on the old bishop. He needed to sit down before he fell. The man was nearly seventy. The haughtiness of royalty faded from Placidia as she went to Germanus and cupped his cheek with her hand.

"You and your companions will have no wants in the one hundred and eighty leagues between here and Auxerre," the Empress whispered.

CHAPTER 72

Within a few days of meeting Empress Placidia in person, Bishop Germanus died. The grand Augusta didn't fail in delivering her promise to Bishop Germanus. She had her son, Valentinian the Third, provide an ivory bier that rode on a whitewashed equipage. The imperial chamberlain had the body of Bishop Germanus embalmed with spices as if he was an Egyptian noble.

An army of imperial servants journeyed to Auxerre with us. Strange tales of miracles sprung up as we traveled through Piacenza on our way to Germanus' fatherland. The last time we traveled like this, we were in Britain and Ambrosius was High Commander. Young Artorius took it all in. The extravagant procession had him awestruck. Its splendid array outshined anything Euthar's army ever exposed him to. Amazingly, the young boy maintained his made-up alias. Out of all the names that he could have picked, Artorius chose Marcellus.

As we settled into Bishop Germanus' private quarters, I remarked, "You have handled yourself extremely well, Artorius. Even though you did well, I was surprised when you used someone else's name. Why did you use that name? Why Marcellus?"

"He is my friend from Britain," Artorius replied with a light smile.

"Oh right, I remember. He came with you when you first arrived in Aureliani," I added.

"That's him," Artorius confirmed. "When we were first taken by the Romans, Uncle told me not to tell anyone my name or who I was. He said that it would complicate things. It might even endanger our lives."

"I guess I might have overreacted," Ambrosius replied.

"I wouldn't say that. I was going to say the same thing," I replied. "There is too much palace intrigue to take chances. Honestly, I wish the bishop hadn't said anything to Empress Placidia. I fear that the place we stayed in had ears. Even our whispers were heard."

"If there was to be any trouble, it should have happened already, right?" Ambrosius added.

"I would figure that they would wait until we left from Auxerre," I added.

"Then, we should never leave," Artorius laughed. We joined him with a short laugh.

"I wish that it was that easy," I replied. "Germanus cast a lot of attention on us. It didn't help having different bishops always around asking him questions."

"Maybe you shouldn't have helped him with Sigisvult's secretary's son or the imperial chamberlain's adopted boy. Oh, and let's not forget about the sick little girl in Autun," Ambrosius remarked. "People thought that breaking the boy's fever and purging the other child of his demonic seizures were the work of heavenly miracles. Don't you think that might catch some people's attention? What name were you using? Maximus the Miracle Maker?"

"Hah, that's funny," Artorius remarked with a laugh.

"No. No. That wasn't it. I can't believe I keep forgetting it. I would crack under questioning." Ambrosius replied.

"It was Budicius," I remarked. "I don't think it will matter much. No one associated the deeds with me. The healing was attributed to Bishop Germanus. Personally, though, I do not think we should linger much longer. We have been here for eight days. We should leave after they bury the bishop tomorrow. You both are welcome at my villa."

"At this point, anywhere is better than here," Ambrosius answered.

"Good, we shall all return home," I answered.

When we returned from Auxerre, we found the villa deserted, but barred shut. Nothing indicated what happen to Nepos, Sevira, or Ulfin. It just seemed as if they took only their personal belongings and left. With no one else, the three of us – Ambrosius, Artorius, and I – tried to restore normalcy to our lives at the villa near Aureliani.

CHAPTER 73

Four years later in the third consulship of Aëtius, we received a letter from Goar, the king of the Alans. The old warrior king planned to marry his third wife later in the year. His first wife had died some time in the reign of Emperor Honorius. Goar married his second wife shortly after Ambrosius and Artorius were carted off to Ravenna as prisoners. He had a son with this wife. The boy was named Beorg.

After informing Ambrosius of the content of the letter, he asked, "Did you want to go with Artorius and me to the wedding?"

"Oh. You were planning on attending the marriage?" I asked.

"Yes," he replied.

I was slightly surprised by his answer. I hadn't realized that Ambrosius and Goar had made that much of a connection. They had only spent a week or two together and that had been several years ago. Other than that, I knew of no other contact or interaction between them.

"Sure, I'll go," I answered. "When did you want to leave?"

"We can leave in the morning if that works for you," Ambrosius said.

"Oh, that soon? Sure, why not?" I asked.

"Good," he replied. "I'll have Artorius gather his things for the journey."

We rode north for the village called Allaines. It was just off the road between Soissons and Tournai. It was a new settlement that King Goar had established and named in honor of his future wife, Helena, and for their people. It wasn't the wisest location to choose. Clodio, a man of noble birth and noted martial skills, was the king of the Franks and was aggressively pushing south toward the Somme River. He and his men had overrun the helpless lands of the Atrebates near Arras. Soissons was in Clodio's sight and Cambrai was within his reach. Still, we headed for Allaines.

After passing Soissons and nearing the Oise River, Artorius rode ahead of us. He was eight years old and well-developed for his age. He was tall and growing every day. As we closed in on Allaines, we casually trotted the horses forward to keep little Arthur in our sights.

"So, why did you want to go to Lord Goar's wedding?" I asked.

"Many reasons," Ambrosius replied.

He said nothing more but still I waited for him to say something more. He didn't. He remained silent, and I did not want to pry.

Several moments later, Ambrosius added, "Lord Goar is the best source to tell me about my father. I still want to know him, Merlinus. I know it might sound crazy, but I still would like to know more of him."

"Fill in some of the blanks," I replied.

"Right," he answered as he looked at me with sadness in his eyes. It was some of the same sadness I saw that night Ambrosius told me that Priscilla had died. It troubled me to think that he had sacrificed so much for her just to lose her. He had intentionally abdicated power to live a humble existence, but still he suffered. His love and son were taken from him. He was a man that had been torn to pieces in three different lifetimes. The first, he only knew through what he had been told. Still, that pain was real. That was apparent from the look in his eyes now. He turned away to hide it. For the seventeen years I had known him, Ambrosius was never one who wanted to express his emotions, whether they were good or bad.

"You're right," I remarked. "Lord Goar is the last of the old guard. It is simply amazing to think that he has been a part of so much, the great winter invasion, serving, and setting up emperors. He's inspiring. He has to be nearly sixty."

"Hah," Ambrosius laughed. "Marriage would be the last thing I would be thinking about at that age."

"That's for sure," I replied.

Later before nightfall, we reached Allaines.

CHAPTER 74

After spending several days with us, Lord Goar stood ready to get married once more. The blonde-haired groom held the hand of his beautiful bride, Helena. She had wheat-colored hair like Goar. There had to be at least thirty years difference between them. Still, her face showed a lover's smile. He returned her smile. The ceremony was splendid.

Ambrosius and Artorius had stood up in Lord Goar's wedding. All three of them wore white tunics with silver chain mail over the top of it. They sported royal blue cloaks with silver-fur collars that ran along their shoulders. They wore white breeches. Thick black leather belts held up their pants and their sheathed swords. Knee-high black leather boots with the tops folded down hugged their calves. Ambrosius and little Artorius wore large black leather gloves that fanned out, covering their forearms. Lord Goar had his gloves off, and Ambrosius carried them.

A silver dress that shimmered in the summer sun draped over young Helena's long slender body; there was nothing fragile or manly about her. She was nearly taller than Lord Goar. Though having long, flowing hair, she wore it up in a braided bun for the ceremony. Silver mess streamers fluttered in the wind. Helena's younger sister, Diana, stood behind Helena and directly across from Ambrosius. The sisters' little niece, April, stood behind Diana and in line with Artorius. Both April and Diana had dresses that matched Helena's.

The day's weather could not have been better. The sky was a light blue with high, white clouds scattered across it. A steady breeze kept the strong summer sun cool. Joyfully, the wedding party gathered on a hill that overlooked the river near Allaines. Finalizing the ceremony, the revelers sang a Scythian marriage song. It echoed across the countryside.

The happy occasion had drawn several high-ranking Roman officers. The officer of Aëtius, Majorian, and the tri-consul himself were said to be en route. They would be there for the nuptial celebration in a short while.

I stood in the crowd next to Claudius, a Gaul who served Goar, along with several other close associates of the Alan warrior king. My heart suddenly sank as I smelled smoke and saw it blackening the sky on the other side of the river where the village, Allaines, stood completely ablaze. Men upon horses and men on foot flooded through Allaines. They were not Roman, or at least not dressed like them. From this distance, it was hard to distinguish anything definitive about them except the destruction they wreaked.

"They leave nothing unburnt, damn it all," Lord Goar cried out. "That bastard, Clodio and his men will pay for this with their lives. Men, to your horses."

As Goar shouted for blood, some of his men had already gathered and mounted up onto the horses on the hill. The Alan men rode hard for the fight. Stunned slightly by the sudden change in events, I stood there watching everything unfold. At that moment from the south, the Romans arrived on the scene. They quickly split and formed into two separate groups. The main group marched up the road toward Allaines and the other took position at the junction where the road split in two. The one road continued north to Allaines while the other veered to the right and headed east across the river and up the side of the hill to where the wedding party still stood. Girders of wood and chains supported the road as it scaled the steep terrain. The second group, which consisted entirely of cavalry, swept into position at the bridge.

The Franks did not retreat. In fact, their shouts and yells grew into a battle frenzy as if burning empty huts gave no honor as killing a man did. They rushed at the Roman lines in a massive mob fashion while their horsemen swung out from the flanks. The clash from the two armies was tremendous. They met head-on in the middle of the road, for many wagons and tents took up the fields leading up to Allaines on the side opposite of the river.

"This can't be happening. Not on this day," Lord Goar shouted. "Where is my horse?"

"My love, calm yourself. You don't want to have another attack. Please calm yourself," Helena begged.

"That's not happening. I can't calm myself, Helena," the old warrior king crowed. "Damn it all, where is my horse?"

"My lord, there are no more horses," Claudius remarked.

"There were only a few that were brought up here on the hill and they are already gone."

"This is outrageous," Goar shouted. "Claudius, stay here with Helena so you can protect the ladies from any harm. I'm marching down there to get retribution."

"Yes, sir," Claudius said as he moved closer to Helena.

"No, my love," Helena whispered. "Please don't go."

The old man fell silent, looked her in the eyes, and said, "I must. I am being disgraced."

"I don't care," she cried.

"I do," Goar said, looked away, and added, "Damn it all, how did this happen? Why didn't our scouts report about the Franks? I'm going down there. I'm not waiting and watching everything stripped from me. I will..."

Oddly, Lord Goar stopped in the middle of his tirade. He had a strange look upon his face and fear suddenly in his eyes. His right hand clutched at his chest over his heart. He gasped for air as if that would relieve him of what suddenly afflicted him. Speechless, he stared at us with bulging eyes. Slowly, he sank to his knees. Immediately, Helena dropped down to her knees next to him.

"My love, my love. What's wrong? Oh no, you're having another attack," she moaned and held him.

Though his mouth hung agape, no words escaped. He simply looked at her and patted her hand with his. Turning from her, he stared at Allaines as flames consumed what remained of it. A tear rolled down from the corner of his eye and Lord Goar expired, overwhelmed with grief. Still on his knees, the old warrior king fell face forward. Before he hit the ground, Ambrosius caught and held the dead king. As the tear on the king's cheek disappeared, many began to roll down Ambrosius'. He shook his head in disbelief. Slowly, Ambrosius laid the king down on the ground and straightened out his legs. Ambrosius looked at the weeping widow. She cried and crumbled, laying her head on Goar's chest. Ambrosius stood up and turned away while little Artorius instantly took his place by Lord Goar. I turned away and looked at the battle still raging.

Unfortunately, Lord Goar was not needed in the melee and had worked himself up for no reason. The Romans had the fight well in hand. They forced the enemy to turn and flee into the wooded countryside.

The short battle had left much mayhem. Splattered blood gleamed in the sunshine as it marred the canvas-covered wagons and tents. Fire consumed other lodging.

After Lord Goar's grand funeral, we returned sadly to Aureliani.

CHAPTER 75

It had been nearly five years since Lord Goar died. The former closeness between Ambrosius and I still hadn't returned. He spent most of his time away from the villa wandering the woods near the river. Artorius was nearly a young man now. It was good to have both of them around the villa, just the same.

Luckily when the one old oak came down last year, it was too far away to take down any part of the villa. Still, rain found its way through the roof of the villa. Water damage had ruined several rooms, including my private quarters. Repairing all the leaks had been a long task that Artorius and I tackled first.

As we worked on the roof of the stables, I noticed a rider rapidly approaching. I got down and started walking toward the open gate.

"What's wrong, Merlin?" Artorius said as I walked past him.

"There's a rider headed here," I answered.

"How many are there?" the boy asked as he followed me.

"There only appears to be one," I answered.

"It must be a messenger," he answered.

"There is a good chance that is what the rider is," I answered.

As the rider neared, I recognized him. It was Annianus. I wanted to close the gate and bar it shut. Nothing good could come out of his visit. The last time I saw him, Annianus asked for a donation to help restore the church of Aureliani. Ambrosius and Artorius were hunting at the time.

"This is not good," I mumbled.

"What's wrong?" Artorius whispered. "Who is it?"

"He's Annianus. He's now the Bishop of Aureliani." I answered.

"He was here when I had to go with King Goar," Artorius replied.

"Right," I remarked.

Breathing out a heavy sigh, Artorius wiped away the sweat on his forehead. It was a hot spring day.

"What does he want this time? I won't have to leave again, will I?" the boy asked in a nervous tone.

"You won't have to leave again if I have any control over the situation," I said.

"Good," the boy remarked. "I don't want to go. I'm fine just where I am at"

I smiled as we kept walking. By the time we reached the gate, the bishop had dismounted and was walking his horse toward us.

"Greetings. The tales are true. You have returned. I had thought that I had driven you from your villa when nothing else could. I thought I had done something that the Bacaudae or even the Empire could not do. That's amazing. I had simply asked you to contribute to the restoration of the city's cathedral and I hadn't seen you since," the bishop chuckled.

"It must just have been bad timing," I lied. "We must just keep missing each other. I had gone on a pilgrimage to Rome."

I had purposely avoided Annianus. Opinions of Annianus had changed. Mine had soured while others sweetened. Annianus used this to his advantage and took the holy see of Aureliani when it became vacant.

"So how long have you been back?" Annianus asked. "I haven't seen either of you two in Aureliani. It's been said that Ambrosius has returned, also. Is this true? Where is he? I don't see him around. Why isn't he helping?"

It had been nine years since Bishop Germanus died. In that time period, neither Ambrosius nor I had journeyed to Aureliani. There was simply no need for it. We had nothing to sell and wanted nothing that the countryside couldn't provide. Annianus' presence was unnerving. I could only think of Attila the Hun as a more unwelcome person.

"Unfortunately, I have no good news to tell you," the bishop said with a short laugh. He tried to make light of the moment but failed miserably. After a moment of awkward silence, the bishop added, "Attila and his Huns are sweeping into Gaul."

It didn't surprise me. I remained silent, not phased by his comment. It seemed fitting to hear him say it. There's nothing sure in this world except death, whether by famine, fighting, or fright. There is no escaping the Scourge of God.

"Did you not hear what I said?" the bishop asked with a skewed expression on his face.

"Yes, I did. But why should this concern me?" I asked.

"He's Attila, the great plunderer of people and prosperity."

"Hah, take a look around, Bishop. This is all I have, a dilapidated estate. I have nothing that a man like Attila would want to bother with," I declared. "Luckily, my only riches have been spared by the elements, my library's roof has no leaks."

"Laugh all you like," the bishop warned.

"What else would you like me to do, Annianus?" I snapped back. "Should I cry over something I cannot control? Attila and his men aren't coming for what I have. I can only prepare and hope by the grace of God that we're spared."

"The grace of God?" the bishop scoffed. "How do you expect to find the Almighty when He hasn't seen you once in the city's church?"

"I doubt that God lingers alone in your church waiting for me to appear. Besides, you can find the grace of God outside of the church."

"That's heresy you speak. Have you not heard of the teaching of Augustine of Hippo? How ignorance and arrogance leads the masses astray," the bishop remarked.

"Many considered Jesus a carpenter, but did he ever once build a church of wood or stone?" I remarked.

The bishop remained silent, though his stare sharpened.

"Some say predestination is heresy," Ambrosius called out as he suddenly joined the conversation. No one had noticed his arrival. Having no horse, he was quiet walking across the leaf-littered forest. The wind made more noise blowing down a beaten path than he did.

"Greetings, Lord Ambrosius," the bishop said in a more upbeat tone when he turned and saw Ambrosius.

"Good afternoon, Bishop Annianus," Ambrosius replied. "Long journey from the city for someone traveling alone."

"Dire circumstances require drastic measures," the bishop replied.

"What disaster is plaguing the world this time?" Ambrosius asked in a casual tone.

"Is that how you see me, harbinger of bad news?" the bishop followed up.

"Oh, you have good news to tell?" Ambrosius quickly replied.

"No," the bishop replied lowly.

Ambrosius smiled and shook his head. "So, what is it now?"

He followed up.

"Attila rides through Gaul as we speak," the bishop replied.

"And? Why does this concern us here? We have nothing that a man like Attila would want." Ambrosius remarked.

"Hah," Artorius laughed. "That's what Merlinus told him."

Ambrosius gave Artorius a stern stare and added, "Why don't you go back to work? If you can't work on the roof, go clean the stables."

Knowing that he should have remained silent, Artorius' head dropped as he added, "Yes, sir."

With a light smile, the bishop remarked, "He has grown into quite the young man."

"He's still a boy," I added.

"So what are you needing from us?" Ambrosius asked. "I doubt that you would have ridden out here if that's the only thing you had to tell us."

Bishop Anianus' smile soured, but he added, "This is true. I could have easily sent a messenger, but there is more. I have come in possession of a letter. I am having difficulty deciphering all of it, though."

"Why the concern with it?" Ambrosius added. "Why are you having troubles with it, if it was addressed to you?"

"It wasn't," the bishop added. "It was sent to Sangiban."

"Why are you intercepting letters addressed to the overlord of these lands? Did you not learn from the last time you meddled into the affairs of an Alan king? People have been executed for less of a reason," I remarked.

"It appears that the letter was sent by Attila," the bishop added. "I can't read it completely, though. It appears that it's written in Greek. You can read Greek, can't you Merlinus?"

I did not want to read that letter. There wasn't anything good to be gained by reading it. Once more, I saw myself being sucked into a vortex of civil chaos. There was no sorting things out, no controlling fate, none of that. I lacked the power to manipulate destiny. I had no delusions of grandeur.

"Can you?" the bishop asked as he held the letter in his hand. Ambrosius looked at me to see if I was all right. I wasn't all right. I felt nauseated looking at the rolled-up letter. I didn't raise my hand. I simply nodded my head.

"Will you?" the bishop asked.

Their mouths hung agape as they waited for my response. As I hesitated, Ambrosius' stare broke as if he suddenly realized why. He turned away and shook his head. Once more, he was disappointed with my cowardly behavior. Once more, the hero within me failed to surface and take control of the situation. Guilt set in. He walked away in the direction of Artorius.

I didn't want him to leave with Artorius. They were the only family I had. My hand reached for the letter.

"I'll read the letter," I called out loud enough for Ambrosius to hear. He didn't even break stride. I took the letter, scanned through it. It wasn't long.

"What does it say?" the bishop asked.

"It appears that it was written by a secretary of Attila, Eudoxius. It's a confirmation letter to Sangiban. The two parties have agreed to a pact. The Alan king shall surrender Aureliani to Attila to maintain his control over the lands where the Isère River meets the Rhône, in addition to the previously received gifts. Attila states that the Huns shall reach Aureliani no later than mid-June," I replied.

"Is there more?" the bishop asked.

"No," I answered.

"I wish there was more," Annianus remarked.

"What more do you really need to know?" I replied.

"Well, it would be nice to know what the gifts were," Annianus remarked.

"What does it matter? You know when Attila will be here." I said.

"Right," the bishop conceded.

"What's next for you?" I remarked.

"We are going to have to go to Arles," Bishop Annianus remarked.

"We? What do you mean?" I questioned.

"I want you to go with me. I need you to go with me. I can't read the letter. You must read it for me," the bishop demanded.

"I already told you what it says," I barked back. "In fact, I will copy the letter word for word in Greek and then translate it to Latin next to it on the same piece of paper. Then you can return the letter to whomever you received it from so it can be delivered to Sangiban."

"I was going to take the letter to Arles and deliver it into Aëtius," the bishop said proudly.

So he could do what with it? Wipe his ass? I wanted to say it to him. Although refined and pleasant-mannered, Anianus' proud righteousness sickened me.

"How can you convince the Roman general that the letter is authentic?" I questioned.

"Why would I ever forge such a document?" the man replied.

"Besides the obvious protection from the Huns, one could use such a letter to discipline Sangiban. Maybe even confiscate his lands. Maybe not the ones near Valence, but you could try to seize the ones here," I stated.

Annianus fell silent. As the simple logic sank in, he just shook his head.

"Not everyone thinks as corruptly as you do, Merlinus," Ambrosius called out.

Turning, I saw him approaching with Artorius. The boy carried a wooden pail while Ambrosius held four wooden mugs, two in each hand. I went to Artorius and helped him with the bucket. As Ambrosius held the mugs out in front of him, I poured them full with well water.

After taking a long draft, Ambrosius remarked, "So when do we leave for Arles?"

I just laughed, because I knew there was no avoiding the trip to the capital of Gaul. I knew I could make a diffcrence but hadn't really wanted to put my neck on the chopping block again. I could only get so many pardons from the powers that be. The death that I had personally witnessed made me aware of that. Still, I hoped it would help to bolster Ambrosius' opinion of me.

CHAPTER 76

We didn't waste any time. Bishop Annianus had arranged everything. We traveled along the Loire River toward its source. From there, we crossed the lands over to Lyons. We traveled down river to Arles on the Rhône River.

The weather in the capital of Gaul was much more pleasant than that in London. A bridge of boats connected the city as it straddled the Rhône. People flooded the street. There was a wider variety of people in Arles. There were Orientals, Persians, and Africans here in noticeable numbers. That was lacking in London.

Artorius needed constant looking after. Everything drew his attention. He wanted to see what everyone was doing, what they were selling, what they were trading, and what they were talking about. There were many armed men throughout the crowds. I assumed that most were Gothic due to their Germanic features and dialects.

We headed for the city's palace. We had hoped to catch up with Aëtius there or, at the very least, someone who had his ear. As we entered, loud, chaotic conversations echoed down the wide, white-washed hallway. We followed Bishop Annianus.

"How do you know where to go?" Artorius asked.

Smiling at the boy, the bishop remarked, "Before the great bishop of this metropolis, Hilary, had died, I came here and stayed for a while. He was generous enough to show me around the entire city and all of its important buildings."

"I see," Artorius remarked. "Good thing that you know where to go because I'm already lost."

Ambrosius, Bishop Annianus, and I laughed as we moved along the colonnaded hall. The voices had nearly became deafening.

Turning left, the bishop guided us into a wide-open room. There were easily a hundred people gathered. Many of them were formally dressed as Bishop Annianus was. Our presence went unnoticed except by a few guards near the entrance. One walked toward us.

"State your business," the guard ordered.

"We are here to speak with General Aëtius," the bishop stated.

With a slow wave of the hand, the guard remarked, "So are they."

"We need to speak with him regarding Attila the Hun," he added.

With a disgruntled look, the guard added, "So do they."

"We have intercepted a direct correspondence from Attila. He is heading for Aureliani. We have evidence that Sangiban, the Alan king, is going to turn over the city without defending it," the bishop stated.

I couldn't believe that Annianus had told this man all of that.

The guard didn't seem impressed by the news. He remarked, "Wait here while I report this to my superior officer."

"Good," the bishop remarked.

The guard walked back to his other cohorts and whispered something in one of their ears. That man's eyes grew keen as he looked at us. His eyes shifted from person to person in our group. He studied the bishop, then Ambrosius, myself, and finally Artorius. His gaze turned to the Roman official at the back of the room, sitting and listening to the delegates as they stood before him pleading their issues. As that man watched the speaker for a moment, he just shook his head. Turning back, he muttered something and the informing guard nodded his head and walked back to us.

"Come back later. You shall have Aëtius' attention," the guard remarked.

"How much later?" the bishop questioned.

Bishop Annianus lacked the finesse of speaking that Bishop Germanus had excelled at. This was evident in the guard's body language, the slight roll of his eyes followed by a heavy sigh.

"Come back in about two hours. There are many folks before you," the guard added.

"Do you think he could be done any sooner. Should I come back in an hour," the bishop pressed.

"You can stay the whole damn time as far as that is concerned, but he will not get to you any sooner," the guard remarked.

"But —," the bishop tried to continued.

Cutting in, Ambrosius remarked, "Bishop, why don't you use this time to show Artorius this great city?"

"But —," the bishop tried to continue, once more.

"Yes. That would be great. Please, Bishop Annianus," the boy begged. "Besides, I'm hungry."

"Very well," the bishop conceded.

Returning about two hours later, we found the room just as crowded if not more so. From where I was standing, I no longer could see the Roman speaking with the delegates. Though we looked around, no one noticed the cohort that we had spoken with earlier. There had been a changing of the guard.

"Oh, this is just great," muttered the bishop.

"Hold on," I remarked as I spotted the guard's superior officer.

"What?" questioned the bishop.

"There is the man that the guard had reported our news to," Ambrosius stated.

"Where? Where?" the bishop remarked as he looked about the crowd. "Oh, there he is. Right, that's him. That's the man. What should we do? I should just go up to him."

"I would advise you to simply place yourself in his line of sight, at first," I remarked.

"You don't think I need to be more direct?" the bishop asked.

"No," I replied.

As we moved into his peripheral view, the man turned toward us and noticed us immediately. He turned to a guard on his left side, whispered something, and then motioned toward us with his head. After looking right at us, the guard nodded his head and moved toward us.

"Come with me," the guard stated, then walked toward his commander. That officer led us out of the crowded hall and into an adjacent room. This room had no windows and only one other door located on the opposite wall from us. As we entered, I noticed the Roman that had been sitting out in the other room earlier. I was surprised to see him. I had assumed that he was still out there even though I hadn't seen him when we had returned. He stood up as we entered. He wasn't what I had expected for the renowned Aëtius. He was of average size, medium build and height. His dark hair receded from his olive-tan forehead. Though I recognized him from Lord Goar's funeral, I hadn't realized that it was him. We had maintained a low profile after the Alan king's sudden death.

"Greetings," the man called out. "I am Aëtius. I've been informed that you may have some information that could be of interest."

"Yes," Annianus added, "Definitely. I believe that you will be extremely interested in what I have to show you. Here."

The bishop handed the letter to the Roman general. With a quick glance, Aëtius laughed and remarked, "Is this a joke? If it is, I don't have time for this."

"What are you talking about? Why would you think that this is a joke?" Annianus replied in a sharp tone.

"Well, first off, why would the writer take the trouble to write in Greek and then translate the message into Latin?" The irritated man replied. "That just doesn't make sense."

"Please, your magnificence," I interrupted. "Allow me to explain. I am the one who copied the letter you hold in your hand."

Though losing the hard tone, the general questioned, "And who are you? And why have I been given only a copy of this supposed letter? Where is the original?"

"I am Merlinus. Currently, I have a villa southeast of Aureliani. You have only been given a copy because the original has been delivered to the person it was addressed to," I declared in an even tone.

"So why was that done?" Aëtius questioned further.

"That way their planned treachery is not changed or revised. This way you may still have the element of surprise if you wish to act upon this information that we have provided."

"How do I know that this is credible information?" the general asked.

"You don't," I remarked. His eyes grew focused.

"I —," the bishop started but stopped as I glared at him.

"I know you have had extensive dealings with Attila. Read over the letter and judge the merit of it," I stated.

Gauging my words, the Roman stared at me for a moment. Without another word, he read through the letter. His eyes moved line by line. They shifted to the edge of the paper. He turned the paper around so I could see the writing. With his free hand, he pointed at a symbol at the edge of the paper and asked, "What is this?"

"Truthfully," I answered, "I haven't a clue."

The bishop turned and stared at me with a shocked look.

Before he could say a word, I added, "I noticed the symbol on the original. I didn't know what it meant, but I figured that it had to signify something, so I copied it."

Saying nothing, the Roman nodded his head in agreement and turned his attention back to the letter.

As his eyes scanned the letter, he asked, "What do you make of the letter?"

"I believe . . ." the bishop stopped as Aëtius gave him a hard stare and then transferred his glance back to me.

"Attila has marched into Gaul and has already sacked Metz. I don't believe it would be unrealistic that the Hun wants more, but doesn't want to sacrifice any more blood than he has to," I remarked.

The Roman glanced at the officer who had led us in. That man nodded his head in agreement.

"Head back to Aureliani. Do all that you can do to prepare the city but do not tip off Sangiban that we know about his planned treachery."

"Is that it?" the bishop questioned abruptly.

"Yes. Now go," Aëtius remarked.

"Aren't you leaving right now, also?" The bishop remarked.

"No," the Roman replied.

"But," the bishop started.

"Come, Annianus. We have done all that we can here," Ambrosius remarked.

CHAPTER 77

Bishop Annianus said nothing good the whole trip back from Arles. He was short with people more than usual, even rude. Artorius remained mute. He realized the magnitude of the situation now. Young Arthur had lost the excitement that he had earlier. It disappeared after the bishop had given us a tour of Arles. The mood of the city had impacted the boy heavily. It left no doubt within any of us that destruction and death charged after us on horseback.

Though he had helped Ambrosius and I restore the gate to good repair, Arthur had become distant and ate very little during the last few days. Ambrosius worried over him. I was worried for him. A boy his age shouldn't have to worry about such things.

One day after returning to the villa in early June, Artorius meandered outside at the back of the villa.

Walking up to him, I asked, "Do you mind if I walk with you?"

"I'm not really headed anywhere," he replied plainly.

"That's fine," I remarked. "I really don't want to go anywhere."

A little smile appeared but then vanished as if he never had it.

"Okay, then," he said as he took long, slow steps. He headed toward the woods behind the villa.

"Is there anything you want to talk about," I asked.

Looking at me with a bewildered look, he replied, "No. Not really. Should there be?" Laughing lightly, he added, "I don't remember doing anything wrong."

"No, I didn't mean that," I replied. "I'm talking more along what may happen with the Huns. It's all right to think about the dangers, but you shouldn't dwell on such things. That's not good."

"I know, sir," the boy replied. "I'm just trying to stay out of the way. I don't want to be a burden on anyone."

"Don't worry, Arthur," I stated. "You definitely are not that. In fact, I know that you've been the saving grace for both your uncle and me.

Without you, we really wouldn't have much reason to look forward to the future."

"Quit fibbing, sir," the boy remarked. "It's not helping me through the moment. Besides, my uncle doesn't need anything. He is stronger than Atlas."

"Anyone is stronger than Atlas. Atlas isn't real," Ambrosius said as he approached from behind us. We stopped and turned toward him.

"Hello, Uncle," Artorius replied.

"Hello, Arthur," Ambrosius remarked. "You know that Merlin tells you the truth. There wouldn't be much left for me, if you weren't here. I've lost a lot in my life and I'm not sure what I'd do if something happened to you. I nearly lost myself with the death of Priscilla. It was your arrival that marked a turning point for me. At that point, I looked past my own problems. Then I thought of your well-being, your happiness. You are the son I always wanted and you have lived your life in a way that would make my brother proud."

"Really?" the boy reluctantly asked, fearing that Ambrosius might be playing with his emotions.

"Yes, that is the truth. You are the world to me and you are truly no burden to carry," Ambrosius added.

"Hah," the boy laughed. "You are stronger than Atlas."

"Only for you," he added. "Well, I didn't mean to break up your conversation, but I was heading out for supper. Arthur, did you want to accompany me on the hunt."

"Sure," the boy replied excitedly. "Did you want to go with us, Merlin?"

"Thanks for asking, but it would be best if I remained behind to man the fort. For once, I am in charge. Everyone must obey my every command."

"There's no one to be commanded," the boy observed.

"There's me, myself, and I," I replied.

"You're goofy," the boy remarked as he shook his head.

"Well, either way, I shouldn't have any troubles with my squadron," I added.

Ambrosius and Artorius laughed.

"Come on, kid. You can't beat Lord Merlin when it comes to words," Ambrosius remarked.

"Right," the boy replied.

I walked over to the stables with them. After equipping the horses, they mounted up and rode out of the gate. Afterwards, I barred the gate.

CHAPTER 78

Terror filled me as I heard Artorius call out repeatedly, "Merlin. Merlin, come quickly. There's trouble."

Going to the gate and letting him in, I asked, "What's wrong?"

"We came across a squadron of Huns. Uncle wanted me to come and get you. He wanted you to ride out to him. He is waiting at the third mile marker heading northeast toward Allainville," the boy stated.

"All right," I remarked as I moved toward the stables. Before going to get a horse, I remarked, "Go to my quarters. Go to the chipped white-marble bust by the window. Lift the head and take it on the bed. After laying it on its side, remove the bottom, gather the coins from inside and bring them to me."

"Yes, sir," the boy replied as he ran toward the villa.

We met at the front gate. He handed me the heavy sack of coins.

"Thanks," I replied. "After I leave, bar the gate."

"Yes, sir."

Mounting, I rode hard for the third mile marker northeast of the villa. I hoped Ambrosius had enough sense not to engage any group of Huns on his own. Nothing could make my anxiety subside. I heeled the horse to a faster gallop.

I didn't travel directly on the road. I rode along the roadside, remaining in the cover of the forest. After passing the second mile marker northeast of the villa, I halted the horse and dismounted. I saw the front of Attila's army approaching. I walked my mount farther into the woods. Completely hidden in deep cover, I remounted and continued for the third milestone. I didn't witness the end of the military procession for some time. The Hunnish army was enormous. It made me feel like there was no hope for Aureliani or Gaul, for that matter.

As the supply train behind the riding warriors passed, I rode less than a hundred yards when I spotted Ambrosius riding hard straight for me.

As we approached each other, he called out at a low volume,

"You've seen them, then? Their army is huge."

"Yes," was my only response.

"Where's Artorius?" he questioned.

"I told him to remain at the villa with the gate barred shut. I didn't want him riding out in the open with us," I told him.

"Right," Ambrosius replied. "Staying behind the wall would be the safest bet for him. This is not good. Attila's army measures over a mile long."

"We need to get back to the villa," I urged.

"Absolutely," he replied.

As we continued for the villa, we saw a squad of five horsemen riding southwest in the same direction. We halted our horses and tried to draw no attention. Immediately, we knew our presence was detected.

The group veered toward us. The head rider yelled, "Don't move!"

We heeled both of our horses into a strong gallop as we turned and headed deeper into the woods. They gave chase. We had the advantage of being familiar with the terrain; however, their superior horse-handling surpassed the edge we would have otherwise had. Neither myself nor Ambrosius were slouches in horse riding, but compared to them, we were novices. As the five Hunnish riders pursued us, the lead horse was nearly on top of me. In the corner of my eye, I saw the horse's head inching up along side of me. I heard it breathing as it frothed from its mouth. The horseman was coming up between us. Although ahead of me, somehow Ambrosius noticed what was happening. Suddenly, he halted his horse with his right hand while unsheathing his sword with his left. Though I doubted that he would hit me, I shifted to the left side of my horse as Ambrosius' sweeping sword gleamed past me. Without a moment to move out of the way, the lead rider fell victim to Ambrosius' blade. Ambrosius decapitated the rider. In that instant, the Hun's head floated forward with the horse while the rider's dead weight pulled his body to the ground. The Hun behind him couldn't avoid the lifeless corpse. It tangled up the horse's legs and threw the rider to the ground with a crippling thud. The other three scattered from the path. As they did, a tree limb ripped down one of the riders from his horse. Ambrosius charged after the horseman to his right as the rider headed in the direction of the Roman road. Following suit, I turned and pursued the last one to the left. As I rapidly gained on the Hun, I realized that his animal had to be lame.

Without hesitation, though, I withdrew the hunting spear secured to my saddle and pierced it through the back of the Hun. I turned and headed in the direction where I last saw Ambrosius.

Riding up to a sharp knoll, I spotted Ambrosius and the last Hun. They sparred like two saber-swinging centaurs. Sparks rained like tiny stars falling through the sky. The impact from their consecutive blows jolted them as they wheeled about attacking each other from the backs of their horses.

There wasn't much room to fight and the stone outcrops divided the clearing into sections. Each of them masterfully used the terrain to try to gain the advantage. Ambrosius wheeled out of the way of the Hun's charge by veering down the side of a short but sharp bank. Hooking back around and climbing up, Ambrosius mimicked the Hun's attack and charged at him. As the sides of the stallions collided and their swords clashed, the two grand warriors fell from their horses.

I watched as the Hun and his horse fell toward the point of the outcrop. Somehow, the Hun brought his left leg clear as his horse slammed hard onto the sharp rocks. His sword, tip down, jammed into the large cluster of stones as the Hun fell clear of the outcrop. The Hun scrambled to his feet and went for his sword. He yanked on it but failed to draw the sword from the stone. I heeled my horse forward. As he spotted my approach, he frantically pulled on the sword. Realizing it was futile, his head turned about looking at his options. Spotting Ambrosius' horse, the Hun went for it. I recognized him immediately. Though gray lingered in his thin beard, I knew that the Hun was Attila. Little had changed for him in the fifteen years since I last saw him. He still had a broad chest with a massive head on his shoulders. He still stared at me with his beady little eyes. The quality of his garments was the most noteworthy change. A silver fur cape hung from the shoulders of his crimson-red tunic. Mounting up onto Ambrosius' horse, the Hun heeled the horse into an instant gallop. I let the Hun flee and went to Ambrosius.

I didn't like what I saw when I reached him. Blood darkened the inner part of his lips. Ambrosius was spitting up blood as he lay on the ground. It appeared that he had landed on some of the jagged rocks and punctured his lung.

"Is it that bad looking?" Ambrosius gurgled. "Merlin, you look white as freshly bleached linen."

It did look that bad, but I didn't want to tell him that.

"Don't say a word. Just rest," I told him as I dismounted and knelt down by Ambrosius' side.

As he laughed with a chilling hiss, he remarked, "Merlin, you know there is no time left for me. I feel it; you see it. Now, there's only one thing left to do. Save Arthur."

"No," I cried. "I can save you."

"If anyone could, it would be you, but I'm beyond even your healing powers. You have given me a life that I wasn't ever supposed to have. If you still feel obligated to give me more, then let me die knowing that Arthur is safe."

"No, I can save you," I repeated. "I will save you."

"I am beyond saving. Take Arthur to my brothers in Britain. Take him to Cai and Geraint," Ambrosius added with his dying breath, "Save Arthur. Promise me, Merlin. Save Arthur."

Jealous of the legendary life Ambrosius led, the gods of fate and free will were allowing him only thirty-seven years on this earth. I considered myself fortunate for witnessing much of it. I had seen the beginning and the end of his years. Strands of gray had crept into his hair though still a young man.

As I watched the last bit of life draining away from Ambrosius, how could I deny his request?

"Please, Merlin! Don't make me suffer any longer," Ambrosius hissed as a bead of blood streamed down from the corner of his mouth. "Save Arthur."

"I promise."

Leon Mintz

The Making of Arthurian Tales

<u>Arthurian Tales</u> rises up from years of research. The author has sown and cultivated the relevant folklore of Nennius and Geoffrey of Monmouth in a topsoil enriched by various fifth-century and near-contemporary chroniclers. Will <u>Arthurian Tales</u> decisively dispel the mystery surrounding King Arthur? Not likely. Though the author presents a plausible "World-Restorer" scenario, the waters of Avallon remain murky to this day. Even if new historical material surfaced, the author doubts that it would decisively settle the issue. There would be those who doubt its authenticity. Technically, the question – did King Arthur ever exist – would remain unresolved.

Still, a hero stands in the shadows of time. We are left with subjective stories about the man, the events in his life, and the ones leading up to it. We must pick and choose what we believe and build our own legends, accordingly. We must decide what seems more likely than not. There are those that have made a respectable career out of this. Scholars and professors highlight that list. The author does not pretend to be either. But having no ties to certain Arthurian dogma, the author has been able to formulate several unique arguments that have the potential of breathing new life into Arthurian studies. These key elements regarding <u>Arthurian Tales</u> follow the time line of <u>Ambrosius Aureliani</u>.

The time line has various markers that require some brief explanations. The symbol ~ marks an event on the time line that has a small variance in the year that it occurred. These events are mostly taken from the Gallic Chronicle of 452. The symbol * indicates an event dated conjecturally by the author. Some of these calculations are achieved by not associating the third consulship of Aëtius with the British appeal to Agitius. The basis for the event was developed by the author independently. In some cases, though, the author utilized the theories of noteworthy individuals such as Ian Wood's opinion on when Germanus became a bishop and Geoffrey Ashe's view that King Arthur was Riotimus. [ ] mark the author's conjecture within an event. The author uses them to establish links with events mentioned by Gildas and the other sources. Starting in 425 and ending in 436, (yr1 through12) appears at the beginning of each year. This correlates with Passage 66 of Nennius.

Many may argue that any story based on these key elements would be ridiculous and need no further consideration. Unfortunately, the Arthurian Age is not well-documented or what had been written hasn't survived to modern times. Possibly, it went up in smoke as many books did upon the order of Pope Leo. Whatever the case, many times, only one source tells of an event and we are left with assumptions that cannot be verified by independent sources. This is what we are faced with when dating the British Appeal to Agitius. In its traditional interpretation, there is an inherent time variance spanning from the year Aëtius received his third consulship to the year he died. Some have even argued that the "tri consul" is not to be used as a time marker, but simply to identify the Aëtius being referred to. Faced with a possible margin of error over a decade long, it does not seem ridiculous to take a moment to entertain a different theory for dating the events within the sources. And from this effort, <u>Arthurian Tales</u> comes to light.

The Chronology of Ambrosius Aureliani

Source Abbreviations

GC - 382 ~ The British soldiers elevated Maximus up as emperor, then, he halted the invading Picts and Irish.

GC - 383 Maximus crossed to Gaul & killed Emperor Gratian near Lyons.

Gi§13 /
PA / N - 388 Valentinian & Theodosius killed Maximus three miles outside of Aquileia.

GC - 391 ~Temples in Alexandria, including the ancient one of Serapis, were destroyed.

OT9 /
JA194 - 405 ~ Stilicho removed troops from Britain to fight Radagaisus at Fiesole.

OT12 - 406 The British army elevated Marcus to supreme ruler.
          Dissatisfied, the army killed Marcus & elevated Gratian in his stead.
OT 9 -   Various Germanic tribes crossed the Rhine nearly unopposed.

OT12 - 407 After six months, the British executed Gratian. Constantine took his place.

The Chronology of Ambrosius Aureliani

                                                                            Source Abbreviations

407 Soon, Constantine took his army to Gaul to validate his claim.   - PA

408 ~ Saxons laid waste to Britain.   - GC

409 The British expelled the imperial magistrates from the island.   - Z

410 British cities received the Rescript of Honorius.   Z / - Gi§18
    Alaric & his Goths sacked Rome & took Princess Placidia as a hostage.   - OT3
    Disease & raiders hit Spain. Famine forced walled cities to cannibalism.   - OT30 / H

411 Lord Alaric died & his brother-in-law, Adaulphus (Athaulf) became king.   - OT10
    Imperial forces killed the usurper Constantine in Arles.   - GC
    Jovinus usurped the Gallic imperial government.   - GC
    * The British appealed to Agitius [Agroetius] for help.   - Gi§20 / GT

412 * The Gallic people removed the magistrates from their offices.   - CL / Z
    * Conscripted, Germanus became the Bishop of Auxerre.   - CL

413 Jovinus the usurper was killed. Pelagius declared the Doctrine of Free Will.   - PA
    ~Enormous famine hit Gaul [& Britain].   - GC / Gi§20.2

414 Holding his first consulship, Constantius shared it with Constans.   - PA
    King Adaulphus married Princess Placidia.   - OT24
    She gave birth to a boy & named him Theodosius in honor of her father.   - OT26
    Their baby boy died in Barcelona & was buried in a silver coffin.   - OT26
    * The daughter [Ahès] of Vortigern [Grallon] had his son, Faustus.   - N/A

415 A servant named Dubius murdered King Adaulphus while in his stalls.   - OT26

416 Goths traded Placidia for grain.   - OT31
    Palladius became consul.   - PA

417 ~Asclepius toppled the statue of Mount Etna.   - OT15

418 Council of Carthage condemned Free Will & Valentinian III was born in July.   - PA
    Honorius established the Gallic Council of the Seven Provinces when   - OA
    Agricola was the praetorian prefect of Gaul.

420 In Constantius' third consulship, Honorius made him a colleague of power.   - PA

421 Agricola became consul. Emperor Constantius died.   - PA
    * A plague hit Farther Gaul [& Britain].   - / CL Gi§22.2

423 Emperor Honorius died on August 27. With the help of Castinus &   - OT41
    Aëtius, John opposed Valentinian III's claim to the Empire.

The Chronology of Ambrosius Aureliani

Source Abbreviations

PA -	424 Soldiers in Arles murdered the Prefect of Gaul, Exuperantius of Poitiers. No authority sought to bring the evildoers to justice. With an Alan army sent by Theodosius II, Placidia & Valentinian III returned to Italy as the recognized Augusta & Caesar.
N - OT46 - PA - JA196 -	425 (yr1) * Vortigern [Grallon, lord of Vorgium] held an empire in Britain. The Alan forces defeated John the usurper & established order. Placidia pardoned Aëtius & sent him after the Goths besieging Arles. Felix became the master of the soldiers instead of Aëtius or Boniface.
PA -	426 (yr2) Barnabus the Tribune killed Bishop Patroclus of Arles.
PA -	427 (yr3) Felix waged war upon Boniface. The Vandals entered Africa.
Gi§23 / N / GM - PA -	428 (yr4) Vortigern & the British Council requested the English to come to Britain. Aëtius took Gallic lands by the Rhine from the Franks. Felix was consul.
PA - Gi§23.5 / N / GM / CL - Gi§25.2 / N / GM - GM / N - GM / N - Gi§25.3 / - GM / N	429 (yr5) Bishop Germanus was sent to Britain upon Palladius' suggestion. * Bishop Germanus battled the Saxons & Picts in Britain on Easter. * The Saxons left. * After Vortimer promised to restore the churches, he died. * On May 1st, Hengist and his men massacred many British nobles. * Ambrosius [& Bishop Germanus] marched out against Vortigern, laid siege to him & burned down his fortress.
PA -	430 (yr6) Aëtius put to death Felix, his wife, Padusia, & the deacon, Grunitus.
PA / N - GM -	431 (yr7) Palladius became the first bishop of the Irish. * With Merlin's help, Uther [Euthar] took down the Giant's Ring in Ireland.
PA -	432 (yr8) Aëtius became consul. Boniface replaced Aëtius as the master of the soldiers by the orders of Augusta Placidia.
GC - CL / GC -	433 (yr9) Defeated by Boniface, Aëtius fled to the Huns after retiring. Bishop Germanus became renown for miraculous deeds.
GC -	434 (yr10) Aëtius came under Placidia's good graces.
GC -	435 (yr11) Tibatto led a rebellion in Farther Gaul against the Roman state.
N - GC -	436 (yr12)* From when Vortigern first reigned to the quarrel between Vitalinus and Ambrosius, twelve years elapsed. Aëtius & his Huns slaughtered Gundahar & the Burgundians.

The Chronology of Ambrosius Aureliani

Source Abbreviations

437 Aëtius became consul.	- PA
Tibatto was captured.	- GC
Rome waged war on the Goths.	- PA
* Uther [Euthar] & Ygerna conceived Arthur after Eastertide.	- GM
438 * Arthur was born in the spring.	- GM
439 Aëtius lost Carthage to Gaiseric & the Vandals.	- PA
440 Deacon Leo restored peace between Aëtius & Albinus.	- PA
441 * Bishop Germanus went to Britain & formally condemned more Pelagian heretics. Afterwards, he helped the son of Elafius.	- CL
~The Saxons subjugated the British provinces.	- GC
442 ~Aëtius gave Farther Gaul to King Goar & his Alans.	- GC
* Bishop Germanus parleyed peace with King Goar & vowed to get it imperially endorsed. Bishop Germanus died while in Ravenna. Bishop Germanus received an imperial funeral procession back to Auxerre.	- CL
443 Pope Leo had great piles of books seized & burned in the city of Rome.	- PA
444 Albinus became consul. By ways of Cain, Attila took his kingship from Bleda the Hun.	- PA
446 With no true contemporary fanfare, Aëtius held his third consulship.	- EC
* Majorian & Aëtius battled Clodio, the king of the Franks at the Scythian wedding [of Goar, king of the Alans. King Goar died.]	- GT / S
448 * Attila received the Sword of Ares from a herdsman.	- PP / Jo
450 Placidia died.	- GC
451 Attila assaulted Aureliani, a city of Gaul.	- Jo / GT
454 Valentinian III killed Aëtius.	- PA

Source Abbreviations

A – Vie de S. Guénolé by Albert Le Grand. *The Saints of Cornwall, Part Two* by Gilbert H. Doble. (Felinfach, UK: Llanerch Publishers, 1997), p. 86

CL – The Life of St. Germanus, Bishop of Auxerre by Constantius of Lyons. *The Western Fathers*. Edited and translated by F. R. Hoare. (New York, NY: Harper Torchbooks, 1954), pp. 283 - 320

EC – Easter Cycle of 457 - Victorius of Aquitaine. Vermaat, Robert "The Text of Victorius' Cursus Paschalis - years 367 - 497 AD" Vortigern Studies. http://www.vortigernstudies.org.uk/artsou/victoriustabel.htm (accessed March 23, 2010)

GC – Gallic Chronicle of 452. *From Roman to Merovingian Gaul*. Edited and translated by Alexander Callander Murray. (Peterborough, ON Canada: Broadview Press Ltd., 2000), pp. 77 - 85

Gi – Gildas. Gildas: *The Ruin of Britain and Other Works*. Edited and translated by Michael Winterbottom. (West Sussex UK: Phillimore & Co. Ltd., 2002), pp. 20 - 28

GM – Geoffrey of Monmouth. *History of the Kings of Britain*. Translated by Lewis Thorpe. Middlesex, UK: Penguin Books Ltd., 2002), pp. 135 - 199

GT – Gregory of Tours. *The History of the Franks*. Translated by Lewis Thorpe. (London, UK: Penguin Books Ltd., 1974), pp. 116; 124 - 125

H – The Chronicle of Hydatius. *From Roman to Merovingian Gaul*. Edited and translated by Alexander Callander Murray. (Peterborough, ON Canada: Broadview Press Ltd., 2000), pp. 85 - 98

JA – John of Antioch. *The Age of Attila*. Translated by C. D. Gordon. (Ann Arbor, MI: Ann Arbor Paperbacks, 1966), fr. 194, pp. 27 - 28; fr. 196, pp. 47 - 48

Jo – Jordanes, *The Origin and Deeds of the Goths*. Edited by Charles C. Mierow (Philadelphia, PA: D.N. Goodrich, 2007) pp. 33 - 43.

N – Nennius. *British History and the Welsh Annals*. Edited and translated by John Morris. (London: Phillimore & Co. Ltd., 1980), pp. 22 - 36

OA – The Gallic Council of the Seven Provinces. *From Roman to Merovingian Gaul*. Edited and translated by Alexander Callander Murray. (Peterborough, ON Canada: Broadview Press Ltd., 2000), pp. 169 - 171

Source Abbreviations

OT – Olympiodorus of Thebes. *The Age of Attila.* Translated by C. D. Gordon. (Ann Arbor, MI: Ann Arbor Paperbacks, 1966), fr. 9, p. 30; fr. 12, pp. 30 - 31; fr. 3, p. 34; fr. 10, p. 35; fr. 24, pp. 40 - 41; fr. 26, pp. 41 - 42; fr. 31, p. 42; fr. 15, p. 35; fr. 41, p. 45; fr. 46, pp. 46 - 47

PA – Prosper of Aquitaine. *From Roman to Merovingian Gaul.* Edited and translated by Alexander Callander Murray. (Peterborough, ON Canada: Broadview Press Ltd., 2000), pp. 62 - 76

PP – Priscus of Panium. *The Age of Attila.* Translated by C. D. Gordon. (Ann Arbor, MI: Ann Arbor Paperbacks, 1966), fr. 8, pp. 72 - 93; fr. 10, p. 93

S – Sidonius. *Sidonius: Poem Letters I - II.* Translated by W. B. Anderson. (London, UK: Harvard University Press, 1996), pp. 77 - 85

Z – Zosimus. *An Age of Tyrants* by Christopher A. Snyder. (University Park, PA: The Pennsylvania State University Press, 1998), p. 22

Other Arthurian Sources

Alcock, Joan. *Life in Roman Britain.* Stroud, UK: Tempus Publishing Limited, 2006.

Alcock, Leslie. *Arthur's Britain.* Middlesex, UK: Penguin Books Ltd., 1982.

Ashe, Geoffrey. *The Discovery of King Arthur.* New York, NY: Henry Holt and Company, LLC, reprinted by Owl Books, 1987.

Bachrach, Bernard S. *A History of the Alans in the West.* Minneapolis, MN: University of Minnesota Press, 1973.

Blair, Peter Hunter. *Roman Britain and Early England. 55 B. C. - A. D. 871.* New York, NY: W. W. Norton & Company, Inc., 1966.

Borer, Mary C. *The City of London.* New York, NY: David McKay Company, 1978.

Bulfinch, Thomas. *Bulfinch's Mythology.* Avenel, NJ: Gramercy Books, 1979.

Clayton, Peter. *A Companion to Roman Britain.* Dorset Press, 1985.

Dalton, O. M. *The Letters of Sidonius -- Volumes I & II.* Oxford, UK: Clarendon Press, 1915.

Other Arthurian Sources

Drinkwater, John and Elton, Hugh. *Fifth-Century Gaul: A Crisis of Identity?* Cambridge, UK: Cambridge University Press, 2002.

Ferguson, John. *Pelagius*. Cambridge, UK: W. Hefner & Sons Ltd., 1956, reprinted Ann Arbor, MI: UMI Books on Demand, 2007.

Galliou, Patrick and Jones, Michael. *The Bretons*. Oxford, UK: Basil Blackwell Ltd., 1991.

Hanson, R. P. C. *Saint Patrick -- His Origins and Career*. Oxford, UK: Clarendon Press, 1968.

Haywood, John. *Dark Age Naval Power*. Norfolk, UK: Anglo-Saxon Books, 1999.

Lapidge, M.; Dumville, D.; and Wood, I. *Studies in Celtic History V - Gildas: New Approaches*. Woodbridge, Suffolk, UK: The Boydell Press, 1984.

Littleton, C. Scott and Malcor, Linda A. *From Scythia to Camelot*. New York, NY: Routledge, 2000.

McClure, Judith and Collins, Roger. *Bede -- The Ecclesiastical History of the English People - The Greater Chronicle - Bede's Letter to Egbert*. Oxford, UK: Oxford University Press, 1994.

Morris, John. *The Age of Arthur*. New York, NY: Charles Scribner's Sons, 1973.

Muirhead, Findlay and Monmarché, Marcel. *The Blue Guides -- Brittany*. London, UK: Macmillan & Co. Ltd., 1925.

Scullard, H. H. *Roman Britain -- Outpost of the Empire*. New York, NY: Thames and Hudson Ltd., 1979.

Stevens, C. E. *Sidonius Apollinaris and His Age*. Westport, CT: Greenwood Press, Inc., reprinted 1979.

Source Web Documents

"Princess Ahez and The Lost City" Folk Tales of Brittany -- Sacred Texts. http://www.sacred-texts.com/neu/celt/ftb/ftbo9.htm (accessed December 9, 2008).

Zosimus, New History: London: Green and Chaplin (1814). Book 6. http://www.tertullian.org/fathers/zosimus06_book6.htm (accessed March 25, 2010).

In the following pages are the seven key elements to Ambrosius Aureliani. Though containing some radical reinterpretations, the elements utilize well-recognized sources to underscore the author's opinions. Their main intent is to provide a way to reconcile the various myths and sources into a more-concise, historical story.

Though brief, each element provides some unique insight on the various issues that shape this heroic genre. The space allotted for these elements does not provide enough room to adequately argue these points beyond a reasonable doubt, but these pages do allow a chance to cast a new light on the subject.

For the novice of Arthurian folklore, little attention to these key elements are required, but anyone familiar with the various works might want to glance through the seven elements. This will help to detach oneself from certain established dogma surrounding King Arthur. By doing so, the known myths and historical events stream together in a more natural flow and Ambrosius Aureliani can truly be enjoyed.

The Key Elements regarding Ambrosius Aureliani

The British appeal to Agitius did not involve the Roman general, Aëtius

The episcopate of Bishop Germanus ran from 412 to 442

The English/Saxons came to Britain in 428 and revolted in 429

King Grallon was Vortigern

King Goar inspired the legends of King/Ban Bors

There existed an association between Ambrosius and the city of Orléans

The Sword of Power and the Round Table were given historical bases

The British appeal to Agitius did not involve the Roman general, Aëtius

The British appeal to Agitius occurs at §20 in the part called Independent Britain in <u>The Ruin of Britain</u> by Gildas (trans. Michael Winterbottom). Traditionally, Independent Britain ranged from the death of Maximus to the third consulship of Aëtius with a possible nine year variance ending at the year that Aëtius was murdered (388-446/454). This time period is strictly based on the assumption that Agitius is Aëtius.

Various writers have debated over the Roman named Agitius, though. In Professor Christopher Snyder's book, <u>An Age of Tyrants</u>, he tells of the discrepancy in the identity of Agitius, stating that it could be Aëtius or even Aegidius. In the notes section of <u>The Ruin of Britain</u>, Dr. John Morris states that Gildas misplaced the appeal within his own narrative. Professor David Dumville has discussed the issue, also. The corruption within Gildas' text and/or the major inconsistency between the sources seems well-documented.

In the section called Independent Britain, the British enemies were the Scots and the Picts. Both brought war upon the British in §14 and §19. They appeared to be the reason for the appeal to Agitius in §20. Finally in §21, the Irish pirates and the Picts returned to their homelands. During this time of truce, the British slipped further into moral decay. Nowhere in Independent Britain did Gildas portray the Saxons as a major problem for the British. In fact, Gildas does not mention the Saxons at all in Independent Britain. Though the Gallic Chronicle of 452 (trans. Alexander Callander Murray, <u>From Roman to Merovingian Gaul</u>) makes note of a Saxon attack in 408, Olympiodorus of Thebes (trans. C. D. Gordon, <u>The Age of Attila</u>) writes that the British discontent with Rome stemmed from Stilicho removing the garrisons that defended the British from the Picts.

The Gallic Chronicle of 452 states that the Saxons subjugated the British provinces after the British had endured a variety of disasters and misfortunes. It was listed as occurring in 441 or 442. Considering this along with the details regarding the traditional time span for Independent Britain, the apparent problem between the sources can be underscored. With the Saxons subjugating the British, at least, four years before the third consulship of Aëtius, it puts the Gallic chronology at odds with the

The British appeal to Agitius did not involve the Roman general, Aëtius

chronology implied by Gildas' writing. This conclusion is made with the assumption that the British would have appealed for help before they were completely subjugated. Based on this, Gildas could not have seen or copied any appeal specifically mentioning the words, tri-consul, if the chronology of his narrative correlates with the Gallic Chronicle of 452.

It seems more likely that Gildas would have identified the wrong man instead of misplacing a major event within his own narrative. This seems to imply that Gildas relied upon an oral source for the appeal to Agitius or personally added the tri-consul gloss to the letter he copied. Either scenario makes the imperial title appear as a corruption within the text if the general chronologies of the sources do not contradict each other or themselves.

In light of these details, the third consulship of Aëtius has not been used to date the events within the writings of Gildas. Still, it is essential to date the events of The Ruin of Britain to use it with other available sources. Orosius, Prosper of Aquitaine and the Gallic Chronicle of 452 document the execution of Maximus as occurring in 388 (trans. Alexander Callander Murray, From Roman to Merovingian Gaul). Gildas mentions this happening in §13 at the end of the section entitled Roman Britain. Professor David Dumville establishes this as his starting point in his work, "The Chronology of De Excidio Britanniae, Book I" (Studies in Celtic History V - Gildas: New Approaches). The event serves well as a starting point for dating this part of Gildas' narrative.

The beginning of Independent Britain at §14 seems to rehash the events that ended in §13. With this assumption, the tyrant is identified as Magnus Maximus and not as one of the three British usurpers that rose briefly to power in the beginning of the fifth century. In §18 and §19, the Romans told the British to defend themselves and gave little prospect of returning. This is interpreted as the Rescript of Honorius noted by Zosimus (trans. Green and Chaplin, New History).

When the Romans left at the beginning of §19, the Scots and Picts wreaked havoc upon the British. The citizens abandoned the towns and the Wall in §19.3 as if to avoid the grips of cannibalism that seized the

The British appeal to Agitius did not involve the Roman general, Aëtius

cities of Spain (Hydatius/Olympiodorus). Echoing the words of Hydatius, the Gallic Chronicle of 452 tells of an enormous famine in Gaul between the years of 411 to 416. Gildas states that disasters abroad increased internal disorder on the island at the end of §19. With the British, also, suffering from food shortages, the famine ran from the Mediterranean to the western shores of the North Sea. This seems like a famine that would still be talked about in Gildas' day.

All the while, the British suffered from attacking barbarians. The British sent out a second appeal. This time it went to Agitius. Gildas mentions the event in the first sentence of §20. Effort should be made to not date this event, at this point. If taken literally, this event had to occur no earlier than 446 based on the year that Aëtius achieved his third consulship. Instead of decades elapsing as traditionally accepted, the dreadful and notorious famine still raged on as noted in §20.2. These events happened within the section entitled Independent Britain and there is no indication that any of these events went past 416 if Agitius is not considered to be Aëtius.

Though still nagged by a spelling discrepancy, during this narrow time period, there was a man of some stature in Gaul with a similar name to Agitius. Agroetius was the Head of Chancery for the usurper, Jovinus, according to Lewis Thorpe's translation of Frigeridus in The History of the Franks.

The second paragraph in fragment 26 of Olympiodorus tells of Roman rule returning to much of Gaul and possibly Britain. It further states that the imperial control remained until the death of Emperor Honorius. Based on this fragment from the Theban historian, this peace would have lasted until 423. Though maybe the conjecture of C. D. Gordon being interjected into the words of the ancient writer, the fragment still notes a small window of time where there was no warring mentioned. This lack of fighting could give the illusion that Roman authority had returned to the island. In §21 of Gildas' writings, there is a period of a truce between the British, the Irish pirates and the Picts. Still the British's every action plagued their salvation.

The British appeal to Agitius did not involve the Roman general, Aëtius

After §21, a plague swooped brutally upon the British people. This plague fell within the section called The Coming of the Saxons in §22.2. An independent reference to this plague can be inferred from Constantius of Lyons in section VIII of the Life of St. Germanus, Bishop of Auxerre (trans. F. R. Hoare, The Western Fathers). Gildas states that the plague laid low so many in such a short period of time that the living could not bury all of the dead. Constantius writes that the illness first struck the children and then the elders, bringing death in about three days.

The plague in section VIII occurred sometime before 429. This year is established by the ability to date section XII in Constantius' writings. Constantius tells of Bishop Germanus traveling to Britain to combat the Pelagian heresy. Prosper of Aquitaine dates this event to 429.

Though there is no known contemporary writers before Gildas that tell of the coming of the Saxons like he does at §23.3, later sources document the event. Nennius (trans. John Morris, British History and The Welsh Annals) and Geoffrey of Monmouth (trans. Lewis Thorpe, The History of the Kings of Britain) describe the event. Nennius gives 428 as the year that the English came to Britain.

In §23.5, the Saxons revolted after being hired to beat back the people of the north in §23.2. Constantius notes that the Saxons and the Picts made war on the British in section XVII while Germanus preached against the Pelagian heresy [on the east side of Britain] in 429. In §24, Gildas elaborates the destruction caused by the Saxons.

In §25.2, the cruel plunderers went home. Described more as raiders than conquerors, it seems inappropriate to assign this to the last British event in the Gallic Chronicle of 452. The famous mentioning of Ambrosius Aurelianus by Gildas appears in §25.3. All dates provided by Nennius that involve this Roman gentleman take place before 441. Upon the removal of the tri-consul reference, the dates provided by Nennius no longer conflict with the British appeal to Agitius.

In §26, the British and barbarians battled back and forth; both sides scored victories. This lasted right up till the siege of Badon Hill.

The British appeal to Agitius did not involve the Roman general, Aëtius

With a liberal view, sections 23.5 through 26 date from 429 to the 470's. The revolt of the Saxons erupted in 429. If Germanus' Alleluia victory was one of the four battles of Vortimer against the Saxons, it effectively dates some of the events in Geoffrey of Monmouth, possibly leading to the dating of Uther's first trip to Ireland. A slightly adjusted version of the dates suggested by the Cistercian monk, Alberic, can be inserted here. Geoffrey Ashe mentions these dates in his book, <u>The Discovery of King Arthur</u>.

The last mention of British affairs in the Gallic Chronicle of 452 happens around 441 as previously noted. After enduring a variety of disasters and misfortunes, the British provinces fell under the authority of the Saxons. The Saxons held this control or maintained an upper-hand against the British to, at least, 452. Otherwise, it seems likely that the Gallic Chronicle would have used different wording in the 441/442 entry or would have noted the power shift that seems to occur later between the two sides.

In Charles C. Mierow's translation, Jordanes indicates that the British had become a force of reckoning in section XLV of <u>The Origin and Deeds of the Goths</u>. The Gothic writer notes that the Roman Emperor, Anthemius, requested military aid from the British king, Riotimus. The year that Anthemius rose up as the Emperor of the West is deduced from Hydatius (trans. Alexander Callander Murray, <u>From Roman to Merovingian Gaul</u>). The British return to power would have been recognized by the year 467 but most likely would have occurred earlier than that.

So, by dropping any concern for the third consulship of Aëtius, the sources can be synchronized into a more concise chronology. The variance in the time of the Agitius' appeal shrinks by two-thirds from nine years to three years. The events of the Anglo-Saxon Chronicles and the work of Bede can be linked to the other sources, but some of the dates are null and void. These works color in the elements of the enemy of the British Romans.

<u>Ambrosius Aureliani</u> falls within the time period of Independent Britain and The Victory at Badon Hill.

The episcopate of Bishop Germanus ran from 412 to 442

In his work entitled "The End of Roman Britain: Continental Evidence and Parallels", Professor Ian Wood provides a strong argument against the traditional years of 418 to 448 for the episcopate of Bishop Germanus. He suggests that Germanus became the Bishop of Auxerre in either 407 or 412. Comparing the Life of St. Germanus, Bishop of Auxerre, by Constantius of Lyons (trans. F. R. Hoare, The Western Fathers) to other contemporary sources, the latter of the two years has been chosen for Ambrosius Aureliani. It should be noted that F. R. Hoare accepted the traditional years for the episcopate of Bishop Germanus.

In section II, Constantius tells that the populace – clergy, nobility, townspeople and country folk – demanded that Germanus was their bishop. The sentence that follows it states that a war was declared by the people against their magistrate and they overthrew the official. The line seems odd at first glance but it echoes the words of Zosimus quoted in An Age of Tyrants. The cited passage told of Roman officials being expelled from Britain, Armorica, and other Gallic provinces around 409. Four men – Constantine, Attalus, Maximus, Jovinus – tried to usurp the Western Empire during the years 407 to 411. Each had magistrates and military personnel, giving rise to several sets of traitors during this time period.

Three interpretations can be made about the ascendance of Bishop Germanus. The first is that the magistrate stripped from his office was not Germanus and the election of Germanus was at the time that this civil war raged. Secondly, Constantius artistically expressed Germanus' ascendance and it had no historical connotation. Or alternatively, Germanus was a magistrate in one of the usurpers' governments. Removed from office but spared by popular-consent, the divine [imperial] authority conscripted Germanus to an ecclesiastical office. This view would accounts for his compulsion to receive the religious position. This would, also, explain why Constantius fails to note any of Bishop Germanus' deeds as a duke. It would be difficult even for a talented orator to honorably mention exploits against the Empire.

Sometime after becoming the Bishop of Auxerre, a plague hit the region. With a reevaluation of Independent Britain by Gildas, there is a

The episcopate of Bishop Germanus ran from 412 to 442

possibility that the plague that hit Britain happen around the same time. Though lacking the year for the plague that Constantius mentioned, it had to occur in between 412 and 429. The end date is based on the bishop's first documented involvement in British affairs, which began in section XII and ran through section XVIII. Much, if not all, these sections occurred in 429 when Prosper of Aquitaine notes Germanus' trip to Britain (trans. Alexander Callander Murray, From Roman to Merovingian Gaul).

The three references to miraculous powers in sections XX, XXI and XXII are dated to 433 by the entry in the Gallic Chronicle of 452 regarding Germanus (trans. Alexander Callander Murray, From Roman to Merovingian Gaul).

In section XXIV, Auxiliaris governed as the Praetorian Prefect of Gaul and warmly received Germanus when he arrived in Arles. Hoare places Germanus' visit between the year 435 and 439 based on his note for section XIX. There doesn't seem to be a reason not to accept this time period.

In section XXV, news of the Pelagian heresy troubling the British reached Germanus at home. This time, he traveled to the island with Severus, the Bishop of Trier. By prior points and with future considerations, the second trip to Britain happen between 435 and 441.

Returning from Britain in section XXVIII, Bishop Germanus confronted King Goar as his Alan tribes and cavalry filled the roads, ready to subdue Armorica. The Gallic Chronicle of 452 places this event around 441/442. The bishop went to Italy seeking a pardon for Armorica. Constantius doesn't give the impression that six years had elapsed between Germanus' trip to Britain and the one to Ravenna.

In section XL, Tibatto incited the people of Armorica to rebel, again. This event does not contradict the events of the Bacaudic revolt in the Gallic Chronicle of 452. Though said to be captured in 437, the Gallic entry does not specifically state that Tibatto was killed like other rebel leaders were. In fact, trouble continued for another eleven years. After being implicated in the Bacaudic revolt, Eudoxius fled to the Huns in 448.

The episcopate of Bishop Germanus ran from 412 to 442

In section XLII, Bishop Germanus died while in Ravenna.

So, Bishop Germanus' expulsion from office and his conscription to the see of Auxerre fits neatly within the chaotic times of 412 while his involvement with the Alan king, Goar, establishes 442 as the end of his life.

The English/Saxons came to Britain in 428 and revolted in 429

The fifth-century events mentioned by Nennius in Passage 66 (trans. John Morris, British History and The Welsh Annals) are taken as being accurate. Many have argued that its elaborate dating is glossed in or false. In either case, it points to an alternative dating for the reign of Vortigern than what is offered by Bede (trans. Judith McClure and Roger Collins, Bede – The Ecclesiastical History of the English People – The Greater Chronicle – Bede's Letter to Egbert). Through the removal of Aëtius time-stamping in Gildas, the sources fall in sync. Passages 43 to 46 by Nennius and sections [vi.13], [vi.14], [vi.15] and [vi.16] by Geoffrey of Monmouth in The History of the King of Britain fill out this fifth-century time line. Bishop Germanus' visit in 429 forms the keystone in synchronizing the three sources.

Both Nennius and Geoffrey tell of four battles that Vortimer waged against the Saxons. Geoffrey elaborates on other events in section [vi.14]. Soon after the fourth victory, Vortimer restored the churches as Bishop Germanus requested.

This gives the impression that Bishop Germanus was still in Britain after the four battles. Due to the timing and their general descriptions, it seems possible that the battle Bishop Germanus had against the Saxons and the Picts on Easter Sunday [April 8th] was one of the four battles Vortimer had against the Saxons.

In comparing the details described in sections XVII and XVIII of the Life of St. Germanus, Bishop of Auxerre (trans. F. R. Hoare, The Western Fathers) to the ones listed in Nennius' passage 44, it seems that the Alleluia victory would have been the battle on the river Darenth or at the ford called Episford. This conjecture comes from the following line by Constantius of Lyons. Many [the enemy - Saxons and Picts] threw themselves into the river which they had just crossed at their ease, and were drowned in it. Other information used to form this conjecture was gathered from Peter Clayton's A Companion to Roman Britain. He tells of the Lullingstone villa that sat on the Darent River not far from the village called Eynsford. The villa burned down early in the fifth century. Though lacking definitive archeological evidence and not suggested by Clayton, the villa's fiery end could be attributed to Saxon rage.

The English/Saxons came to Britain in 428 and revolted in 429

According to Geoffrey of Monmouth, Vortimer laid siege to Thanet in his fourth and final battle against the Saxons. During a parley between the opposing sides, the Saxons sailed off to Germany in their longships. Vortimer was poisoned shortly after ordering the churches to be restored in section [vi.14].

John Haywood cites in his book, Dark Age Naval Power: (with a small professional sailing crew) In fair weather, each voyage across the North Sea would have been measured in days rather than weeks and the risks would have been slight. In terms of traveling time the 300-mile voyage between Jutland and the Thames estuary would have been no longer than a 60 mile-long journey overland.

The Saxons returned. During a meeting set up by Vortigern, Hengist and his men massacred many British nobles on the first of May, the date agreed upon in section [vi.15] and described in section [vi.16] of The History of the Kings of Britain.

It seems possible that one of the four battles of Vortimer, his death and the British massacre occurred in a rapid succession between Easter Sunday [April 8th] and May 1, 429.

King Grallon was Vortigern

The legends of King Grallon and Vortigern reek with debauchery and incest. As divine punishment for his sinful daughter, Grallon's city, Is [Ys], was submerged by the sea (Muirhead, Findlay, <u>The Blue Guides -- Brittany</u>). Nennius tells of Vortigern's fathering his daughter's son, Faustus (trans. John Morris, <u>British History and The Welsh Annals</u>). Both men lived in the fifth century based sources written centuries later. Though these events may not have occurred, it is still worth gleaning for details. This literary sifting has led to the belief that King Grallon was Vortigern.

King Grallon's activities centered around the Bay of Douarnenez in western France. The Life of Winwaloe written by Wrdisten presents this as an accepted truth in the second half of the ninth century (<u>The Saints of Cornwall, part two</u> by Gilbert Doble). Wrdisten describes Gradlon, Courentinus, and Winwaloe as three great luminaries and pillars of Cornouaille. Tutualus, a famous monk, preceded them. Findlay Muirhead states that the town named Douarnenez owes its name and origin to the priory of St. Tutuarn, founded on the neighboring Tutuarn-Enez, now called Ile Tristan. Allegedly, Is [Ys] was located in a lagoon on the Bay of the Departed. This bay forms the bottom point of the Bay of Douarnenez. Some Gallo-Roman remains are located in the nearby hamlet of Troguer.

Patrick Galliou and Michael Jones in <u>The Bretons</u> state that over sixty percent of the documented salting units in western France are located on the bay's shores. Based on the total volume generated, the authors figure, these fish-salting units produced more than what was locally or regionally consumed. They theorize that the surplus was shipped to other parts of the Empire and to the shores of Britain. They further speculate that the salting industry was extensively developed to supply the military markets of the British and Rhenish *limites*. These units had reached a "corporate-level" by the third century AD. From an inscription of that time, one learns of the worshiping of the Greek god, Poseidon Hippios, in the bay area. Galliou and Jones mark salting tanks just south of Quimper on a map. In <u>Muirhead's Brittany</u>, King Grallon established Quimper in the fifth century, calling the area Cornouaille (Cornwall), a name brought over from Britain. In the neighboring area of Quimper not a great distance from the church of Combrit, the remains of a Roman villa and baths were discovered. Farther south, one will view Ile-Tudy and Loctudy.

King Grallon was Vortigern

Besides holding sway over land by the sea, the saints associated with King Grallon reinforce his strong link to fish. It has been put forth that St. Winwaloe used a small almost black bell to attract fish. According to another source, St. Corentin had a miraculous fish that he would eat for his daily meal. Afterwards, the fish would reappear in a pool near his cell.

King Grallon could have been controlling the garum industry in the area. If Grallon ran this type of operation, two things become apparent. He dealt more frequently with sea-faring men, ranging from the Franks, the Goths, the Irish to the Saxons. Secondly, he had a source of wealth beside any generated by his lands in Armorica or possibly those in Britain. With this capital available and the increased day-to-day interaction with sailors, it does not seem extreme that Grallon hired Saxons to beat back the people of the north.

Logistically, Grallon's presence in western Armorica and possibly in western Britain would explain the need to hire out the defenses of the eastern shores of Britain. King Grallon's own fleet would have been busy guarding his personal interests. Safe harbors on both sides of the channel would have facilitated patrolling the western waters.

In passage 66, Nennius states that Vortigern came to power in 425. In the Life of St. Germanus, part 3, passages 47 and 48 compiled by Nennius, different stories spell out the eventual end of Vortigern. In one, Bishop Germanus drove Vortigern into exile twice. Vortigern fled first to Gwerthrynion and then to his fortress in Demetia. The bishop followed Vortigern and laid siege upon him. Fire rained down from the heavens and destroyed the fortress of Vortigern. In the last paragraph in section [viii. 2] of The History of the King of Britain by Geoffrey of Monmouth, the army of Ambrosius and the other Brits laid siege to Vortigern's fortress and used weapons of fire to burn up the tower. Another version tells of him wandering about and dying without honor.

In "Princess Ahez and The Lost City", Grallon and his men became lost in a forest. They came upon the hermitage of St. Corentin. The monk fed them with a single fish. Miraculously, the fish regenerated itself. For his hospitality, Grallon made Corentin the first Bishop of Cornouaille.

King Grallon was Vortigern

Possibly in gratitude, St. Corentin passed down the events of King Grallon's life in a favorable light. Vortigern's incestuous affair with his daughter was cast as the fault of King Grallon's promiscuous daughter.

To help establish a floriut for King Grallon, one could further review the religious figures surrounding him. In the chapter entitled "De altitudine et nobilitate Cornubie", Wrdisten implies that Grallon, Courentinus, and Winwaloe were contemporary while Tutualus was already established in the area and/or was from an older generation. According to Butler's Lives of the Saints, King Childebert insisted that Tudwal should become the Bishop of Tréguier. This occurred when the religious man was in Paris obtaining confirmation of his titles to land from the Frankish lord during the sixth century. Doble notes that the mentioning of Tutual puzzled many scholars due to the assumed association with the Bishop of Tréguier. This has led to the opinion that Tutualus and Tudwal are two separate individuals.

A much later source, the Sanctoral of Quimper of 1500, states that Grallon sent Corentin, Winwaloe and Tudy to Martin [Tours] to have him consecrate the most fitting candidate of the three. Corentin was chosen. Though Gilbert Doble dismisses this information as untrustworthy, his reason seems contested by other details he provides. Doble states that no Breton writer before the twelfth century would have written that St. Corentin was consecrated in Tours due to the primatial dignity of Dol. Still though, Doble establishes strong ties between Cornouaille and St. Martin of Tours. The monks from the abbey of Marmoutier near Tours proudly retained the body of St. Corentin during the Norman invasion of the tenth century. St. Corentin received an honorary mention in the litany of a psalter of Tours used at Christ Church, Canterbury, in the eleventh century. The influence of St. Martin traveled near and far. By the late fifth century, the prestige of Tours seems undeniable based on the letter from Sidonius to Lucontius regarding Perpetuus raising a new church over the shrine of St. Martin (trans. O. M. Dalton, Letters of Sidonius). Dated to the ninth century, the Book of Armagh has the Life of St. Martin copied within its pages according to the book, Saint Patrick – His Origins and Career, written by R. P. C. Hanson.

King Grallon was Vortigern

Winwaloe traveled to an island called Laurea to learn from Budoc the Zealous. The writer of the Life of St. Winwaloe, Wrdisten tells of Tudual carrying coals across an island. This same feat is noted by Doble being done by Bothmael, a companion of Tudy, in the Vita Maudeti. Gregory of Tours tells of Bishop Bricius of Tours, carrying burning coals in his cassock. In <u>The Western Fathers</u>, F. R. Hoare believes that the design for Martin's community near Tours was that of a laura. St. Martin's biographer, Sulpicius, tells that the hermitage was located on a bend on the River Loire with a high mountain wall behind it with one narrow approach [nearly an island].

This seems to offer a thin chance that Winwaloe traveled to the hermitage of St. Martin which could led to the following conjecture about the Sanctoral of Quimper of 1500. It seems possible that it provides a general chronology of religious figures in Cornouaille. Tutualus came first and Winwaloe followed. As the Christian element developed even further, King Grallon sent Corentin to be consecrated as the first bishop of the area. The desire of King Grallon to have his bishop consecrate by a Bishop of Tours does not seem hard to fathom.

Albert Le Grand tells us that in his time several parishes on certain days would sing a service to repose the soul of King Grallon according to Doble.

King Grallon and Vortigern appear to be contemporaries operating in the same general region during the fifth century. It seems likely that both had dealings with the Saxons. In turn, the sexual controversies surrounding their daughters, now, seem less coincidental and this portrayal more convincing.

King Goar inspired the legends of King/Ban Bors

In <u>Bulfinch's Mythology</u>, King Arthur and His Knights, Chapter VIII, the following is stated, "King Ban of Brittany, the faithful ally of Arthur was attacked by his enemy Claudas, and after a long war saw himself reduced to possession of a single fortress, where he was besieged by his enemy. In this extremity he determined to solicit the assistance of Arthur, and escaped in a dark night, with his wife Helen and his infant son Launcelot, leaving his castle in the hands of his seneschal, who immediately surrendered the place to Claudas."

In the book <u>From Scythia to Camelot</u> by C. Scott Littleton and Linda A. Malcor, the authors suggest that Ban is a title much like Riothamus is considered.

Helaine and Elaine were identified as the wife of Ban and Bors in the Arthurian myths. In Chapter VIII of King Arthur and His Knights, the myth tells how, "(Helen) she was joined by the widow of Bohort, for the good king had died of grief on hearing of the death of his brother, Ban. They had two sons."

It seems possible that Helaine and Elaine could be variations of the same woman's name. Bernard Bachrach did suggest that the Alans were polygamous in <u>A History Of The Alans In The West</u>. Bachrach cites Salvian as the source of this information. Salvian was a younger contemporary of King Goar in fifth-century Gaul.

These various details and opinions can be construed as King/Ban Bohort being at war with Claudas. And eventually, his enemy took over all of King/Ban Bohort's territory. Breaking the king's spirit, King/Ban Bohort died of grief. Two wives and three sons survived him. One was his namesake; the other two were Lionel & Launcelot [Lancelot].

In <u>The Age of Attila</u>, Olympiodorus tells how King Goar helped Jovinus usurp the Empire just before Constantine died in 411. Jovinus' reign lasted only for a few years when Dardanus executed him in 413 after his capture. The Alan king ruled for many years though his reign remains somewhat obscure and its true duration uncertain.

King Goar inspired the legends of King/Ban Bors

Alexander Callander Murray provides the following translation for the Gallic Chronicler of 452 in <u>From Roman to Merovingian Gaul</u>. Murray states, "The lands of Farther Gaul were handed over by the patrician Aëtius to the Alans to be divided with the inhabitants. They subdued those who opposed them with arms, drove out the owners, and obtained possession of the land by force."

W. B. Anderson notes that King Goar settled near Orléans around 442. Constantius of Lyons tells how Bishop Germanus of Auxerre confronted the Alan king in Armorica.

In <u>A History Of The Alans In The West,</u> Bernard Bachrach states, "With the aid of toponymical evidence it is possible to ascertain the probable location of at least some of the settlements established for Goar's followers. Allains (Somme) is located some thirty miles to the east of Amiens and protects the roads leading from Cologne to Amiens and Soissons. Twenty-five miles to the south-southeast is Alaincourt (Aisne) which commands the roads from Tournai to Soissons and Tournai to Rheims."

In <u>The History Of The Franks,</u> Gregory of Tours states that Clodio was a man of high birth and marked ability. It is alleged that he was a king of the Franks that lived at Druisburg in Thuringian. Gregory states that Clodio attacked and captured Cambrai after his spies told him what he needed to know. Afterwards, he occupied the country up to the River Somme.

In the panegyric to Majorian translated by W. B. Anderson, Sidonius orates how Aëtius defended Turoni [Tournai - instead of Tours as W. B. Anderson suggests - this is based on their geographical position.] sometime before they fought together where Cloio the Frank had overrun the helpless lands of the Atrebates.

These lands might be referring to the people of Civitas Atrabatum, Arras, which is about thirty miles northeast of Allains near the Somme River. Since the early part of the fifth century, various Germanic barbarians had troubled the neighboring region.

King Goar inspired the legends of King/Ban Bors

Sidonius further tells of a Scythian [Alan] wedding party that is attacked near the village of Helena. Though not clearly stated, it appears that Cloio/Chlogio and his Franks attacked in the middle of the ceremony when the Romans arrived in Vicus Helenae shortly afterwards. Interestingly enough, the village bears the same name as Ban/Bors's wife, Helen. W.B. Anderson notes that the date of the attack by Clio/Chlogio and his Franks occurred some time after 440 and may have been several years later.

It has been assumed that it would have been before 451 AD due to the fact that an Alan by the name Sangiban controlled Orléans at the time of Attila's invasion of Gaul according to section XXXVII of The Origin And Deeds Of The Goths.

In the folklore, Bors the younger has been mentioned. He is portrayed as one of the sons of Bors the elder. This legendary son appears as the cousin of Lancelot and a great knight of King Arthur in the various myths.

In The Discovery Of King Arthur, Geoffrey Ashe argues that a man identified as Riothamus was King Arthur. The author goes further and cites Sharon Turner as stating, "Either the Riothamus was Arthur, or it was from his expedition that Geoffrey [of Monmouth], or the Breton bards, took the idea of Arthur's battles in Gaul."

W.B. Anderson states that Anthemius was created Augustus on the 12th of April, 467. According to section XLV in the translation of The Origin And Deeds Of The Goths by Charles C. Mierow, Jordanes states that the new emperor sent his son-in-law, Ricimer, against the Alan king, Beorg, and his army. Ricimer destroyed King Beorg and his army in the first engagement. It is in this same section that Jordanes tells of the events surrounding Riotimus and his activities in Gaul.

By comparing the above details, there seems to be a parallelism between Goar and Bors. It appears that Claudus, the enemy of King/Ban Bors, could have been Clodio/Cloio, the king of the Franks.

King Goar inspired the legends of King/Ban Bors

This Germanic ruler captured Cambrai and invaded the lands up to the river Somme. Allains on the river Somme was in the lands controlled by Goar, at one time. This site could have been Vicus Helenae where a Scythian wedding party was slaughter when the Romans, Aëtius and Majorianus, battled the king of the Franks.

About twenty years after these events, an Alan by the name, Beorg, became king and was a contemporary of the British king, Riotimus, who is suspected in being King Arthur, the fabled ally of King Bors.

There existed an association between Ambrosius and the city of Orléans

In §25.3 of <u>The Ruins of Britain</u>, Gildas identifies Ambrosius Aurelianus as the leader of the wretched survivors [of the Saxon revolt], but provides little else about this Roman gentleman. Geoffrey of Monmouth mentions a man named Aurelius Ambrosius in <u>The History of the Kings of Britain</u>. Many assume that these two men are essentially the same man. Another legendary man connected to Ambrosius Aurelianus is referred to by Nennius. The Welsh called him, Emrys.

Various arguments can be presented in regards to the proper form of his name. Many may assume that it is the standard type of name utlitized by the Romans. This assumption begs the question. What are the other parts of his name? With no further details provided in the major sources, a different interpretation has been made regarding his name. In <u>Arthurian Tales</u>, this enigmatic figure is portrayed as a Roman named Ambrosius that resided near Aureliani at various times.

Geoffrey of Monmouth presents several interesting details about Aurelius Ambrosius. When Aurelius and Utherpendragon were children, the brothers were originally given to Archbishop Guithelinus to be brought up. After their father's murder and the death of the archbishop, the brothers were taken to Little Britain so Vortigern could not murder them. A lord by the name of Budicius took them in. Though noted as the king of Brittany, Geoffrey of Monmouth states nothing more about this Budicius or the range of his power.

Within this information, a noteworthy point is the lack of similiarities between the names of Ambrosius and Uther. It gives the impression that the brothers were actually raised by two separate families, with the first being Roman while the latter possibly Alan. The conjecture regarding Uther is based on the brothers commanding an Armoric cavalry when they returned to Britain, the details provided by C. Scott Littleton and Linda A. Malcor in <u>From Scythia to Camelot</u> about the title Pendragon, and the various spellings for Goar noted by Bernard Bachrach in <u>A History of the Alans in the West</u>.

There existed an association between Ambrosius and the city of Orléans

Geoffrey of Monmouth states that Utherpendragon and Aurelius Ambrosius still lay in their cradles when Vortigern crowned their older brother, Constans, the king of Britain. This gives the impression that the two younger brothers were both babies at that time and relatively the same age. This raises the possibility that they were twins.

Going with the assumption that a Roman family adopted Ambrosius, his name could have derived from his caregiver or from the region he lived in while exiled. Each scenario could imply that he resided in or around the Gallic city of Aureliani (present-day Orléans, France).

Tangent details provided by near-contemporary writers form the bases to these conjectures. An association between Ambrosius and the locale can faintly be seen in the writings of Jordanes. In section XXXVII of <u>The Origin and Deeds of the Goths</u> as translated by Charles C. Mierow, Jordanes states that the Alani king, Sangiban, promised to surrender Aureliani to Attila the Hun.

A precedent for someone living in the area with part of his name is established in a story from Gregory of Tours that was passed down by Fredegar. In the book, <u>From Roman to Merovingian Gaul</u> by Alexander Callander Murray, it states that Clovis sent a certain Roman called Aurelianus to inspect the king's future wife, Chlothild. Aurelianus lived in the region of Orléans.

Though an example of a name-place in Britain based on Aurelianus seems lacking, Dr. John Morris identifies Ambrosden, Amberley, and Amesbury as examples of locations named after Ambrosius in <u>The Age of Arthur</u>. If these examples are named after a person, it seems more likely that the person was known as Ambrosius or Emrys but not Aurelianus while in Britain.

Considering these various factors has led to the view that the Roman gentleman mentioned by Gildas was widely known as Ambrosius and, at one time or another, lived near Aureliani, but also fought battles in Britain.

The Sword of Power and the Round Table were given historical bases

Liberties were taken in the development of the Arthurian themes regarding the Sword of Power and the Round Table. Still, fifth-century events anchor them within <u>Ambrosius Aureliani</u>.

Littleton and Malcor bring up two influential points in <u>From Scythia to Camelot</u> about the Sword in the Stone myth. The authors ask why the whole episode is absent from British chronicles, as well as from Geoffrey's Historia. Secondly, the authors tell that the earliest appearance of the Sword in the Stone myth occurs in the writings from the regions settled by the Alans around Orléans.

This has led to the belief that the Sword of Power did not originate in Britain but somewhere in Gaul. Interestingly enough, contemporary and near-contemporary writers tell a tale about a noteworthy sword in the fifth century. Based on the known travels of its wielder, this sword rode through the region near Orléans.

King Bleda died in 446 according to the Gallic Chronicle of 452 in <u>From Roman to Merovingian Gaul</u> by Alexander Callander Murray. Sometime afterwards, a herdsman drew the Sword of Ares from the earth and gave it to Attila the Hun. In <u>The Age of Attila</u>, Priscus records this contemporary event and Jordanes passes the tale down in <u>The Origin and Deeds of the Goths</u>.

Gregory of Tours tells that Attila was turned away from Aureliani and that city of Gaul survived the Scourge of God.

In this mist of details, the Sword of Power will appear for the future king to claim.

The Sword of Power and the Round Table were given historical bases

According to the French writer that introduced the theme of the Round Table, Wace states that the tales of Arthur were not all lies nor all true. Geoffrey Ashe makes note of Wace's statement in <u>The Discovery of King Arthur</u>. This leaves us the task of once more, sifting through the various legends for an underlying history.

Geoffrey Ashe further cites a myth that Merlin made the Round Table for Uther. Geoffrey of Monmouth tells how Aurelius Ambrosius had Uther travel to Ireland with Merlin. They took down the Giant's Ring and brought it to Britain as a monument for the nobles massacred on the first of May [in 429 - based on the documented revolt of the Saxons by Constantius of Lyons].

With the trip to Ireland happening sometime after the massacre, the taking of the Giant's Ring is cast in the context of Palladius' trip in 431. Ambrosius, Merlinus and Utherpendragon [Euthar] take down the Giant's Ring on behalf of the Roman Church. The pagan symbol falls victim to the wrath of Christianity like the ancient temple of Serapis in Alexandria and the consecrated statue of Mount Etna on the island of Sicily. Unlike the others, Merlinus preserved it by moving it to Britain.

In <u>Ambrosius Aureliani</u>, this stone monument is not portrayed as Stonehenge, but instead as an enormous stone hoop, a ring that a giant could wear. Through the process of moving it, the idea of the Round Table develops within Merlinus.

A Map of Western Europe

For the most part, modern-day name-places are used except for Aureliani and Vorgium, which are Orléans and Carhaix, respectively.